MW01134235

Books by Alina

The Holbrook Cousins
   The Successor
   The Screw-up
   The Scion

The Frost Brothers
   Eating Her Christmas Cookies
   Tasting Her Christmas Cookies

The Svensson Brothers
   After His Peonies
   In Her Candy Jar
   On His Paintbrush
   In Her Pumpkin Patch
   Between Her Biscuits
   After Her Fake Fiancé

Weddings in the City
   Bridezillas & Billionaires
   Wedding Bells & Wall Street Bros

Check my website for the latest news:

http://alinajacobs.com/books.html

TASTING HER

Christmas Cookies

TASTING HER

Christmas Cookies

A HOLIDAY ROMANTIC COMEDY

ALINA JACOBS

Summary: Down-on-her-luck baker Holly needs to win The Great Christmas Bake-Off. Grouchy, Christmas-hating billionaire—and, inexplicably, bake-off judge—Owen Frost isn't making it easy. Kitchen sabotage, crazy family members, and tasty desserts abound! 'Tis the season for a sexy, funny, holiday romantic comedy!

*To my great-aunt, whose cookie
recipe inspired this story.*

On the second day of Christmas, my true love gave to me...

CHAPTER 1

Holly

C hristmas has always been my favorite holiday. My first Christmas memory is when my mom dropped me off at my grandmother's house then took off to find herself. Talk about being home for Christmas! The tiny 1950s-style bungalow was stuffed with all things yuletide: lights in every window, a nutcracker collection on the bookcase, and antique ornaments on the Christmas trees in every room. To six-year-old me, it was magical, though in hindsight it might have been veering dangerously into *Hoarders* territory.

Even more magical was how none of those decorations came down in January. The neighbors complained bitterly when Granny's elaborate nativity scene lit up the sky in August. But my grandmother loved all things Christmas. Some might even call her a fanatic. Every six weeks, she even installed a whole new set of Christmas trees, supplied by her boyfriend, who owned a tree farm. Every night, I would drift off to sleep lulled by the blinking lights. That kicked off eight years of nonstop Christmas, and it was just the way I liked it. My grandmother and I baked cookies, decorated wreaths, and sang carols all day every day.

I didn't see my mother again until I was fourteen and my grandmother died. Granny and her Christmas tree farmer boyfriend were doing a raunchy role-play of Mr. and Mrs. Claus. She went with a smile on her face and cookie crumbs on her collar. Best way to go if you ask me. My mom missed the Christmas-themed funeral. I barely had time to pack all of my grandmother's decorations into a way-too-expensive storage unit before my mother dragged me back to her new husband and his deranged teen daughter.

They did not love Christmas. Instead of nonstop wholesomeness and baking Christmas goodies, it was nonstop drama revolving around my crazy stepsister, Amber.

I would be minding my own business, baking Christmas cookies and watching *Holiday in Handcuffs* in July, as one does, and Amber would storm into the kitchen, accusing me of trying to move into her territory because I dared to talk to some guy she liked. *We had a group project, Amber, so I don't know, excuse me for trying to not flunk out of high school.*

Ahem. Got a little carried away.

My stepfather regularly threatened to cancel Christmas when he would hear us arguing. One year he actually did, picking up the Christmas tree and throwing it out onto the street in a fit of teenage-girl-drama-fueled rage. He also threw out his back, prolonging the Christmas misery.

But my Christmas cheer would not be snuffed! As soon as I could, I escaped that house and into the money-burning embrace of culinary school. When you think about

Christmas, what do you think of first? The presents? The twinkling lights? The happy families gathered around the fire? For me, it was the desserts. I loved the rich cakes, exquisitely decorated cookies, and homemade candy. Desserts were my specialty. I could make a buttercream so stable you could caulk a tub with it. My piecrusts would add years to your life, and I have been told my sugar cookies will cause a religious experience.

I wanted to be the next Christina Tosi with Milk Bar or Chloe Barnard with Gray Dove Bakery, but my big break as a dessert chef never happened. After graduation, I took a series of jobs at restaurants that were all horrible and awful in their own unique special way.

Somewhere around chopping my thousandth pound of onions to the tune of an angry chef screaming at the dishwashers, I realized I only had so many Christmases left—and I wanted to spend them baking. So I quit my job and started a subscription baking company. Every month, my subscribers received a beautiful box filled with yummy baked goods in the mail. I had a kick-ass Instagram account with beautiful photos. I was on my way to success!

And just to spoil it, yeah, turns out that wasn't a smart decision. I was up to my eyeballs in credit card debt before you could say "deck the halls." I had started hemorrhaging money out of the gate. New York was expensive, and I was illegally subletting a bed in a studio apartment plus renting a shared kitchen space. My subscriber numbers were in the toilet, and I had had to resort to posting slightly raunchy photos on Instagram to generate any visibility. My costumes were starting to border on bodice ripping due to the amount of unpurchased desserts I ate. The topper on the Christmas tree? Someone had complained to code enforcement and we had all been evicted from the shared studio.

And lo on the third day of the month before Christmas did my true love give to me a mountain of debt, a failing business, and a Christmas stocking's worth of broken dreams.

But I had one more cookie in my arsenal. I had managed to secure a spot in *The Great Christmas Bake-Off*. There was a huge payout for the winner, enough to wipe out my debts, including the payments I was behind on for the storage unit with my grandmother's Christmas decorations. Best of all, it came with housing.

It was a new Christmas season! This was my last chance, my big moment. I had to win the bake-off. Christmas and my grandmother's beloved holiday decorations were on the line.

"I am going to win *The Great Christmas Bake-Off*!" I yelled out. I was in front of a huge tower with a sign on top that said Quantum Cyber. It glowed against the grey winter sky. Some billionaire trying to overcompensate for his tiny Christmas package probably built the skyscraper. Still, it was going to be my home away from—well, basically just my only home for as long as I was in the bake-off.

A Goth girl was leaning against the door inside the sterile lobby space, inspecting the black polish on her nails. She let out an exaggerated sigh when I walked into the building, dragging all my worldly possessions behind me on a trolley.

"Once again we come to the worst holiday season," my friend Morticia said. People always found her strange and a little scary. And once you got to know her... you realized your first impressions were in fact correct.

"Santa's going to bring you a lump of coal," I said, hugging her.

"Better coal than anything related to the Christmas bake-off," she complained. "You should see these people. You better win every round so I'm not stuck here by myself!"

"How's your decorating job going?" I asked her as she picked up one of the bags that was listing on the tower of boxes on the cart.

"I'm a serious artist. The only reason I'm here wasting my talents is because Penny McCarthy wanted me to help her with the *Vanity Rag* videos. They're partnering with the bake-off."

"How's your foster sister?"

"Snagged herself a billionaire. She's very proud," Morticia replied dryly.

I followed Morticia to the bank of elevators. She pulled a key card out of a purse shaped like a spider. If Christmas was my holiday, Halloween was Morticia's. She even had extra black lipstick on to combat all the Christmas cheer floating around.

"I can't believe I made it through," I said as the elevator took us to the 95th floor of the building.

"It's because of your Instagram account. Seriously, Santa is bringing you clothes and a Bible for Christmas," she said, adjusting the spiky choker she was wearing.

"My Instagram account brings in a lot of subscribers for the Taste My Muffin baking box," I retorted.

"I'm sure, especially seeing that sexy pilgrim outfit you posted yesterday on Thanksgiving."

"Hey, I got a hundred new subscribers thanks to that picture. All the boys want to buy my baked goods."

Morticia smirked. "They're paying to taste your cookies."

CHAPTER 2

Owen

Christmastime—darkness, death, holiday parties. Thanksgiving wasn't even over—I still had leftovers in my fridge—yet here I was at the season's first holiday party. It was for the kickoff of *TechBiz* magazine's annual ranking of the best technology companies to work for. The magazine was trying to stir up press for the competition. The rankings were big news in the business world. But why it had to be rolled into a Christmas party was beyond me.

It was a typical generic corporate Christmas party. Here was the spread of cured meats and cheese, there a punch bowl of warm eggnog.

"Do you want a sip?" a woman in a tailored skirt suit asked, slinking up to me.

"No, thank you, Sloane."

"You know I'm on the selection committee," she said craftily, drifting her manicured fingernails up my suit jacket sleeve. "Maybe if we have a repeat of our date from a few months ago, I could put in a good word for you." She licked her lips.

I tamped down a shudder. I'd gone on one date with Sloane six months ago, and she hadn't left me alone since. Thankfully, Evan Harrington, whose hedge fund owned the magazine, stepped up onto the stage.

"They're about to start the presentation," Sloane said, turning to leave but not before her hand brushed dangerously close to my belt buckle.

"You sure you don't want to give her another shot?" Walker, my chief operations officer joked, nudging me as he returned from the snack table. "You're getting older."

"I'm not that old," I hissed as Evan clinked his glass for our attention.

"Your younger brother Jack is going to be engaged any day now," Walker whispered back. He was a Svensson. There was an excessive number of them, and they were all brothers—or half brothers in some instances—and they were all obnoxious, from the smallest, cutest little boys to the biggest, meanest Svenssons, who currently had a sizable portion of my company by the balls. Greg and Hunter Svensson had originally invested in my company and owned a large percentage of it. I tried to give them a wide berth.

"At the very least, she could give Quantum Cyber good marks in the contest," Walker said out of the side of his mouth. "Greg's not happy with the recruiting numbers. He and Hunter are afraid we're going to lose our edge."

"We're not losing our edge," I hissed back. A server came around with desserts. I waved her away. I was not a sweets person. Walker took two of the mini donuts covered with chocolate frosting and red and green sprinkles.

"Thank you all for coming," Evan said into the microphone. "We like to think the *TechBiz* list of the best places to work in the tech industry makes or breaks companies. Recruitment season for this year's graduates is starting in a couple of months. Ninety-nine percent of grads say that they use our detailed write-up and ranking system to decide which companies to accept an offer from or to even bother applying to. It's also used when smaller start-ups decide to sell. So put your best foot forward! I hear Holbrook Enterprises is the company to beat!"

We applauded politely as Walker and I glared over at the Holbrooks in the corner. Holbrook Enterprises had been at the top of the list the last two years, while my company had ranked tenth. Tenth!

"You'd think paying people a shit ton of money would be enough, but you would be wrong," I said, glowering.

"People want atmosphere and a nice place to work," Walker said, grabbing a mini cupcake off a tray. "They want fun activities, Christmas parties, nice food, and a CEO they feel like they could have a beer with." I did not score well on any of those counts.

"You're just very frosty, Owen, get it? Because Frost is your last name?" Walker said, elbowing me in the ribs. See what I said about Svenssons? Obnoxious.

I spent the rest of the party pretending to be nice to my competitors and avoiding Sloane.

"Man, you go on one date with a woman in this city and it's like you agreed to marry her," I complained to Walker under my breath.

"It's the population disparity. There are more women than men who are young professionals. It's flipped in San Francisco. Women are very territorial in Manhattan," Grant

Holbrook said loudly, swaggering over, arm around his wife, Kate. She looked up at him in bemusement then hugged me and Walker.

"Merry Christmas!"

Grant's cousin Carter yawned beside him. "This party is boring. Holbrook Enterprises has a bomb-ass Christmas party planned. My wife—"

"You two literally are not even engaged," Grant interjected.

"If I say it out loud, one day it will be true," Carter said sagely. "She's got a ton of Christmas-themed cocktails planned."

"You guys shouldn't even bother applying," Grant said to me in that casual asshole way the Holbrooks had. "I have a Christmas wish list of companies I want to buy, and I think Santa's going to bring me everything I want."

"Honestly, I don't know how Grant manages to function given that he has to haul around his massive fucking ego," Walker slurred. He had snuck a huge container of the boozy eggnog out of the party and almost sloshed it on me as we got into my luxury sports car. I would also have bet good money Walker had Christmas cookies wrapped in a napkin snuffed in his pocket. My COO had a sweet tooth.

My only vice was fast cars. In my tower, I had a whole floor of them. Usually I was too busy to drive them, but sometimes, late at night, when the roads were clear, I would take them out, zipping down the long avenues or out into the countryside.

My COO pulled a Christmas cookie out of his coat pocket, showering me with crumbs. I sighed. "I'm already ready for Christmas to be over."

"Buckle up, Blitzen, because we are just getting started!"

I dropped Walker off at his condo building then drove home to the Quantum Cyber tower. My offices were in two-thirds of the building; the rest of the floors contained one of Archer Svensson's hotels. Several condos were also part of the hotel. I owned three of them.

I loved my penthouse. It occupied three stories, with a sick roof deck and a master suite that was bigger than most Manhattan apartments. So sue me. I liked nice things.

To combat all the sweetness from the holiday party, I opened the fridge and pulled out my Thanksgiving leftovers. One thing I would say for the Svenssons: they could throw a good Thanksgiving. Or rather, their girlfriends could. Cornbread stuffing, deep-fried turkey, green bean casserole—I snacked on it as I went upstairs to the master suite.

Curious. The bathroom light was on. Usually I was particular about turning the lights off. Maybe the holidays were starting to mess with my brain.

The room was hot. I threw open all the French doors to the balcony. It was way too warm; I usually kept the penthouse just warm enough so the pipes wouldn't freeze. I started to undress, stripping down to my boxer briefs, ready for an ice-cold shower. Cold water was better for one's health. I hung my pants on a hanger that had been lying on the bed. Also curious. Usually I didn't leave the hangers strewn about the room. I was about to pull the boxer briefs down when I realized there was someone in the room with me.

CHAPTER 3

Holly

I was huffing and puffing as I pushed the trolley into the private elevator lobby.

"Man, I need to cut down on the holiday treats!"

"Don't blame the holidays. You've been stress eating since March," Morticia said. I stuck my tongue out at her.

"Not that it doesn't look good on you, though your Christmas mugs do runneth over," she said, gesturing to my chest then helping me roll the trolley over the hardwood floors. "Gunnar Svensson, one of the show's producers, thinks people will love you. I really talked you and your baking boxes up to Penny. She wants to do a special for the *Vanity Rag*. She's basically running things over there. Good thing, especially since Evan Harrington is a moron."

"He's rich and handsome!"

"And engaged to a harpy."

"This is the place where the contestants are staying?" I said in awe when we walked into the penthouse. It was huge!

"*Vanity Rag* doing a web special on decking the penthouse halls," Morticia explained as we went back to heaving the cart. "I need to buy decorations."

I had a flash of an apocalyptic holiday scene—black snow, a burned tree, a weeping angel—it would look like *The Nightmare Before Christmas*.

"I'll come with you to help pick out décor," I said hastily.

"Good choice," Morticia replied.

"This penthouse is nuts." I said, trying not to drool. "There is an actual staircase! I can wrap it in garland, real garland that smells like pine, with cranberries, big white ribbons, and fairy lights!"

Morticia smirked and tucked a strand of her long black hair behind her ear, showing the piercings. "I knew you would want to jizz Christmas all over this place."

"How is Romance Creative able to afford all this?" I asked her.

"They worked out some deal with the tower owner to film *The Great Christmas Bake-Off* here," Morticia said, sauntering into a large living room. It was fancy but bare.

"I hope this is on the list to be decorated."

"Of course," Morticia said.

"And no skeleton reindeer or creepy elves on the shelf," I added.

"The elf on the shelf is not creepy!"

I froze. The voice that haunted my Christmas nightmares—*Amber*.

"Heya, sis," she said, sauntering down the stairs.

I glared at her. "Don't tell me you're part of the bake-off. No. I literally cannot have this. You ruined enough Christmases for me. I cannot take another!"

When I went off to culinary school, Amber had decided that she would go to culinary school too. I did my best to avoid her, but I believed in spending the holidays with family, even if it killed me, so I had to see her over breaks. At the very least I didn't have to work with her at my various restaurant jobs.

"You always do this!" I yelled at her, "You stalk me and try to ruin my life! It's just like culinary school when you flirted with the dean so he would give you my schedule so you could take the same classes as me."

"I'm not here for *you*. I'm here to snag a billionaire," she said, admiring her freshly manicured nails. "Rumor has it one of the Frost brothers is going to be a judge. Chloe landed Jack Frost last year. Now I want my own billionaire too. I even adjusted my look," she said, fluffing her hair, which she had dyed a peroxide blonde.

"Gag," Morticia said.

Amber glared at her. "Naturally, Holly, you would be friends with the queen of the dead."

I stepped between them before Morticia could plant her heavy boot in Amber's face.

"Don't you dare try to steal my man," Amber warned me. "You were always trying to steal my boyfriends."

"No I wasn't. I literally was not trying to steal any of those crusty males you were stalking. You have the worst taste in men."

"Liar!" Amber hollered.

"I cannot even believe I'm having this conversation. St. Nick, give me strength! I am almost thirty. I am not acting like a teenager around you. I refuse!" I said, throwing up my hands.

Amber flounced away.

Morticia gave a black-eyeliner stare at Amber's back. "She was picked to add drama, so I've heard."

"Which means she's going to be here for the majority of the competition."

"Yep."

"Great. Just great. I need a drink."

"Do you want a white Christmas or a red Christmas?" a fun-looking girl with a pixie cut asked, holding up a bottle of wine in each hand.

"Just put an IV of each in each arm, please, spirit of Christmas alcohol," I said, following her to the couch, where she had glasses laid out.

The girl laughed. "I'm not a Christmas spirit, just Fiona!"

"Good enough for me!" I said as she filled the glasses.

"To Christmas baking!" We clinked glasses.

"I couldn't help but overhear," Fiona said to Morticia, "but are you the one who got us all private rooms?"

"Morticia has ways," I said.

"Thank every spirit of Christmas. I've done another competition like this, and we were four to a room. One person got sick, and it spread like wildfire," Fiona said.

"And that's why I insisted we use a huge penthouse," Morticia replied, sipping the dark-red wine. I'd never seen her drink white. "I did make sure Holly got the best room, though if I'd known how cool you were, I'd have made sure you got the second best," Morticia continued.

"What I have is actually bigger than my entire apartment in Manhattan that I shared with two other people, so *namaste*," Fiona said, making a little bow.

"For what it's worth, Amber did get the worst room." Morticia smirked.

"I'll drink to that!"

Morticia hadn't been lying, I decided later, after Fiona had helped drag my bags and boxes upstairs to the master suite. At least, I assumed that was what it was, because if it was just a normal bedroom, the actual master suite might make me spontaneously combust. The suite was enormous and luxurious. My toes sank into the carpet of the private sitting room, which led into the bedroom. A king-size bed was centered along a wall facing a set of French doors that led to a private balcony that looked out over the Manhattan skyline. There was a huge plush robe in the walk-in closet. I stripped down and put it on then walked into the master bathroom and just about died.

"Totally decorating this for Christmas," I said, switching on my phone. I needed to do an Instagram story for my measly number of followers. They were a small but dedicated fan base. Instagram had been propping up my existence for the past year. At first, it was supposed to be all baking. Then I started filming myself in cute outfits baking. I felt a little dirty, but then most of the messages were nice. A few were creepy, but I blocked the senders. None of the guys seemed normal enough to risk swapping messages with.

"We are having a Christmas bath scene in the near future," I said to the camera, "with holiday bath bombs and themed cocktails. But unfortunately, it won't be tonight. The bake-off starts tomorrow, baking fans!"

I looked longingly at the bathtub. Then, making sure the phone was definitely not recording, because I did not need to be *that* kind of Instagrammer, I took a quick shower. I seriously could not get over how huge the bathroom was. I could live in it. With a toaster and a mini fridge, I would totally be good.

After wrapping myself in the robe, I tied a T-shirt around my hair. I had frizzy hair on a good day; keeping my curls manageable was a perpetual struggle. I applied a gingerbread-cookie-scented moisturizer while my videos uploaded. Because I was busy scrolling through my phone and answering comments as I came out of the bathroom, I didn't notice the half-naked man until he swore.

I looked up and screamed.

"Help! Help! Stalker!" I shrieked and ineffectively pointed at the stranger. Between the rippling muscles, the washboard abs, and an ass I could bounce a quarter on, I hoped he wasn't actually here to hurt me, because he could do some damage. Pointing and shrieking wasn't going to stop him. Fortunately, he looked more shocked and horrified than angry and violent.

"Stop screaming!" he bellowed. A freezing breeze blew into the room. It was as if the man had brought the rage of winter into the master suite with him. He looked like it, too, with his ice-blue eyes and silver-white hair. "This is my penthouse. You are not authorized to be here. That makes you the stalker!"

I stopped screaming. It clearly wasn't helping anything. I also couldn't help but notice that the bathroom wasn't the only thing that was huge in the room. With him wearing nothing but boxer briefs, I could tell Santa had brought the handsome man a very large Christmas package indeed. The breeze blew in from the balcony, swirling the strange man's clean and masculine scent around the room. I forced myself to ignore it.

"Get out of my house," Big Christmas Package said flatly.

"You get out!" I shrieked. "I'm a bake-off contestant. This isn't your room!"

"What the—" he grabbed his clothes, tugging on his pants. "*The Great Christmas Bake-Off*? I cannot have Christmas invading every element of my life. This is ridiculous. Christmas is ridiculous. It's such a stupid, childish holiday." He punctuated his words by snatching up articles of clothing.

"Hey now!" I said, hands on my hips, fear subsiding. "Christmas is never ridiculous. It's the best holiday ever. And if you can't see that, well then, you're just a grinch, aren't you?"

He advanced on me. I was suddenly very aware of how large he was. Christmas package notwithstanding, this dude was *tall*, broad shouldered, with rippling muscles. He could probably split me in two.

Yes, please.

"You're some stupid little baker who never outgrew the childish fantasy of Christmas," he sneered.

My nose was inches away from his chest. He glowered down at me. I was too angry to be aware of his half-naked body. Okay, maybe I was like fifteen percent aware. But the majority of my energy was focused on being offended on behalf of Christmas.

"Don't insult baking," I said, giving him my best "I want to speak to the manager vibe," though it was ruined by the fact that I had to crane my neck up to see him and that

I was completely naked under the robe. "And never insult Christmas!"

His nostrils flared slightly.

"Men like you constantly belittle the work that women do to keep cultural traditions like Christmas alive," I continued, poking him in the chest.

"We decorate homes to make them cozy."

Poke.

"We cook holiday dinners and bake festive desserts."

Poke.

"We host parties that bring families and friends together."

Before I could poke him again, he grabbed my hand in his much-larger one. Then, realizing what he'd done, he quickly released it.

"I will not stand for your bad attitude!" I declared.

He glared down at me, strong jaw clenched, eyes cold as a frozen lake. "I can't even believe this," he finally snarled. He grabbed his briefcase and stormed out, still shirtless.

"Oh my God!" Fiona exclaimed, wide-eyed, as she ran into the room. She hugged me then pushed me to sit on the bed. "Are you okay? Who was that? Why was he in here? Someone call the police!"

"I knew it! You're trying to steal my boyfriend," Amber yelled at me, rushing into the room. "That's Owen Frost, and he's mine!"

CHAPTER 4

Owen

What was that girl doing in my bedroom? I fumed as I stalked out of the penthouse. I paced around in the elevator lobby. I was still shirtless. I didn't even have my shoes on. The elevator dinged, and the doors opened.

"Look who's back!"

"Belle?" I said.

My older sister leaned casually against the wall of the elevator. She had my coloring, and though she didn't quite have my height, she was still tall. When we were kids, she would be the one to take care of me and my younger brothers because my own mother couldn't be bothered. She had disappeared for several years and shown up again last Christmas. My brothers and I were all afraid she would leave again one day. Therefore we would do anything and everything to keep her happy.

Belle, of course, knew this, and like any big sister, she took full advantage. I had decided she enjoyed seeing how far she could push us.

Belle smirked. "Is that how you decided to introduce yourself to the contestants? You're going to be a very distracting judge," she said, motioning me inside the elevator.

"I am *not* judging. And where are all my clothes?" I asked as she pressed the button for the floor below.

"In your other condo," she said.

"You moved all my stuff?"

"We needed the bigger condo for *The Great Christmas Bake-Off*. You're one single man. You don't even have a girlfriend. There's no reason for you to own such a large penthouse."

"But I need it!" I protested as I slipped on my shirt.

My sister glared at me over her shoulder. "I think you'll just have to survive in the two-story condo with the custom marble accents for the next four weeks."

"We agreed that Romance Creative could have one of the unused lower level floors for the studio space and the smaller condo for the contestants' housing. My penthouse wasn't anywhere in the negotiations," I grumbled.

"Well, they can't live here," Belle said as I followed her into the condo she had been staying in the past few months.

Dana Holbrook and Gunnar Svensson, the owners of Romance Creative, the reality-TV production company behind the bake-off, were at the dining room table.

"There's our judge!" Dana exclaimed. I glowered at her. She smirked.

"No," I said flatly. "I have squatters in my penthouse. They're probably up there making cupcakes and gingerbread houses. I refuse to be a judge."

"But I already promised the advertisers there was going to be a Frost brother," Penny McCarthy said, smiling up at me. She was Garrett Svensson's girlfriend and had organized the Thanksgiving feast we'd had yesterday. Garrett could be vindictive at the best of times. I was sure he wasn't happy his girlfriend had immediately gone back to Manhattan to work. Best to tread carefully. I didn't need Garrett Svensson on my case.

"Seriously, you're going to try and convince me to be a judge after I had to listen to your obnoxious cousins at that horrible *TechBiz* holiday party?" I said to Dana.

"*Vanity Rag* needs a Frost brother," Penny interjected.

"Surely you would rather have someone with baking experience," I said.

"I've been running analyses," Penny said, "and our magazine will have an estimated forty-percent-higher engagement if you're in the bake-off."

"Just do it," Belle coaxed.

"Will I get a cut of that profit?" I grumbled.

Dana raised an eyebrow. "I'm on a group chat with my cousins and brother, and they were all crowing about how a Holbrook was going to be on top of the *TechBiz* list. Again. I believe," she said, scrolling through her tablet and pulling up the previous year's list, "that your company was not given high marks for coolness, approachability of their CEO, and bonding experiences."

"How about," Penny said, looking up at me, "if we throw you guys a holiday party! That would really put you on the map."

"I don't know if the bake-off is really the demographic we go after," I said. "We recruit women, yes, but our employees mainly consist of stereotypical tech bros."

"Yes," Penny said, "but their girlfriends and their moms love *The Great Christmas Bake-Off*. When the programmers are thinking about where to apply for a cushy tech job, if their mom or girlfriend is like, 'We really love Owen!' that's good for you."

"Do you want to be on top of the list, or do you want to be at the same party next year while my cousins act like obnoxious toddlers bragging about who got the bigger ice cream cone?" Dana asked.

"Take it from me," Gunnar said. He had longish blond hair and always reminded me of a stoner. "Desperate times call for desperate measures."

"Is it really that desperate?"

But I did need to win. Greg and Hunter Svensson, who were big investors in my company, had been on my case at the last board meeting about recruitment, talent retention, and staying competitive. At the very least, this might show them I was doing something. And Belle clearly wanted me to. I owed her big-time for what had happened.

"Fine, I'll do it."

"Of course you'll do it!" Belle retorted.

"Contest starts bright and early tomorrow morning. Wear something sexy!" Dana called out as I went to my smaller condo.

As I showered, I thought about the girl I had surprised. If she was one of those obnoxious Christmas lovers, she and I were not going to get along.

I scowled at my reflection in the mirror.

I forgot my Thanksgiving leftovers.

I really did hate Christmas.

CHAPTER 5

Holly

Morticia's voice blared through a megaphone, waking me out of a very pleasant dream. There was an ice prince, shirtless, of course, who looked very similar to the handsome stranger who had been in my bedroom last night.

His name is Owen.

"First day of the bake-off, people. You will be on camera. Make sure your makeup looks nice and you're wearing something decent," my friend announced.

I yawned, crawling out of the giant bed. The handsome guy had said it was his bedroom. Did he sleep in this bed? Did he do *other things* in this very bed?

The door swung open; the megaphone shrieked. "You have half an hour," Morticia told me.

"I can't do my hair in thirty minutes!" I yelled, running into the bathroom. My hair was a rat's nest. That was what I got for going to sleep with it not completely dry.

Morticia brought me a coffee while I pinned up the frizz as best I could and threw on my comfy shoes. She looked down her nose.

"I'm sorry, did you not hear me when I said you're going to be on TV?" She went into my closet and pulled out a red sweater dress, a push-up bra, and heels.

"I can't wear that! I need my Crocs and my sweatpants!" I complained.

Morticia looked nonplussed. "I thought you were trying to use the bake-off competition to increase your Instagram presence and get people to buy—" she sighed "—baking boxes. You can't look like a homeless person."

She stuck the dress out to me. "Put this on. Friends don't let friends go on camera with sweatpants and saggy boobs."

I compromised with Morticia on the high-heeled shoes, instead opting to wear black tennis shoes. If I tried wearing those heels in the kitchen, I was going to trip, fall, and break my neck trying to take a cake out of the oven.

As soon as I put the dress on, I realized that it wasn't large enough to hold both me and all the cake I'd been stress eating the past few months.

"Time to bake," Morticia said from the doorway.

Too late to change. I ran to the elevator.

"I look like a mess," I complained to my friend, adjusting the dress in the reflective paneling in the elevator and slathering makeup on the bags under my eyes.

"You need another coffee," Morticia said, stabbing more bobby pins into my frizzy hair. "And considering that your last Instagram post was you in way less clothing, eating a cupcake, I feel like you're overreacting. Sex sells baked goods."

When I walked into the studio space, it felt like Christmas. I was immediately hyped. For all her acerbic anti-Christmas comments, Morticia was a good artist, and the decorated space was warm and festive without feeling cheesy. There were garlands and lights strung around the perimeter of the large studio. The palette was whites and golds, with pops of dark reds. It felt like everything had been dusted lightly with powdered sugar. Brighter lights shone over each baking station. I rummaged through the boxes under my table. We each had a set of the high-end Platinum Provisions cooking tools. I whistled. This was thousands of dollars' worth of stuff.

Dana Holbrook and Gunnar Svensson, the producers, were talking to a tall, willowy woman at the front of the room. I recognized her as Anastasia, the host of the show and owner of the Whimsical Dining blog. Dana nodded as she and Gunnar walked off the set. They looked up to the front of the room. The camera guy signaled, and the willowy woman smiled brightly.

"Welcome to the second season of *The Great Christmas Bake-Off*. Just like last year, this contest is all about the bakers, the desserts, and of course, Christmas! We don't believe in gimmicks. The contestants have hours, sometimes a full day, to complete their desserts. Also, like last year, we have a fantastic panel of judges. Anu and Nick are back! Anu Pillai, a chocolatier and baker from Li'l Masa bakery in NoLiTa. Then we have Nick Mazur, a pastry chef and restaurant owner with businesses all over the New York area. Finally, we have Owen Frost, founder and CEO of

Quantum Cyber. He does not do any baking, but he's very good-looking, so here he is!"

OMG. That was the guy who had been in my-slash-his room the night before. He sat at the reclaimed-wood judges' table, back straight, wearing a dark-navy suit that made his hair and icy-blue eyes pop. Something else down in the South Pole was popping too. I must really be going through a dry spell if I was freaking out over some guy who said he hated Christmas.

I internally flipped out. Did he recognize me? I really wished I had changed my outfit now. I must look like a drugged-out stripper.

You are not Amber. You are not going to freak out over some egotistical billionaire, I chanted to myself as Anastasia continued to talk about the rules of the competition. Owen scowled as he surveyed the contestants.

I forced myself to concentrate. *Think of the prize money! Think of the debt you're going to pay off! Don't get distracted.*

"The first challenge," Anastasia said, "is the Shimmy Down the Chimney Challenge. You have until this afternoon to create a fun, festive dessert that's tasty enough to make reindeer dance and Santa shimmy on down the chimney!"

I'd like Owen to shimmy down my chimney.

But he was watching Anastasia. I sighed. She was willowy and pretty, with a curtain of chestnut hair. *I bet Christmas-hating billionaire Owen goes for women like her.*

I pulled at my skirt some more and adjusted my top. I seriously needed to cut back on the sweets. I looked up from adjusting my boobs. Right. I was on camera. Better stop touching myself inappropriately. Owen's gaze flicked in my direction. His eyes narrowed slightly.

I slept in your bed last night, I mouthed to him.

His eyes widened slightly, and he scowled.

"You're trying to steal him! I knew it!" Amber whined nasally. She had managed to worm her way to a station next to mine. "Owen is mine," she continued. "I already have a bombshell Christmas dessert planned. Owen is going to come crawling for my sweets."

"Whatever. You want some sort of Christmas-hating ice prince, fine with me," I said, taking out the pans I would need for my dessert. "In fact, if you're chasing after Owen Frost, then I know something's wrong with him."

I went to collect my ingredients. Amber and Owen could spiral into a descent of Christmas-ruining madness, but I was going to bake. I had the perfect dessert planned: chocolate pomegranate tarts. Chocolaty, rich, with a smack of pomegranate, they were a more adult Christmas dessert. It would be very sexy to eat a piece with a glass of wine by the fire, a Christmas tree softly blinking while you fed a bite to your paramour curled up beside you under a fur throw.

My pastry dough was perfect, if I did say so myself, and I could fill it with literally anything. In the pantry, I grabbed pomegranates, bricks of deep-brown chocolate, heavy cream, sugar, flour, and butter. I was planning on making several smaller tarts—not too small, because then it was all crust—but if they were too big, one might as well be eating chocolate pudding.

Using a food processor so as to not overwork the crust, I began cutting the butter into the flour. I was regretting wearing the sweater dress, which rode up whenever I raised my arms above boob height. I was also regretting not getting up earlier so I could shower. That clean, masculine scent from Owen's room clung to me; anytime I moved my hair, I could smell it. It was distracting.

"I can't believe I was in his bed. Did they even change the sheets before we arrived?" I muttered as I made the dough. "What if he sleeps nude? It would be like I was sleeping *with* him. Naked."

I jumped when a man said behind me, "I assure you, I do not sleep naked."

CHAPTER 6

Owen

When Anastasia started the clock, the contestants scurried to collect their ingredients. One woman with frizzy hair looked oddly familiar. If I hadn't known any better, I would have thought she was the girl who had been in my room last night and who I thought was going to bludgeon me with a Yule log when I told her I despised Christmas.

"Since there's so much time in the competition," Dana said as the camera guys moved around to take close-up shots of the contestants, "we want the judges to mingle a little bit and talk to the contestants about what they're making. Just don't get in the way. Owen, why don't you start over there near Amber and Holly?"

"Who's Holly?"

Dana glared at me. "Did you seriously not read the packet?"

I shrugged. Dana tapped her foot. "Red sweater?"

The girl.

"I have to go to work," I complained. "I can't be here all day!"

"Do your interviews, and then you can go. Your company headquarters is upstairs. It's not like your commute is long."

I strode over to Holly, determined to get this over with. She was chattering to herself, puffs of flour coming out of the noisy machine she was using.

Aren't bakers supposed to be crazy? And now she was in my house. *So are all those other people.*

Yes, but Holly was sleeping in my bed. I would never be able to clean out that scent of cinnamon and sugar.

I waited impatiently as she kept talking to herself.

"I sleep partially clothed," I said finally butting in. I could not be here all day. The smell of sugar and the strong pine scent from the garland were starting to give me a headache.

"You do?" she asked me. Her eye was twitching a bit, as if she wanted to look me up and down.

"Of course. Sleeping when it's too hot is the worst."

"I thought you hated winter," she demanded.

"I hate Christmas, but winter is the perfect time of year," I retorted.

Zane, one of the camera guys, was framing his shot, and he motioned for me to start talking about her dessert.

Let's get this over with.

I gritted my teeth. "Would you care to talk about what you're baking?"

Holly adjusted the sweater dress. I tried not to stare. It hugged her curves, the knit collar dipping down to frame her cleavage.

Be calm.

I didn't need someone like Holly in my life. I had gone on that one disastrous date with Sloane six months ago, and I would never date a woman again. No, I needed to concentrate on my business.

"I'm making a chocolate tart," Holly said, tucking a lock of hair behind her ear. "The key to a good tart is the crust—it should be buttery, just a little sweet, slightly crunchy, but still tender. Like a good man!"

"You like your men buttery?" I asked, confused.

"I don't mind it when my men are a little greased up," she said, doing a little shimmy. Her tits jiggled in the low-cut neckline. I looked up at the ceiling. Someone had hung a whole reindeer family up there.

"But for the tart, we don't want the butter hot. I need it ice-cold. Like you, Mr. Frost!" She winked. It was… well, it was sexy. But I only noticed it in an objective, dispassionate way.

I stood there while she made the dough. I didn't know how long Dana wanted me to talk to the contestants. If I left too early, Dana would storm upstairs and find me and drag me back to the studio. She did not screw around when it came to her business.

I watched as Holly made the crust, narrating as she mixed the flour, salt, and sugar. Then she dumped it out on the counter and began working it with a metal torture-device-looking thing.

"This is a pastry blender," she explained. "I start the dough with a food processor but like to finish the job by hand. Otherwise I think it gets the dough too excited!" She stuck her tongue out slightly as she added the egg yolk, vanilla, and cream.

"Now," she said, rolling it into a long yellow tube of dough, "we put it in the fridge so it gets nice and stiff."

Zane smirked behind the camera. Was there something going on with them? I had assumed Holly was flirting with me, but had she been flirting with Zane?

I shook my head as I took off the microphone. What did I care? I had a company to run.

I had barely made it upstairs to my office when Walker Svensson, my COO, accosted me.

"Dude, you didn't tell me!" he said around the candy cane he had in his mouth like a cigar.

"What?" I said irritably.

"You're judging the bake-off! Did they give you anything to eat? Are you suffocating in sugar? You have it all over your suit."

I scowled and looked down. There was powdered sugar on my bespoke suit jacket. I brushed at it angrily but only smeared it around.

Great. Holly ruined my suit. I knew The Great Christmas Bake-Off *was a mistake.*

"That was a brilliant move," Walker said as I followed him to the C-suite offices. "Everyone's talking about it."

"Like our employees?" I frowned.

"The office manager is scheduling a viewing party with food and everything," he said. "Also, Penny just called and said she want to have the bake-off contestants do a holiday party baking competition for one of the episodes. And she's decorating the main lobby as part of the *Vanity Rag* digital content, so that will for sure get us more points on the *TechBiz* list."

"I can't believe the list is so subjective," I complained. "Why can't they measure actual metrics? They're just going to come, talk to people, and hand out surveys on how the employees feel. You can't measure that!"

"You can't fight it. You have to let the sea of public relations take you where it wants you to go," Walker said, making hula dance moves. I resisted the urge to snatch the candy cane out of his mouth and stab him with it.

"Don't forget we have that meeting with my brothers coming up," he continued.

Speaking of wanting to stab people. "I do not have the patience to deal with Greg and Hunter," I said, sitting down at my desk.

"Last board meeting of the year," Walker said. "Maybe we can have one of the contestants cater it. Are there any cute ones? Who knows, maybe Santa will put a girlfriend for you under the tree this year!"

"I would never date one of the contestants," I said. "It would be nonstop baking and Christmas all year round. I'd go insane."

CHAPTER 7

Holly

"**Y**ou *are* trying to steal him from me," Amber spat as soon as Owen left. "You were flirting with him."

"I wasn't flirting. I can't help it if his candy cane was happy to see me," I said, knowing it would rile my stepsister up.

Her face went red as if she were about to explode.

"Relax, it's just a joke," I told her hastily. "We were having a conversation. It was all for the show."

"You don't even know anything about him," Amber said as she went back to angrily pitting cherries. "I've read all about him online. He's a billionaire and a visionary. He built his company, Quantum Cyber, from nothing. He made billions on Bitcoin. He's revolutionized cybersecurity. I saw his TED talk; it was inspiring."

"He sounds insufferable," I said as I carefully removed seeds from the pile of bright-red pomegranates.

"He had a terrible childhood with a cold mother," Amber continued. "He needs a good woman to take care of him."

"And you're going to be the one to help him," I said, trying not to gag.

"Of course. Once he realizes we're meant for each other, he'll whisk me off to his castle," she said dreamily.

"He has a castle?" I asked, raising an eyebrow.

"He will once I tell him to buy me one," Amber insisted as a cherry pit flew out of the metal device and hit me in the face.

"Oops," Amber said. She'd clearly meant to do that.

The first tart would be a vanilla-bean custard on a pomegranate crust, with a brûléed sugar crust on top. The caramelized sugar would be as golden as the Christmas ornaments that sparkled around the room. To make the crust, I lightly folded in the bright-red pomegranate seeds, speckling the dough pink and red.

The second was a chocolate tart crust with a pomegranate filling and a thin layer of chocolate ganache on top. This tart would be less sweet but very rich. The third type would be a chocolate tart on a vanilla butter crust, with a layer of pomegranate reduction with candied pomegranate seeds to decorate it and provide a little tartness.

I was straining my pomegranate juice as Penny and Morticia skirted around the cameras to come talk to me.

"Morticia says you make baking subscription boxes," Penny said excitedly.

"Yes. I need to send another batch out tonight actually." I gestured to my tarts. "Since I'm already in the mood, I may make tarts, along with cookies."

"Can we do a special on your Taste My Muffin baking boxes?" Penny asked. I'd heard Morticia talk about the bubbly redhead but never met her. And what I'd heard had made me slightly jealous. Penny seemed like she had her shit together—fun creative job, rich, handsome boyfriend, clothes that were free of batter and flour.

"Sure!" I replied.

"I've seen your Instagram. It's so much fun!"

"You mean raunchy," Morticia said.

"Guys like a little excitement," Penny said, lightly nudging me with her hip. "Hey, I'm not judging! I have my Queen of Tarts baking brand. My videos attracted all sorts of random guys!"

"I'm surprised Garrett hasn't made you give it up," Morticia said.

"I think he's pretending that if he ignores it, it will go away. Not that I have time to do videos for my channel anyway. Though I did want to be on this season of *The Great Christmas Bake-Off*," she said wistfully.

"Seems like you got the better end of the deal," I said, hoping I didn't sound jealous.

"To be honest," Penny said, "I'm actually not that great a baker. You're doing very fancy stuff here."

"It's just a tart."

"Hardly! I don't think I could ever make my chocolate mousse so creamy!" Penny said, bouncing on the balls of her feet. "So, can you do the subscription baking boxes tonight? I need content to feed the digital beast."

"Sure!" I said. Then I chewed on my lip. "So are we really living in Owen's penthouse?"

"Oh my God! Morticia told me what happened. I'm so sorry about that. Belle, his sister, told us we could use his condo since it's bigger and there will be better camera angles. I guess he never got the memo."

I thought about Owen shirtless in the bedroom, his intense blue eyes, his chiseled, muscular body.

"He's grouchy and set in his ways. Don't mind him," Penny assured me.

"But where is he staying if we're in his house?" I asked in concern.

"He has another condo," Penny assured me. "It's much smaller, but he'll live."

CHAPTER 8

Owen

I t was nonstop baking when I went back down to the studio for the final judging later that afternoon. Holly was the first contestant to present. Based on my conversation with her earlier, I was expecting a simple chocolate tart. That was not what was set before me.

"In the spirit of Christmas and making people shimmy—" she did that motion that made her tits jiggle again "—I've prepared Christmas tarts three ways," she said as I carefully cut each of the perfect round little tarts in half. The red one looked like it would be less sweet. The pomegranate glaze was sticky and slightly tart, and the vanilla custard stuck to my tongue. I swallowed. I needed a glass of water, or better yet, some whisky.

"It's fine," I said, pushing the plate away.

"Fine?" Holly said. "Well, I suppose that's the best I get from the Christmas-hating grinch."

No one talked to me like that. Who did Holly think she was?

"I love the presentation on these," Anu gushed. As a pastry chef herself, I was sure she had more relevant comments to make than anything I could come up with.

"I love how instead of doing several radically different tart flavors, they were all variations on a theme," Anu continued. "It's subtle but clever."

"Yes, it shows a lot of thought," Nick added. "Also, if I'm not mistaken, you're a bit of a familiar face?"

Did they date or something? Also, why do I even care?

"Yes, I worked at one of your restaurants last year on the pasta line," Holly replied.

Wait, she did? That seemed like a waste of talent. Even if I didn't care for the dessert she had made, I could see she knew what she was doing.

"I hope you had a good experience!" Nick said with a laugh. "If you ever come back to one of my restaurants, I'll have to put you on the dessert station. As you can see, I ate all of mine!"

"As did I," Anu said, smiling. "I'm about to eat part of Owen's too."

"I think we'd all like a bite of Owen!" Holly said, looking at me from under her lashes. She and Anu laughed, as did Anastasia.

The next contestant was Amber. She watched me as though she might actually take a bite out of me.

"And what did you bake for us?" Anu asked.

"This is a cherry spice cake trifle. I made my own boozy cherries and layered them with a caramel nutmeg custard, holiday ginger-and-orange spice cake, whipped cream, and candied walnuts."

I looked down at the tall crystal glass.

"It's very rustic," Nick said after a moment.

"I know the secret to a man's heart," Amber declared. "He wants simple, honest food."

I wasn't sure how to eat the dessert. As much as I didn't care for Penny's tart, I'd rather eat that than the trifle. Somehow it was both too sweet and too flavorful.

Nick dumped his glass out on the table and dissected it, tasting each piece. "There's a lot going on, and none of it is very good."

"Owen, thoughts?" Anu asked as she took a small bite.

"I think Holly's dessert was better."

Amber's face screwed up when I said that.

Fiona was next. She had made a more restrained miniature orange cheesecake with candied cranberries and other winter fruits.

"If you want to make a rustic yet refined dessert, this is the way to do it," Anu said. "Nicely done."

The rest of the contestants hadn't done anything all that interesting. There was a smattering of cakes and pies, but for the most part, we were served ice cream after ice cream. I didn't care for desserts, and I really hated ice cream. Why ruin something cold with all that sugar and milk?

"A lot of restaurants, many of mine included," Nick explained to me after Anastasia had herded the contestants to the greenroom, "have cut desserts from the menu and don't employ a pastry chef, let alone a whole crew. They'll have, say, one of the line cooks make ice cream because it's cheap and easy. So now not just on TV shows like this but everywhere really, all these kids know how to do is make ice cream."

"Some of it was imaginative," Anu said diplomatically.

"What about that parfait that Amber made?" Nick asked.

"I don't know anything about desserts, but why is she even here?" I said. Anu made a face at the mention of the parfait. "Let's boot her."

Gunnar came over, fiddling with his headset. "Just a note: Amber is our drama for this season, so you guys can't boot her for several more episodes at least. Cool?" He flashed a thumbs-up. "You're doing great! You're already trending on Instagram, Owen. All the celebrity blogs are talking about your being a judge."

"Great."

"You ready to announce?" Gunnar asked.

"We've made our decision. Owen, are you okay?"

"I'm fine with whatever you all want. You are the experienced chefs."

"And you're here as eye candy!" Anu giggled.

The contestants filed out, lining up in front of us. Holly was directly in front of me. She kept fidgeting with her dress, smoothing it down, running her fingers along the collar. Was she flirting with me?

"Would Holly and Jin-Yoo please step forward?" Anu said. "Jin-Yoo, while the ice cream was tasty, it just wasn't as complex or imaginative as the other desserts. You had several hours to cook. We expect a bit more from contestants. Holly, your dessert was classic tart, yet had a subtle refinement and intelligence about it. Congratulations, you've won this round. Jin-Yoo, best of luck."

I checked my phone as I handed back the microphone after the cameras finished their close-up of Jin-Yoo's teary face as Anastasia hugged her.

I had ten messages, and they were all from my brother Jack.

CHAPTER 9

Holly

I was riding high on my first big win. Maybe I could do this! Maybe I could turn my life around. I didn't want much. Just a kitchen big enough to make a wedding cake and a freestanding tub. Ideally, the tub wouldn't be in the kitchen, but I could make it work if I had to.

I did feel a little bit bad that we had kicked Owen out of his own home, though it was a very nice penthouse.

"Such a pretty kitchen!" I purred, hugging the white marble countertops as Penny and Zane set up to shoot. "Seriously, I bet Owen doesn't even cook in here. Speaking of which, I'm starving."

"There's leftovers in the fridge from Thanksgiving," Morticia said with a slight smirk.

"OMG! Thanksgiving leftovers!" I dumped the turkey, corn-bread stuffing, and sweet potatoes on a plate and heated them up in the microwave while I sketched out what I was going to bake.

"I have to send out boxes for my new subscribers from November," I said. "I was thinking tarts, chocolate chip-mas cookies, and gingerbread cookie bars. I have a hundred and twenty boxes to mail out."

"That many?"

"Yes, and that was just from Thanksgiving week!" I told Morticia. "Ever since the drum up for *The Great Christmas Bake-Off* started, I've had more people wanting to order a Taste My Muffin subscription box!"

"Seems like a lot," Morticia said as I blew on the turkey and stuffing. She took out a fork and snuck a bite.

I smiled at her.

"No," Morticia said, eyes narrowing.

"Please?" I wheedled.

"I'm not helping you bake."

"But you're a good baker!" I cajoled. "You helped me in college." We had both gone to the same university, but I was in culinary school while she was in art school. I had dormed in a pod with Morticia and her identical twin, Lilith.

"Just help me! You know the gingerbread cookies take forever."

Morticia heaved a sigh. "Fine." She tied up her long hair. "But I get the last of the leftovers."

"We're ready to start filming whenever you are," Zane said, motioning to his camera.

I narrated as I mixed up the ingredients for the chocolate chip-mas cookies. I used chocolate chunks, of course, but to give it that Christmas pizzazz, I added in green and red sprinkles and white-chocolate chips.

"The trick to the perfect chocolate chip cookie is to take the pan out of the oven every three minutes and slam it," I said.

Morticia raised an eyebrow at the camera. "Heh. Slam it. Can you tell she has sex on the brain?"

"I do not!" I sputtered. "Don't sully chocolate chip cookies with that kind of talk."

"She wants a certain someone to sully her." Morticia smirked.

"Ignore her, please," I said, waving a hand in front of Morticia's face. "Now," I told the camera, "I'm going to use an ice cream scoop to make even balls."

"Balls." Morticia snickered.

Owen's balls looked nice in those boxer briefs.

I refused to give in to the naughty portion of my brain. I was not getting coal for Christmas.

"Remember to check the oven temperature, because you can never be too careful," I said, checking the thermometer. "It looks good, so I'm going to slide in three pans, since this is a big oven."

"Three at a time, Holly? Good gracious," Morticia remarked as she creamed butter and sugar for the gingerbread cookie bars.

I just need one big… Shut up brain. Think of cookies and frosting.

Owen Frost… yum.

No, not that kind of frosting.

The timer beeped.

"Time to bang!" I chirped then mentally face-palmed.

Morticia was grinning. "Bang… frosting?"

I slammed each cookie tray on the counter once then put them back in the oven.

"Getting a little hot in here," Morticia said.

While the cookies cooled, I made the gingerbread cookie bars and Morticia made the tarts. I was all tarted out, so I was glad she was doing it. It was dark when we finished. Morticia and I laid out the red-and-white boxes while Zane took B-roll of the piles of finished baked goods.

"How do you make sure they don't break up in transit?" Penny asked as Morticia helped me carefully pack the baked treats into the boxes.

"These are special boxes."

"I designed them," Morticia interjected. The boxes had little inserts that fit the various pans I used for making cakes, loaves, cupcakes, or bars. We carefully packed the boxes, nestling the baked goods in tissue paper decorated with candy canes, snowflakes, and the Taste My Muffin logo. As a final touch, I added a letterpressed note describing what each item was. I took a few pictures to post to Instagram.

"These are ready to go!" I said as Morticia helped me load the boxes onto the cart.

We took the boxes downstairs. I had arranged for a courier pickup, and a big truck waited by the front door to the lobby.

"Something in here sure smells good!" the courier said hopefully. I handed him a package of gingerbread cookie bars.

"For the road."

He smiled. "Merry Christmas!"

After sending off my baking boxes to their new homes, I took a few pictures out on the street then recorded a video for my Instagram story.

"As you can see, it is starting to snow," I said into the camera, shaking snowflakes out of my hair. "Though some of all this white stuff on me is powdered sugar. I've been baking, as usual!"

I watched my phone upload the video. The comments came in as soon as it was posted.

"I love Christmas!" I sang, twirling around in the snow-flakes. I was so absorbed that I didn't realize anyone was watching me until a man grabbed me!

CHAPTER 10

Owen

"**M**y second-favorite brother!" Jack announced when I walked into Frost Tower. Yes, my little brother had named a whole tower after himself. The lobby was decorated for Christmas, and Jack stood in the middle of it smirking, surrounded by a frankly excessive Christmas scene.

"Like my sign?" Jack said, pointing to a neon sign displaying the Frost Tower and Grey Dove Bistro logos.

"It's fitting considering that this tower was a failure until Chloe came along and saved both your ass and your tower," I replied.

"It's a very nice ass," Chloe said, skipping out of the Grey Dove Bistro, the restaurant she owned. Chloe and Jack had met during last year's filming of *The Great Christmas Bake-Off*. I wondered if he had asked me to come over so he could rub the whole bake-off situation in my face.

Someone, save me from the bake-off. Not only did I have to eat sweets, but my Thanksgiving leftovers were still being held hostage in my occupied penthouse.

"Recovered from Thanksgiving?" Jack asked with a grin as we waited for the elevator.

"We should ask the Svenssons to make more food next year," I said.

"Or you could get off your lazy butt and drive to Harrogate bright and early to help cook," Jack said as the elevator dinged.

"There were like fifty turkeys. I'm amazed that they all disappeared!" Chloe said.

"Well, I can eat a deep-fried turkey all by myself."

"Yeah, I saw," Jack said with a smirk. He and Chloe looked at each other and laughed. It was nice to see him happy with Chloe. I definitely was not bugged at all that my younger brother had met the perfect woman and fallen in love before me. Nope. *Not at all.*

"So we have some news!" Jack said when we were in his penthouse.

"You and Chloe?"

Chloe nodded excitedly.

"Sit down. You might want a drink."

Jack poured me two fingers of the whisky that I'd been craving all day to wash away the taste of the desserts. Chloe was bouncing up and down on the couch with excitement.

"You are going to be a great-uncle!" Jack exclaimed.

"Ta-da!" Chloe said.

"What, you guys are pregnant?" I said in shock. "Wait, that's not right. That would make me an uncle, not a great-uncle."

"He's so confused!" Chloe laughed.

"I'm only a great-uncle if my nephew has a child," I said, frowning. "Who has a secret child? Wait, it better not be Jonathan!"

"Actually, it's Milo," Jack said.

He whistled, and his huge silver-and-grey husky padded into the room, tongue lolling. He came right to me, butting his shaggy head against my pants. I was immediately covered in fur.

"Milo had puppies?"

"Dude, no, that is not how that works. And you call yourself the smart one!"

I stood up and put Jack in a headlock. He shoved me off, laughing.

"Milo knocked up a dog at the groomer's," Chloe explained.

"I thought he was fixed?"

"So did I," Jack said grimly.

"So how is this your problem?"

"He knocked up an award-winning Dalmatian," Chloe explained. "Ginny, from the Scottie Dog Groomers and Pet Boutique, said the Dalmatian's owner sued."

"Thankfully, only one of the puppies is Milo's," Jack said. "We had a pupternity test done and everything. The rest of them are all Dalmatians."

"Ginny's insurance settled with the Dalmatian's owner on the condition that Ginny keep the puppy."

"But she said it's Milo's problem, ergo, it is now my problem," Jack said.

"Mazel tov!" I said, raising my glass.

Jack poured me another while he and Chloe exchanged a look.

"Do you want to see the puppy?" Chloe asked.

"Sure, I guess," I said, trying to figure out what was going on.

She disappeared for a minute.

"So how's the bake-off?" Jack asked, grinning. "Find a cute girl?"

"No. You know I'm done with dating."

"You can't let Sloane turn you off of love!" Jack exclaimed.

"Who are you, and what did you do with my cold-as-ice brother?" I remarked, feeling his forehead.

"You're soft on the inside," Jack cajoled. "You still talk to Mom and Dad."

"I shouldn't," I sighed. "But I keep thinking they'll have a revelation and apologize."

Jack snorted. "The Svensson brothers think you're lonely."

"I'm not."

"Also, they want me to make sure you don't go after Meg."

"What? Hunter's Meg? Why would I?"

"You made the comment at Thanksgiving that you would pursue her. It's been a serious point of contention. Liam showed me the group chats," Jack said seriously.

"It was a joke, and also Hunter would probably light my tower on fire. I'm not an idiot," I retorted.

"We know, but they're all concerned. You know how tightly wound Hunter is," Chloe said, coming out with a bundle of floof in her arms. "Isn't he cute!" Milo wagged his tail as Chloe placed the puppy gently in my arms.

"He definitely doesn't look like he came out of a Dalmatian," I said, inspecting the puppy. He was the spitting image of Jack's husky.

"Do you love him?" Chloe gushed.

"A dog can add a lot of value to a person's life," Jack added. I looked between him and Chloe.

"No, thank you."

"Take the dog, Owen."

"I don't have time."

"*I* don't have time," my brother insisted.

"He pees everywhere," Chloe explained, "and I just had the penthouse redecorated. He's ruined several very expensive shoes and a nice couch I had imported."

The puppy stuck his tongue out and licked my face.

He *was* cute.

"He likes you," Jack said. "Just take him for a little while."

"Also, he's a good chick magnet," Chloe added with a giggle. "Put a little Santa hat on him, and women will flock to you!"

Chloe proved more right than she probably knew. I had taken the train, as it was rush hour. The puppy was in my jacket, looking around intelligently at his surroundings.

"Are you going to help me steal my Thanksgiving leftovers?" I whispered to him as I rounded the corner to my tower...

... and immediately crashed into Holly. The puppy yelped as she screamed. I grabbed Holly around the waist before she could tip over. She was wearing ridiculous high heels.

"You should pay attention to where you're going!" I growled. "Dangerous men look for girls like you who are wandering around totally oblivious."

"You mean dangerous like you?"

CHAPTER 11

Holly

"I'm not dangerous," Owen countered.

"It's good that we cleared that up!" Something furry stuck its head out of his overcoat.

"You have a puppy!" I squealed. Owen winced. I ignored him. "Hi! You're so cute! What's your name?" I said to the puppy.

"He doesn't have a name," Owen said, peering down at me.

"You have to name him Rudolph!"

The puppy barked. "He's not staying," Owen said.

"Of course someone who hates Christmas also hates puppies."

"I don't hate puppies," Owen said tersely.

"Great! Because you're perfect for each other!" I swooned, taking out my phone. The puppy mugged for the camera.

"You have no shame," Owen scolded the dog.

"He's too innocent!" I cooed at the dog. The cuteness was overwhelming. "Wait, hold him up! Shots of attractive men and cute dogs are gold! Once Penny sees you have a puppy, she's going to go nuts! You'll be plastered all over the *Vanity Rag* website."

I took the puppy out of Owen's arms, tipping him over in the crook of my own arm and snapping pictures.

"Who is the absolute cutest thing in the world?"

The dog was either exceptionally friendly and photogenic, or more likely, he smelled the turkey on my breath.

Owen was studying me intently.

"He's cute, isn't he?" I said, kissing the puppy on his little black nose. "You should keep him."

Owen didn't say a word. Instead, he stepped up to me, cupping my face slightly. Was he about to kiss me? Not that I was complaining. I would totally make out with him then yell at him about Christmas, of course, but I can compartmentalize.

Owen leaned in close to me. His breath felt cool against my mouth. He closed his eyes and—sniffed?

"You smell like—" he sniffed again.

"I smell?"

His eye twitched slightly. "You smell like Thanksgiving leftovers!" he snarled. He turned my face and swiped a thumb over my cheek. "Is that gravy?"

I made a face. "There were the most delicious leftovers in the fridge. Morticia said I could have them."

"They weren't hers," Owen said flatly, releasing me. "They were mine."

"I'm sorry!" I looked up at him, wide-eyed. "They were really good. Best turkey I've ever eaten. Really life changing."

His lip curled back, and he snatched the puppy from me. "People who eat another person's leftovers don't then get to pimp out said person's dogs for Instagram likes."

"I'll make it up to you. I ate something of yours, so you can eat something of mine!" I struck a little pose.

"How is eating you out a fair trade? Shouldn't you be offering a blow job in exchange for eating leftovers?" Owen asked, confused. Then he looked horrified.

"I meant, I would *make* you something to eat," I clarified, feeling slightly flushed at the thought of him tasting my Christmas cookies. "I'll make you a roast beef or something or, hell, another turkey. But sure, I mean, I can totally also give you a blow job." I smiled at him. So twist my arm. I wanted to open that Christmas package early.

"I'm sorry. My apologies," Owen said abruptly, turning and leaving only snowflakes in the space where he had been.

CHAPTER 12

Owen

I tossed and turned all night. I couldn't sleep. I alternated between apocalyptic scenarios in which Holly went on a nuclear public relations campaign against my company and then fantasizing about what it would be like to actually taste her Christmas cookies, so to speak.

The dog didn't help, either. Someone had decided he wanted to be named Rudolph. I tried calling him Monster or Gremlin, but the puppy ignored me. When I called Rudolph, though, he came running. With his tiny bladder, I had to race him all the way downstairs every few hours.

At this rate, I should pitch a tent in the lobby.

I felt less than sharp the next morning, which was bad, because I had a meeting with Svensson Investment. Greg Svensson was mean on a good day. The holiday season made him unbearable.

"What am I going to do with you?" I asked the dog. It was clear I couldn't leave him in the condo. Picking him up, I took Rudolph (*dear God, why did that have to be his name?*) down to the main lobby with me. Several of the bored-looking software engineers perked up as soon as they saw the dog.

"Whoa!" one guy said. "Best CEO ever! You brought a puppy to work!"

"He's not staying."

"You're not keeping the dog?" another programmer asked in horror.

One of our marketing interns whipped out her phone to take videos of the puppy wriggling in my arms, tail wagging. I recalled how terrible my CEO relatability scores had been in the last *TechBiz* report. Pictures of me with a puppy would probably go a long way to helping Quantum Cyber beat the Holbrooks.

Guess he's staying.

"I'm keeping him," I assured them. "I just need someone to puppy sit. He's not housetrained yet."

"My brother has a dog-sitting start-up," the programmer offered. "I can email you."

"Thanks."

I had been planning on paying the receptionist to take care of the dog. I couldn't just leave Rudolph with her now, though. That would look like puppy abandonment. I would ruin all the goodwill I had just built up.

Penny and Holly and the other contestants streamed off the elevator. I peered at her. She liked dogs. And Holly had eaten my leftovers, so she owed me a favor. But then I had asked her to suck my dick, which was, in hindsight, not what I should have done. I weighed my options. Talk to

Holly? Pretend I didn't see her and take the dog with me to Svensson Investment to face Greg's wrath?

Holly waved to me, so I headed in her direction.

"Good morning, Rudolph!" she said.

"I'm sorry for last night," I said gruffly.

"Last night was amazing!" she said, squeezing my arm. Amber looked as if she was having some sort of fit. "No need to apologize!" She winked at me.

I pressed my lips together. "I hate to ask you to do this, but I have a puppy emergency."

"A cuteness emergency?" she asked, scratching Rudolph behind one floppy ear.

"I need someone to pet sit. I know it's—"

"I accept!" Holly squealed, snuggling Rudolph, since apparently this was my life now and I had a puppy named Rudolph.

"He needs food, a collar, a leash, and a bed probably. Here." I pulled out my wallet and handed her my credit card. "Buy him whatever he needs."

"I think Rudolph might need a new pair of Louboutins and a Coach bag!" she said, hugging the puppy.

"Honestly, if you keep him out of trouble, I'll overlook any shoes or jewelry he might require."

The Svensson Investment tower loomed in front of me. I squared my shoulders.

"How's our favorite puppy-owning CEO?" Walker said in greeting, clapping me on the shoulder. "Where's your new furchild?"

"Did Jack tell you?" I frowned.

"Dude, it is all over Twitter. It's trending!" he said glee-fully, sticking his phone in my face. The comments under the picture ranged from wholesome to... less than wholesome.

"I think you've acquired like seven new stalkers," Walker said, swiping through his phone as we went into the building to the elevators.

"I cannot afford to deal with that right now. Sloane is bad enough," I complained as we rode up to the upper-level conference rooms with the million-dollar skyline view.

"Look on the bright side," my COO said as we stepped off the elevator, "this is good publicity. Maybe it will help us edge out the Holbrooks. I know Kate definitely pimps photos of Grant and his chunky corgi on the Holbrook Enterprises Instagram account. This is going to be awesome!"

When we sat down in the conference room, however, Hunter and Greg, Walker's brothers, did not share his enthusiasm.

"I cannot believe you got a puppy while your company is in shambles," Greg said, glaring at me.

So it was going to be that kind of meeting.

CHAPTER 13

Holly

"All right, listen up!" Penny said, clapping her hands. Rudolph barked.

"He's the most adorable dog!" Fiona whispered to me. "His feet smell like pupperoni!"

"I should take him," Amber whined. "Owen and I are practically dating. You promised you weren't going to get between us."

"I'm not handing over Owen's dog to you!" I exclaimed.

"Girls!" Penny ordered. "Part of being in the bake-off is participating in creating digital content for *Vanity Rag*. Now, we want all the viewers to learn a bit more about the contestants. The first episode is airing in a few days. We need a lot of content online. It is in your best interest to participate. Be charming! Feel free to talk about your endeavors. Also, if you have any ideas for content, I want to hear them."

Penny motioned around the lobby. "Today, we're decorating for Christmas. Owen Frost and Walker Svensson have generously allocated money to add some festive cheer to the lobby. We are going to take some footage of you all talking about your ideas."

"We should have a romantic Christmas theme," Amber said, waving her arm. Dana Holbrook was surveying us, arms crossed, looking very chic in her pencil skirt and silk shirt. She directed one of the cameramen to follow Amber. Of course. Crazy people sell.

Amber took a deep breath, stepped in front of the camera, and then she was off.

"What these girls don't understand is that men like women who can bake and decorate and look sexy while they do it." Amber hiked up her boobs. Morticia and I looked on in horror.

"I'm here to win the competition and to win Owen Frost. I know all these girls here, and some of them are trying to steal *my man*!" Amber said, turning to screech at us. "But you won't get away with it! He and I are meant to be together. Everything I do, I do for him!"

"What a train wreck," Morticia said, shaking her head.

"You're telling me. I had to live with her for years. Thanks, Mom, for giving me a crazy stepsister for Christmas."

"And thanks, Dana and Gunnar, for subjecting all of us to her," Morticia added.

"How are we supposed to decorate by committee?" I asked Morticia as we walked around.

"It's just for show. Penny wants me to clean up whatever you guys buy," Morticia said. "Because apparently that's what I do—clean up whenever the Polar Express jumps the tracks."

"The ceilings are so high in here," I said, looking up. "Let's hang lights and garlands from the ceiling, so it looks like a winter fairy forest. Also, we need a giant Christmas tree, plus a few smaller ones. And as much as I despise Amber, I do sort of like the idea of a romantic Christmas theme. The lobby has little niches, so we should make them semiprivate spaces. Obviously we don't want people boinking in the lobby, but they could be nice little moments."

"Color palette should be silver, white, gold, and green. We don't want a lot of red. If it happens, it needs to be desaturated and matte, not a shiny, glittery red," Morticia added, sketching on her small drawing pad.

I nodded, looking over her shoulder. "I'm feeling like I want a very retro, very mod Christmas. Also, I have a miniskirt and fake eyelashes I want to bust out," I said, snapping pictures.

"Quantum Cyber could have their holiday party down here," Morticia said as she sketched out a scene. "Penny wants one of the bake-off challenges to be the holiday party. If we decorate this place nicely enough and don't have giant pictures of Owen everywhere—" She glared back at Amber, who was still going strong. "It should look nice."

"Let's go shopping."

The snow flurries from the night before had stopped.

"I'm dreaming of a white Christmas!" I sang. I handed Rudolph to Morticia, who took him as if I had handed her a live bomb, so I could take selfies in the streetscape. Wreaths and huge red bows hung from the streetlights. The street's trees were draped in fairy lights and glowed softly against the grey winter sky.

"You need to buy this dog a leash and a harness," Morticia said flatly. "I'm covered in fur."

"I'll order something on Amazon."

"There's a dog boutique nearby," she said, shoving the puppy back into my arms. "We're going there now."

The Scottie Dog Groomers and Pet Boutique wasn't far. The shop was bright and airy, with a section of organic dog treats, along with harnesses and—

"Costumes! He needs a sweater."

"Does he?" Morticia wrinkled her nose. "These are all so… festive. Here," she said, shoving a black collar and harness at me. "These are his size."

"They're black! It's Christmas. He needs a holiday leash," I said, browsing through the options and selecting a red-and-green leash with snowflakes embroidered on it. There was a matching collar and harness. I tried them on Rudolph.

"Very festive!" I told him.

"Is that it?" Morticia said, clearly annoyed. "We need to shop for the lobby."

"I want to find him a sweater."

"He's a husky."

"Hi. I'm Ginny, the shop owner. Can I help you?" She was a pretty young woman, but her pleasant expression soured slightly when she saw Rudolph. The puppy wagged his tail.

"Ugh," Ginny said. "I really should ban him from the store, except he's so cute."

"He's just a puppy!" I cried. "What could he possibly have done?"

"His father knocked up one of my clients' show dogs," Ginny said, shaking her head. "There were lawsuits out the wazoo. You are in possession of probably the most expensive puppy in Manhattan if you go based on the insurance payout."

"Geez," I said, looking down at Rudolph. "He's definitely a billionaire's dog then."

Rudolph seemed a lot happier now that he had a harness and could sniff to his heart's content. The puppy bounced around from a tree to a stoop to a friendly doorman. I was constantly trying not to trip over the leash.

"I hope he manages to keep up the energy," Morticia said. "We have a marathon shopping session ahead of us." She pushed through the door to a high-end home-goods store.

"The dog needs to wait outside, please," the saleswoman said when she saw me.

Owen had acted as if he didn't like the husky, but I would have bet all my Christmas cookies that if anything happened to the puppy, he would be furious.

"We're here to buy decorations for *The Great Christmas Bake-Off*," I explained. "Owen Frost is partnering with them, and we need enough Christmas decor to fill the lobby of his company, Quantum Cyber."

As soon as the name dropped and I waved around Owen's credit card, the salespeople were all over us. A pillow was procured for Rudolph, and the manager literally closed the shop for us and insisted on leading us through the several floors of home decor.

"We have all our Christmas products out, as you can see," she said.

Morticia showed her the sketches, and we explained the theme. "We need a mile of garland," I added.

"Some of that we'll have to ship, but you can see our samples," one of the saleswomen explained as I admired the lengths of garland. It was a nice sage green, interspersed with fairy lights that glowed warmly.

"I want a few of those abstract trees," Morticia said, pointing to a crop of white, almost skeletal trees.

"I guess they don't look too bad," I said. "They're sculptural."

Another saleswoman led us through the furniture.

"We need cozy benches," I said, admiring a white tufted couches and loveseats.

"We should have some other types of seating arrangements too," Morticia said. "These leather chairs will look great draped with one of those fur throws."

"These will be a nice arrangement next to a Christmas tree."

"Right, the trees," I said. "We need ornaments."

"We have several sets of crystal ornaments," the saleswoman said, leading me into another room. The glass ornaments sparkled in the light.

"These might be a bit much," I said hesitantly.

"You wouldn't use these exclusively," the saleswoman said. "Just to add some sparkle."

"All right, let's do it!"

Morticia added several huge white, silver, and gold bows to our order, then we were ready.

"We'll have the items that are in stock delivered today, and the rest of the items we'll have rushed as soon as they package them from the warehouse," the store manager said pleasantly as she swiped Owen's credit card. "Would you sign please?"

I stared at the total, the six-figure number swimming in my vision.

"How—how did we spend that much money?"

"It's a huge lobby," Morticia answered. "Besides, Penny said it was okay."

"All right, I guess," I said, signing the receipt. "I hope Owen doesn't freak out."

CHAPTER 14

Owen

The text interrupted Greg's tirade about Quantum Cyber not having an adequate staff of computer programmers. I stared at it coldly.

"What the fuck?" I said as I read the text message.

Belle: *Don't freak out, but you're going to see a $108,000 charge on your credit card for Christmas decorations.*

"Who spends that much money on Christmas decorations?" I said aloud.

"Probably the Holbrooks," Walker replied. "Their decorations are all over social media, tagged of course, with #TechBizTopCompany. All the tech blogs are already speculating on who's going to be at the top of the list."

"And that brings us back to the topic of the meeting," Greg said. "For the last two years, Owen, Quantum Cyber has not been hiring the best and brightest. We're opening that new facility in Harrogate in partnership with Svensson

PharmaTech. At this point, I'm highly doubtful that we will have qualified workers to manage it."

"It's this idiotic *TechBiz* list," I said, trying to keep my cool. "Not only do the Holbrooks vacuum up all the good workers, but they also have first dibs on any start-up trying to sell."

"It's all because of the corgi," Walker said. "Kate and Grant just post random pictures of him. Look, here's another one. They decorated their sign, and they have Gus the corgi in front of it. It's so blatant. All Kate wrote is, 'You know you want to work here.' Here's another picture of Grant and the corgi in matching hats."

"And yet here you are, Owen," Hunter said. "Complaining as opposed to taking actionable steps to correct the problem."

"He's trying," Walker protested, attempting to stick up for me. "We have a nice Instagram post with him and the puppy. Penny's decorating the lobby."

"It's all so petty," I complained. "Quantum Cyber pays very well, and our employees have a lot of autonomy. The Holbrooks are terrible, but they throw up a picture of a corgi in a Santa hat in front of a Holbrook Enterprises–themed Christmas tree, and everyone is falling all over themselves to work there."

Hunter gave me a flat look. "People are sheep. They want a shallow Instagram moment, and they want to feel good about where they work. You two need to try harder. You know how I feel about the Holbrooks. I'm taking this as a personal affront if their company is at the top of the list again this year. If the Holbrooks are using the holidays to lock in the top spot on the *TechBiz* list, then Owen, you better get on board with Christmas."

"I need a drink," Walker said after several more hours of Greg and Hunter picking apart the company finances, the progress of the new gene therapy facility in Harrogate, and their general disappointment with me.

"Both Hunter and Greg are usually difficult to deal with, but Greg especially seemed in a worse mood than normal," I remarked.

"It's because Crawford came back," Walker said.

"Your brother? I thought you said he moved to Tokyo."

Walker shrugged. "He's back. Greg won't even let us say his name. He's still furious at him. I didn't think he could despise anyone more than Hunter, yet here we are."

"Speaking of people we despise," I growled. Sloane was waiting in the lobby. She waved to me, uncrossed her legs, and stood up, smoothing her hands slowly down her body.

Holly does it better.

"You should be nice," Walker insisted. "Give her the Owen Frost five-star treatment. Can't hurt to have an edge in the competition. We do need to, if not win, at least achieve a higher ranking. I did a poll of our employees, and eighty percent of them wouldn't recommend the company to a friend because it's not a fun place to work."

"It's a company specializing in cybersecurity and cryptoanalytics. There's nothing fun about that," I retorted.

"Exactly," Sloane said, sauntering up to us. "That's why you have to try extra hard to make it exciting." She slid her hands down the collar of my jacket, pretending she was doing it to smooth out my tie.

"I really enjoyed our last date," she said. "We should do it again."

"It was six months ago," I said, trying to push her off me.

"You're a busy man. I can come by tonight and wear something sexy. I'll be your elf on the shelf."

"No, thank you."

"You need to relax," she said. "Being a billionaire and running a huge company must be stressful. I can help you strategize about increasing your *TechBiz* ranking."

"I am not interested," I said firmly. "I have a lot on my plate right now."

"We'll catch up later," she said, her hand drifting around my waist before I pushed past her.

"I can't believe you're rejecting her, dude," Walker said as the valet handed me my keys. "She's pretty, and she could help your business. Win-win."

"Lose-lose. She's crazy. We went on one date. Sloane hasn't left me alone since then. I've tried ignoring her. I've tried telling her clearly that I do not see a future together. It's like she doesn't even hear me. Every few days, she texts me. It's insane! Six months, this has been going on. Isn't she exhausted? It's not like she doesn't have a job." I blew out a breath. "I will never date again."

"You could string her along long enough to beat the Holbrooks and get my brothers off our case."

"That sounds like dealing with the devil. Besides, I already am making enough deals with evil spirits. I have all that Great Christmas Bake-off nonsense, which I know is going to come back and bite me."

As I pulled up in front of my tower and handed the keys to the valet, I remembered how much *The Great Christmas*

Bake-Off was already ruining my life. When I walked into the lobby, it looked like a storage facility. Six figures' worth of Christmas decorations filled the space. Holly was happily skipping through the maze of boxes like a demented ballerina in *The Nutcracker*.

"What the hell?" I growled. People were going to think my company was going out of business.

Holly stopped and blinked at me, and Rudolph ran over to greet me. I picked him up and walked over to her. Holly pulled a wad of receipts and my credit card out of her coat pocket and handed them to me. I took them silently out of her hand.

"Merry Christmas?" she said sheepishly.

CHAPTER 15

Holly

I hadn't had a lot of time to go through the decorations the night before. Owen, a scowl firmly on his face, had picked up the dog and disappeared upstairs. After a full day of shopping, I didn't have the energy to go through each box. Instead, I sat in bed and ate a bowl of peppermint ice cream and chatted with my fans on Instagram while old holiday cartoons played on my laptop.

The next morning, I had a sugar hangover. I sucked down coffee while Zane clipped on my microphone.

"Today," Anastasia said after the judges had all sat at the reclaimed-wood table, "is the Santa's cookie challenge. It's not Christmas without Christmas cookies. And we have the queen of Christmas cookies, Chloe from the Grey Dove Bistro, here as a guest judge. Chloe, do you have tips about cookies that could help the contestants?"

"I love a good sugar cookie!" Chloe said. "At the Grey Dove Bistro, we make several thousand cookies and decorate them by hand every day for Greyson Hotel Group to give as welcome gifts to patrons. Remember to keep the dough cold. A steady hand while decorating is also important. Also, I feel like there's no such thing as a bad cookie. Good luck!"

I was excited for this challenge and knew exactly what I was going to make: my grandmother's famous sugar cookies. They were light and fluffy and practically melted in your mouth. I would frost them with a layer of buttercream and a sprinkle of rock sugar. They were my favorite Christmas treats in the world, and I was determined that my baking would bring Owen some Christmas cheer. Who in the world hated Christmas and baked goods? No one, that's who. Owen just needed someone to remind him what the holiday was all about.

These cookies were sweet, but everyone I fed them to said they were addicting. The buttercream didn't use all that much sugar, and it tempered the sugar cookie dough. Even Morticia liked them, though she always requested Halloween shapes.

I was making candy canes, stars, bells, Christmas trees, stockings, and snowmen. The cookies were tasty, but I was worried that they wouldn't be enough to win. I chewed on my lip and looked around in the pantry. I didn't want my dish to be a sad plate of a few cookies. It needed to be a true platter with a mound of cookies.

Last Valentine's Day, I had made cookie sandwiches with this recipe. Maybe I could do something similar for Christmas and have a beautiful plate. For Valentine's Day, I had used raspberry jam in the middle and either frosted the top piece, left it plan with a sprinkling of colored sugar, or drizzled ganache over it.

For this challenge, I decided to do all of the above and filled my basket with ingredients then toted everything back to my station. These sugar cookies seemed simple, but they did take a while to make. There was a lot of waiting—waiting for the dough to chill, waiting for the cookies to bake, waiting for the pans to cool.

Since the dough needed to be good and cold, I made it first. The dough wasn't that difficult to make. Cream the cold butter and the sugar, add the salt, flour, and baking powder then the eggs. When I was done, I had a buttery-colored plank of dough. I put it in the freezer to chill then set about making the filling.

Instead of raspberry jam, I reduced raspberries to a rich red syrup. I also made an orange reduction, zesting several organic oranges and squeezing the juice. I didn't add any sugar. I wanted the tang to contrast against the sugar cookie. Since it was Christmas and I wanted to have something green, too, I made the final reduction out of key limes. I strained all three fruity sauces and set them aside to cool.

The dough was finally cold. I split it into portions and rolled the first ball out on the parchment paper.

To make the sandwiches, I cut out a large star and cut a smaller star out of the middle of it for the top of the sandwich so you could see the filling inside. I repeated this for the other shapes like the Christmas trees and the bells. After I had a nice set of tops, I peeled the remaining dough off the parchment paper and put in in the fridge to cool again. When I got back to my station, a cookie tray had appeared next to my rolling pin. I looked at it suspiciously.

"I had to borrow your cookie sheet for a second," Amber said innocently.

"Uh-huh." After all her accusations of me trying to steal Owen, I didn't trust her. I inspected the sheet and all the cookies I had rolled out. The cookie sheet was the kind I preferred, constructed of two pieces of metal with an air pocket sandwiched between. It *seemed* fine. I checked my oven temperature then took out two more cookie sheets and slid the pieces of parchment paper onto them. I put them in the oven and set a timer.

I was rolling out the next set of cookies when a whistling sound came out of the oven. Zane and another camera guy raced over, hoping to capture the drama.

"It's nothing. Sometimes ovens make noises," I assured them.

Bang! I was cut off when an explosion came from the oven.

"What in the world!" I raced to open it. "My cookies!"

They were ruined. Somehow, one of the cookie sheets had literally exploded. The cookies had been knocked off in the carnage and were smoldering at the bottom of the oven. Struggling not to cry, I turned off the oven and grabbed an oven mitt. Anastasia came over with a fire extinguisher.

"What happened? I thought baking was supposed to be safe!" she exclaimed.

"Something was wrong with the pan," I bit out. I couldn't remember which cookie sheet was the one Amber had given me. But she was working at the next station over with a smug look on her face.

"What did you do?" I yelled at her.

"I didn't do anything!" she protested.

"You took one of my cookie sheets, and now my cookies are ruined. I know you did something. I want to review the footage," I demanded.

"All I did was use the sheet and wash it. Maybe some water got in the air pocket. I don't know," Amber said in feigned innocence. "We can't *know*. You can't blame me for your issues, Holly."

I tried to stay calm. I didn't need to go viral for screaming at a fellow contestant, even if I did want to shove her face-first into a bowl of icing.

None of the cookies in the oven were salvageable. I threw them all away, trying not to swear. I had made extra dough, but I couldn't afford to mess up anything else. We had to make four identical plates, one for each judge and then one that Romance Creative would use to take photos and videos of our dish. That meant a lot of cookies.

Checking the clock, I rolled out and cut more cookies, carefully monitoring the oven while they baked. I repeated the process several more times then let the perfect sugar cookies cool. I could not frost them when they were at all warm because they would break.

"Can you watch my station, please?" I asked Fiona. "I need some chocolate and a double boiler."

"Sure!" she said. Then she lowered her voice to a whisper. "I saw Amber dunk that cookie sheet under water. I bet she tried to fill up the air pocket on purpose."

"Of course she did," I said.

While the cookies cooled, I made a glossy chocolate ganache, mixing the heavy cream and rich, dark, unsweetened chocolate together. It was a special imported Dutch cocoa that made an almost black chocolate. It also turned pretty hard when it cooled, which was good, because I didn't want it to smear on the cookies.

Thankfully, they were cool. I mixed up a huge bowl of buttercream frosting using good European butter, confectioners' sugar, heavy cream, imported vanilla extract, and sea salt. I usually added a bit more salt than other people. As in life, a little salt made one appreciate the sweet things even more!

I tasted a big dollop of the frosting.

"Delicious! I could seriously eat buttercream frosting just by itself," I announced.

Fiona giggled from where she was mixing up royal icing. "I know, right?"

I started with the cookie sandwiches. I spread one of the fruit glazes I'd made onto the solid bottom cookies then carefully lined up the top ones and pressed, making sure not to crack anything. On some of the shells, I had sprinkled large rock sugar granules before putting them in the oven. Those sandwiches were ready to go, and I set them aside. The second set received a drizzle of ganache.

The clock was ticking down. I carefully frosted the remaining cookies with a layer of buttercream. It shouldn't be smooth, because I wanted it to be a bit rustic to catch the sugar. I arranged them on the platters with a few minutes to spare.

"Hands up!" Anastasia called as the buzzer sounded.

I looked over at Fiona's dish. She had beautifully decorated chocolate cookies that resembled tiny works of art. I looked back at my cookies. Maybe they weren't good enough?

CHAPTER 16

Owen

"How's Rudolph?" Chloe asked after the contestants were all furiously making huge batches of cookie dough. I was not looking forward to having to eat ten rounds of dessert. I had doubled my run that morning to make up for it.

"Unfortunately, he's very attached to the name."

Chloe giggled. "Huskies are smart dogs!"

"He's a handful. I should go check on him actually."

I had left the puppy with Walker that morning, and my COO had insisted on bringing the dog to the office.

He better not have peed on my carpet.

A gaggle of my employees was playing with the dog when I strode into Walker's office.

"You didn't tell me you bought him a costume!" Walker said, trying not to laugh and failing. Rudolph, true to his name, was dressed as a reindeer, complete with a noisy bell-studded harness and reindeer antlers. He raced around in a circle then tripped over his feet and collapsed on the floor. "I'm glad Santa doesn't have to rely on him, because nothing would be delivered," Walker joked.

I was barely able to complete any more work in the next few hours. Between the puppy's admirers coming to visit and take pictures and the barrage of text messages and calls I was getting from Sloane, I couldn't concentrate.

Rudolph whined, and I took the excuse to go outside for a break. There was a park near my tower, and I took the dog there to burn off some energy.

"Does he have snowflakes and candy canes on the leash?" I complained. Of course that was what Holly had bought for him. *Six figures on Christmas decorations, then she decks the dog out in Christmas.*

"I don't understand why you hate Christmas. I always tried to make Christmas perfect." Dr. Diane Frost, researcher extraordinaire and, according to Jack, the world's worst mother, stepped out from behind a tree.

"Mom? What are you doing here?" I asked in shock. "Are you stalking me?"

"I can't come see my son?" she said, reaching up to hug me. She was a slightly older version of my sister, Belle, but with none of the humor. She had the same height and blue eyes, but her hair was brown, not our white.

"Several of my children refuse to talk to me. I don't understand. I've given you all everything," she said in disbelief.

Jack felt she was the worst mother in the world. I took a more nuanced view. She certainly wasn't great, and what she had done to Belle was terrible, but Diane wasn't all bad. She was my mother after all. That had to mean something.

"I met your girlfriend the other day," she continued. "She and I had a very nice chat over coffee. I really like her. I think she will be a good wife and mother. And she has a high-profile job. You two are perfect for each other."

"Girlfriend? That's news to me."

"Sloane is very much in love with you!" my mother said with a laugh, as if I was just joking. "Sloane told me all about how she's going to help you with your contest."

"Sloane isn't my girlfriend. She's—" *What, a stalker? Men couldn't really be stalked, could they? Sloane wasn't dangerous, just delusional.* "We are not together," I said flatly.

"You're not getting any younger," my mother insisted. "You've done so well in your career. You own all this property. Now you just need to get married and give me grandchildren. All my friends have grandchildren."

"This is so typical," I said in annoyance. "You didn't even ask me how I am. You just jumped straight to what you want."

"I'm *so sorry* you think I'm such a terrible mother that you won't give me grandchildren," Diane said dramatically.

My mother did this every single time I interacted with her. It was as if she sought me out to make herself feel validated.

"If you want grandchildren, maybe you could go adopt a child out of foster care," I suggested. "There are lots of needy kids."

Diane jerked back as though I'd slapped her. "No! I could never. I need nice grandkids, not rejects. I want to have a picture-perfect Christmas morning, watching them open their little presents, giving them their stockings."

I didn't want to listen to her anymore. "I have to go back to work," I said, picking up Rudolph.

I left Rudolph with Walker then went to the studio to judge the bake-off. The encounter in the park had reminded me why I had been trying to limit my contact with my mother. She was so self-absorbed and a bit of a snob. After that terrible family experience, all I wanted was a drink and to work on my new computer code. Instead, I had to eat multiple Christmas cookies.

Against my better judgment, I checked all the messages from Sloane. As I scrolled through them, I saw a picture of her and my mother. I sent it to Jack.

Owen: *This is why I refuse to date.*

Jack: *Wow! Your stalker and Mom. You need to cut her off.*

Owen: *You know I can't do that.*

I was in a terrible mood when the first batch of cookies was brought out. All the talk dredged up memories of Christmases past. Most children loved Christmas. I had dreaded it.

My mother would become extra demanding. She would make us all scrub the house, then she would dress us in matching outfits. Belle would be put in charge of wrangling me and my four younger brothers. My sister spent the entire month of December in a terrible mood, because what teenager wants her mom micromanaging her whole holiday and treating her like the live-in maid and chef?

Belle would yell at my brothers and me until everything was perfect for the lavish holiday parties my parents would throw for their work colleagues. The only food my mother would make herself was macarons. Belle cooked everything else, from all the perfectly constructed hors d'oeuvres to the impeccably decorated cakes and cookies.

My mother and father were obsessed with making sure their neighbors and colleagues thought the Frost family was perfect. Diane would force all of us kids to decorate the whole house for Christmas. Garlands on the staircases, candles in the windows, and the large blue spruce tree in the living room all went up right after Thanksgiving. My mother would order us to rehang the ornaments until they were perfect, and heaven help us if we dropped one.

No, Christmas was a terrible holiday. Usually I tried to avoid it. But here it was staring me in the face.

"I have an array of chocolate holiday sugar cookies with royal icing," Fiona said.

"What do you think, Owen?" Chloe asked me brightly.

I picked up the cookie gingerly and broke off the smallest piece I possibly could.

"It's sweet," I said. "And tastes like chocolate."

Chloe rolled her eyes and patted me on the head. She broke the cookie in half and showed the camera.

"See how the cookie looks layered? You can tell Fiona didn't overwork the dough." Chloe took a bite. "It's light and flavorful and has a nice bite. This is a very nice cookie! Also, making a chocolate sugar cookie is more difficult than a plain sugar cookie, because you have to balance out the chocolate and subtract that amount in dry ingredients. People think baking is just some sort of girly thing to do while you sip wine, but baking is a science. The ratios, temperatures, and processes have to be exact, or you won't get excellent results."

"I agree with everything," Anu said. "Fiona, you're lucky to have the dessert queen looking over your cookies."

"They're beautiful cookies," Chloe continued. "Look at the intricate icing work. This winter lace pattern is perfect. It's like art. Did you see that, Owen? She put snowflakes on it." She stuck a cookie in my face.

I grunted, earning more eye-rolling from Chloe.

Holly was up next.

"I heard you almost blew up the kitchen," Chloe joked as Holly set the platters of cookies before us.

"What?" I growled. "Are you seriously trying to burn down my tower after you subjected my dog to a Christmas costume?"

Holly's eyes narrowed. "He looks cute in that costume. Every other normal person feels a sense of warmth at the sight of a puppy in a costume. But of course not Owen Frost."

I glowered at her.

"Don't worry about the accident. It all worked out," Holly said to Chloe. "And I was able to make all these cookies."

The sugar cookies were piled with fluffy white frosting. I poked one suspiciously.

Chloe picked up a star and took a bite. "These are delicious, if a bit rustic. They sort of dissolve in your mouth. They're really addicting! Try it, Owen," Chloe coaxed.

I picked up a frosted candy cane. I appreciated that it wasn't pretentious. It was a cookie. It didn't need to have a detailed depiction of the *Mona Lisa* on it. I took a bite of the cookie, bracing myself for the sledgehammer of sugar to my teeth. But it didn't happen.

The word *dissolve* made it sound as if the cookie had no substance. That was not the case. This cookie was like eating a cloud. It tasted—happy. It wasn't too sweet, either. It was perfectly balanced.

"These just feel very homemade," Nick said, inspecting the cookies critically.

I couldn't really concentrate, as I was having a religious experience. The slightly savory buttercream frosting, the crunchy sugar crystals, the cookie dough that wasn't overly sweet. I stuffed the rest of the candy cane into my mouth.

"If you compare these to the cookies we just saw," Anu said, "those were professional cookies. These are… I don't know if I would even put these on Instagram."

"Sometimes rustic cookies are good," Chloe said. "These are tasty and addictive. You feel like you could eat one after the other then look around and say, 'Hey, who ate all my cookies?'"

Maybe they weren't Instagram-worthy, but that was why I liked them. They were honest. My mom would never have served cookies like these at her holiday party. I was about to take another cookie but scowled. I didn't want to think about my mom right now.

"You don't like it?" Holly asked. She was annoyed at the comments.

"Those three are the chefs," I said gruffly. "If they say they're bad, then they're bad. They don't look like Fiona's cookies. I guess you could have used one of those bag thingies." All the while, my thoughts were spinning. How would I sneak out the rest of these cookies?

"You mean an icing piper," Holly said through gritted teeth. "Why are you even judging the baking contest if you don't even know what anything is called?" Her voice became shrill, and her cheeks flushed. "And why are you even judging something called *The Great Christmas Bake-Off* if you don't even like Christmas?"

"Thank you, Holly," Anastasia interrupted.

Holly stalked off to the greenroom, and I had to contend with a parade of cookies. Nick and Anu weren't as harsh with the other contestants. None of them made simple cookies like Holly's; they all had fussy, fancy cookies.

I tried to look around as the stagehands swapped out the plates of desserts. Where had they taken Holly's cookies? Surely they didn't toss them. Were they eating them?

"Who do you want to pick as the winner?" Anu asked Chloe as the last contestant was escorted to the greenroom.

"Holly's cookies were just too homemade. They were very lacking in professionalism," Nick interjected.

"They tasted good at least," I retorted. "Especially compared to that guy with the purple hair. His cookies tasted like grass."

"They were vegan," Chloe added.

"You can make a tasty vegan cookie, but those weren't it," Anu said with a shudder.

"They were beautifully decorated though," Chloe said. "But yes, of course it's better to serve something tasty than beautiful and borderline inedible."

We finished the discussion. Then it was time to announce the decisions.

"Fiona," Chloe said when the contestants all filed in front of us. "Your cookies were beautiful, tasty, and technically perfect. Congratulations! You win this round! Would

Holly and Waldo step forward. Waldo, while we appreciate you trying to bring something different to the world of baking, a kale and applesauce cookie just didn't bring on the Christmas spirit. Holly, your cookies were simply lacking in finesse and aren't what we expect to see at this level of competition," Anu added.

Holly pursed her mouth angrily. She didn't even seem to be scared of being sent home.

"Holly, you're safe for another round. Step up your game."

CHAPTER 17

Holly

"How dare they?" I fumed after all the contestants had sat in front of the camera as Dana asked for our reactions. "Those are my grandmother's famous sugar cookies," I said, pacing around the master bedroom in the penthouse. Morticia sat on the bed. "Everyone loves those cookies. You remember Mimi's boyfriend? He was sick, and I sent cookies back with you. Everyone thought he was dying, and the cookies gave him another year to live."

"It probably was the antibiotics," Morticia said, flopping back on the bed.

"It was the cookies!" I exclaimed.

"We need to decorate the lobby," Morticia said in a bored tone. "Fiona just texted me and says she's down there already."

"And Owen." I continued to seethe as I followed Morticia downstairs with my decorating kit. Yes, I had a decorating kit. Yes, I was delusional and thought that one day in the near future, a craft room would simply sprout up in my nonexistent dream apartment.

Instead, I was confronted with a sea of boxes when we stepped off the elevator into the tower lobby. More had been delivered since yesterday, and there was a maze of cardboard.

"I can't believe they put him on the judge's board. Isn't that just the worst? Owen Frost is just a pretty face. He has no idea what's going on. You can tell he thinks the whole thing is stupid." I angrily tore into a nearby box.

Morticia took out a huge knife and started cutting the plastic ties that held the boxes together. We spent the next several hours unboxing and decorating. I even livestreamed some of my decorating to my followers.

Zane also came down and shot footage of the decorating process. Making the lobby into a winter wonderland lifted my mood. Screw those judges if they didn't like my cookies. I was going to enjoy the Christmas season and enjoy baking.

"We made a fair amount of progress," I said, looking around. It was dark outside, and Quantum Cyber's workers had mostly left for the evening. A few of the hotel guests were milling in the lobby, watching us bring Christmas to the space.

"Come help me position this last tree," Fiona said.

We rotated it until it was straight. We were still waiting on the giant tree I'd ordered to tower in the atrium space. The garlands were waiting to be hung as soon as a scissor lift was delivered.

"The furniture looks amazing!" Fiona gushed, snapping pictures for her own social media.

"Hey, six figures should get you something nice," I said, admiring how we'd used the various chairs, ottomans, and benches to create cozy spaces. Fairy lights softly glowed, nestled in the garland that was draped along the walls.

Morticia had put her art degree to good use and had made several metal sculptures in the months before the competition. There were winter scenes with reindeer, elks, and even one with cute penguins. The metal sculptures were lit up, and instead of fake snow, we'd used white fur throws to give a more abstract winter feel.

"It's beautiful," Fiona sighed.

"I think we need some more plants," I said. Morticia scowled. "Just some poinsettias," I told her.

"Gross. They smell."

"We need some more live greenery," I countered.

"Maybe a few dozen more Christmas trees," Fiona added. "It supposed to be a winter wonderland."

"A few dozen more?" Morticia said in annoyance.

"Just some small ones."

"I'm trying to make this a high-end Christmas experience," Morticia sniffed. "I have a vision."

"You've been trying very hard," I said, patting her on the shoulder. Her black leather jacket was covered in spikes, so I did it gingerly. "I didn't see any skeletons or jack-o'-lanterns wearing Christmas hats, so good job!"

"Really? Because I feel like that life-sized animatronic elf is pretty creepy," Fiona commented.

"What elf?" I asked, frowning.

We followed Fiona back to the bank of elevators. There on a shelf was a literal life-sized elf.

"Are you sure this isn't one of your grandmother's old ventriloquist's puppets?" I asked Morticia softly.

"It's creepy enough to be one," Fiona whispered.

The elf peered at us with lifeless eyes.

"I'm not a puppet," the elf said, head swinging to look at us.

Fiona and I screamed and clung to each other. Morticia hissed.

"Amber!" I said as the elf hopped down to the floor. My stepsister was wearing heavy makeup along with the green felt costume.

"I'm trying to surprise Owen," she said.

"He's going to be surprised, all right," Fiona said, slowly backing away.

Amber adjusted her costume then hopped back up onto the shelf, striking a sexy pose.

"Well, I think I need a drink," Fiona said as she swiped the key card to the elevator. "Care to join me? I'm trying out new cocktail recipes. The penthouse came with a fully stocked bar. I was planning on drinking my way through it."

"As much as I like Christmas and alcohol and Christmas-themed alcohol, I really need to do some more pics for Insta," I said. "It's snowing outside, and I need to snap a few shots."

"Okay! Need help?"

"Nah, I got it. It's tedious and cold. Besides, I have a tripod."

As soon as I was back to my room, I changed into a cute Christmas costume. It was a red-velvet sleeveless dress with white fur trim, matching elbow-length gloves, and a giant silk bow that went around my waist. Red stiletto boots and a furry white hat completed the look. I loved dressing up. It was probably left over from my childhood dream of being a Christmas unicorn princess.

"You're going to catch tuberculosis," Morticia said when she saw me.

"Drink for the road?" Fiona asked, handing me a martini glass with a red liquid in it.

"Don't mind if I do. Yum! This is good!"

"It's a Christmas cosmo," she said. "I figured since we're in a swanky Manhattan condo, we should channel our inner *Sex and the City*. It's a pomegranate-cranberry juice blend, garnished with lime twists."

"Amazing! I won't be out that long. Save me some more!" I called out as I left.

Amber was still perched on the shelf when the elevator doors opened. Owen must have been safely hidden upstairs. Lord knew I would avoid Amber if I could.

There was a park near the tower. It was lushly landscaped, with petunias and other winter flowers in artful beds. The fountain in the center of the park was iced over and lightly dusted with snow. The lighting was like a spotlight.

"It's like the movie *La La Land*—except in New York in the middle of winter!" I said, happily striking a pose. Then I shivered. I was seriously regretting sacrificing warmth for a good picture.

CHAPTER 18

Owen

I stayed late in the office, partially because I needed to do work and partially because I was scheming about how to steal more cookies. Unlike most people, when I decided I wanted something, I went after it. Of course, I didn't rush in blindly; I analyzed my goal rationally. If it was a worthy goal and achievable, I went for it, like a wolf after an elk.

That was how I had made billions on Bitcoin when other people were joking about it on TV. That same mentality was also how I had grown my company when everyone was wondering how data analytics and cybersecurity could possibly work together. And that mind-set was how I was going to get those cookies. They were seriously addicting.

My plan was simple: take Rudolph downstairs to the studio and poke around for the cookies. Surely the production company didn't throw away perfectly edible food. If anyone asked, I would shove the dog at them to distract them then make a hasty exit.

Except when I went into the studio, there wasn't a single crumb to be found.

"Owen, what are you doing?" Belle called out as I was prowling around the greenroom.

"Just looking for my cuff link."

My older sister looked at me suspiciously. I kept my face a smooth, cold mask.

"You're such a weirdo," Belle said.

I gestured to my puppy. "Isn't he cute?"

"What are you really here for?" my sister said.

"Sorry, he has to go out," I said, picking up Rudolph and heading to the elevator. He was making that dancing motion that let me know his puppy-sized bladder was about to give up the Ghost of Christmas Past. I mentally cursed at the Christmas reference. It was infiltrating everything. There was no escape from the holiday.

As soon as I stepped off the elevator in the lobby, a giant elf launched herself at me.

"Owen! What a surprise!"

Rudolph barked.

"Sloane?"

"It's Amber," the girl said, annoyed. "From the bake-off. Who is Sloane?" Her eyes, heavy with makeup, narrowed.

"No one." I sighed and looked down at the dog, figuring she had startled him so badly that I might need to call the custodians.

"Funny we should bump into each other like this," Amber said with a high-pitched laugh. She was wearing pointy elf ears, and her hair was shellacked into a cartoonish swoop away from her face.

"Uh—"

"We should totally grab a drink!" she suggested.

"I can't. I have to—" I held up the dog then made a hasty retreat to the park my company owned near my tower.

Even though Rudolph's mom was a Dalmatian, in the snow, the puppy was all husky. He bounded ahead of me, snapping at the snowflakes. I watched him and also tried to figure out how I was going to acquire more of those cookies. The simplest solution was to just ask Holly. I thought about how furious she had been earlier. No, that was not a solution.

Rudolph stopped in front of me, ear cocked. I was on the lookout for any other members on the laundry list of crazy women in my life. I stood still, trying not to breathe, then glided into the trees, glad it was snowing so my hair wouldn't stand out. Rudolph, completely oblivious to any of my silent hand signals, bounded forward. I moved slowly through the woods to the other side of the park, near the fountain. A girl was there taking pictures.

"Holly," I breathed. She looked… well, she looked good. The strapless dress hugged her curves, and she posed in front of the camera, tossing her hair and making sexy faces. Then she made a few silly faces, laughing. I smiled in spite of myself.

Holly didn't see Rudolph, who had chosen that time to try out his hunting skills. The little puppy crept around the fountain. Holly was posing on the edge of it. In those high heels, she was going to fall if the puppy scared her.

My company owned this park, plus I was out here with Holly alone. I could just see the headlines—"Billionaire Kills Baker!" The Svenssons would have a fit. *TechBiz* would vote my company the worst ever.

I sprinted out of the woods toward the dog.

CHAPTER 19

Holly

My snow pictures were going to be amazing. I had on my red stilettos with the metal heels, and I was feeling like a supermodel perched up on the edge of the fountain. I was about to do an over-the-shoulder wink when I saw a man barreling toward me.

I screamed, and since I wasn't all that coordinated unless I was making a seven-tiered cake, the shock immediately sent me off balance. My heels slipped on the icy stone.

The man skidded then grabbed me before I could fall.

"Police! Help! Stranger danger!" I swung at his face with my fists, though my gloved hands couldn't do that much damage.

"I'm not a stranger," a familiar deep voice said irritably.

"Oh, bedroom stalker, it's you!"

"I wasn't stalking you. It was my house and my bedroom," he said, setting me down. "Apologies for scaring you. I was trying to save you from the big bad wolf."

"Huh?" I looked down. Rudolph pounced on my furry hat, which had been knocked into the snow.

I rolled my eyes. "Oh, thank you, kind savior. Whatever would I have done without you to protect me?"

"He could have frightened you," Owen insisted mulishly. "You could have had a concussion."

"Instead, I had a huge man run at me. That is way less frightening than a cute puppy."

Owen's mouth was a thin, hard line. "What are you even doing out here?"

"Taking pictures. Follow me on Instagram at Taste My Muffin!" I said, flashing a peace sign.

The frown on Owen's face deepened.

"If you wondering if it is some sort of blatant sexual innuendo," I chattered on, still a little more shaken than I cared to admit, "yes, yes it is."

"I'm surprised you didn't name it Tasting Her Christmas Cookies."

"Look at you making a joke! And here I thought someone who hated Christmas and was the CEO of a data analytics firm was going to be stiff and überunimaginative."

"It takes imagination to do computer programming," he said, offended.

"I know it does! I'm teasing," I said, stealing my hat back from Rudolph. "I follow Grant Holbrook on Instagram. His company does computer programming–type stuff."

Owen snarled, "No they don't. It's all lightweight user interfaces."

"Okay, Mr. Gatekeeper. Do I detect some snobbery?" I teased.

He scowled.

"Don't take it personally. A good-looking man and a corgi? You can't buy publicity better than that!" I said, collapsing my tripod.

Owen sighed. "I wish I could. I need to—well, never mind. It's not any of your concern."

"You want to win the *TechBiz* competition?" I asked, raising an eyebrow.

"How did you know?"

"Instagram. The hashtag is in every post on the Holbrooks' feed," I explained.

"I need to win that competition. The Holbrooks are insufferable," he said.

"And to that end, I've spent all afternoon decorating your lobby. You're welcome. It looks awesome, by the way," I told him. "I'll come take some pictures of you and Rudolph next to the holiday lights. Some nice casual pictures, just like, 'Oh, don't mind me, I'm just sitting here sexily under the tree with my Christmas package on full display with my supercute puppy. Vote for me! My company is awesome!' I'll make sure I fluff up your stocking first. You'll bring all the girls to your Christmas tree yard!"

CHAPTER 20

Owen

Had Holly been flirting with me?

The question bounced around my head all night. It didn't help that Rudolph wanted to go out every two hours. I thought he would have been tired, but no. I hauled him downstairs. At night, the lobby did look magical, like a winter scene from *The Nutcracker* or one of those old holiday movies my sister used to watch.

Holly was fun. And clearly I needed to seem fun if my company was going to beat Holbrook Enterprises.

I didn't bother trying to sleep after Rudolph did his business. Instead, I surfed the internet while the puppy snoozed at my feet. I was trying to find that sugar cookie recipe. I was now officially obsessed. It was like trying to figure out a line of code; I couldn't rest until I solved it.

There were thousands of cookie recipes on the internet. I wrote a script to analyze all of them and find commonalities. I let it run while I lifted weights.

The code was done when I went back into the home office. The summary said that the main similarities for sugar cookies were butter, sugar, salt, vanilla, eggs, and flour. Not in that order. There were hundreds of various combinations of the ingredients. Baking was clearly much more complex than I'd originally thought. This was going to take awhile. I put in a grocery delivery order for enough of each ingredient to make five hundred cookies. Then I went to work.

Normally I loved my office. I had a huge corner office with floor-to-ceiling glass. White marble accents made the space feel like winter when the sun reflected on freshly fallen snow. There was a balcony with French doors that I kept open all winter to keep the room freezing cold. It overlooked the little park in which I had surprised Holly the previous night.

I was looking forward to sitting alone in my office, taking a couple of conference calls, and working on some computer code.

Except when I arrived, Rudolph in tow, my office was packed with Svenssons. Almost identical with broad builds, blond hair, and grey eyes, the Svensson brothers numbered around a hundred, a byproduct of a polygamist cult and an insane father. They ranged from toddler age to adults. The small Svensson brothers were endearing. The big ones? Insufferable.

"Get your feet off of my desk," I growled to Archer. He ignored me.

"I demand a cookie tax. Walker said you were thick in *The Great Christmas Bake-Off*," Archer declared. "I'm totally judging next year."

"What do you know about baking?" Mace, his twin and CEO of Svensson PharmaTech, scoffed.

"I know that I like cookies!" Archer waggled his eyebrows at me. "I hear you've been tasting some Christmas cookies lately, if the pictures on Instagram are any indication."

"What pictures?" I asked.

Archer whipped out his phone with a smirk. I swept his feet off my desk—it's marble; seriously, it stains—and peered at the phone.

The Instagram handle read @TasteMyMuffin. There was a picture of me, Holly wrapped in my arms, lifting her in front of the fountain in the park.

The caption read:

Just what I need on a cold night! Manhattan's hottest CEO *wink* to rescue me from a big bad wolf. #QuantumCyber #TechBizBestCompanyList

"You were busy last night," Archer said with a laugh. "And to think, Walker was afraid you would stay a bachelor forever!"

I ignored him and grabbed the phone, swiping. The next image was a video clip of Rudolph attacking Holly's hat.

"While I'm glad to see you are actually trying to win this competition," Greg said acerbically, "maybe you should be courting actual business writers and not half-baked Instagram influencers."

Icy anger trickled through me. I turned on Greg. "Don't insult her. She's trying to help me unasked and unpaid."

Greg glared flatly at me.

"Don't mind him," Mace said. "He's mad about Crawford."

"Don't say his name," Greg spat.

"I don't care what—or who—you do," Hunter said coldly. "You need to have a better standing for recruitment by any means necessary. Walker has told me that one of the judges, Sloane, is making advances on you. Stop rebuffing her. You need every edge."

Walker made a subtle "stand down" motion. I gritted my teeth. I did not have the patience to deal with the Svenssons today.

"See," Garrett drawled, "this is why I don't come into Manhattan. You all spiral into pettiness. Who cares about some idiotic magazine contest?"

"You guys at PharmaTech don't actually have to compete for workers," Walker complained. "Anyone who wants to work in the biotech sphere is beating down your door. Quantum Cyber has to compete with Google, Facebook, and the Holbrooks."

"Whatever. I refuse to waste my time on this any longer," Garrett sneered.

"Literally no one asked you to come here," Walker said, grabbing a pitcher of water and herding his brothers into the adjacent conference room.

"We need to talk about the new gene therapy center. Your algorithm is key," Mace began, opening up his laptop. "Since I know you're frosting deep in the bake-off, we figured it would be easier to come to you."

"Walker said it was fine," Archer added. "And we had to drop off the surprise for the next bake-off episode. Also, Garrett wanted to come spy on Penny."

"I don't need to be physically present to spy on someone," Garrett replied.

"Yes, but why are *you* here?" I said to Archer. "You own hotels. You have nothing to do with this."

"One word," he said. "Cookies!"

CHAPTER 21

Holly

I stood, yawning, in the lobby early the next morning. We had to film a shopping segment for the bake-off. Dana was tapping her Louboutin as she waited for all the contestants to show up.

"Where is Amber?" she asked.

There was a shriek, and Amber stormed into the lobby from the elevators.

"You!"

"Here we go," I muttered to Fiona.

"I guess she saw your Instagram post," Fiona said.

"You're trying to steal him from me," Amber shouted, her voice echoing around the huge lobby. "You're trying to steal my boyfriend again!"

"Owen isn't your boyfriend!" I yelled back as I ducked a swipe of Amber's nails.

"Girls!" Dana barked.

Zane, camera on his shoulder, tried to avoid Amber as she lunged at me again.

"If I had wanted to be a middle school teacher, I would have," Dana said in annoyance. "Today you are all going shopping for ingredients. With the magic of TV, viewers will see you go shopping after Anastasia announces the contest theme. Do make sure you're wearing what you're going to wear tomorrow."

I looked down. I had put on a semisexy outfit because I was planning on taking more pictures after the shopping trip.

"Guess I'm going to be baking in this tomorrow," I said, hoisting up the top. It was an Austrian-inspired gingerbread-girl dress. The bodice was laced up and low-cut. Hopefully we weren't going to be doing a "love your grandma" challenge.

"Tomorrow's theme is kids' Christmas," Belle said. "We'd like to see fun, whimsical desserts."

Ooof. I was definitely not dressed appropriately. I raised my hand.

"Unless you need me to call 911 for some godforsaken reason, you better put your hand down," Dana warned. "You are all going shopping now. Be on good behavior. The last thing we need is to have your nonsense splashed all over the tabloids."

We followed Anastasia to a nearby specialty foods store.

"What are you making?" Fiona asked me as we browsed the aisles.

I loved food shopping. Really, I loved any kind of shopping, but with food, there were so many possibilities! What fancy dessert was I going to bake?

"Since it's for kids, it needs to be fun, but it also needs to be easy to actually make. I was thinking of baking an icebox cake, but I don't want to do a no-bake cake. This is *The Great Christmas Bake-Off*, after all."

I decided to make a multilayered sponge cake with custard cheesecake, fruit, chocolate, and mousse. When they announced it was a kids' challenge, I knew Dana and Penny were too smart to pass up an opportunity to have a pack of adorable, photogenic children in the studio. This type of cake would be good for multiple kids because each one could make a layer.

While browsing through the store, I selected various fruits and chocolates. The specialty store had very nice oranges. In the olden times, oranges and other citrus fruits had only been in season in the winter. It had been fashionable to give citrus fruits as gifts. They were definitely going in my dessert.

After I had finished collecting my ingredients and checked out, I went outside to snap photos for my Instagram story. I was framing the perfect shot of the window display when an elf approached me.

"Amber?" I asked, confused. She couldn't have had time to change. I peered at the elf. She had a cold expression, ice-blue eyes, and long brown hair. She was also very tall. I'd worn heels, and I still had to crane my neck. "Do I know you?"

"I'm Dr. Diane Frost, Owen's mother," the tall woman said. She gazed at me. "So you're the one my son has been after. I'll have you know I take pride in the quality of my children's choice of life partner."

"That's nice," I said, starting to back away. I'd lived with crazy for years when I'd had to occupy the same house as

Amber. I knew better than to poke crazy. I wanted to leave crazy way the hell alone.

"You aren't what I envisioned," Diane said, nostrils flaring. Geez, I wasn't even sleeping with the guy, and yet I had all his family drama spewing all over me.

"Well, I hope you get that checked out! Have a nice life!" I said, flashing her a thumbs-up and scurrying back to the bake-off group. *Hope I never see you again.*

"Who was that?" Fiona asked as we walked back to the tower.

"Crazy lady."

"It's Manhattan. I once saw guy having an entire conversation with a pigeon. You just have to let these things go."

"I made alcohol," Morticia said in a bored tone when we were back in the condo and had put away our ingredients.

"What is it?" Fiona asked.

"Alcohol," Morticia repeated.

Fiona shrugged and picked up a glass. "Can't beat that."

"Ooh!" I said, clapping my hands after I'd taken a burning sip of whatever the hell that was. "Take cute pictures of me. Like a sexy *Mad Men* Christmas with my drink. Please, Morticia, you're such a good artist!"

"I know you're trying to flatter me, and it's working," she said, picking up my phone.

I struck a Betty Boop pose.

"I hope you're not going to be like that when the kids are here," Morticia commented.

"Hardly," I said, smooshing my boobs up even more in the tight-fitting bodice. "Though I think I better find an apron that provides some coverage. Otherwise these babies might be a bit much."

Morticia lowered the phone. "Call me crazy, but since you still claim to be running a baking Instagram account, not an escort-for-hire Instagram account, maybe you should put some baked goods in the picture?"

"She had her muffins!" Fiona giggled. The alcohol concoction was clearly hitting her fast.

I took another sip of my own. "I don't have any cookies. Except for the extra-special Christmas cookie!" I said, pointing down to my hoo-ha. Fiona and I collapsed into a fit of giggles.

"Three hundred twenty-five days until Halloween, three hundred twenty-five days until Halloween," Morticia chanted and went around to the other side of the kitchen island. She pulled out a box. "I have some leftover cookies here. Use these in the picture."

"You like these?" I held the mitten cookies up to my chest and blew a kiss to the camera.

Morticia snapped a few more pictures. "Just post one of the photos along with a donation link. I bet you make this month's student loan payment."

"My grandmother always said to use the gifts God gave you, whatever they may be!" I said, flipping through the pictures.

"I'll drink to that!" Fiona said.

CHAPTER 22

Owen

notification came into my phone, making it rattle on the glass conference table. I tried to force myself not to look at it. I'd set the notifications to let me know when Holly posted a picture on Instagram. But only because I wanted to know if she was doing any more buzz for my company.

My hand twitched. I tried to concentrate on the financial report Garrett was giving. He paused and glared at me.

"Go ahead and look at it. You clearly aren't going to pay attention until you do."

"I don't—"

"Go ahead. We're waiting."

I picked up the phone and swiped at the notification. A very suggestive picture came up. Holly was blowing a kiss for the camera, and two of *the sugar cookies* were held up to the mounds of her breasts, which threatened to spill out of the bodice. The caption read:

I know you want to get your mittens on my cookies!

"Geez," Walker said, looking over my shoulder. "Now I see why you were out in the middle of the night."

"That's not—I have a puppy that I am now responsible for, thank you very much."

I snuck another glance at the picture then set the phone down.

Walker was still looking at me. "Three, two, one," he said.

"What?" Then it hit me. Holly hadn't just sent the picture to me, obviously—it was a social media account after all. But that meant that *everyone had seen it.* I was suddenly, irrationally furious.

"And there it is." Walker patted me on the shoulder. "We might as well call it quits, you guys. He's going to be stewing over Holly the rest of the day, poor big idiot."

"I'm not an idiot. I can handle myself," I snarled, shaking him off. "Go through the rest of the report, Garrett. Please."

I was wound up tight through the rest of the meeting. I'd barely said ten words to Holly that weren't related to the bake-off or how much I despised Christmas. Why was I suddenly so possessive? It was irrational. I wasn't irrational; I thought deeply about things then made decisions and followed through decisively. I was the very definition of a cold, rational man.

Furthermore, Holly, with her Christmas excess and crazy outfits, was not the type of woman I had ever imagined myself being with.

It's the cookies. She put some sort of spell in them.

No, that would be crazy.

"Owen, so you're in agreement?" Greg asked, interrupting my thoughts.

"Uh, yes, that sounds great." I said, trying to look as if I'd been paying attention.

"Wonderful. I'll have my little brothers delivered to your house in the evening. I'm sure all of my half brothers will be looking forward to their six-week-long snowboarding retreat. Do be mindful. Several of the children have developed the rather unfortunate habit of throwing random items such as clothes, Rice Krispies treats, and once even a toaster out the window. While that's not much of an issue on a private estate, I hope your liability insurance covers people throwing things off your balcony."

"Wait! I don't want to take all your little brothers!" I said, panicking slightly.

"Then pay attention and don't agree to things when you have no idea what's going on," Hunter snapped.

"It's Holly," Walker said sagely.

"Honestly," Archer said from the corner, where he was playing games on his phone—how he ran a multibillion-dollar hotel conglomerate was beyond me—"You should have Holly come and organize all your fun workplace activities. That contest is based on employee surveys, right? So foster some good cheer and host a boozy party at two in the afternoon."

"I can't just throw parties in the middle of the workday," I protested.

"Of course not. That's why you have Holly do it!"

I stewed about Holly the rest of the evening as I assembled with Gunnar, Dana, and several other Romance Creative workers in my condo. The TV was set to the Internet-streaming channel. A countdown clock of happy elves tossing numbers on the timer was ticking down to the premier of *The Great Christmas Bake-Off*.

Belle was setting up another flat-screen TV that displayed several stats, including number of viewers and shares on social media.

"I made snacks!" Penny called, bringing in a charcuterie tray from the kitchen. Garrett followed his girlfriend with several more dishes.

"I didn't peg you as a Christmas Bake-Off fan," I said to him, snagging one of the pinwheel sandwiches off the tray he held.

"I'm supportive," he said, settling on the couch and wrapping an arm possessively around Penny. She giggled and fed him a bite of sandwich.

I was suddenly jealous. Not that I wanted Penny—Garrett would flat-out murder me if I even thought that—but I wanted what Garrett had. When I'd originally agreed to go out with Sloane six months ago, she had seemed perfect. She checked all the boxes: Ivy League educated, good career, slim and tall, with conservative fashion sense.

I had been ready to find a partner, a girlfriend and eventual wife I could settle down with. Then Sloane had turned into a disaster, and I was in damage-control mode. But now there was Holly.

The timer on the screen reached zero. The cartoon elves cheered, and the theme song played.

"I had to basically sell my soul to Lilith and Morticia to get them to create that little cartoon," Penny explained with a laugh.

Morticia was standing in a corner, glowering.

"Don't you feel a little bit of Christmas spirit?" Penny teased her friend.

"Never."

That was how I felt unless I was looking at Holly in a sexy costume or Holly's Christmas cookies or Holly in that outfit *with* the Christmas cookies. I jumped up, suddenly warm, and threw open the French doors to the balcony.

"It's freezing in here," Gunnar complained.

"Shhh, it's starting," Belle said.

Upbeat Christmas music played while the contestants baked. I sucked in a breath when the show cut to a close-up of Holly, hair swept into a messy updo, that ridiculously festive and ridiculously short sweater dress emphasizing her curves.

"There's a lot of people watching," Penny said, chewing on her lip. "Are all those people going to crash the system?"

"Of course not," I retorted. "My company runs the server infrastructure for WebFlix. You could have ten times as many people watch it all at once and not notice a difference."

"Hopefully we have that many," Dana said, making notes on her tablet as the episode played.

"How are the stats looking?" Gunnar asked, looking at the adjacent screen.

"Shit, we're up to eight hundred thousand," Belle said. I watched as Holly presented her dessert on screen.

"Owen's really hitting it out of the park," Garrett remarked. "That shot where Anastasia asked him a question and he just scowled up at the ceiling and grunted was particularly insightful."

"He's eye candy," Dana said.

"He's definitely helping to sell the show," Gunnar said, scrolling through his phone. "From the stats, a good thirty percent of the comments are about Owen. This woman said, 'I want to smear him with frosting and lick it all off'."

"He's drawing in viewers," Belle said. "We're at one point three million!"

"Fantastic!" Dana said, pleased. "I think we had that many viewers during the season finale last year. We're going to blow those numbers out of the water this season!"

"Someone needs to give Owen a crash course in baking. We're trying to ensure his company does not fail the *TechBiz* ranking again," Garrett said. "He can't just sit there with a blank look on his face. That does not inspire confidence."

CHAPTER 23

Holly

'd stayed up late into the early morning, first watching the premiere of *The Great Christmas Bake-Off* then interacting with fans online. The Taste My Muffins baking subscription boxes also experienced a surge in subscribers, which I was grateful for. I'd received another note from the storage facility where my grandmother's Christmas decorations were. The owner said I needed to make some sort of payment or they were going to auction off my unit. I didn't even have to check my accounts or my credit card to know that I did not have enough money for that month's payment.

I sent an email back begging for an extension until Christmas. By then I would have won the bake-off, and everything would be perfect!

A few hours later, I had stuffed myself back into my gingerbread girl dress and was standing in the studio at my station. Today I would be vigilant. After Amber's attempt to ruin my cookies in the last episode, I wasn't letting anything slide.

"Welcome to the next episode of *The Great Christmas Bake-Off*," Anastasia said. "Christmas is about family, and there's something about experiencing Christmas through the eyes of a child to make the holiday extra special. And that makes children's Christmas our theme of the day. Contestants, your challenge is to create a dessert that is enjoyable for children to both eat and bake! And to help you, we have brought in a few children. We're borrowing the Svensson brothers! Come on out, boys!"

This wasn't a few children, I thought, as two dozen blond-haired, grey-eyed boys, in a range of sizes and ages, streamed into the studio. The younger ones looked around in awe at all the Christmas decorations.

"We have assigned several children to each station," Anastasia explained.

Someone must have already told them where to go, because the boys all sorted themselves out so there were around three kids at each station. Fiona was teamed with three very happy teenage boys who were clearly over the moon to be working with the pretty baker.

I seemed to have been assigned the youngest Svensson brothers. One of them barely came up to my knee. I bent down to talk to them at their level. Zane zoomed in with the camera. The youngest boy immediately looked freaked out.

"What's your name?" I said, trying to use my best this-is-going-to-be-amazeballs-and-totally-not-scary voice.

TASTING HER CHRISTMAS COOKIES • 131

The small child looked between me and the camera, wide-eyed. "I'm Davy," he said finally.

I let out a breath. Meltdown averted.

"I'm Henry," his slightly older brother announced. "I'm five and a quarter."

"Are you really!"

"I'm Andy, and I'm six," said the third boy.

"Are you ready to help me bake?"

They nodded.

"Great! Because I really need your help!"

On the outside, I was the fun, Christmas-loving baker. However, I was silently wondering if I was actually going to be able to finish this dessert. The other stations with the older kids already had their ingredients selected, while I had just finished introductions.

The three teens at Fiona's station expertly chopped nuts and stirred sauces in a double boiler. She had basically been given three sous chefs. Someone had clearly taught them something about cooking.

I doubted that knowledge had trickled down to my three. Davy clung to my skirt as we went over to the pantry to pick up my ingredients. Andy and Henry did at least help me carry things back to my station, and they didn't even drop anything. Henry stood on tiptoe to push his items onto the counter. Andy was barely tall enough to peep over the top of the table, his eyes clearing the counter.

"Can you pick them up?" Zane asked in a low voice. "They're out of the frame."

"Am I supposed to hold them and bake?" I whispered back.

Zane shrugged. One of the assistants brought out two milk crates, and Henry and Andy clambered onto them.

"Perfect," Zane said, flashing me a thumbs-up. "Just set Davy on the table."

"Oh my God," I muttered, picking him up. He watched wide-eyed as I set about making the yellow sponge cake batter for the cake layer while Henry and Andy whipped cream cheese.

I started several saucepans of fruit to cook on the stove. I had to make two cakes, one for the production crew to photograph and one to present to the judges.

"I feel like they should have parceled the kids out better," I said to Fiona as she and the three teenagers moved like a choreographed ballet in the tight space. "Maybe we could trade?"

She giggled. "I don't know, Isaac," she said to one of the teenagers. "You want to switch?"

"I'm good," he replied, deftly removing the seeds from a vanilla bean with a chef's knife.

I wish one of these kids could handle a knife.

At least Andy and Henry were halfway competent. I wasn't sure what to do with Davy. He was maybe three? He sat on the large table, watching me intently.

"I want to help," he piped up.

"Um, okay, how about you—" I looked around. "You can start on the whipped cream. We need a lot of it to make the custardy layers fluffy and light!"

Davy nodded solemnly as I gave him the bowl of whipped cream, which was big enough for him to sit in. The whisk was as long as his arm.

"This is a lot," he said as he stirred it with two hands. He was occupied, but baking the cakes was slow going. I couldn't just cook; I was also basically babysitting.

"I feel like this is turning into a gimmick," I said when Anastasia came over. "Not that I don't enjoy the world's cutest sous chefs!"

"I'm not sure why they were parceled out like that, honestly," she said, laughing. "But seriously, this footage is going to be gold!"

I was finally able to put the sponge cake in the oven to bake while I strained the fruit filling and portioned out the whipped cream cheese. Then I helped Andy and Henry stir the fruit in. Davy was still slowly whipping the cream as I started the custard. I had just turned my back for a second when there was a crash and a *clang*!

The whipped cream had fallen and splattered all over the floor. I hurried to grab a towel.

"You're fine," I told Davy. "We have so much whipped cream it doesn't even matter." I patted the splatters on his pants as his lower lip trembled. "See, you didn't get anything on your nice outfit," I assured him, trying to keep him calm.

A production assistant hurried to mop up the whipped cream.

"See, it's all cleaned up," I told Davy.

His eyes watered, his lips parted, and he *screamed*.

"Oh dear," I said, picking him up. I looked to his teen brothers.

Isaac shrugged. "Davy's a crier. He'll go for the next few hours."

"He's messing up my sound," Zane said as I patted Davy on the back. He screamed and writhed in my arms.

"Maybe one of my older brothers is around," Isaac said, looking around as he expertly whipped cream. "Garrett can sometimes make him stop crying."

Zane made hurry-up motions as I tried to rock Davy and stir my custard before it burned. Owen came into the studio, annoyance clear on his face. He stormed over to me, Belle following behind him.

"We can hear him screaming in the Quantum Cyber offices upstairs," Owen complained. "Isaac, where are your brothers?"

The teenager shrugged.

"Honestly," Belle complained. "Gunnar just disappeared."

"The Svenssons are flaky as hell," Owen said, looking around in frustration. "Someone's going to call the police. One of the interns said she heard him screaming from the street. She thought a raccoon was trapped or something."

Davy screamed even louder, and we all winced.

"Give him to me," Owen said. "I got it."

"Do you?" I said skeptically. "He's purple."

Owen glared at me.

"Fine. He can blast your eardrums," I said, handing Davy over. As soon as Davy was in Owen's arms, though, he stopped crying. The purple subsided, and he hiccupped.

"I know," Owen said, his voice low, almost a purr. "Baking is rough, isn't it? I bet you'd rather execute a corporate takeover or monopolize a market." He bounced the kid in his arms. I felt my ovaries pop. There was something about a powerful man in a suit cuddling a little kid that made me lose my *Pfeffernüsse.*

Owen snuggled Davy in his arms then lightly pressed his nose to Davy's small one, grinning at him. Davy giggled. A nuclear bomb went off in my womb. In the distance, sirens.

"That's it. I need a baby right now," I said under my breath.

"I know, right?" Fiona said, laughing.

"You should take one of my brothers," Isaac offered.

CHAPTER 24

Owen

I had been planning on returning to work, but I ended up remaining in the studio the rest of the day. As soon as I tried to put Davy down, he threatened to scream. He also didn't want to come up to my office and color. He wanted to watch Holly cook; nothing else was acceptable. Therefore I was also going to be watching Holly cook.

With Davy out of the way, Holly seemed like she had the cake a little more under control. She was very patient with Andy and Henry, which was impressive, because the Svenssons did not inspire patience.

"That looks like a very intense cake," I told her as she meticulously fitted a layer of baked cheesecake over a firm, red-colored custard.

"I might have been a little ambitious," Holly admitted as she helped Henry pour in the next layer of cream cheese and whipped cream over the top. She jiggled the tall cake pan, her chest bouncing with the motion, and carefully carried each cake to the fridge.

"We're making the candied pomegranates, cranberries, and orange peels to go on top for decoration," she explained to the boys. "Then I'll make ganache, and that's it! We'll have two beautiful cakes."

I set Davy back on the counter, and he sort of helped dissolve the sugar in water while Holly sliced several oranges. Henry and Andy seeded a pomegranate as Holly boiled the orange peel.

"We have to boil it off and change the water a few times to remove the bitterness and cook the peel," she explained, "before we actually candy it."

The candied fruit was done by the time the last layer on the cakes had set. Holly poured the glossy chocolate ganache over the top of the cakes, and Davy helped sprinkle the candied fruit on top.

"We'll let this set in the fridge," Holly said. "Now, let's clean up! It's important to make sure your station is nice and tidy and the baking equipment is clean."

Watching Holly with the boys was stirring something in my cold heart. She was so wholesome and adorable with them.

You're going soft.

"The cakes should be ready now," she said, glancing at the clock. The station was clean, and the boys were waiting excitedly for the cake reveal. Holly brought them separately from the fridge.

"That's a big cake," I remarked as she set the second one carefully on a crystal cake platter.

"It's a whole ten inches," she said, sticking her tongue out.

"Impressive."

"How are you going to take it out?" Henry asked.

"Very carefully," she said, running a dish towel under hot water and wringing it out. She pressed it quickly to the sides of the round metal cake mold.

"Everyone, cross your fingers," she said and slowly slid the mold up.

"Wow!" the kids exclaimed. Davy applauded. The cake was impressive. It resembled a rock formation worn away by a river that revealed the layers of sediment. I didn't know how she had done it, but on several layers, there were cutouts of various fruits. For example, the orange custard layer had little orange fruit candy canes pressed against the side, and the grapefruit layer had thin slices of grapefruit stars.

"Just in time too," she said as she put the finishing touches of sprigs of mint and other edible greenery around the cake.

Davy had enjoyed watching the cake being made, and he did not want to retire to the greenroom with the rest of the contestants. He sat in my lap as each of the contestants, with their groups of Svensson brothers, presented their desserts. Fiona's group had made a seven-layer Christmas cake. Somehow she had engineered it so that when she cut into it, there was a whole Christmas scene of Santa, Rudolph, and the elves.

Holly's, I felt, was the most impressive.

"I was a little worried when you said icebox cake," Nick said as he took a forkful of the cake. "But this is so fruity and refreshing. I love the detail you put into it."

Anu addressed the children. "Did you all have fun making it?" They nodded silently, a bit overwhelmed at being the center of attention. "This does seem like something you could actually do with children of all ages, not just something you could give them to eat."

"Have you guys tried it?" Nick asked. They took a bite. I gave Davy a bite of mine.

"It's really good," Henry said. "We should make this every day." We all laughed.

"I think it's a special-occasion thing," Holly told him, ruffling his hair.

"It's definitely a good activity if it's day five of Christmas vacation and it's sleeting outside," Anu said. "You could keep kids occupied for hours!"

❄ ❄ ❄

"And?" Nick asked when the last contestant had presented. "Who do we like as the winner?"

"I think the guy who made the little pudding cups is definitely out," Anu said. "Not only did they look like alien eggs, they also tasted mealy."

"Holly should win," Davy piped up. We were now on hour seven of him being glued to me. There was not an adult Svensson in sight.

"That works for me," Anu said. "I loved the flavors in her cake. And the height was impressive. It had structural integrity. Also it seemed fun for kids without being condescending."

Holly and the boys jumped up and down and high-fived when we told them they'd won. I forced myself to keep my eyes on her face and not on her tits when they threatened to spill out of the low-cut bodice.

I tried calling Walker then several of his brothers while interviews were being done. None of them answered their phones. The filming was done, and the Svensson brothers were milling around in the studio when Walker finally responded.

Walker: *Just take them to your apartment. Someone will come get them in a little bit.*
Owen: *I've been babysitting them all day.*
Walker: *Think of this as a test for when you and Holly have a million kids.*
Owen: *Two, maybe three max.*
Walker: *Have you even asked her out yet?*
Owen: *She's a contestant. I shouldn't.*
Walker: *Ah yes because we don't want to corrupt the integrity of* The Great Christmas Bake-Off, *now do we?*

Holly was laughing with the Svensson brothers. They were all sampling the cakes.

"I'm hungry," Henry complained when I walked over.

"But there's all this cake!" Holly exclaimed.

"I want macaroni and cheese."

"Your brothers aren't ready to come pick you guys up," I told them, "so you're going to hang with me."

"They're not?" Holly said, shocked.

I shrugged. "The Svenssons leaving their little brothers just lying around is pretty standard."

"But it's dinnertime," Andy complained.

"Can we order pizza?" Isaac asked me.

"I know Mace doesn't want you eating garbage for dinner."

"Are you going to cook?" he asked incredulously.

I looked around helplessly. I could barely cook for myself, let alone twenty kids.

Holly was clearly struggling not to laugh. "Why don't I come up and cook?"

CHAPTER 25

Holly

"I can't believe you, you hussy," Amber spat at me.

"Relax. I'm just being helpful," I said as I rode up in the elevator with the other contestants. I wished Amber had been sent home, but at least it hadn't been me.

Once at the penthouse, I collected my spices then added the box of leftover cookies from the last competition. Hopefully Owen had more in his condo than energy drinks and frozen dinners.

I felt slightly nervous when I went downstairs. It was freaking me out that I was going into Owen's home. Well, technically, I'd already been in his home and been sleeping in his bed, but he wasn't in it. This was where he currently lived, his personal space. Would it smell like him?

I stood at the front door then heard Owen bellow. "Get down off of there! Don't climb the curtains!"

I knocked tentatively. Several small feet pounded toward the door.

"Hi!" Andy said as the door opened a crack.

"You shouldn't just open the door to strangers," Owen said.

"You sound like such a dad," I teased him as he opened the door the rest of the way. His jacket and tie were off. He gestured to my container of cooking supplies.

"Honestly, you don't have to cook. We can order something. Not pizza," he said before Henry could open his mouth.

"I thought you said you were being forced to stay in the smaller condo?" I asked him as I walked in.

"I am. This is tiny," he insisted, taking the boxes from me. The muscles under his shirt rippled with the motion.

"It's two stories," I said skeptically. There was a staircase off in the corner.

"I know," Owen said seriously. "Tiny. My penthouse is three stories. This is like one and a half. I only have six bedrooms."

"What could you possibly need with all that space?" I said, trying not to drool as I thought about completely clearing out whatever he had in there and setting up a craft room. Plus, I could have a whole room—no, *two* whole rooms—dedicated entirely to Christmas stuff. I could turn one into a second kitchen...

Owen shrugged. "It's nice to have extra space." He set my boxes down on the counter in the huge kitchen.

"Why is it so cold?" I explained. The double French doors to the balcony were open, letting in the frigid winter air.

"Seriously?" Owen said. "It's incredibly warm in here."

I rubbed my hands together and blew on them. "We need to heat things up in this kitchen." I unpacked my boxes then turned to Owen's cabinets. "What do we have to cook with?"

"You brought cookies?" Owen asked from his spot at the giant kitchen counter.

"Yes," I said, opening his fridge. "I had some left over. They aren't going to last, so we might as well eat them." If I hadn't known any better, I'd have thought I saw him quickly reach into the bag and take one out. Must have been my imagination, though.

The fridge contained more than I was expecting.

"You have greens for salad," I said, surveying the contents, "and you have chicken. Lots and lots of chicken. Why do you have so much chicken?"

"It's good protein," he said. "Makes you buff." He flexed his biceps. My brain chose that moment to beat me over the head with the image of Owen standing before me shirtless.

Yum. Muscular man.

I wiped my mouth.

"Do you have flour?" I said, opening all his cabinets. "And you do! Perfect. We will be making Holly's famous chicken tenders, a favorite of men of all ages from very small to…" I snuck another glance at Owen looking positively edible as he leaned casually against the counter. "Very large."

I pulled my apron over my head. Owen was right there, untangling my hair from the clip in the back.

"Thanks," I said. His hand brushed the back of my neck, making me shiver.

"Why don't you all play hide-and-seek?" he said to the Svensson brothers. "I'll help Holly cook."

"You don't know how to cook," Davy insisted before Isaac picked him up.

"See, this is why I need a large condo," Owen said matter-of-factly after the boys and Rudolph scampered off.

I snorted and took the chicken from the fridge. I was very aware of Owen in the kitchen with me. Usually I was not an anxious person. I liked to think that my time in the restaurant trenches had made me impervious. Owen, however, was making me slightly nervous. He watched me intently as I moved around the kitchen. I was starting to rethink the decision to offer to cook.

"I was thinking," I said, starting to ramble to fill the intense silence. "I'm going to make fried chicken strips and a big salad, but I should probably make some carbs, or they're going to be hungry again in an hour. I guess you don't have any pasta? But at least you have cheese. That's something." I opened the fridge and bent over, pawing through the cheese drawer. There were blocks of various kinds of cheese. I found some sausage as well.

A strangled cough came from Owen's direction.

"You can spare some cheese," I said, picking up several large pieces. "Hopefully you don't mind me using all of it?"

"Not at all. It was left over from the premiere of *The Great Christmas Bake-Off* last night," he explained as I dumped the ingredients on the counter.

I'd spent the last several years living in tiny shared apartments. I'd never had this much counter space all to myself. I wanted to just sprawl on the marble, but that might be weird.

"I can have pasta brought here if you need it," Owen offered.

"Like, Santa brings it?"

He smirked. "Like I can ask the concierge to go purchase some."

"That seems excessive. You have eggs, flour, and salt, so I can make it," I assured him as I cleared off the counter. "Why do you have so much flour, by the way?"

"Part of an experiment," he said gruffly.

"Uh-huh." I narrowed my eyes at him, but he didn't crack.

"I'm going to make *spätzle*, a German pasta," I told him, dumping cups of flour on the counter. I made a well in the flour and added the wet ingredients. "I just have to brown it in a skillet and add cheese sauce. Everyone loves it."

"Do you need help?" Owen offered, undoing the cuff links on his shirt and rolling up his sleeves.

"Um, sure." I swallowed. The tendons and muscles on his forearms rippled as he began mixing the flour, eggs, salt, milk, and white pepper together.

"Am I doing it right?" he asked, noticing me watching.

"Yeah, just use your hands to really work it," I said, lightly placing my hand over his much larger one. "Don't be afraid to be forceful. This isn't pastry dough. It likes it rough."

"It does, does it?" he murmured, his breath drifting across the back of my neck.

I turned my head and was caught in his gaze. I took a breath, inhaling that clean masculine scent like basil and fresh snow. "I'm going to make the—" I gestured helplessly to the stove.

I started making the cheese sauce while Owen made the dough. While I cubed the cheddar, Gruyère, and other cheeses he had in his fridge, I also heated the oil to fry the chicken tenders. Some wise soul had built a literal deep fryer into the counter. As a self-proclaimed fried food junkie, I was in heaven.

While I worked, I snuck glances behind me. Watching Owen knead the dough with his hands, the way his broad shoulders tapered down to his waist, was doing... things to me.

"Is this going to be enough?" he asked, gesturing to the balls of dough stacked on the counter.

"Sure! Plus you have some meat that I'm adding. You have a really nice, thick sausage, which is just what I like!" I said cheerfully.

CHAPTER 26

Owen

I couldn't quite tell how Holly felt toward me. If the kids hadn't been there, I probably would have pushed her against the counter and slid my hands up that impossibly sexy dress. While that would let me know immediately one way or the other how she felt, I forced myself to remain in control.

"The nice thing about spätzle," Holly said, demonstrating how to make the small noodles, "is that you don't have to use a special machine to make the shapes, you simply roll it out. It should be rustic and handmade."

"Like your cookies," I said with a small smile.

"Yes!" she practically shouted. "*Exactly* like my cookies." She put her hands on her hips and looked at me. "I'm still a little mad that you didn't fall to your knees in front of me."

I mean, I sort of want to right now...

"Everyone has a religious experience with those cookies," she said and returned to whacking the chicken into strips with a cleaver.

Now's your chance. Ask her to make them.

But I hated admitting I couldn't solve a problem myself. My whole company was centered around solving complex data problems. I was a billionaire. Magazine articles had been written about my brilliance with cryptocurrency. I should be able to make cookies; it was just embarrassing otherwise.

"I'm not a person who like sweet things," I replied.

"Even after a taste of my Christmas best, you're telling me you don't want to put your mouth on my cookies ever again?" she said with an overly dramatic pout, looking up at me from under her lashes.

"I—" I clamped my mouth shut. Holly looked too kissable.

And fuckable.

But maybe she wasn't actually flirting. Maybe she was just being friendly. Belle would kill me if I scared Holly. But she'd come up here willingly…

"What should I do with all these little spätzle noodles?" I asked her after I had a huge pile of them.

"We're going to brown the spätzle in the pan with the sausage," she said, banging her spoon on the rim of a cast iron skillet.

I scooped the little noodles off the cutting board. They spattered when they hit the pan.

"Stir that," she said, resting her palm on the underside of my forearm. Her hand was warm against my skin. I wanted to crush her to me.

I stirred while she finished cutting up the chicken strips then dipped them in a spicy batter. She was humming "Rudolph the Red-Nosed Reindeer" as she worked.

"How's that oil looking?" she asked. "Hot enough?"

I peered around on the stove top. "I don't see it."

She pointed. A few feet away from the stove was a container of oil sitting in the countertop.

"That's the garbage can," I said, confused.

"Oh, sweet winter child, no," Holly said with a laugh. "I'm about to blow your mind. And maybe you." She muttered the last line under her breath.

"What?" I said, thinking I must have misheard.

"What? You have a deep fryer in your countertop. You're really living large here," she said, shaking off the last strips of chicken.

"Aren't you supposed to separate those?" I asked in concern as she dropped the batter-drenched strips of chicken into the oil.

"It's better this way, trust me," she said.

The smell of fried chicken brought the kids in.

"I just have to make a salad," Holly told them.

They immediately jumped into action, tearing lettuce for the salad and slicing up the few vegetables I had in my fridge. They even made a vinaigrette.

"I'm very impressed," Holly said, surveying them. "I always wanted a big family but thought it might be a little too chaotic. But if they can be trained to cook, eh, why not have ten?"

"Seriously, you want this many kids?" I asked her as the young Svensson brothers worked like little elves to set the table.

She thought for a moment as she mixed up chipotle aioli for the chicken tenders. "Maybe not this many."

The condo had a huge farmhouse-style table that I usually just used to spread out my work. Now it sat all twenty-five of us. Holly was laying everything out buffet style on the kitchen island when the front door beeped, alerting me that someone had punched in the key code.

"Hey, we got here just in time for dinner!" Walker said gleefully, trotting into the open living and kitchen area.

"Hell no," I argued. "You can't just leave your little brothers then show up when it's time to eat."

"We have enough food," Holly said, touching my arm. Several more Svenssons piled into my condo. "I think we have enough?"

CHAPTER 27

Holly

The Svenssons waved goodbye to me as they ate the last of the leftover cookies.

When the last one was out the door, I slumped on the couch. We had barely had enough food. I felt terrible. I prided myself on feeding people and throwing amazing parties. What else did I have going for me?

"I demand a redo!" I told Owen as he poured two glasses of amber whisky.

"For what?" he asked, handing me a glass.

"It wasn't my best work," I railed. "I didn't have time to plan. I was working in less-than-ideal conditions."

"They ate it, and they liked it," Owen said with a shrug and took a sip of his drink. "We didn't even have leftovers."

"Exactly!" I said, jumping up and pacing around his living room. "That's the problem. If you don't have leftovers, you didn't make enough food. I am shamed!"

He laughed and reached out to stop me, his hand resting lightly on my waist. "You were perfect. Thank you."

I wrinkled my nose. "I'll do better next time. We'll bring the Svenssons back, and I'll cook an insane feast."

"Please spare me," he said with a slight smile around his mouth. His hand was still on my waist. I really felt like he wanted to kiss me, but then sometimes I had gut feelings that turned out to be indigestion.

I stepped away, breaking the contact, and took another sip of the whisky.

"I really appreciate you coming by," Owen told me.

"Next time, I'm making you some Christmas cookies," I said stubbornly. "I know there's a recipe you'll love. It is my lifelong dream to see your eyes roll back in your head when you eat my cookies."

That sounded dirty, Holly. He's going to think you're just like Amber.

"Guess I better go before I say anything else inappropriate!" I said with a too-loud laugh, hightailing it to the front door.

Owen caught up to me as I was staring at the door, trying to figure out how to open it. It had a fancy high-tech lock. He spun me around, large hands resting on my hips.

"Maybe I just need another taste of your cookies. I'll take it a little slower, really savor the flavors," he murmured.

I looked up at his blue eyes. He was ridiculously tall. If this had been happening to anyone other than me, I would have said this was the start of a Christmas romance story for the ages.

Ha! Who was I kidding? The most I could hope for was a tumble under the Tannenbaum, then we'd go our separate ways. Like I said, modest dreamer—food, sex, a place to stash my baking gear, and Holly was good.

I stared up at him, willing him to kiss me.

But he stepped back instead. "Goodnight, Holly."

"Did he frost your Christmas cookies?" Morticia asked when she saw me. She was sketching designs for the penthouse Christmas decorations in the living room.

"Unfortunately, no, he did not touch my Christmas cookies, baked or otherwise. Not that I have the wherewithal right now to try and fight off Amber for him," I replied. But the thought of Amber sticking her claws into Owen really made me want to go all *Holiday in Handcuffs* on someone.

Even if Owen didn't like Christmas or Christmas cookies, he was still a good man. I knew what kind of girl Amber was—flaky, manipulative, destructive. I didn't want Owen in her crosshairs, even if he did hate Christmas cookies.

Down, brain. Think of your financial situation. I need solutions, not more problems. Owen is a grown man. He can handle himself.

My brain bashed me in the face with another image of Owen half naked, the bulge of his Christmas package visible in his boxer briefs.

Yes, I thought, *grown male.*

My phone buzzed. I had ten more new subscribers for the Taste My Muffin baking subscription box.

"Can you still help me bake?" I begged Morticia. "I have three hundred boxes to mail out."

"Fine," Morticia said, prowling around the kitchen. "However, we do not have enough flour. Or butter."

"Guess we're going shopping!"

"Can you afford it?" she asked in a genuine display of concern.

I tamped down thoughts of losing all my grandmother's Christmas decorations in the storage unit. The baking boxes were an investment toward saving them.

"Hey, my credit card debt needs more debt to keep it from feeling so lonely!"

We left earlyish the next morning for the store. My years of working in kitchens had put me on the "work until three a.m. and sleep until noon" schedule then rinse and repeat ad nauseum until you just randomly quit one day and start a failing baking subscription service then in a fit of delusion join a Christmas baking TV show that will magically make your problems go away.

Fiona rode down in the elevator with me.

"Thanks for coming with," I told her.

"I love shopping! Plus I want to take pictures of the Christmas displays," she said happily.

Morticia had a long black scarf wrapped around her neck, probably more to ward against the Christmas spirit than the cold. I peered at her.

"Do you have red glitter in your scarf?" I asked, pointing.

"I better not," she hissed, clawing at the scarf. "It's tinsel from your ridiculous sweater."

I was wearing a fun sweater that I'd bought on impulse.

"This is a nice sweater!" I protested, looking down. The sweater depicted a corgi wearing a Santa Claus hat. His nose blinked red.

"It's cute, Morticia! I should buy you one!" I teased.

"You put that on me, you're losing a finger," she threatened.

The specialty food store was crowded. Fiona grabbed a cart.

"What are you making? I'm sure you'll need butter," she said, loading up the cart. "And cream."

"I want to make Christmas rum-punch pound cake, hot cocoa brownies, and crème brûlée sugar cookies," I said.

"So chocolate and more chocolate!" Fiona laughed.

Morticia dumped an armload of ingredients into the cart. "Here are more oranges," she said. "And booze."

"I don't think we need two bottles of rum."

"One for us, one for the cake."

Fiona and I looked at each other and nodded. "I'm okay with that."

"Why am I not surprised?" A woman who looked exactly like the mean girl from any high school movie crossed her arms, leg jutting out in a model pose. She was well-dressed, but in New York City, if someone was talking to strangers, that meant either they were trying to sell something, or they were crazy. My default with dealing with crazy people in New York City was to purposefully and vigorously ignore them.

"I'm assuming you have no idea who I am," she said as we all tried to move around her. "I'm Sloane."

We all shrugged.

Sloane's nostrils flared at the slight. "I am currently the most important woman in Owen's life. His company needs my company to vote for Quantum Cyber as the best place to work. He's going to do anything and everything I ask of him in order to win that prize."

"Doubtful," I said hotly. "I've been helping him, too, and I'm not trying to exploit him."

I usually wasn't one to fight over a guy. I mean, come on, I did have some standards. But Sloane was really pissing me off. I was over there minding my own business, buying my weight in butter, and she just came over swinging her Christmas stocking around.

"Of course someone like you would think she had a chance with Owen."

"Is all of this," she gestured to the packed grocery cart, "for Owen, or are you all going to eat butter and sugar while watching movies?" She turned up her nose.

"What's with Owen and attracting crazy women?" I said out loud. "You're going to have to get in line, because my stepsister, Amber, also thinks she has a claim to him."

"Is she another roly-poly baker like you?" Sloane said, smiling. It did not reach her eyes.

"Men like something to grab onto," Fiona said hotly.

"She does have a lot, doesn't she," Sloane sneered.

"Right, because she actually cares what some Upper West Side Becky has to say," Morticia snapped.

"You'll see," Sloane said with a smirk. "Don't even waste your time with Owen. He's mine."

CHAPTER 28

Owen

After the Svenssons had left the previous night, I'd prowled around the condo. All I could think about was Holly and how to make up an excuse to spend more time with her. My phone buzzed with texts from Sloane. I ignored them in favor of scrolling through Holly's Instagram. There was photo after photo of her striking fun, sexy poses in ridiculous, over-the-top outfits that usually featured a low-cut top and some sort of cinched waist that hiked her tits up.

I opened the windows at either end of the condo to bring in a frigid cross breeze. I was reaching a boiling point. Rudolph, worn out from chasing the Svensson kids around all evening, snoozed peacefully in the Christmas-themed bed Holly had purchased for him. It was a giant reindeer head, and the antlers flopped slightly in the breeze.

Though I had gotten a taste of the Christmas cookies she had brought over, I really wanted a taste of a different kind of cookie. I would have to settle for the sugar cookies, though. I'd reworked my computer program to give me the most likely combination of ingredients to make Christmas cookies like Holly's.

The first recipe looked, to my untrained eye, to be similar to what Holly had made in the bake-off: flour, sugar, butter. Should be easy. I creamed the butter until it was sort of smooth. I added the other ingredients, and the dough seemed fine. I rolled it out and cut out shapes. I didn't have a cookie cutter, so I freehanded it. This was just for a test.

While they baked, I made buttercream frosting.

"I mean honestly, how difficult could it be?" I said to the sleeping dog.

The fire alarm went off.

"Shit." The cookies had spread across the cookie sheet, and some dough had dripped onto the bottom of the oven, where it was burning cheerfully.

"Fuck," I yelled. I tossed the whole thing into the sink and turned on the water, making it sputter.

Cookie log: attempt one, I wrote. **Failure.**

On to attempt two.

The cookies were much more difficult than I had thought. I finally had to call it quits in the early hours of the morning. I did have an actual company to run.

"I need a better recipe," I said to Rudolph when I took him outside. "Also, my buttercream sucks." It was disgusting and somehow tasted both greasy and too sweet.

Rudolph was starting to become a problem. I kept him with me, but I needed a dog nanny or dog babysitter. I texted Walker as I rode the elevator.

Owen: *Dog daycare. We should offer that at Quantum Cyber.*

Walker: *Sounds like a crazy idea… a crazy good one! Look at you being fun and hip.*

Owen: *It's not about hipness, it's for convenience. Plus Rudolph needs socialization.*

Walker: *Ha! You're such a dog dad now.*

Owen: *… No.*

Walker: *Absolute dog dad.*

I left Rudolph with my secretary. She gave me a guilty look when I asked her to mind the dog for a few hours.

"Or not?" I asked with a frown.

"I might have let your father into your office," she admitted. "He wanted to see you. He said it was an emergency."

I sucked in a breath. I did not have the bandwidth to deal with my father this morning.

"You know my parents aren't supposed to be up here," I reminded her.

"I'm so sorry. He's just…" she made a helpless gesture.

"Yeah, I know. He steamrolls himself wherever he wants to be." I shook my head, bracing myself.

My father was sitting on my desk when I walked into the office.

"Owen, my golden child," he boomed. We were the same height. He was a slightly older version of me and my brothers, with the same prematurely white hair. There I liked to think the similarities ended. My father was self-absorbed, had a massive ego, and looked down on anyone who didn't act how he wanted them to act. My whole childhood had been an obstacle course of trying to make him proud of me—until Belle left, when I just sort of stopped caring.

"You didn't have to come here," I said, willing him to leave. "I'm sure you're needed at the hospital."

"I have a spinal and brain surgery on a toddler to perform in an a few hours," he said. "It's the one from the robbery that was in the news. They're making a documentary about the child's road to recovery. I, of course, am an integral part of that."

"You do save lives," I said neutrally.

"The parents said they didn't want any other surgeon than myself. Of course, someone has to be the best," he said smugly. "Not that you'd know anything about that, what with the fact that your company has not been anywhere near the top of the *TechBiz* list the last few years."

There it was.

"You couldn't just send me a passive-aggressive email instead of coming to berate me in person?" I said, forcing myself to sound cold and bored. If my father sensed weakness, he pounced.

"I have faith in you, son," my father said, clapping me on the shoulder. "You were always my favorite child. You're just like me. I know you'll be back on top in no time."

I shrugged his hand off.

"Besides," he continued, smiling conspiratorially, "I hear from your mother that Sloane is looking out for you. You made a good choice in her."

"There is not and never will be anything between Sloane and me," I replied.

But it was as if my father didn't even hear me. "She told us when we had her over for dinner that she's looking to have a baby within a year after you two are married," he barreled on.

"I am not marrying her."

"Of course you are," my father said incredulously. "Your mother and I like her very much. She'll make a great wife. Not like your brother Jack and that baker."

"Chloe is a wonderful person and owns a very successful franchise," I retorted. I could feel my blood start to boil.

Stay cold like ice, I chanted to myself. I forced myself to relax.

"Still," he said. "She's nothing like Sloane, who is the perfect corporate wife. She and your mother went engagement ring shopping by the way, so expect information from her about Sloane's choices," he called over his shoulder as he left.

I threw open the doors to the balcony after he left and stood outside, letting the cold numb me. No wonder Sloane wasn't taking the hint if my parents were egging her on and feeding her delusions. One thing was for certain: Sloane was not the type of woman I wanted to spend the rest of my life with.

The woman I wanted was messy, curvy, and baked like her life depended on it.

I just needed a way to make Holly mine.

CHAPTER 29

Holly

The next day was spent decorating the penthouse. I tried to act happy for the cameras as Fiona and I wrapped garlands around the banister. After the common areas were decorated, I tackled the Taste My Muffin baking subscription boxes. I had hundreds to mail out, but it was difficult to concentrate.

I hated to admit it, but Sloane's words had cut. Owen had barely said anything to me. Yet here I was obsessing over him. I wasn't crazy like Amber, I assured myself. I just wanted to take a sleigh ride on him. Naked. And maybe smear him with frosting and lick it off those washboard abs and see just how big his Christmas package really was.

"You sure you want to do that?" Morticia asked.

I yelped. Had all that tarot reading and making offerings to spirits given her the ability to read minds?

"Honestly, it wasn't that dirty."

"You're being weird," Morticia said, "and you're also about to pour a cup of salt into that cake batter."

"Crap," I said, hastily stepping back.

The rest of the baking took me a lot longer than it should have. I accidentally tipped half a bottle of vanilla into my cookie batter and had to start over. Morticia finally kicked me out of the kitchen.

"I'll finish this. You're going to send me to an early grave," she said, taking the spatula out of my hand. "You're distracted. I told you I cannot be trapped here the rest of December with the Christmas bake-off idiots. If you get kicked off because you're dreaming about some billionaire who can't even work an oven instead of coming up with an award-winning dessert, I'm not helping you bake a single thing ever again."

She handed me a plate of hot chocolate brownies. They had homemade marshmallows on top.

"Go stuff a brownie in his mouth and then stuff his candy cane in your Christmas stocking and get your head in the game," she ordered, practically shoving me out the door then slamming it behind me.

The faint strains of Mozart's funeral requiem filtered through the shut door.

I sighed. Should I really go see Owen? I could just eat all these brownies by myself.

Maybe I'll take him one, I thought as I swiped my key card to go down a floor. The elevator let me off at the private lobby to his condo.

"Here we go!" I said, trying to hype myself up. Coming over to make dinner for starving children was one thing. That had been an innocent pretense to spend time with him. Now it was evening; I was dressed in the semirevealing outfit I'd worn while making baking videos. I had a plate of brownies. It was clear I was there for one thing.

"We're going to jump down the chimney," I chanted to myself. I bounced up and down, raised my hand to knock… then immediately turned around and headed to the elevator.

"Nope, not happening."

I had already swiped my key card when the fire alarm went off inside the condo. There was cursing, and a dog yelped.

What in the world? I banged on the door. "Owen! Owen!"

Heavy footsteps approached the door and it swung open. The fire alarm blared, strobe light flashing. I squinted at Owen, who stood in front of me, holding a sheet of very burnt cookies.

"You're making cookies?" I exclaimed in shock and horror.

Owen grimaced. His normally perfectly controlled demeanor was askew. He had batter on his cheek. His platinum hair hung in his face, and his shirt was rumpled, with the sleeves rolled up and several buttons undone.

"I, uh—I don't have to explain myself to you!" he shouted back over the blaring siren.

I pushed past him, set the brownies on the counter, and fanned the fire alarm.

Rudolph was barking, all four feet leaving the ground with every yelp.

"Shhh," I told the husky puppy. "Honestly, Owen, are you trying to burn this tower down? I could have come and baked you cookies if you'd just asked."

"I have it under control," he said in a clipped tone, dumping the pan and all the cookies into the trash can. I snatched the oven mitt from him and pulled the pan out.

"You're going to be sorry when it melts the plastic," I told him, putting it in the sink. "What were you trying to do?"

Owen shrugged helplessly.

I narrowed my eyes at him, trying not to smile. "It was my sugar cookies, wasn't it?"

"No," he said mulishly.

"Yes, it is!" I crowed. "I knew it! I knew you wanted my cookies. Admit it!" I sang, dancing around him. "My Christmas cookies are life changing."

He grabbed me suddenly, pressing me against his body for a brief moment. His teeth caught his lower lip. He grinned slightly then released me.

"Are you hot? Because I'm really warm. I think we need to open a few more windows in here," I squeaked. I hustled over to the French doors out to the balcony, throwing them open to let the winter air inside.

Owen watched me from across the room. Why was I acting so weird? I had actually come up here to tempt him with a very Merry Christmas after all.

"I thought I could make the cookies," Owen admitted after a moment. "I had a computer program and everything." He gestured to his laptop.

I peered at the recipe on the screen. "Good gracious! I'm not surprised the cookies burned with the amount of sugar you're using."

Owen scowled at the computer and muttered, "Worthless program."

"If you wanted my Christmas cookies," I said with a wink, "you should have just asked. I'd be happy to give you a taste!"

"I'll file that away for later," he said, that deep voice wrapping around me.

"Or we could do it now," I offered, not sure which type of cookies I was offering.

Owen closed the distance between us. "You're going to give me a taste of your Christmas cookies?" he asked, eyes dark. We were inches apart. His hands came up to rest on my waist.

"I mean, if you really want them," I said and swallowed.

"I do."

Owen was so freaking intense; I'd never been with any man like him. The guys I normally dated were some flavor of hipster with interchangeable man buns working on their new song, failing nonprofit, or great American novel.

Yet here was Owen. He was the CEO of his own company, possessed more real estate than I would even know what to do with, and had a body that looked like someone had chiseled it out of ice.

It was suddenly a little too much.

I pulled away and clapped my hands. "Cookie time! I'm going to teach you how to bake!"

Owen growled slightly in the back of his throat but followed me around the kitchen. I opened the fridge. It was stuffed with butter and cream.

"Oh my goodness, either you're going overboard on the Bulletproof coffee or you're planning on making enough cookies to feed your entire office."

"I wanted enough to run experiments."

"Uh-huh, well, let Holly show you how it's done," I said, and started creaming the butter and sugar in the stand mixer.

"You don't need a recipe?" Owen asked. He was standing right behind me, his breath slightly cool on my neck.

"Please. I could make these cookies in my sleep." I snorted, measuring out the flour. I had Owen crack an egg in a bowl and whisk it up with the vanilla. Then I mixed it in with the dry ingredients.

"Perfect!" I said, taking a pinch of cookie dough and eating it.

"That has raw eggs in it," Owen protested.

"It's from farm-raised, free-range chickens," I countered. I took another pinch and held it out to him.

"Eat it!"

Owen grabbed my hand and carefully licked the dough off. The feel of his tongue on my fingertips kicked off a rousing round of Christmas carols in my hoo-ha.

"Is it tasty?" I squeaked.

"Very good," he said against my hand. He pressed his lips to my fingertips then released me.

"So I'll just put this in the fridge. It needs to cool down."
And so do I!

Wait, what was I thinking, trying to bang one of *The Great Christmas Bake-Off* judges? I was about to default on my student loans. The storage unit with all my grandmother's beloved Christmas decorations was about to be auctioned off because I couldn't pay the bill. And here I was jeopardizing my only shot to fix everything.

But Owen looked so delicious standing there, and I had never been the most rational person. Exhibit A being quitting my job and starting that ill-advised baking subscription box company.

"So what do we do to pass the time while we wait?" The look on Owen's face said he had one and only one idea in mind.

"Buttercream frosting," I practically shouted and dumped the ingredients on the counter.

"Because you want some frosting on your cookies?" Owen said, slow smile spreading on his face.

"Well, when you put it like that, it sounds dirty. Christmas cookies are supposed to be wholesome," I said, measuring out powdered sugar.

"Are they?" he said in his deep voice. "Because there's that whole naughty-nice dichotomy with Christmas."

"I've been very nice this year," I said primly. "And I expect Santa to bring me a very nice Christmas package all wrapped up in a bow."

"I'm sure I can put a bow on my package if that's all it takes to convince you to put your hands on it."

I switched on the electric mixer, hoping it would drown out the slight moan that escaped my lips when I thought about Owen's Christmas package.

When the frosting was done, I slowly licked a spoonful of it. Owen followed the motion with his eyes.

"It's very tasty buttercream," I told him. "I would lick it off of literally anything."

CHAPTER 30

Owen

"If you want my tongue on your whole body, then you can cover yourself in frosting," Holly added, scooping up another dollop of frosting and sticking her finger in her mouth.

Erotic was the only word for it. Before I knew what was happening, I had taken two steps across the kitchen and grabbed her hips, my hands pressing against her, feeling the softness of her curves through the skirt. Holly arched up against me in surprise, her chest heaving in the laced-up bodice.

She blinked up at me. My hands drifted up the curve of her back, one hand tangling in the tousled brown curls, the other cupping her face.

"I think the cookie dough is cold enough now," Holly said slightly breathlessly. "I should start rolling it out. Otherwise we'll be here all night."

That was perfectly fine with me, but I stepped back and let her take the dough out of the fridge.

"I have cookie cutters," I offered when she'd rolled out the dough. I'd thought about taking notes, but I could really only concentrate on Holly—the way she moved, the graceful way she smoothed out the dough. The intensity of her expression as she baked almost reminded me of me, of how I could be so absorbed in a programming problem.

I loved the way she bit her lower lip as she decided on the best way to cut out the cookies. After pressing the cookie cutters into the dough, she carefully stripped away the excess and slid the parchment paper onto the cookie sheet and put it in the oven. The puff of air as she closed the oven sent the skirt rustling up, exposing a hint of creamy inner thigh.

Get it together.

"Now we wait," she said.

I knew how I wanted to spend the time. Holly was watching the cookies through the glass of the oven. I wrapped my arms around her and nuzzled her neck. She squeaked then laughed.

"I hope you're not trying to distract me," she joked. "If I burn those cookies, I'll never be able to live it down."

I wanted to pick her up and carry her to my bedroom; the cookies could just burn. But I also wanted to savor this, to unwrap her like an exquisitely decorated package.

She moaned slightly as my hands drifted up to cup the swell of her breasts. I kissed her neck, moving up to nip her earlobe. I spun her around to face me, fully intending to claim her mouth like I intended to claim her body.

But there was a slight hesitation in the way she chewed on her bottom lip. All I wanted to do was kiss that mouth myself. But I didn't want any reluctance on her part. I only wanted unbridled desire.

"I think the cookies are about done," Holly said, turning away from me and breaking the tension. "So now that you love Christmas cookies," she continued, taking the sheet out of the oven, "I need to help you bring Christmas to the rest of your life."

"You already have my dog bedazzled in Christmas cheer," I replied as Holly used a metal spatula to place the cookies on a cooling rack and took them outside.

"I'm going to decorate your house. Oh, I should have ordered you a Christmas tree!"

"I don't need a Christmas tree."

"You do! Christmas trees show your employees that you aren't some sort of modern-day Ebenezer Scrooge, counting pennies and keeping the heat off."

"Nothing wrong with the cold. It's good for your circulation."

"You need to have a big holiday extravaganza for your employees," she insisted.

"Like a black-tie Christmas party?" I asked, confused.

"Too formal. I'm thinking more like a casual holiday party."

I was skeptical.

"It will be fun! Booze, a holiday party, and a self-deprecating CEO will make your employees all love you and the company. I'll decorate, your employees can take nice photos, and you can reap those sweet, sweet social media points."

I *had* wanted to spend more time with Holly. Maybe this was the way to do it.

"Fine."

"Really?"

"Yes. Plan my holiday party."

"This is going to be the best Christmas you've ever had!" she promised, nudging me with her shoulder and heading out onto the large balcony. She picked up a cookie and inspected it.

"These are ready to frost. Heh, get it?"

Though I wanted to really give her some Owen Frost on her cookies, Holly was all business as she decorated, expertly twirling the knife to frost the cookies and sprinkling them with a glitter of sugar.

"Taste," she ordered. Holding a small star up to my mouth, she slid the cookie inside. My tongue flicked against her fingertips, and she shivered.

"Delicious," I said, locking eyes with her.

"And now you can make cookies."

"Correction. Now I can watch you make cookies. I still don't think I'd be able to replicate it."

"Don't worry! You can call me whenever you have a craving for something sweet."

"I have one now," I said, pressing against her, letting her feel the hardness of my length. "I want you," I breathed against her mouth.

"I, um—" She pushed away. "I think maybe we should probably keep this professional, you know, since you're a judge and I'm a contestant. It might just be better if we didn't do this."

What the—

"Enjoy the cookies!" she called out as she practically ran out the front door.

"Fuck," I said, staring around at the empty condo.

I absently cleaned up, the cookies taunting me.

How did I seriously fuck that up?

CHAPTER 31

Holly

The next day, I was in a daze. We went shopping, and I mailed my subscription boxes. But all I could think about was Owen.

"So you seriously didn't unwrap any packages or let him put his hand in your stocking or any other sexual Christmas innuendos?" Fiona whispered as we stood in the studio space for another morning of baking.

I shook my head. "I chickened out."

"Did you see it? Was it huge?"

"I don't know!" I groaned.

"I bet it was huge," Fiona said matter-of-factly. "I mean, it has to be, right?"

"Don't make me feel worse," I said, smoothing my skirt and trying not to look at Owen as he sat down at the judges' table. He stared straight at me, as if he could eat me right up. I fidgeted with my necklace as Dana signaled to Anastasia.

"From *White Christmas* to *Miracle on 34th Street*, the 1950s cemented our current image of Christmas as a lavish, joyous occasion. Fresh off of winning World War II with all the handsome GIs returning and wanting to start families and create picture-perfect moments, the fifties embodied the excess and extravagance of Christmas. They had new gadgets and canned food. The fifties housewife was willing to experiment to make her Christmas more festive than anyone else's in the Junior League. Today, our contestants are going to be creating desserts that evoke the 1950s aesthetic. Contestants, you have until this afternoon. Let's bake!"

I had worn my 1950s outfit with the corseted waist and the flared skirt with a mountain of petticoats that ended right at my ankles to reveal my cute red-and-green heels. The bodice had off-the-shoulder chiffon, and I wore a fake pearl necklace. I'd even managed to wake up early and convince Morticia to help me curl my hair so it hung around my face in a perfect fifties coif.

I went into the pantry and looked around. The fifties had been a time of great change, both in the world at large and in the world of food. Jell-O, canned food, boxed desserts—the decade had been all about novelty. However, food choices had also tended to be rather bland. Deviled eggs with a dash of paprika was about as crazy as the average housewife wanted to get with her flavors.

Since the fifties had also been the atomic age and people had given home chemistry sets to their children for Christmas that included, among other things, radioactive uranium ore, I decided to go retro atomic for my theme, and that meant molecular gastronomy. The whole point of this food movement was to use chemicals and processes to transform the physical properties of ingredients while leaving the essence of flavor.

I couldn't have a fifties Christmas dessert without Jell-O, and that was what I decided to build my dish around. Not Jell-O exactly but a nice custard. And unlike the fifties, I was also going to turn up the volume on flavor—way up.

"You looked dressed for the part," Anastasia said as I laid out all the tools I needed. "Are you about to conduct an experiment?"

"A tasty experiment!" I said with a laugh. "Those avant-garde desserts you see on Instagram tend to have a lot of components arranged on a dish. You have to include several sauces, little crumbles, and small single tasty bites."

"I can't wait to see it," she said, moving on to talk to Fiona.

Along with the eggnog custard, I was going to make a baked Alaska truffle, since that was a dish fifties housewives used to slave over to make perfect for their dinner parties. I was also including a tart, fruity molded gelatin. I couldn't resist. There was something about Jell-O that was whimsical. However, I was going to make one that was tasty.

Because they were all very different elements, the flavor profiles would need to work in harmony. To go against the spice of the eggnog, the baked Alaska truffle would have chocolate sorbet. The molded gelatin would be cape goose-berry, a flowering plant that produces tart orange berries hidden in little translucent husks.

First up was the gelatin, since it needed to set. I wanted to display the molded dessert in the husk just to make it a little more interesting.

"That looks toxic," Fiona joked as she looked over at the bright-orange liquid I was stirring.

"I know, right?" I said, adding in several gelatin sheets. I poured the thick liquid into the mold then started on the eggnog custard. In my Christmas world, eggnog should be thicker than heavy cream and contain copious amounts of rum. I grated nutmeg and cinnamon into the double boiler while I stirred.

Now that I was comfortable with my desserts, I couldn't help but notice that Owen was still in the room. Normally he hightailed it out of there as soon as the camera crew took their shots of the judges. Except there he was, studying me.

I took a sip of the rum. I still wasn't sure where we stood. He had kissed my neck, and I had made excessive jokes about his dick then fled like a teenager when he tried to kiss me.

"Stop staring at my boyfriend!" Amber screeched, causing me to almost spill the hot eggnog custard all over the table.

"He's not—you know what, never mind," I said, trying to keep my hands steady as I poured the last of the hot liquid into the last mold.

"You do realize," I said, turning to Amber after I jiggled the molds, "that you're not the only person trying to lay claim to him, right?"

"You—"

"Not me," I said, holding up my hands. "This girl named Sloane."

Amber's eyes narrowed, and she went back to furiously chopping walnuts.

"Setting crazy after crazy," Fiona remarked. "Nice."

"Hopefully they'll keep each other occupied," I said.

"So you can slip in there."

"I don't know. He's a judge."

Fiona shrugged. "It's the holidays. Everyone knows things can be wild. There's all those memes about people going sexually crazy at holiday parties."

CHAPTER 32

Owen

knew I should go up to my office and work, but Holly was so mesmerizing.

Walker: *Earth to Owen. Were you kidnapped by the elf on the shelf?*

Owen: *I'm at the bake-off.*

Walker: *Seriously? What about the TechBiz contest? We still need to figure out what we're doing. They're going to start doing surprise walk-throughs any day now.*

Owen: *Relax. I have it under control. I hired Holly.*

Walker: *Uh sure ok so that seems like it's going to turn into a problem. She's going to be working for you, but then you're also sleeping with her.*

Owen: *I'm not sleeping with her.*
Walker: *Could have fooled me.*

I wanted to, though. The fifties had really known how to dress women. With every motion, the full skirt swished around her legs, her ankles delicate in the heels, her waist cinched in that hourglass figure. She looked like a Christmas present I wanted to carefully unwrap. Her motions were expert yet feminine, but when she used a blow torch to caramelize the sugar, the way she stood with her legs spread made her look ever so slightly dangerous.

I felt as if I could stare at her for hours. When I looked up at the clock, I realized I had.

"I'm excited to see these desserts," Nick said. "It seems like everyone's found their groove."

Unfortunately, I had to sit through several desserts before Holly's.

"Fifties housewives were very proud of their cakes," Amber said. "And it was in vogue to make them shaped like animals, trains, or flowers." She presented each of us with a cake shaped like the head of a reindeer.

"Did you go out and decapitate these poor animals yourself?" Nick deadpanned.

"Is all the fruit sauce around the bottom supposed to be blood?" I asked her.

"Only the blood of my broken heart, Owen," she said.

Anu raised her eyebrows. "Let's cut this open and see how it looks inside," she said, sticking a fork into the reindeer's head.

"This isn't made out of Rice Krispies, is it?" I asked Amber, tapping the antlers. "Correct me if I'm wrong, Anu, but aren't the contestants supposed to do better than Rice Krispies treats?"

"These are special Rice Krispies," Amber insisted. "They're made with almond flour, and there's a surprise inside."

"It's all you, Mr. Badass Billionaire," Nick said.

I broke one of the antlers, and red sugar spilled out.

"That's very upsetting."

"The cake tastes pretty good though," Anu said. "If you just ignore the packaging. I do like the moistness of the cake and the way you layered it with the black current liqueur frosting, the ganache, and the fudge. The fifties did like hokey stuff, but at least it's tasty. You have the flavors, and you don't taste pure sugar or cardboard like you do with a box cake."

The rest of the desserts were all along the same vein. There were several variations of Jell-O cakes. Fiona at least had an imitative take on a French 1950s dessert called poached pears belle Hélène. She had made a perfect trio of French pear dumplings with cinnamon chocolate sauce and salted caramel ice cream.

"With Julia Child, Americans were just waking up to the joys of French cooking," she told us as we sampled the dessert.

"Very rustic," Anu said. "But refined. The chocolate sauce is the perfect consistency, and the caramel ice cream is actually very good."

"You know how tired I am of ice cream," Nick said. "But I feel like I could eat this all day."

"You did have all day though," Anu said, "and while this is tasty, we would expect something more with the time you had."

"And for the final contestant," Anastasia said. "Holly."

"Ready for another taste of my Christmas cookies?" Holly said, winking at me. "Though today it's not cookies. Instead, this dessert is a reimagining of the perfect 1950s Christmas. We have a baked Alaska truffle, with chocolate sponge cake and dark chocolate and sea salt sorbet surrounded by a layer of chocolate and then a layer of scorched meringue."

"How did you manage to keep it round?" Anu marveled, picking up the truffle.

"A good housewife never tells her secrets," Holly said with a playful smile. "Also on the plate is an eggnog custard and a cape gooseberry gelatin."

"This is magnificent," Nick said. "I seriously need to take a picture. This is crazy!" He snapped photos with his phone then took a bite of the gelatin. "Lovely. I love that you took the crappy processed fifties food and completely reimagined it while still keeping the essence. It's brilliant."

I scooped up several of the golden balls on the plate.

"Those are spice peach and rum spheres," Holly said.

They burst in my mouth.

"The sauces are excellent. This is an award-winning dish," Anu told her. "After those Christmas cookies, it's nice to see you strive for more."

"There wasn't anything wrong with the cookies," I growled. Holly smiled at me sweetly.

"I think the winner is pretty clear here," Anu said after Holly went to the greenroom.

"Who are we getting rid of?"

"That reindeer head was disturbing," Nick said. "I'm going to have nightmares."

"It was better than the Jell-O layer cake with the fruit," I said.

"I know. And you know me, I like my alcohol," Anu said, "but with all the liquor Farrah put in the Jell-O, I felt like I was back in college doing Jell-O shot after Jell-O shot. Bad decisions all around."

Holly clapped her hands and bounced up and down when we told her the news.

"Congratulations, Holly, and thank you, judges," Anastasia said as Farrah was led off, sobbing, to give her postshow interview.

I wanted to nab Holly, but the production crew whisked her away to give the postcontest rundowns that the producers would edit into the episode. I should have at least gotten her number. Then I could text her under the pretense that we should plan for the *TechBiz* visits.

I went back up to my condo, absorbed in how I was going to reel in Holly. I wanted her begging and pleading for me. I didn't notice the life-sized elf leaning seductively in the condo entryway until I almost ran into her.

Sloane. She sauntered over to me. The elf costume was really more in the direction of lingerie, I decided.

"Just the man I wanted to see," Sloane said, unlacing the bodice of the elf costume. Suddenly she grabbed me. The elevator dinged just as Sloane pressed her mouth to mine.

"I, uh—I'm sorry," Holly said as I scrambled to push Sloane off. Holly stepped back on and mashed the door close button before I could yell out to her.

I shoved Sloane away.

"Her? Honestly, you can't be serious," Sloane sneered, looking between me and the elevator. Her eyes narrowed. "I'm the perfect woman for you."

"You need to leave," I said, wiping my mouth. I was covered in her red lipstick. "I don't know how you even snuck up here."

"Holly has you under some sort of spell," Sloane said angrily.

"No," I said, furious. *Stay cold.* I could not afford to have her bad-mouth me to the *TechBiz* people.

"I have work to do. I'll talk with you another time," I told her. I went into my condo without waiting for her to answer me.

I was angry that Holly had seen Sloane kiss me. *Calm down. You can explain to her what happened.*

I couldn't have ruined my chances with Holly. I hadn't even kissed her yet. Well, not on the mouth.

CHAPTER 33

Holly

"Celebrate?" I asked Morticia, desperate for anything to keep me from showing up at Owen's condo like a stalker. I wanted him, but he was so intense, and it really wasn't a good idea, especially if I was going to be working for him.

But I wanted to see him. Maybe I could pretend I wanted to talk about the holiday party? But then I really should schedule a meeting. Workers don't just show up at their boss's house in the middle of the night to "work on a project." That would earn a serious eye roll.

"I have to work," Morticia said with a dramatic sigh.

"Fiona?"

"I'm meeting a friend from college for drinks."

I went down to the lobby to be as far away from Owen's condo as possible.

Do not think about Owen.

I tried making a list on my phone of all the things I wanted to do for Owen's holiday party, but the reality was that I was too wound up about Owen to think of anything coherent.

My phone buzzed with an email notification, and I almost dropped it. The message was from Walker, detailing the *TechBiz* contest and his thoughts. I wrote him back with my ideas. In the back of my mind, I wished it had been Owen to write me.

You're obsessed and crazy.

Yes, but I wanted him.

Holly: *I'm going up.*

Morticia: *To the great Christmas tree farm in the sky? I'll throw a nice funeral for you.*

Holly: **Eye roll* no, to see Owen.*

Morticia: *No don't do it, you're too young! You have so much more to live for than a dickwad billionaire. He doesn't even like your holiday.*

Holly: *I can make him like it. I have all those super-duper sexy outfits I bought drunk shopping. I can make even the most hard-core grinch sing Christmas carols if I walk up wearing a sexy candy cane outfit.*

Morticia: *Oh right, the candy cane stripper outfit with the matching pole. Honestly, for someone who complains they never have any space or money, you sure have a lot of stuff.*

Holly: *It's a collapsible pole. I use it for exercise.*

Morticia: *You hear that? That's the sound of me choking because I'm laughing so hard.*

Holly: *I'm going if only because I need some positive affirmation that I am a sexy desirable woman.*

Morticia: *I was in the studio today. He definitely desires you.*

I swiped the key card and pressed the button for Owen's floor. What was I going to say to him? "Hi, I need you to light up my Christmas tree?" "Hi, I'm Holly, and I'm horny?"

But when the elevator doors opened, it looked as if Owen had already found someone to not just light his Christmas tree but set it on fire. There was Sloane, in a super-sexy elf costume with thigh-high stiletto boots, locking lips with Owen.

"Well then," I said, stepping back on the elevator and mashing the buttons until the door closed. "That's awkward. And unexpected."

Holly: *Owen's making out with Sloane.*
Morticia: *I knew he had bad taste.*
Holly: *What do I do?*
Morticia: *Key his car.*
Holly: *I'm not going to key his car. That's crazy! Ugh now it's going to be awkward.*
Morticia: *When are you not awkward?*
Holly: *I was dreaming of a white *cough* Frost Christmas *lonely warbling intensifies**
Morticia: *315 days until Halloween, 315 days until Halloween.*

I paced around in the penthouse living room, nursing a glass of Owen's expensive liquor that I had stolen from his bar. I felt stupid for even thinking I had a chance with him. Then I was angry. He had definitely been flirting with me in his condo. He kissed my neck first and did that thing with his tongue on my hand. I wasn't going to be the one moping around like a sad sack. Owen needed to be taken down a peg. He was like one of those self-absorbed alphahole billionaires in those romance novels I always told myself I was never going to read another one of and then totally did.

I marched to the elevator, tapped my foot as it slowly took me to the next floor down. Sloane wasn't in the foyer when I stepped off the elevator.

"I guess they took their little Christmas sex pageant to the bedroom," I fumed and pounded on the door and mashed the doorbell. I was mid mash when it swung open. Owen was rubbing at his face with a towel.

"Oh, I'm sorry," I said in my best sassy voice. "Did I interrupt?"

"No," Owen said, frowning.

"Oh."

My whole speech went out the window. I had been expecting drama, fireworks, maybe even a girl-on-girl fight, though in this corset, I figured my odds weren't that great.

"Well, I—" I looked up awkwardly at the ceiling.

Owen licked his lips. "What are you doing here?" he asked, his deep voice flowing round me.

"I, um—I was just going to—" I panicked and flailed. "Ask you about the company holiday event because I'm working for you now." I looked down at my feet. "And I guess that means I shouldn't sleep with you."

"Am I supposed to pretend I didn't hear that?" he said, voice dropping an octave.

The corset was getting a little tight. I fanned myself, trying to get air down the bodice.

Owen stepped through the doorway. His large hands encircled my waist, caressing me. He bent down so that our mouths almost touched.

"You know you want to kiss me," he stated.

"Full of yourself much?" I whispered, mesmerized by his mouth.

"Always," he said. "I was waiting to hear you beg for me, but I don't think I can wait any longer." Then he closed the distance between us.

His mouth was soft, making me melt like a marshmallow over a fire. I wrapped my arms around his neck. He tipped my head slightly back as he lazily explored my mouth. I could see now why Sloane had jumped him in the hallway. I didn't think I'd ever be able to find any man who was a better kisser.

Owen leaned back, looking slightly smug at my expression.

"I can't even imagine why I didn't do that two days ago," I said.

"It's really all I could think about," Owen replied, cupping my face.

CHAPTER 34

Owen

My phone rang just as I was starting to tug Holly inside.

"I should go," she said, the spell broken. "It's late."

"Please—" But she pulled away. I had expected that she would simply fall into my arms and into my bed. It seemed that Holly was a slightly more difficult puzzle, however.

"*What?*" I growled into the phone. "This better be an emergency."

"Hi. How is everyone's tenth-favorite CEO?" my brother Jack asked. "The Svenssons have been asking if you reviewed the report about the gene therapy center in Harrogate. They have to submit paperwork to the FDA."

"I can't believe you interrupted—" I snapped my mouth shut.

"Interrupted what?" my younger brother practically yelled into the phone.

"Never mind."

"Tell me," Jack demanded. "Is it the baker? Walker said you were after one of the contestants."

"I'm not after her. I—look, drop it. Tell the Svenssons I'm working on reviewing the report."

"Really? Because apparently Walker sent everyone your IT logs, and it says you haven't opened an email since two p.m."

I did actually work the next day. Rudolph lounged out on the balcony off my office while I reviewed the reports. My company was making a huge investment in the gene therapy business.

While usually I prided myself on being able to be one hundred percent focused under any circumstances, today it was difficult. My thoughts wanted to wander to Holly and the kiss. It was everything I'd thought it would be. Now I wanted more.

My phone beeped. If it was Jack...

Unknown number: *Santa's sleigh to HQ. Do you read me? Over.*
What the hell?

I texted Walker.

Owen: *Do you know this number?*
Walker: *Yeah that's Holly. I told her to get with you on the TechBiz holiday party stuff.*

Walker sent me her contact card, and I added it to my phone.

> **Owen:** *Do you ever get tired of Christmas?*
> **Holly:** *How'd you know it was me and not one of your crazy stalkers?*
> **Owen:** *Tech genius and billionaire.*
> **Holly:** *You asked Walker, didn't you?*
> **Owen:** *How did you know?*
> **Holly:** *Christmas savant.*
> **Holly:** *And Walker told me. He also wants me to bring fun and Christmas cheer to your office. And the dog daycare?*
> **Owen:** *Right.*
> **Holly:** *Want to meet tomorrow?*
> **Owen:** *Fine.*

I wanted to meet right now. If my office wasn't all glass, I would fuck her here. But she had run off last night. I'd better be patient. I could do that. I was successful because I remained cold and rational when everyone else was freaking out. When Bitcoin tanked and everyone including Walker was telling me to stop investing in it, I had poured more money in. And it had paid off.

But it didn't seem as if Holly was all that impressed by my business prowess.

The thought that I would see Holly again soon was enough to get me through the rest of the day. After a contentious conference call with Svensson PharmaTech, my day was over. I clipped on Rudolph's harness. I needed to buy him one that wasn't so Christmassy. But Holly had bought it, so maybe I would keep it.

Unfortunately, I couldn't see to that tonight. I had drinks scheduled with my siblings. Ever since Belle had returned last year, we had tried to get together more often. My youngest two brothers were in college still, but Jonathan, Jack, and Belle were already at the bar.

"They said we could sit outside in the courtyard," Belle said, giving me a hug.

The waiter looked at us nervously. "It's cold outside."

Belle shrugged. She was wearing a sleeveless silk top. "The cold never bothered me anyway. Besides, the dogs can run around."

Jack's husky, Milo, promptly picked up Rudolph by the scruff of the neck and took him outside. There was frost on the metal café furniture in the small courtyard. People gaped at us through the windows.

"Owen has a girlfriend," Jonathan blurted out as soon as we were seated.

"It better not be Sloane," Jack said.

The server, bundled up in a puffy coat, brought out a tray of whisky. "I warmed it up," he said, steam rising from the cups.

"Cheers!" Belle said, clinking glasses.

"So did Mom tell you about Owen's girlfriend?" Jack asked Jonathan.

Jonathan looked askance. "She showed up at my office."

"Dad showed up at my office too," I growled.

"They still want grandchildren," Belle said, rolling her eyes and taking a sip of her drink. "I guess they've given up on you, Jack."

"Even if I had a kid, I wouldn't let her see it," Jack said, scowling at his drink.

"So if it's not Sloane, who's your girlfriend?" Belle asked me. "It better not be one of the contestants. I saw you flirting with Holly ineffectively."

"It was effective," I bragged. "She's showed up at my apartment several evenings this week."

Belle sighed and sipped her drink.

"You can't date a contestant. You're a judge. As soon as you do something dumb and break her heart, she's going to turn around and sue the production company. Stay away from Holly."

"But I have her working with me to help win the *TechBiz* contest," I countered.

Belle was appalled. "Well then, seriously, don't start anything with her. You're on thin ice," she warned. "This is a bad idea."

I knew it was a bad idea. But I couldn't stay away from Holly.

CHAPTER 35

Holly

I was giddy about seeing Owen the next day.

"What should I wear?" I asked Morticia. I was going to meet him in his office, so it wasn't like we were going to have some sort of torrid affair in the middle of the afternoon.

"Something that makes you look like you aren't there for a booty call."

I chose a red-and-black pencil skirt, a flowy black top, and a chunky gold necklace with a snowflake pattern. I put my hair up in a bun. Black heels finished the look.

"Do I look like a professional woman?" I asked.

"You look more like Santa's little helper, but sure," Morticia said, reaching down my shirt to tighten the bra straps and hike my boobs up.

I had my laptop and my Christmas-themed notebook. The pages were decorated with little Christmas scenes, and it came with several pages of stickers because secretly I'm a twelve-year-old girl. Still, I was nervous as I took the elevator down to the Quantum Cyber offices. I wasn't sure where Owen and I stood.

With all of Owen's complaining about not being at the top of the *TechBiz* list, when I stepped off the elevator to the company's office, it looked like the headquarters of a successful tech company to me. All the girls wore leggings, boots, and flowy tunic tops. The men were high-end casual in jeans and three-hundred-dollar T-shirts.

"I'm here for a meeting with Owen," I said after greeting the receptionist. She was wearing a reindeer headband that jingled when she smiled at me.

"Just a moment," she said.

While I waited, I looked around. The whole headquarters was white marble and glass with blue accents. It was like an abstract winter wonderland. There was a huge atrium that opened up to five stories. There were actual trees inside basking in the winter sun that streamed in from the huge expanse of glass.

"These towers are like another world," I said.

"I know, right?" the receptionist said as she directed me to the elevator. "I hear you're here to help us decorate. Can I request those big hanging snowflakes? I want a winter fairy-tale land!"

"Absolutely!"

Owen was seated behind a huge desk in his office. The wall of windows behind him framed him against the winter sky. He looked up at me and smiled imperceptibly.

"Come in, Holly," he said, standing up. Was it going to be a professional greeting?

Owen wrapped me in his arms and kissed me, his tongue claiming my mouth. Okay, not professional.

"Aren't people going to see in?" I croaked.

"No. Walker's out. My secretary and her wife are taking their dog to a therapy appointment. I had my schedule cleared for you. We're alone." He leaned down again, tipping my head back to kiss me as his hands roamed over my back and down to cup my ass.

"Though there is a bit too much glass to fuck you on my desk," he whispered against my mouth.

This was a different Owen than the one I had been dealing with previously, the one who baked cookies and played with his puppy. This Owen Frost was all business. And it seemed that he had zeroed in on one purpose today—me.

"I guess we should talk about the festivities," I said, a little breathless after he released me.

He gestured wordlessly to the chair opposite his desk. But instead of sitting across from me, he sat on the edge of the desk.

"Trying to get a good view down my blouse?" I joked, shifting in my seat.

"Maybe," he said, his deep voice rolling around the room.

I shivered slightly.

"Cold?"

"Hot."

"Am I making you nervous?"

"You're making me horny," I muttered.

Owen's smirk widened. He leaned over to kiss me, his hand drifting down to cup my breasts. He unbuttoned the top two buttons of my blouse, and his hand pushed inside my bra, his touch making the nipple erect. I moaned softly as his hand drifted down. I widened my legs slightly.

"This pencil skirt is a little tight," I said, whimpering slightly and straining against him.

He leaned back, looking slightly smug at the expression on my face.

"What the—"

"You can't open your present before Christmas."

"You're not going to make me wait until Christmas?" I said, aghast. "I think I'll combust."

"It's winter," he said. "I think you'll be fine."

He wanted to play hard to get? Fine.

"I guess we should go over my plans for your Christmas festivities to help increase your company's ranking," I told him, buttoning up my blouse. "Can I plug my laptop in somewhere so you can see my screen?"

Owen's eyes narrowed slightly.

"What?" I said in pretend innocence. "I came here to have a professional meeting. I don't know what you were thinking was going to happen."

"Give me the laptop," he said, voice gravelly. He pressed some buttons, and then what was on my screen magically appeared on the large TV mounted on the wall.

"Magic!" I patted his very firm buttocks. "You're not just a pretty face after all."

I gestured to the screen. "So here's the rankings. Your company pays the best and was voted as highly cutting-edge and pretty well organized. But oh look, you got a frowny face for being cool and unapproachable and not having a fun workplace culture."

"Such a racket," Owen complained.

"This is a good place to be. You have a nice cake with good crumb integrity and flavorful fillings. You just need a little frosting. Fortunately for you, I love decorating and throwing parties. So here's what we're going to do. We're not just having a holiday party. It's going to be a full-blown winter festival."

"I don't—"

"Shhh. Trust Holly. We're going to have all your employees showcase what they've been working on all year. Invite the *TechBiz* selection committee, and boom, one-stop shop to show how awesome you are. Time it just when they send out all those surveys to the employees," I said, gesturing with excitement. "Also, because people think you're a sociopathic grinch, we'll have an event that makes you seem personable, warm, and caring."

"I'm not warm."

"You aren't," I agreed, "though sometimes you make me really hot."

There was that slight smirk again.

"Since you're the self-proclaimed prince of winter, we're going to test that out," I told him. "All your employees love dogs and animals. We're going to make you the star of a little fundraiser. I think I can make it go viral too. I'll have to see how much your employees pimp it out on social media."

"What do I have to do?" he asked.

"Now that *is* a surprise. But don't worry, it's going to be epic."

"I'm a little worried. I'm also a little worried that the winter festival won't be fun enough. You said that a holiday party should have booze."

"The actual booze-soaked holiday party is what's happening with *The Great Christmas Bake-Off*," I explained.

"We're having it in the main lobby, which I've poured my heart and soul into decorating. There will be themed cocktails, desserts, and other snacks. Everyone loves it when their boss pays for food and alcohol."

Owen scowled.

"I know you hate Christmas," I said, exasperated, "but I'm trying to help you here."

"It's not that," he said. "I just hate that Sloane will be there." He grabbed my hands. "I hope you don't think there was ever anything between her and me."

"She was sucking your face in the hallway, but you're a big boy, and lord knows I've made questionable decisions."

"The only woman I ever want is you." Owen said then crushed his mouth to mine.

CHAPTER 36

Owen

Kissing Holly was like drinking hot chocolate: smooth, creamy, filling and warming my insides. I wanted to steal her away to a cabin somewhere and make love to her as the snow fell softly outside and a fire roared in the hearth. Just the two of us, together.

"So you're okay with the plans?" she said softly.

Sex in a cabin? Absolutely. But…

"Right, the winter festival. Yes, that sounds fine."

"I guess I'd better go get started then," she said.

I pulled Holly into another kiss. She tasted like gingerbread and spices.

"We could just go away," I offered.

"I have the bake-off tomorrow. We're supposed to go shopping," she whispered against my mouth.

"You could skip it," I replied. "Quit the bake-off. We'll go to a chalet in Switzerland."

She giggled. "You just don't want to judge anymore!" She squeezed my arm. "Besides, I need to work on helping you win that *TechBiz* contest. It's important."

"I suppose," I said, pulling her in for another kiss, reveling in the way she melted against me.

"Also, um—" She looked down.

I pulled her chin up. "What?"

"I think I need your credit card again." She smiled sheepishly.

I pulled it out and handed it to her.

"It's okay to use this one? It's not maxed out?" she said, inspecting it.

I shrugged. "It doesn't have a limit. It also has some sort of concierge service attached. I never use it, but it's part of the monthly fee. You should try it out so I get my money's worth."

Holly looked slightly shocked. I leaned down and pressed my mouth to hers.

"I could do this all day," I murmured against her lips, my hands caressing her curves.

"I can't," she said, smiling, though she wasn't actively trying to leave.

"Stop by tonight," I told her, kissing her once more.

"I'll see where I'm at. I want to do a good job! I have standards to uphold."

I'd scheduled a lunch meeting with the C-suite executive team.

Beck, Walker's brother and the chief financial officer of Quantum Cyber, was back from our Boston office. He pointed to the spreadsheet up on the screen.

"Why in the world did someone spend over one hundred thousand dollars on Christmas decorations?"

"It's for the *TechBiz* contest," Walker explained, taking one of the sandwiches from the platter.

"That thing?" Beck sneered. "I thought with making the investment into the gene therapy data algorithms, we wouldn't have to compete so much for talent."

"We still need to," I told him.

"But Christmas decorations?" Beck said, clearly scandalized. "When have we ever decorated for Christmas?"

"We do now," I said coldly. "Get into the Christmas spirit."

Beck stared at me with his mouth half open. "Who are you?"

"Owen found a girlfriend. One of the bake-off contestants," Walker said. "He's a changed man."

"So that's why you decided to be a judge," Beck said thoughtfully. "Maybe I'll do it next year."

"She lets him eat her Christmas cookies and everything," Walker said.

"That's not appropriate talk for a workplace environment," I growled.

"Get your mind out of the gutter, Owen!" Walker exclaimed, grabbing his chest and pretending to be scandalized. "I meant she makes you baked goods."

"*You* are eating cookies now?" Beck asked, shaking his head. "I wasn't even in Boston for two weeks, and it's like the world is completely different."

Later that evening, after a long day of meetings, meetings, and more meetings, I went up to my condo. I was going to change into workout clothes then take Rudolph for a run. Over the last two weeks, the puppy had grown. He also was a ball of energy that had been cooped up in my office all day. I was secretly hoping Holly would be there waiting for me. But while there was a woman waiting for me when I stepped off the elevator, it wasn't Holly.

"Owen," Amber said. She was dressed in an even sexier elf costume than when she'd ambushed me in the lobby a few nights ago. "I made you some cookies." She shoved a plate at me.

"Please go back upstairs," I said, ignoring the plate and making a mental note to tell Dana to keep the contestants out of my private area. But then I thought about Holly. I needed her to be able to come and go as she pleased.

"I know you love family, and I do too!" Amber launched herself at me, clinging to my suit jacket. Rudolph barked as I entered the code to unlock my door. "We'd be perfect together."

"Find someone else," I told her, prying her fingers off me. "I'm not interested."

Amber started dramatically sobbing. I shut the door in her face. I really wished it had been Holly instead.

I texted her while I changed clothes.

Owen: *Your sister was up here.*
Holly: *Stepsister.*
Holly: *And here I was thinking you had texted me something exciting, like a naughty pic.*
Owen: *You already saw me naked.*
Holly: *Partially. I didn't get the best bits.*

A naughty picture? Usually I would never be so reckless, but with Holly, all I wanted was her. Since I was changing anyway, I ran downstairs and pulled one of the sugar cookies she had made out of the container. It was shaped like a Santa hat. I framed the shot as best I could and sent her the picture, holding my breath as I finished dressing.

Her response came as I left the condo.

Holly: *I think you need a bigger cookie.*

CHAPTER 37

Holly

"Good morning, and welcome to another episode of *The Great Christmas Bake-Off*. This show exists because of the fans who tune in for every episode. We love fan participation, which is why today's episode is the fan-favorite challenge. Fans from around the world have voted on what dessert they'd like each contestant to cook. Contestants, open your envelopes and see what you're going to be making today, then turn on your ovens, and let's get baking!"

My oven had been on all night. The picture Owen had sent me had made sure of that. I mean, I knew his Christmas package was big, but damn. I didn't think I was going to be able to concentrate. But I needed to. It didn't help that I was wearing a marginally too-sexy outfit. To engage my fans, I'd had them vote on what I should wear for the episode. Unfortunately, I'd made the mistake of not trying the clothes on before putting them up for a vote. This one was once again way too snug—another casualty of my stress eating problem.

It was a sexy nutcracker outfit with thigh-high black boots. I had thought it would be fine because it was a flared skirt with a military-style jacket. What I'd failed to account for was the deep V-neckline and the fact that I couldn't button the top buttons on the jacket. My boobs were swollen from all the salty food and sugar and alcohol I'd been consuming. All I could think about when putting on the outfit was Owen taking it off me.

At least I could move in it. For my dessert, the fans wanted me to make a *croquembouche*. A classic French dessert, it was a tower constructed out of cream puffs, and then the whole thing was wrapped in gossamer strands of pulled sugar.

While somewhat time-consuming, the dessert did look impressive. For the bake-off, however, I knew I couldn't just make a classic *croquembouche* and call it a day. To pump up the volume, I was going to make mine look like a Christmas tree, complete with edible ornaments. The trick was going to be making sure it wasn't cheesy.

Back when I was still in culinary school, my pie-in-the-sky dream had been to own an awesome dessert café. In addition to beautiful tarts, cupcakes, and cookies, I would also make wedding cakes, mainly because I wanted to craft sugar flowers like Sylvia Weinstock. I loved how the hundreds of handcrafted sugar flowers cascaded over the towering wedding cakes she produced.

To make a winning dessert, I was going to do something similar with the *croquembouche*.

"I'm jealous of the dessert you were given," Fiona said. "I have to make a Christmas punch."

"How is that supposed to be a dessert?" I asked her.

"I don't know," she said with a sigh.

"Ice cream?" I suggested.

"That's all I did at my last job. Hopefully inspiration strikes me in the next thirty minutes."

I spent the next half hour making cream puffs. The trick was to precook the dough before piping the cream puffs. Otherwise they wouldn't puff up.

After the large batch of dough was cooked, I piped it onto baking sheets in little balls and stuck the trays in the oven. While they cooked, I started on the decorations for the *croquembouche* tree. I needed to make ornaments, a tree topper, greenery, and winter flowers. The flowers would all be molded sugar, but I didn't want everything to be made out of the same material. I wanted some variety in the flavors.

Each of the ornaments should be a type of candy. I would make chocolate sugar truffles and blown-sugar ornaments to hang off sugar branches. I was trying for a more abstract tree, which was good, because I did not have time to make hyperrealistic sugar art.

To make the flowers, I first made the fondant and added tylose powder to make a gum paste. Because these were going to be poinsettias, I colored the sugar a deep red then rolled it very thin.

I didn't need a mold to make the petals; I freehanded them then used a fondant tool to furl the edges of each petal. When the cream puff shells were done, I removed them from the oven and let them cool while I finished making the flowers. Fortunately, we had most of the day. Otherwise I didn't think I would be able to finish.

While the flowers dried, I made the branches the ornaments would hang on. Then I turned to the ornaments.

I checked the clock. The day was already half over, and I still had a series of truffles to make in addition to the filling for the cream puffs. Since the cream puffs were the base of the dish, the filling took precedence. I made a vanilla custard filling in the double boiler, adding cognac for extra flavor, mindful of the clock. It was going to be close. While that cooled, I made the truffles.

Truffles traditionally were simply chocolate with cream added—ganache essentially—then rolled into a ball. Truffles could be rolled in dark chocolate powder, nuts, or dried fruit. I wanted mine to be fairly colorful, so I crushed freeze-dried raspberries and coated the chocolate. The rest I coated in candied orange peel, chopped hazelnuts, or bitter powdered chocolate. I set them in the fridge then turned back to my cream puffs.

The custard was cool, so I piped it into the cream puffs. They were perfect little golden balls filled with a tasty surprise.

Don't think of Owen. Plus his balls aren't at all little.

"Ready to assemble!" I said, admiring all the beautiful pieces of my dessert. I set up the large crystal platter and began carefully stacking my cream puffs. They needed to form an even, round pyramid. The cream puffs stacked nicely, and I set the final one on top and went to retrieve my truffles from the fridge.

I had just pulled them out when I heard a scream. Then Fiona shouted, "Oh no, Amber, what did you do?"

"Shit," I cursed, running back to my station. I was too late.

"I'm so sorry," Amber said, looking at me with what I was sure was feigned surprise. "I was trying to use this

Platinum Provisions icing piper and the top just flew off. It
was an accident, I swear!"

I looked around. The floor was covered in cream puffs.

"How could you?" I said, in shock.

"Oops," she said, smiling meanly. "I guess you won't
really have time to finish your dessert. Too bad!"

My heart was pounding. I had an hour. An hour to bake
cream puffs, make more custard, then fill them and assemble
the *croquembouche*.

"Fuck."

I put the truffles at my station and asked Fiona to watch
them. Then I ran to the fridge and grabbed the ingredients
to make cream puffs *again*.

"I'm so stressed," I muttered, taking a swig of cognac to
calm my nerves. Now I knew why the chefs I'd worked with
were all so insane.

"This is a bake-off; it's supposed to be fun, wholesome.
This is ridiculous," I groaned as I stirred the two pots on the
stove, one for the custard filling and one for the cream puffs.

"Are you going to make it?" Anastasia asked, coming
over.

"Maybe," I said with a smile that was more of a grimace.
If all the cameras hadn't been watching, I would have just
dumped all the batter on Amber, called it quits, and run
away to the Caribbean to do catering on a cruise ship. But
I had to try to finish, if for nothing else than to stick it to
my stepsister.

The cream puff dough was done, and the custard burbled along. I piped out the cream puffs on the baking sheet,
stirring the custard occasionally.

Cream puffs in the oven. Stir the custard. Look at the clock. Drink cognac while wondering why it took the cream puffs so damn long to bake.

The gossamer copper-colored spun sugar was a hallmark of the dish, and I couldn't present a *croquembouche* without it. While the cream puffs baked, I heated up the sugar, checking the candy thermometer to make sure it didn't burn and turn bitter. Though not traditional, I was going to form it into a ribbon that would cascade elegantly over the *croquembouche*. It was a little more refined than throwing sugar around willy-nilly like a spider web. This was supposed to be Christmas, not Halloween.

Finally the cream puff shells were done. I molded the sugar into the gauzy ribbon while the pastries cooled.

"Twenty minutes!" Anastasia called out.

"Crap!" I took another long swig of cognac to steady my nerves then piped the custard into the cream puffs. They weren't quite cool, but this was what I had to work with. I prayed to the kitchen gods that the truffles wouldn't melt.

"Ten minutes!" Anastasia called as I carefully stacked the cream puffs into a pyramid then began decorating the cream puff tree, taking swigs of cognac to try to calm down.

"I'm not going to make it," I said, heart yammering as I carefully placed the sugar flowers and the sugar holly branches among the cream puffs, careful not to disturb them. The truffles went on last. The pastry was still slightly warm.

"Please don't melt!" I begged. Finally, I draped the golden spun-sugar ribbon around the tree.

"Time!" Anastasia called as I adjusted a sugar flower.

"Fuck, I need a drink," I said, slumping to the floor, taking the bottle with me.

CHAPTER 38

Owen

The tension in the studio was palpable when I walked in a half hour before the timer buzzed.

Holly was running between her table, the stove, and the fridge. I watched her frantically assemble a pyramid of little pastries. She had to use a step stool to get the last of them on the top of the tower.

"That's insane," I said to Anu.

"Yes, and this is the second time she's done it. You missed the part where the first tower was knocked over."

We applauded when the timer was up.

Holly took a long swig out of a bottle of amber liquor. She looked wrung out. I wanted to pick her up, take her up to my condo, and ease the tension in her forehead. Unfortunately, there was a long night of Christmas Bake-off judging between me and my desire.

The first contestant was a girl who had hot chocolate as her fan-favorite dish. She had made a deep-fried hot chocolate ice cream. It was weird, though.

"Did you roll this in bread?" I asked, confused.

"It kept falling apart," she explained. "I needed to keep the shape."

"The fudge is nice," Nick said, picking at the breading around the ice cream.

"Next up, we have Amber," Anastasia said. "Her fan-choice dish was peppermint bark."

Amber handed each of us a peppermint tart. I took a bite and didn't know if I wanted to sneeze or spit it out. My mouth burned.

Nick wasn't so polite. He spat it back on the plate. "Seriously, did you just pour peppermint essential oils into this? It's way too much."

"I wanted the peppermint flavor," Amber said. "You know, peppermint is good for a lot of things—if you have a cold or nausea or if you want to make sex with your man interesting." She looked pointedly at me.

The bite of tart was still burning my mouth. I spat it into a napkin one of the production assistants handed me.

"I don't want that anywhere near my junk," I said.

We all gulped water while the next dessert was brought out.

"Honestly, anything has to be better than what we just ate," Nick said, blowing his nose.

Thankfully, Fiona's dish was fruity and refreshing.

"My fan-choice dish was Christmas punch," she said. "I made a pomegranate-cranberry sorbet with an orange-and-apricot-and-brandy sponge cake. Also on the plate is a fizzy cranberry-ginger raindrop cake as well as a pomegranate-and-cognac reduction."

"Amazing!" Nick said. "There's only one issue." He removed the sprig of mint garnish. "Let's not."

Holly was next.

"I must say I'm impressed that you managed to pull through," Anu said.

"She worked in one of my restaurants," Nick said with a laugh. "That means she excels under pressure."

Holly smiled tipsily. She wavered slightly in her heels as she described her dessert. It was even more impressive up close. If that was what she did with just flour, eggs, and sugar in such a short time, I had no doubt that her plans for the *TechBiz* competition were going to be brilliant.

"I think you might have needed a little more time," Anu said, inspecting the tower, "but still, this was very ambitious, and you can see each of these elements was executed flawlessly."

I took a bite of one of the cream puffs. Holly was clearly trying not to laugh.

"What?"

"Nothing," she said, giggling.

"She's drunk," Anu said.

"The makings of a great chef," Nick added.

Anu and Nick decided to give the win to Fiona. Holly was runner-up this round. I knew she was disappointed, but she was whisked away for a postcompetition interview before I could talk to her.

Actually, I didn't want to talk. I wanted to make out with her and take her out of that outfit. The curve of her breasts peeked through the deep V of the top. I wanted to run my tongue over the creamy stripe of skin between the thigh-high boots and the hem of the skirt then lick my way up.

It was pitch-dark when they finished filming. The contest had run late that day. I took Rudolph out. The dog-sitting start-up had set up temporary shop at my office, providing some much-needed interaction for Rudolph. But he still had energy to burn.

Sloane texted me while I was out.

Sloane: *Lonely? I'm in the area. Let me come by and cheer you up.*

Ignore. She'd better not show up. The only reason she had been able to sneak upstairs was because of the *TechBiz* competition; we'd had to give the committee access to our facilities.

When I returned to my condo, I was on edge, half expecting her to be waiting for me. She wasn't, and unfortunately, neither was Holly. I prowled around the condo, trying to convince myself that it wasn't a good idea to sneak upstairs to my penthouse and into the master bedroom to surprise Holly. I poured myself a drink to try to take the edge off. The doorbell rang.

I ignored it. It was probably Sloane. The bell rang again, and Rudolph went crazy. Steeling myself, I checked the camera, but it was not Sloane; it was Holly. She blew kisses to the camera, then her hands slid up her top and started unbuttoning the bodice. I practically sprinted to the door and wrenched it open.

"I thought that would get your attention," she said.

CHAPTER 39

Holly

Owen didn't say a word when he opened the door. He stared at me as though I was his main course and dessert.

"I'm drunk and might be convinced to make a bad decision," I told him, licking my lips. "Such as sleep with the bake-off judge slash technically my boss."

Owen pulled me inside and pushed me against the wall, crushing his mouth to mine. He tasted rich, like expensive liquor. His tongue claimed my mouth as his hand pushed up under the short skirt to caress my ass. He trailed kisses to my tits, pulling one out then the other to lick and kiss the soft skin.

I moaned, legs trembling slightly, my arms around his neck as he kissed his way down. I widened my legs for him as his hand pushed under my soaking panties. Whimpering, I pressed against his hand. Owen stroked me, teasing me, as he kissed me. One hand tangled in my hair as the other rubbed my clit. I had already been hot and bothered when I was outside his door, and Owen was quickly bringing me to the edge.

I clung to Owen as two fingers dipped into my opening then trailed back to circle and tease my clit. I whimpered and moaned against his mouth, my hips making little circles against his hand. He kissed back down to suck on my breast, nipping and rolling the nipple in his mouth, as his hand stroked my pussy.

Moaning, I clung to him as he stroked me, working my clit. I made whimpering, pleading noises as he kissed back up to my neck and up my jaw, using two fingers to roll my clit as if he was making candy canes. My legs trembled, and my body tightened as I came.

I panted against his mouth as he kissed me. His cock was hard through his pants, and I unzipped them. I needed that hard length inside me.

"I think I want my Christmas present early," I breathed.

Owen lifted me, and I wrapped my legs around him. He kissed me as he carried me to the couch.

"Only naughty girls open their presents early," he said, his deep voice sending delicious vibrations through me. He tossed me onto the couch. I landed on my hands and knees, and Owen positioned himself behind me.

"I want your cock," I moaned.

"I want a taste of your Christmas cookies first," he said, one hand tangled in my hair. He tipped my head back to kiss me as his hand pushed back under the wet panties, stroking my pussy. I moaned from the back of my throat as two of his fingers entered me. I gyrated against his hand.

"No fair," I croaked as his fingers moved back to my clit.

He chuckled then eased my panties down. They trapped my knees together, so I couldn't spread my legs wide enough to entice him to stick that big cock into me. I moaned as he undid the bodice of the nutcracker outfit, one hand cupping my tit, rolling the nipple in his fingers. His hands slid down my back to cup my ass.

"I think you really did turn me into a Christmas cookie addict," he remarked then pressed his mouth to my pussy.

His tongue felt even better than his hands. I cried out as his tongue dipped into my opening then made little spirals up to my clit. I cursed, trying to spread my legs more. Owen laughed, his voice sending vibrations through my pussy. There was a tearing noise, and the lace panties ripped. Owen tossed them to the floor.

"*Fuck me*," I begged, spreading my legs wider for him.

He ignored me and kept up the same steady motion with his tongue. His large hands held my hips in place as Owen sucked and licked my clit, almost bringing me to the edge again then not letting me finish. He traced every line of pleasure. I was a sweaty, pleading mess. He slid two fingers back into my opening, crooking them as he worked my clit.

I could barely hold myself up. My knees trembled, and my legs felt like they were going to give out when finally Owen made me come with a series of high-pitched cries. Spent, I half collapsed on the couch.

"You know," Owen said before I drifted off into a land of happy singing elves and friendly reindeer, "I almost expected you to yell 'Merry Christmas.'"

"Next time," I slurred.

I woke up the next morning with a start.

"Crazy drunk dreams," I said hoarsely, groping around for the water I usually kept on the nightstand. It wasn't there. I blinked in the light that streamed through the windows.

Wait, why is the view different? Was I in Fiona's room? That couldn't be right. I sat up, yawning, and looked down. I was completely naked.

Crap. What the hell happened? I drank too much for sure. But it was starting to come back to me—Amber ruining my dessert, the abundant cognac.

The door opened, framing Owen.

Right. And *that*.

CHAPTER 40

Owen

was expecting next time to be in five, maybe ten minutes. I was pretty sure I could make her come again. It was addicting to watch Holly come undone. My cock ached as I thought about the noises she made.

But that wasn't going to be happening tonight, it seemed. Holly was sound asleep, sprawled on the couch. As much as I wanted her to wake up, straddle me, and ride my cock, that was going to have to wait. The first time I fucked her for real, I wanted to take my time, and I wanted her to be alert enough to feel every second of it.

Rudolph chose that moment to creep back into the living room. He licked Holly's hand.

I picked her up. She murmured sleepily in my arms as I carried her upstairs to my bedroom. Her clothes were half off and her panties were somewhere downstairs, so I figured it was fine to undress her the rest of the way. I kissed her then covered her with the comforter. I watched her sleep.

Now what?

If I lay in the bed next to her, I knew I wouldn't sleep at all. I would count the seconds until she woke up. All I wanted to do was fuck her. Sliding my fingers into her had been intoxicating. I was still hard. I forced myself to calm down and went out to stand on the balcony in the cold, looking out over the city's night lights.

The next morning, I heard Holly awake and talking to herself. I went up, fully expecting to fuck her, but she looked freaked out when I opened the door.

"Oh my God!" she shrieked. "Don't look! I don't have any clothes on!"

I dutifully turned around while she pulled a sheet over herself.

"I feel like this might be a little bit of shutting the door after the reindeer has already left the barn," I told her.

"And now he decides to make Christmas references," she huffed.

"Well, last night my face was in your—"

"Yes, I know where it was," she snapped. "But that was when I was dressed. Things were held up and in place. Also I had the extra confidence boost of half a bottle of cognac."

"Unless you bought it half full, the bottle was mostly gone. You left it outside my front door," I informed her.

"No wonder I can barely remember anything," she muttered to herself.

"I can jog your memory," I said helpfully, turning around. The sheet was wrapped around her like a toga. I could make out the outline of her rock-hard nipples through the Egyptian cotton.

"It's a weekday. I can't just stay here in your bed all day," she protested.

"You could."

"I have to plan your winter festival. I have a to-do list," she said.

"And it doesn't include finishing what we started last night?" I asked, slowly approaching her to see if she would back away.

She didn't.

I wrapped my arms around Holly, pulling her into a kiss. Her hands left the sheet to wrap around my neck. The sheet slid down, exposing her tits. Unable to contain my desire, I decorated her skin with light kisses from her collarbone to the swell of her breasts. Holly gasped then moaned.

I pulled the rest of the sheet down. That snapped her out of the spell.

"I need to shower!" she practically shouted and ran to the bathroom, slamming the door.

"Are you all right?"

"Yep, perfect! Never better! I'll make you breakfast when I'm done."

Rudolph padded into the room. He had a scrap of lacy black cloth in his mouth.

"Drop it," I told the puppy, reaching for him.

He zigged around me and scratched at the door. Holly opened it, and Rudolph squeezed inside.

"How come the dog gets to come in?" I complained.

"He's cute, and he gets separation anxiety," she called.

"But he ripped your underwear."

"You did that."

230 · ALINA JACOBS

I snorted, wondering what she would do if I just opened the door and invited myself inside. But no. The first time with her needed to be perfect, not a quickie on the vanity.

"Just sit tight," Holly said. "I'm going to make you a bacon pie for breakfast."

"A bacon pie?"

"Yes. Corn, cheddar, bacon, pickled onions. It's amazing."

I blew out a breath. My phone rang before my dick could talk me out of waiting for a better moment to fuck Holly. I went downstairs to take the call.

Dana was on the line. "Don't forget that we're doing *The Christmas Bake-Off* at your holiday party in a few days," she reminded me. "Please make sure your employees have signed waivers."

"Are the contestants going to give my employees food poisoning?" I demanded. "The *TechBiz* representatives are going to be there. They cannot have food poisoning. I'll be at the bottom of the rankings."

"Who knows?" Dana sighed. "With all the backstabbing going on, anything could happen."

"We should get together with Penny and Holly to talk about the holiday party," I said.

"What does Holly have to do with it?" Dana asked.

"She's helping us with increasing our fun rating in the *TechBiz* competitions."

Dana was silent, then she said, "Owen, you cannot date one of the contestants. And now you have her working for you? Are you even paying her?"

"Uh—"

"At least don't sleep with her until the competition is over."

"Define sleeping with?"

"For goodness' sake, Owen."

Holly came downstairs with Rudolph after Dana hung up. She had put on a pair of my boxers and one of my shirts with the sleeves rolled up. I could make out the outline of her tits beneath the expensive fabric.

"I'm going to make you something nice for breakfast," she said, waltzing to the kitchen.

"I already see what I want right here," I said, sliding my hands under the shirt and kissing her.

"I look like a mess," she said. "You don't want me like this."

"Of course I do," I said seriously.

Holly kissed my jaw then spun away to grab the remote. "I'm still going to make breakfast. But I need Christmas shows on. WebFlix has a twenty-four-seven Christmas channel," she said as Frosty the Snowman popped up on the screen. He was arguing with an elf; there was a lot of hand-waving. It seemed everyone found Christmas stressful.

Holly went back to rummaging in the fridge. Rudolph stood right underfoot. I tried to call the dog away.

"He knows I'm making bacon," Holly said with a laugh, taking out the meat.

The bacon sizzled in a pan while she mixed up a pie-crust. She rolled it out and pressed it into a pan. She stuck the dough in the fridge while she pulled the bacon off the stove, taking the pieces out to cool.

"I'm a little scared at how well you can use that knife," I told her as she sliced red onions and jalapeños very thin.

"This was my life for years," Holly said with a laugh as she mixed them with lime juice, salt, and sugar. "When I landed my first restaurant job, I would have to chop a bag of onions a day. Some of them in rings, some sliced, some minced. It was a lot of onions. The trick is to make sure your knife is very sharp." She cut them deftly.

"Piecrust is going in the oven," she said. "And now to make the filling. I don't want it fluffy, so I'm folding in the eggs," she explained, sprinkling salt and pepper on them then adding the bacon, cheddar, and corn. She poured it into the piecrust and arranged the sliced onions on top.

"It's like a soup muffin," I remarked.

"Oh, those muffins Chloe makes? Yeah, those are really tasty," Holly said, smiling. "But not as tasty as you!"

CHAPTER 41

Holly

I wasn't sure why I was so freaked out by being with Owen. Maybe it would have been easier if we'd just fucked and then I did the walk of shame back to my room.

But instead of just getting his jollies and going to sleep like you'd think a billionaire like him would do, he put me first. Now he seemed perfectly content to let me wear his clothes and walk around barefoot in his condo.

"So is this your usual morning routine?" I asked, sitting down on the couch next to him after I slid the pie in the oven.

"It's usually a little more hectic," he admitted. "But I already did my workout and took Rudolph for a jog and answered emails."

"What time did you get up?" I asked in surprise.

"Never went to sleep."

"Too bad, because I slept very well," I teased him.

He grabbed me by the waist, and I straddled his lap. I could feel his hardness through his pants. I leaned forward and kissed him softly.

"I don't want to mess up your suit," I murmured against his mouth.

He unbuttoned the dress shirt I was wearing, kissing down from my neck to my collarbone to my tits, sucking and teasing one nipple then the other until they were hard little pebbles.

"You won't mess it up," he said. His hand cupped my ass then snuck under the shorts. I was wet and aching for him. I ground against his hand as he kissed me, his tongue dipping in and out of my mouth. He pulled us back down on the couch. It was so large that Owen could stretch out fully. I was still straddling him. He pushed the shorts down, and I spread my legs, moaning.

"I want your cock," I said hoarsely, all earlier hesitations burned away with aching need.

"As soon as that timer goes off, you're going to want to jump up and check the food. I'm going to need more time than that," he said, thumbs rubbing circles on my lower back.

"No one likes a braggart."

Owen chuckled then grabbed my hips, pulling me up toward his head. I was practically sitting on his face.

"This is an awkward angle."

"Mmm," he said. His tongue flicked out and touched my clit. "This is perfect."

I gripped the armrest of the sofa as Owen's large hands dug into my hips and ass. He took his time, tracing every fold, every line of my pussy.

"I thought you wanted to fuck me," I whimpered.

"I want to make you come first," he whispered, going back to sucking my clit, making little circles around it with his tongue. My chest was tight, and I was panting, my hips trying to grind against his face.

"I really want your cock," I moaned, back arching and arms trembling as I tried to keep myself from collapsing.

"You also said you didn't want to mess up my suit," he said, pressing his thumb into my opening as he continued to work my clit with his tongue.

My thighs trembled, and my hips made needy little circles. I whimpered, clutching the fabric of the sofa as I came with a cry.

The timer buzzed.

"Shit," I panted, half sprawled over the edge of the couch. "The food."

"Told you," Owen said, scooting me off him. He stood up and didn't look at all rumpled.

I swiped the hair out of my face. "Show-off."

He smirked and went to pull the breakfast pie out of the oven. I stumbled over after taking a few moments to catch my breath.

"Looks good," I said, inspecting the pan. "Still slightly jiggly."

Owen bent down to kiss my tits through the shirt. I was immediately wet. I wondered if he was going to bend me over the counter and fuck me. It would be good. But I'd just had an orgasm, and better judgment was trying to prevail. This thing with Owen had all the ingredients for a perfect disaster.

I sliced the quiche and plated the pieces, taking them to the couch. It sure had seen a lot of action.

"So this is your morning routine?" Owen asked, turning the question back on me as I blew on a bite of the quiche.

"What, sex with a hot guy? Hardly. Lots of cheesy, carby foods? Totally. Though this is a little early for me. Usually I'm up all night and sleep late unless I have to go in and cook brunch." I shuddered.

"You don't like brunch?" Owen asked. "I thought all girls liked brunch."

"I liked brunch until I had to cook it for a thousand hungover, entitled Beckys and their shallow friends. But yes, if I don't have to cook it or have to listen to people constantly complaining that their eggs are undercooked—spoiler, scrambled eggs should not be little rubber pellets—then yeah, I'm down, especially if there are mimosas involved." I finished my quiche and looked at the clock. "I need to prep for the holiday festival."

"Oh, about that." Owen looked sheepishly at me. "You didn't tell me how much you needed to be paid for it."

"You gave me free rein with your credit card and three of the most amazingly big Os I've ever had," I said lightly. "I don't even know what to charge you. I'm not like a real decorator. I just love Christmas, and I did some event planning in my days with the restaurants."

"I'll have Beck send you a proposal, and you can see what you think," he said firmly.

Especially since now that Owen wanted to pay me, I didn't know where we stood. I had been thinking maybe I was doing a favor for a guy I liked. Now he was like, "Oh, you're an employee." And he'd suggested it right after we—well I guess just I—had sex. Was this a roundabout way of him paying me for it? Was that just how billionaires operated? They assumed that if they wanted something, they had to pay for it? No problem, just pressing a button. Was there going to be some sort of weird nondisclosure clause about his super-special tongue-on-clit technique?

But it wasn't as if I didn't need the money. I had been ignoring the notices from the credit card company about late payments, and there was a new email from the storage company reminding me I needed to pay up.

All my subscription baking boxes and weird outfits had not yet netted me any sponsorship deals. Unless I won *The Great Christmas Bake-Off*, I was going to have nothing for Christmas. Actually no, not nothing; I'd have all my debt to keep me company.

I was a wreck when I went back upstairs.

Morticia was waiting for me in annoyance in the kitchen. "Did you complete a successful sexorcism?"

"I didn't have sex with him."

"Then what were you doing up there all night?" she asked tartly. "Making cookies?"

"I made Owen a quiche," I said primly. "Which he ate. He also ate me out."

"So breakfast and a striptease. Someone got his Christmas present early."

"Ugh."

"You said you wanted me to help bake," Morticia reminded me. "We have a very busy schedule. We need to finish decorating the lobby and you have subscription boxes to assemble. Or I suppose you could go back downstairs and try to convince your billionaire boy toy to give you an engagement ring, and you can leave us all and go off to Christmas fairyland."

I grimaced. "Owen's not a boy, and that thing he's wielding is definitely not a toy."

"Did you even see it?"

"I saw part of it."

Morticia shook her head. "You need to test-drive the car before you sign for it."

I changed and showered again. Then I was ready to bake.

"We have to send out two hundred boxes," I said, looking at the list. "How about making white-chocolate-and-raspberry cheesecake squares, chocolate-almond pound cake, and bread pudding with amaretto sauce. Those should travel well," I said. I turned on a Christmas movie and tied on an apron.

"No. I refuse to watch the Hallmark channel," Morticia said, hefting a spatula threateningly.

"It's Christmastime."

Morticia stared at me flatly.

"*The Nightmare Before Christmas*?" I offered.

"I accept."

We baked while Jack Skellington sang about discovering Christmas.

"See, even the Pumpkin King loves Christmas."

Morticia glared at me as she mixed the cheesecake batter. "That is not a Christmas movie, it's a Halloween movie, which is the only reason we're watching it."

CHAPTER 42

Owen

had meetings all morning and through lunch. When I
went back up to my office, I froze outside the door.

"What the—" It looked as if a Christmas bomb had
gone off. Holly was smiling in the middle of it all.

"Isn't it nice?"

"I thought you were decorating the main office," I said
with a frown.

"You're going to have a meeting with the *TechBiz* representatives in here," she said. "Your office needed some
Christmas cheer. We had leftover decorations from the
lobby."

There was garland hanging from the windows. Gossamer
snowflakes glowed. A basket of winter fruits and flowers
sat on the small refreshments bar. An actual Christmas tree
stood in the corner.

"I kept it pretty minimalist," Holly explained, trotting along beside me as I walked around my office. I really did not want all these Christmas decorations in my space, but Holly had put them up, and I didn't want to hurt her by removing them.

"It's very festive," I said finally, since it seemed as if Holly was expecting some sort of response.

She beamed and went to pack an enormous box of decorating supplies. "The holiday party is tomorrow, so act like a normal Christmas-loving person. The *TechBiz* representatives will be there. They need to see that you aren't Owen Frost the Unfriendly Snowman. Maybe you can practice smiling in the mirror."

"I'd rather spend the day with you," I told her.

"I'm busy today. I have a to-do list," she said, whipping out a fuzzy red notebook and a pen with a bobblehead Santa on it. "I have to go to the post office and then pick my outfit for tomorrow."

I took the notebook out of her hand and put in on the desk then pushed Holly back against the edge of it.

"Just wear what you're wearing right now," I said, my hands creeping up the skirt. I wanted nothing more than to bend her over the desk and fuck her.

Breathlessly, Holly said, "Someone's going to see!"

"Isn't that why you put up all these decorations—to provide some cover?" I said, the grin on my face dangerous.

"I don't think it's that much cover," Holly said.

I stepped back while she adjusted her dress and licked her lips. "I have to go before the post office closes."

I kissed her once more before she left.

The office felt colder without Holly there. I looked around at the Christmas decorations. On second thought, they weren't that bad. There weren't a lot of blinking lights and red and green sparkly ornaments. Holly had used sage-green garlands, lots of silver and white and gold, with soft fairy lights. It felt more like a winter wonderland than a Christmas mall scene.

But it wasn't as calming as she probably thought it would be; I was antsy. I needed Holly. Instead, I opted for a walk. Rudolph needed to go out.

I picked him up from the doggie daycare. I'd given them a temporary spot in the tower until their permanent space was constructed. Already the new amenity was a huge hit with my employees. There were several dogs playing in the room that had been allocated for the service.

One of the workers handed me Rudolph's leash. The puppy was hanging from it by his teeth, three of his four paws off the ground.

"We really did try to tire him out," the woman said. "We took them all to the park and ran around. This dog was never cold or tired. You must have your hands full!"

"He had bacon for breakfast this morning," I explained, dragging Rudolph away. "You better not get expelled from daycare," I warned him in the elevator. The puppy was oblivious and hopped around as soon as we were outside in the cold.

Figuring he was tired of the nearby park, I took him to another park several blocks away. He jumped in piles of dead leaves and snapped at the snowflakes that had started to fall. After a good hour of running around, I took him back to the tower.

Up ahead, I saw Holly, huffing as she pushed an empty metal cart. I snuck up on her then grabbed her, spinning her around and kissing her. She screamed and beat me around the head with her purse.

A young woman walking a miniature horse wearing tennis shoes, a custom blinking sweater, and a hat festooned with poinsettias and sprigs of garland passed us and gave us a suspicious look.

"It's fine, I know her," I assured the horse girl.

"Very well," Holly added.

"Weirdos," the girl muttered.

Holly and I barely held it together until she had passed out of earshot. Then we started laughing.

"Why are you even out here?" Holly asked.

"Rudolph needed to burn off some energy," I said. The puppy was chewing on the leash, tired of standing still.

"Switch?"

She took Rudolph, and I pushed the cart.

"Honestly, you make it look so easy," she said, squeezing my arm.

"You could have told me you needed these taken to the post office," I told her.

"They needed tracking, and I didn't have enough time to order the pickup," she explained. "Because I was distracted." She shoved me playfully.

"Am I distracting?"

"Very."

"I'll make a note to be less distracting."

"But that's how I like you," she replied, licking her lips suggestively.

CHAPTER 43

Holly

Though all I wanted to do was let Owen distract me for the rest of the afternoon, we had to finish decorating the lobby for the holiday party.

"Where is the tree?" Penny fretted while Morticia rearranged furniture. "We need the big tree. I was planning on uploading a tree-trimming video."

Jazzy, poppy Christmas carols played over the sound system. Several of Owen's employees had come down, waiting to gawk at the giant tree that was supposed to be delivered. An impromptu party broke out, with a big bowl of Christmas punch and a tray of baked snacks that I had whipped up. I poured myself some punch.

"Man," I wheezed, "someone spiked this."

I sipped and contemplated my life. The situation with Owen was making me slightly anxious. Was it going to be a fuck and dump? What was his deal? The only time I'd

244 · ALINA JACOBS

interacted with billionaires like him was when I had been catering charity events. Then all I'd asked was, "Care to try a lobster popper?"

Now I was supposed to navigate a complicated—I didn't even know what we had. Was it a relationship? Casual fuck buddies? But we hadn't really actually had sex. Was this some sort of weird self-deprivation thing he was doing? Maybe he was secretly crazy.

A truck blared its horn outside, jerking me out of my spiral of doubt and paranoia.

"Are we going to have a big tree like this upstairs?" one of Owen's workers asked me.

"Not this big," I told them. "We wouldn't be able to bring it up there."

I wasn't even sure we were going to get this tree inside the building.

"Can we remove this glass?" the tree delivery guy asked me, pointing to the front doors.

"Uh, let's not," I said.

Owen came down, Beck and Walker trailing him.

"Half of my employees are missing," Owen said with a frown. "But it appears they're all here." People had their cell phones out, recording.

"The tree won't fit through the opening—it's too big," I told him. "Should have used lube, I guess, or given it a bit of a warm-up."

Owen bit his lip slightly and bent down to whisper in my ear. "We could have tested how big it was earlier." He straightened up. "Maybe take it back out and bring it in through the loading area?"

"Sure thing, chief."

The workers tried to take the tree back out. There was a cracking sound, and all the onlookers oohed.

"Let's not do that!" Penny practically yelled.

The workers tried pushing the tree the other way. It was stuck.

"Call the fire department," I suggested.

"We cannot call the fire department. It would be all over the news," Owen said, horrified.

"Too late for that," Morticia said, gesturing to the onlookers. Zane and his camera panned around us.

Owen took off his suit jacket and undid his cuff links, handing them to me.

"We'll just brute force it in. The pointy end of the tree is already facing the right way, so with some finagling, it has to come in."

Walker and Beck looked at each other, shrugged, and removed their jackets.

"Holly, hold the doors back," Owen ordered. He grabbed the tree and pulled, muscles bulging.

"It's like everything I ever wanted all in one package," I said happily to Morticia.

"I would have expected you to want him in a Santa hat," she said. "And nothing else."

"Might be a little dangerous with all the branches," I said, getting whapped in the face with one as the tree lurched forward.

"Walker and Beck, grab it around the trunk and pull," Owen told his CFO and COO.

With the three strong men pulling, the tree lurched another few feet.

"Pull!" Owen commanded. A few more heaves and the tree was inside!

Everyone applauded.

"It's like a movie!" I exclaimed, throwing my hands up in celebration.

"There's tree sap in your hair," Morticia said.

"Crap!" I pulled a tissue out of my pocket and blotted the spot.

"Oooh," Morticia said, making a face. "Bad idea. Now you have a tissue stuck to your head. Gonna have to cut it out."

"No," I moaned, picking at the tissue.

"I still think you're sexy, even with Kleenex and tree jizz in your hair," Owen whispered in my ear. He kissed my neck softly and took his cuff links from me.

I was feeling warm and tingly watching him roll down his sleeves. He raised an eyebrow when he saw me drooling.

"What? You guys all know that women go Christmas crackers for a nice forearm."

"You make it sound so dirty," he said.

"It's very dirty."

While the tree was being tilted upright, two of Owen's employees came down with a big box.

"Let's see what you made."

"We cut snowflakes out of old computer parts," one of the guys said, showing me. "And we have old motherboards we laser cut with the Quantum Cyber logo."

"See, Owen?" I said. "You can't tell me you don't want these types of Christmas ornaments."

He inspected one. "These are pretty cool."

It took the rest of the afternoon to trim the tree. While that was in progress, Owen brought me some WD-40 to remove the pine sap from my hair.

"Don't look at me," I said to Zane as Owen dumped the chemical in my hair and carefully wiped the sap out.

"All gone," he said after a moment.

"Now I smell like chemicals," I complained. "I need a shower."

"I could help you wash that off," he said, his voice low in my ear.

CHAPTER 44

Owen

Holly blushed slightly at the comment.

"I should probably not," she demurred.

My phone rang. It was Mace Svensson. "Come see me tonight," I told her before I answered.

She went even redder, and her eyes were dilated and little glassy.

I went upstairs to my office to take the conference call with Mace and Garrett about the gene therapy facility. I was only half paying attention, though. The rest of my attention was on planning a perfect evening for Holly. It had to be flawless and romantic.

After the call was done, I ordered food from a nearby Italian restaurant. Then I went back to my condo to set up. The most important part of a plan was executing the details properly. I had a list of small touches that would elevate the evening into a memorable one.

Fire in the fireplace. Check. Intimate table for two. Check. Food delivered right on schedule. Check.

Then I turned on—*shudder*—Christmas carols. Holly would appreciate the touch, though.

As I changed clothes, I texted her a picture of me in a Santa hat and nothing else.

Owen: *Dinner and yuletide entertainment?*

Holly: *You are literally my dream man. I'm going to eat Christmas cookies off of you, so be prepared!*

And a perfect woman. Check.

I set the table and lit the Christmas candles and patted myself on the back for having had the foresight to order them. I checked my suit in the mirror. Perfect. Holly was going to be here any minute. The doorbell rang. Right on schedule.

I opened the door. There was Holly in what looked like a Rockette's outfit that consisted of a super-short red-velvet-and-fur–trimmed coat. She had a party horn in her mouth and blew it at me when I opened the door.

"I brought peppermint schnapps and eggnog-flavored vodka. It's disgusting!" she said cheerfully. Her enthusiasm flagged a little bit as she looked me up and down.

"I guess I seriously misread the Christmas-themed nude photo you sent me, because this is not the evening I pictured."

"I have a nice evening planned," I said, leading her inside the condo.

She whistled. "Yeah, a seriously nice evening."

I pulled the chair out for her.

"I am not dressed right," she said, opening the bottle of peppermint schnapps and taking a swig. The candles flickered. "Seriously misread it," she muttered.

"There's antipasti," I informed her.

She took another swig of the peppermint schnapps. "Where's the Santa hat you were wearing earlier?"

"I thought you might want to be wined and dined first," I said. I took the schnapps away and poured her a glass of wine.

"I mean, I came here to get fucked. I have all the tree sap out of my hair, and I even took a shower. I'm raring to go."

"And here I planned this nice dinner date," I said, leaning back in my chair.

Her eyes narrowed. "I feel like you're teasing me. All the dirty, flirty comments. Now you're Mr. Three-Course Dinner and Two Hundred-Dollar Bottle of Wine."

"It was a thousand," I corrected.

"Yeah, I'm seriously underdressed," she said under her breath.

"Do you want to take off your coat?" I asked.

"I'm not wearing much under this," she said.

"What are you wearing under it?" I asked, sipping the wine.

"I'm all wrapped up like a present."

That got my dick's attention. *Wrapped up how?* it wanted to know.

"Buuuut," she drawled, smirking at my expression. "Now that you mention it, maybe I do want a five-star evening. Wine me. Dine me," she said, swirling the goblet. "Give me the true Owen Frost treatment."

She speared one of the olives on the plate and slowly stuck it in her mouth, her lips making a little O shape.

"Yum! I love the feeling of balls in my mouth."

My pants were uncomfortably tight.

"But the bigger question is," Holly continued, "is sausage the next course?"

I set my wineglass down and stood up. "You know, I was trying not to treat you like a sex object but rather like a woman with thoughts and feelings."

"Yeah, and I appreciate that, except all my thoughts and feelings revolve around sex and Christmas, which is why I really needed you to answer the door in nothing but a Santa hat," she countered. "Maybe Santa's utility belt too."

"I don't have a utility belt."

"Next time," she told me. "Now about that dinner. I'm starving for some meat."

I narrowed my eyes at her. "You can't just say you're wrapped like a present underneath that—I hesitate to call it a coat since it barely covers anything—and then just want to sit here eating dinner."

"But you planned it so nicely," she said, taking a sip of the wine. "I don't want to steal your thunder."

"Steal it."

"Santa baby," she sang as she slowly removed the red coat. "I want you coming in my chimney tonight!"

The coat dropped and revealed Holly literally wrapped as a present. It was like a one-piece bathing suit with eighty percent of it missing. The single ribbon between her legs hid not much at all. It made a red line up to her tits, wrapped around her back, and made a bow in the front.

I swallowed, my cock aching.

"Do you know why Santa's so jolly?" she cooed. "It's because he knows where all the naughty girls live!"

CHAPTER 45

Holly

loved costumes, especially Christmas costumes. I wondered if I had gone a little overboard on this one, though.

"You look like you're going to combust," I said. "Fire and ice don't mix, Mr. Frost. Could be dangerous."

"I assure you I will not spontaneously combust," he said, undoing his tie and hanging it, along with his jacket, carefully over the chair. Then he stepped up to me. His fingertips lightly caressed the bare skin that was not covered by the ribbon. It was supposed to be a fun, sexy outfit. As such, it did not cover much. I shivered as he ran his fingers lightly over me.

Two fingers hooked under the ribbon that went from my tits straight to my pussy. Owen pulled on the ribbon, and I gasped as it rubbed against my clit. He smiled slightly then pulled me to him by the ribbon. I fell into his arms, stumbling on my tall heels.

I moaned as he kissed me, his tongue tangling with mine, one hand gripping my ass as the other toyed with the ribbon, giving me delicious friction between my legs.

"I want your cock," I said against his mouth. I reached for his pants and undid the buckle. I threw the belt to the floor and unzipped the fly with a rasp. I palmed his cock, and he grunted slightly. His fingers went down to tease my pussy as I rubbed his cock through the boxer briefs.

"Fuck me," I moaned. I nipped his lower lip.

He growled then picked me up, wrapping my legs around his waist. I ground against him, the motion making that ribbon that ran right along my pussy rub my clit as he walked up the stairs.

"I've been wanting this for days," he said against my mouth.

"I've wanted it since I saw you in my room," I panted.

"My room," he growled, planting kisses along my collarbone. He pushed me back on the bed. I tangled my fingers in his hair, pulling him back down to kiss him.

"I told you I want my Christmas present now."

"So demanding," he said, the smirk on his face letting me know he had every intention of drawing this out.

I grabbed his shirt collar and pulled. The buttons popped off his shirt and bounced around the room. Owen's chest was just as drool worthy as I remembered. I thought maybe I had exaggerated it in my wet dreams and daytime fantasies, but nope. His chest was amazing. I could make out the outlines of every muscle, from the hard plates of his pecs down to his washboard abs, culminating in the V that pointed like a sign down to his Christmas package, the bulge clear through his pants.

"You're a naughty girl," he said, grabbing my wrists and pinning me back on the bed.

"Too bad you left your belt downstairs," I said, panting as he carefully kissed my tits through the thin red fabric.

"I can punish you in other ways," he said, "but sometimes pleasure is the best punishment."

I cursed as he slowly ran his tongue down the ribbon, the red fabric painting a neon line to my pussy. I arched back as he licked me through the fabric. I spread my legs for him, and he pushed the strip of silk aside, licking a stripe along my folds. I whimpered as he worked my clit with his tongue. My chest heaved. Owen sucked on my clit as he used two fingers to tease my opening, dipping in then making snowflake patterns in the wet hot warmth of my pussy as he coaxed me over the edge with his tongue. I cried out, my nails digging into his broad shoulders as I came.

"You still didn't say Merry Christmas," he said.

"I thought you hated Christmas," I panted. The orgasm had slaked my lust only slightly. I felt that I could easily go another round.

"If I can have you wrapped up like this under my tree, I'll have Christmas every day," he replied.

I sat up on my knees and struck my best fifties pinup girl pose, channeling my inner Bettie Page.

"You want to come give me a white Christmas all over my face?" I cooed, batting my eyes, licking a finger and trailing it down my tits and down the ribbon to my pussy. I was aching for his cock.

Owen stood at the foot of the bed.

"I've been a real naughty girl," I said, slowly crawling across the bed to him.

Owen stripped off his pants and threw them to the floor.

"I want to see what's in your stocking," I told him, pulling down the boxer briefs. His cock sprang out, huge and thick. Owen definitely needed a size XL stocking.

"And a Merry Christmas to me," I said, rubbing my hands together. "I might need two hands for this." I reached for his cock. Owen swore as I ran my hands down the length. "Is it weird that I kind of wish you had a bow around it?"

"Yes, that's very weird," he said as I put the tip of his cock in my mouth, licking the slit. I slid several inches into my mouth, humming "Rudolph the Red-Nosed Reindeer" around his thick shaft.

His fingers dug into my hair, and he pulled me back. I released his cock with a pop of my lips. Owen, I was pleased to see, was breathing a little erratically. His cock jutted out like the North Pole.

"I want to fuck you," he growled.

"Have you been a good boy this year?" I teased.

"Of course," he said in that sexy deep voice. He kissed my neck. His cock pressed against my thigh, and I whimpered, spreading my legs for him. "And that means I get to open my Christmas present early."

He tugged me upright. Then he pulled on the ends of the bow sitting at my breasts. It tugged a little then gave. The red ribbon pooled on the bedspread.

"But then you won't have anything for Christmas," I said. I was on my knees, hands braced on his shoulders.

Owen pressed kisses to my neck and jaw, hand sneaking between my legs to stroke me softly.

"I'll have it again several more times, in fact, before Christmas," he replied then crushed his mouth to mine.

"You gonna let me ride your sleigh, Santa?"

"Don't call me Santa," he growled, pushing me back on the bed. I gasped as he lightly bit my neck then my tits. He sucked on a nipple, rolling it in his mouth. He trailed kisses down to my pussy, and I moaned as he licked me, the tip of his tongue darting out to flick my clit.

"Your tits are amazing," he said, kissing back up, nuzzling one and caressing the other with his hand.

"You're such a tease," I moaned, reaching between his legs for his cock.

"I told you I'm taking my time. Christmas isn't just one day, it's twelve, remember."

"If you keep me here for twelve days without making me come," I warned, "I will make this the worst Christmas you ever had."

Owen chuckled then flipped me over. I screeched in surprise. Owen grabbed my wrists, pinning them above me so I was half arched with my ass in the air.

"We don't want you to combust," he said. I could hear the smirk in his voice. He stroked my pussy, and I ground back against his hand. When he ripped a condom packet, I moaned with anticipation.

"*Fuck me.*"

Owen rolled on the condom then teased my clit with his cock. I moaned again, my head hanging forward and my hips grinding against his cock.

"My pussy is so hot and tight for you," I whimpered, needing his thick length in me.

"You want my cock?" he whispered in my ear, still rubbing it against my clit.

"Yes," I choked out.

Owen turned my head to claim my mouth. Then he grabbed my hips and thrust into me. I cried out as his thick cock filled me then moaned as he slid back out. I made little whimpering, panting noises every time he fucked me. He was huge, but I was so needy and wet that I welcomed every long, hard inch of him. Owen reached up to pinch my nipple, teasing it as he fucked me with an easy rhythm.

"*Faster*," I begged. He ignored me in favor of trailing his hand down to my pussy to stroke me, rubbing my clit. I ground back against his hand then back against his cock.

"Please," I begged, "faster. I need to come."

He grabbed my hips and fucked me for real. My fingers dug into the bedspread as he jackhammered into me, my tits bouncing and brushing the expensive fabric with every thrust. His fingers went back to my clit, rubbing me, bringing me close to the edge. My legs trembled, and my body tightened as I came, Owen drawing out the waves of pleasure. His rhythm got more erratic, then I felt him come inside me.

He collapsed next to me. I patted his thigh.

"I'd say Merry Christmas," I slurred, "but that was better than any Christmas I've ever had."

CHAPTER 46

Owen

I kissed Holly, basking in the feel of being inside her. She felt decadent, like the chocolate tart she'd made during the first bake-off competition. I kissed her lazily, claiming every inch of her mouth.

"You know," she whispered against my lips, "if you feed me, I'll probably be up for another ride in the sleigh." She kissed along my jaw to my neck. "Also," she continued, running her nails along the ridges of muscles on my chest, "I believe I was promised a wholesome romantic evening."

"I never intended it to be wholesome," I said, trailing my fingers along her curves, cupping her soft breasts. Holly was mine now. I was never giving her up.

She swung out of bed. I admired the arc of her ass as she bent down, picked up my shirt, then snapped back up.

"What in the world?" I exclaimed, propping myself up on my arm.

"You never saw *Legally Blonde*?" she said. "It's a great Christmas movie."

"I thought that was about a lawyer?" I frowned.

"Yes, but," she said as she put on the shirt, "it has a Christmas scene in it, which makes it a Christmas movie."

"Is that really how it works?"

"Absolutely! Anything is a Christmas movie if you try hard enough."

"You're just going to do that and then not come back to bed?" I called out as she walked out of the room. I stared at the doorway in mild disbelief. Then I jumped out of bed and pulled on pants to run down the stairs after her.

"You said there was Italian food," she called back to me. "You better have ordered garlic bread and tiramisu. Otherwise I'll just be like the Ghost of Christmas Past, never to grace your bed again."

I grabbed her.

"If you're that easily bought, I'll have tiramisu brought to you every single day," I growled, grabbing her and kissing her, my hands roaming over her back and down to her ass.

"I'm starving," she murmured against my mouth. "I had sex and alcohol. Now my brain wants food. Though if you're really antsy, I can definitely eat and fuck."

"That sound like a choking hazard," I said, following her through the condo.

"I don't know, a cupcake piled high with extra frosting? I could totally ride your dick and eat that," she said cheerfully.

My dick thought that was a very good idea and was actually committing to literally bake a cupcake and frost it just to try that out.

"I think the food might be cold now, though," I said. "I should have put it in the oven before we…"

"You were distracted," Holly said, turning around and pressing kisses against my bare chest. "But hey, you've been distracting me a lot lately, so fair's fair. So what did you get? Chicken parmesan? Fettuccini alfredo? Orrr," she said when we stared at the scene in the kitchen. "Husky *à la Italiene*."

Instead of the neat paper sack of Italian food, there was a small husky covered in tomato sauce. He was lying on the ground, belly round. He wagged his tale and burped when he saw us.

"What are you doing? You're ruining my evening!" I scolded him.

"Fortunately, he only stole one container," Holly said, giggling as she set the empty vessel on the counter and picked up the bag holding the rest of the food.

"There were supposed to be five meatballs plus pasta. That dog ate all of them." I shook my head at Rudolph. "Geez, you need a bath."

Holly pulled a bucket out from under the sink and set it in the basin. She poured soap in it and ran the hot water. I stuck the puppy in the soapy water, and he howled while I cleaned the tomato sauce from the floor.

"At least he licked most of it up," Holly said and laughed as she rinsed Rudolph. "Though watching a man clean is very sexy!"

She wrapped Rudolph in a towel, and I reheated the food. The candles had burned down, but Holly seemed pleased as we sat at the table.

"Oh my God, I didn't even realize you had a Christmas-themed tablecloth!"

"I aim to please."

"Yes, you do," she said, scooping a pile of pasta onto her plate. "Dinner. Sex. Alcohol." She toasted me. "Merry Christmas to us!"

"I really need to stop fucking you on a weekday," I told Holly the next morning in between kisses. She was about to leave. "I want you all to myself for at least a weekend."

Actually, for my whole life.

"I'm going Christmas food shopping," she said. "The holiday baking party is tomorrow. You know, I should buy you a red suit with snowflakes all over it," she teased.

"Please don't."

"You know you want it!"

"I really don't. I'd rather have you in a red suit."

CHAPTER 47

Holly

As much as I wanted to play Mr. and Mrs. Claus in Owen's condo, I had to leave early the next morning. It was the day of the Quantum Cyber company holiday party. And *The Great Christmas Bake-Off* was providing the desserts.

Sometime in the night, the Romance Creative crew had moved all our baking stations down to the main lobby. Now all the contestants were assembled with their baking equipment. Hundreds of Owen's employees were downstairs to witness the filming.

"Welcome to another episode of *The Great Christmas Bake-Off*," Anastasia announced. "What's Christmas without a holiday party? The company holiday party is practically a meme at this point—drunken shenanigans, people making silly faces on the copier, awkward games. But for the Quantum Cyber employees, our bake-off contestants are here to turn up the volume on your holiday party! While the savory food is being catered, our bakers are bringing the desserts. The contestants have to make enough so that each employee can sample their sweets. The employees will vote on their favorites using the company app. The judges will give their feedback for the camera, then we'll announce the winners. Bakers, start your ovens."

I was a little thrown off by my baking station being laid out differently from usual, but soon I was back in the groove. I'd done catering in my early days of food service. Usually for dessert, we'd made cake and cut it up with scoops of ice cream. But I wanted something to impress. From dealing with the crowd a few days ago for the tree trimming, I knew my dessert ought to include alcohol. It also had to be something I could make to feed almost a thousand people.

The answer? Christmas cookie shots. As much as I loved my special sugar cookie recipe, I needed something to hold up to the Christmas cocktail I was going to pour into each cookie. I decided to make a couple of flavors. Otherwise it would be boring, and I was not boring!

The first cookie shot was a bourbon hot chocolate in a more robust sugar cookie that was crunchier and denser. The second was gingerbread cookie shot glasses holding a dirty gingerbread martini. And for the third option, because things are better in threes, I was going to make a fruity vodka pomegranate-rosemary cocktail in a fruitcake cookie cup, which was a modified oatmeal-cranberry cookie.

I did a quick calculation. That was a lot of cookies and a lot of alcohol. I wanted people to be able to have one of each; I didn't want people to have to choose. It was part of being a good hostess—and I couldn't forget that I needed to win this competition. When I had looked at my phone after my very pleasant evening with Owen, I'd found a ton of messages from the bank and credit card companies about missed payments.

I could not afford to lose.

"Game face, Holly," I told myself, striking a power pose. I was wearing another fun outfit. I had on fur-lined ankle boots and a short red coatdress like Christine Baranski in *How the Grinch Stole Christmas*. I had even put my hair in a shellacked updo like hers and glued a snowflake beauty spot on my cheek.

I was feeling the holiday spirit as I mixed up the sugar cookie dough. To make it dense, I used more flour and eggs. I put that dough in the fridge then started on the gingerbread cookie dough, zipping along on my baking high.

The only problem? My outfit was starting to get in the way. My sleeves had fur cuffs, and I was afraid they were going to shed and contaminate the food. I was in mid strip when Owen walked up with Rudolph.

"I don't know whether I should be worried or turned on," he said in that deep voice that gave me a flashback of last night.

"I have a bright-red romper on underneath it," I said, sticking my tongue out at him and handing him the coat to hang up somewhere away from my dough.

"I like your outfit," Owen said. "Come upstairs and let me take it off of you."

"I am making three thousand cookies," I told him. "I don't have time to christen your office."

"Three thousand? That seems excessive."

"You have a ton of employees," I said, measuring out flour.

Owen hovered next to me. "You smell like sugar cookies," he murmured. "You should skip this contest and come upstairs."

"I have baking to do!" I said and sent him away.

I took a deep breath and went back to my gingerbread cookies. I had to mix up several batches of the dough. Fortunately, I was used to making large batches of cookies. Hello, failing subscription baking service!

The gingerbread was spicy and slightly sweet with a hint of bitterness from the molasses. I stuffed it into the fridge next to the sugar cookie dough then started on the last set of cookies. I mixed bags of dried cranberries, macadamia nuts, and some oatmeal into the cookie dough, turning it caramel colored. It, too, went into the fridge. Then I strategized. I was going to bake the cookies into cups, line them with chocolate to create a moisture barrier, then fill them with booze.

I had mini muffin tins to form the cookie shot glasses. The oatmeal cookies and the gingerbread cookies I wasn't too worried about; they were hardy. Sugar cookies could be finicky, however. I didn't want them to taste raw. I made balls of dough, careful not to overwork them, and put each one into the mini muffin pan, slid them into the oven, and crossed my fingers.

My gamble paid off. I took them out halfway through the cooking time and smashed them in the cups, creating little bowls. Then I put them back in the oven, and when the timer went off, I had perfect little sugar cookie shot glasses.

Romance Creative had given us three ovens each since we had to bake for a crowd. I was grateful, though it was a lot to juggle. I was quickly running out of counter space.

"Coming through!" Amber shouted, practically running as she carried a huge sheet cake. I grabbed my cookie pans before she could accidentally knock them off the table. I hissed; they were still hot.

"Stop trying to sabotage me," I snapped at my stepsister.

"I'm not trying to sabotage you," she retorted. "Stop being so full of yourself. Just because you're sleeping with Owen—and yes, everyone knows—doesn't mean people are out to get you. Get over yourself!"

"I'm not full of myself," I countered hotly. "This is the third time you've tried to ruin my dessert!"

"I don't care about a winning the Christmas bake-off," Amber said. "I'm here to snag a billionaire boyfriend."

"I don't see how," I said, taking the cookie cups out of the pans to cool.

"He's going to get tired of you soon enough. Besides, I know his habits. I know what he likes," Amber insisted.

"No you don't."

"I've been following him," she said. "I have a lot more material for my scrapbook. See?" she said, taking out her phone and swiping through several pictures of Owen.

"You are a lunatic."

"I'm doing what has to be done," she said, tossing her head with a tinkling of the bells on her costume. "Just like how Meghan Markle went after her prince, I'm going after my winter prince. He and I are going to have a beautiful wedding. I have my dress all picked out. My dad said he was going to pay for my dream wedding to my dream man. And Owen is the man I want."

"Whatever."

I stewed as I finished making the next thousand cookie cups. As much as I loved Christmas baking, this holiday party bake-off was becoming a little tedious. Especially since Amber was crisscrossing the room being obnoxious. She was wearing her elf-on-the-shelf outfit, and it jangled with every step she took. Between that and the ticking clock, I was starting to feel slightly frazzled. Maybe I had been too ambitious.

I had the last set of cookies to go—the oatmeal cookies. I babysat them while they baked. As they cooled, I started mixing the cocktails.

First was the syrup. I could have bought ginger syrup, but I wanted a nice kick, so I was making it from scratch. I chopped up several pounds of ginger and set it to simmer in a pot, where it burbled happily.

Then I started with the bourbon hot chocolate. Using two huge soup stock pots, I slowly brought milk up to temperature, whisking in the chocolate powder. Since the cookie was very sweet, I only added a scant amount of sugar. I wanted these to be boozy. What was the point of an alcoholic dessert if you didn't get a buzz? So I took the hot chocolate off the heat to cool before I added the bourbon.

Next was the fruity cocktail. The onlookers, many of them taking an extended lunch break that was turning into an early holiday party break, cheered as I poured bottle after bottle of vodka into a big tub. I glugged in gallons of pomegranate and cranberry juice then smoked sprigs of rosemary, rolling them in my hands to release the oils before throwing them in.

"It's beautiful!" someone called out. More cheering.

Last was the dirty gingerbread martini. I wheeled over a crate of Kahlúa and another of Baileys Irish Cream. That went into the tub first then the vodka. This cocktail was just alcohol, alcohol, and more alcohol with some flavored syrup. I tasted it.

"*Man*," I said, the back of my throat burning, "that is strong."

I checked the clock. I needed to coat my cookies. I set white and dark chocolate to melt on the stove as I mixed the bourbon with the now-room-temperature hot chocolate. The lobby was getting crowded. Dana was telling everyone to start lining up.

The chocolate didn't take too long to melt, I was happy to see. Using a plastic brush, I started coating the cookies, trying not to rush as I painted the inside of each cookie cup. I decided to pour the cocktails as needed. I was seriously afraid the chocolate wasn't going to hold up for very long.

All the contestants were rushing back and forth putting finishing touches on their dishes. I was almost done; I had beautiful stacks of cookies all lined up and ready to go. I was giving my cocktails another mix when Amber ran past my station, bells jingling. I saw what was about to happen a second before her hand "accidentally" caught the pan of extra white chocolate. It flew into an arc toward my cookies.

"I'm *so soorrryy*!" Amber said. I heard it in slow motion, and I dove in front of the stacks of cookies, sacrificing myself for the pastry shot glasses.

I was splashed from head to toe in white chocolate. But better me than the cookies. I stood there, blinking.

"So this is what you're after, Owen?" an upper-class voice scoffed. "Honestly, it's almost a cliché."

CHAPTER 48

Owen

I prided myself on being a decisive person. Once I decided that I wanted something or that I was going to invest in something or develop a new technology, I didn't waffle; I committed and, more importantly, followed through.

I wanted Holly. There was no reason I could see why it wouldn't be a good idea to spend the rest of my life with her. Therefore, the only logical solution was to start shopping for engagement rings and make her my wife before New Year's.

"Geez, you really fell hard for her," Walker said when he stepped into the elevator with me as I was taking Rudolph back upstairs to my office.

I jerked my head up. "You don't know what's going on."

"Either Holly worked her Christmas magic, or the wicked witch of Christmas cast a spell on you, causing you to hum Christmas carols."

"I'm not humming," I scoffed.

"Except you are." Walker pressed his phone and played back an audio recording of someone humming. Rudolph cocked his ear and whined.

"You can't tell it's me."

"Rudolph knows who it is!" Walker laughed. "Are you ready for doggie daycare?" he said, riling up the dog. Rudolph barked playfully. "You are?"

"He ate all my dinner yesterday, so don't act like he's so awesome," I said. Walker snickered.

Rudolph, to his credit, did follow me out of the elevator when I whistled to him.

"He seems to have been learning a lot in doggie daycare," Walker commented as we walked down the hall to the C-suite offices.

When we approached my office, Rudolph stopped in his tracks.

"I guess I spoke too soon," Walker joked. "What's the matter, Rudolph, buddy? Do you need to go out?"

"Or maybe he's scared," I said. There, in my office, was Sloane. She was leaning against my desk.

"'Tis the season for winning the *TechBiz* contest," she said when she saw me. She sauntered up and kissed Walker on the cheek then me, though I would have bet anything she didn't try to feel up Walker's Christmas package.

"I'm here to do the walk-through," she said. "I heard you have a holiday party today. Since I'm in charge of the company culture rankings, I needed to be here. Though sometimes people do really naughty things at holiday parties."

"We keep a level of professionalism at all our company-sponsored events," I said firmly.

"That's no fun," she said with a pout and flicked her hair. It smelled like expensive imported perfume. Perhaps it was supposed to be alluring. But I was now firmly in the camp of wanting my woman to smell like sugar, spice, and spruce trees.

"Why don't you give me a tour through your office," she said, "then we'll go join the party."

I spent the next several hours with Sloane. First I gave her the grand tour of the office. Fortunately, Walker and Beck were there through parts of it. Then she interviewed several of my employees, asking how they liked the company. As the CEO, I was not in the room for that, so I had a reprieve. Still, it grated on me that Sloane was here. I wanted to spend every waking moment with Holly.

"I had lunch ordered for you all," my secretary said helpfully. "From the nice French restaurant on 42nd Street."

The caterers set up the lunch while Sloane conducted her last interview.

"Are you hungry?" I asked politely when she was finished.

"How thoughtful," she said, stroking my cheek. "I was just texting your mom about what a wonderful son she raised."

We literally went on one date. Why are people so delusional?

"Interesting," was all I said.

I was going to try to keep the meeting strictly professional. But then Walker and Beck texted, bailing out. They had emergency meetings scheduled with their brother Greg about an investment side deal they were involved in.

Owen: *I'll never forget this. I was going to name my first child after you but no more.*
Walker: *You'll be fine. Just sit on the opposite side of the table.*

Sitting on the opposite side didn't help much.

"This is a very romantic date," Sloane purred as she dished some of the pear and endive salad onto her plate. She ate it slowly, staring at me the whole time. I jumped when her bare foot stretched out to rub my crotch.

"How's your food?" she asked.

"Fine."

"Don't tell me you're still hung up on that chunky little baker," she said with a laugh. "Honestly, Owen, you know your parents won't approve. Not only that, but you can't take her to a nice party. Look what she wears! She might show up to the *TechBiz* black-tie party in a cheap dollar-store gingerbread maid outfit."

"It's not any of your concern."

"But it is your concern if I don't give you high marks in culture. Sure, your company has the highest salaries and with the gene therapy collaboration with PharmaTech, you have high marks in innovation. But your company culture marks are terrible. If I were you, I'd want to impress me, the person with all the power," she said.

"Wouldn't it be unethical if I agreed to go along with what you're implying?" I said through gritted teeth.

"As if this competition is ethical." She snorted. "Honestly, there are so many bribes floating around. Like this very nice lunch."

"Speaking of food," I said, wiping my mouth. "They're going to start judging soon. Can't miss it."

"I did want something a little different for my dessert." Sloane walked around the table and ran her hands up my suit jacket. "You sure you don't need a little stress relief, Mr. Billionaire? You have a lot of weight on those broad shoulders."

"I'm perfectly fine, thank you," I said, twisting out of her grasp and opening the door. "After you."

She sauntered beside me, using any and every excuse to touch me. It wasn't a long elevator ride, but my jaw was clenched the entire time. We arrived in the main lobby just in time to see Holly get coated with white chocolate.

"You need to go sit over at the judges' table. We need to start filming," Dana said, hurrying over to me. She looked Holly up and down. "Holly, honestly. Go change. You're one of the first to present."

"Are you all right?" I asked her after Dana left.

"Totally," she said, rolling her eyes. She was caked in white chocolate.

Sloane looked between us then ran her hand down my back, letting it linger at my hip. "I'll come find you later, Owen."

Holly looked annoyed after Sloane sauntered off.

"Do you need to use my shower?" I asked her.

She sighed. "I need a long soak, but I would never be able to finish in time. The show must go on." She picked up her red velvet coat.

"You're going to ruin that."

"Actually, I ruined it four hours into a nine-hour marathon baking session when I wasn't paying attention and splattered egg everywhere."

"I didn't realize baking was such a hazardous sport."

"That's why I have a hat," she said, putting the red Santa hat on her head and tightening the belt on the coatdress. She blew me a kiss. "You can lick all this off me later."

I started.

She laughed. "That perked up your south pole, didn't it?"

I sat at the judges' table, all my employees gawking as the first contestants presented their dishes. Holly's was definitely the most imaginative.

"This is really cool," Nick said. "Like very cool."

"I love that you can taste all the flavors," Anu remarked. "The cookie isn't too doughy; it's the perfect texture and a great counterpoint to the cocktail shots."

"Also, kudos for not skimping on the alcohol," I said, toasting her with the vodka cranberry shot. All my employees hollered.

"Hey, everyone," Anastasia said after the last contestant had presented. "The judges aren't deciding this round, you are. You've heard their comments. So vote on the app, then let's party. Hit it!"

Christmas rock music blared out of the sound system. I milled around, talking to my employees as they sampled the desserts. Holly's cookie shots were a big hit. I toasted several of the employees in line, and we did cookie shots together.

"Coolest CEO ever!" one programmer said, taking a selfie with me.

I wanted to talk to Holly, but Dana motioned to me.

"She wants more B-roll, I bet," Holly said.

Before I left, I whispered in her ear. "Don't forget I'm licking that all off of you."

CHAPTER 49

Holly

"So you're the famous Holly," Sloane said later. The line had died down somewhat. I was sticky and smelled like chocolate, and I felt sweaty and dumpy beside her.

Sloane's lip curled as she looked me up and down. "Just because he's sleeping with you doesn't mean he wants to marry you," she said. "You with your cookies and your silly outfits. You're not the type of girl a man like Owen marries. He can't take you to a nice fundraiser. You're the train wreck that's freaky in bed. He doesn't want to show you off to his friends."

"Oh, you must have pegged me for the wrong type of girl. See, I don't fight over men. You want Owen? Fine. He can make his own choices. He's a big boy. *Very big*, as I would assume you know—but maybe not," I said as her expression darkened.

"He's just using you," Sloane sneered before she left. "He's going to get his jollies, and then come New Year's, the resolutions will hit, and he'll realize he needs to make better life choices. And those choices won't include baked goods or bakers."

"Don't listen to her," Fiona said. I poured a cookie shot for myself and one for her. "Maybe she'll get run over by a reindeer."

"I'll toast to that."

I left the rest of the drinks and cookie shot materials out so people could help themselves. It looked like I'd severely overbaked. There were still piles of cookies and enough alcohol to take a bath in. Which I still sorely needed.

As I walked around the party, I took video for my Instagram story. I went to one of the out-of-the-way niches, hoping it would be a little quieter. The music was booming. I wasn't the only contestant that had supplied copious amounts of alcohol. It was only six in the evening, and the Quantum Cyber lobby was hopping like a club at midnight.

I was intent on recording myself, explaining why exactly I was covered in chocolate, when something big appeared in my peripheral vision. I jumped, and Owen grabbed me, clapping a hand over my mouth before I could scream. I darted my tongue out and licked his palm.

He started to pull me to him. "Covered in chocolate, remember," I said, pushing him away. "Don't want to mess up your suit. Though later, if you aren't tired of me, we can drink the rest of the booze, get naked, and smear chocolate all over each other."

"I'd rather do it now," he said, kissing me.

"You're supposed to be schmoozing with your employees."

"I know," he whispered. "But I'm really horny."

I was immediately wet. "I'm not sure how to help with that," I said, fidgeting. His eyes were an intense, deep blue.

"Really, you aren't?"

"Someone could see. Also, I'm covered in chocolate," I reminded him.

"This niche is pretty out of the way," he countered, "and you're only covered in chocolate on the front."

"What if we get caught?"

"Guess we'll have to be quick." He kissed my neck and turned me around.

"Someone will hear," I protested as his hand pushed between my legs. But I didn't protest all that hard. I was aching for him. My panties were drenched through. The music was loud, and I could tell Owen was going to make me come quickly.

"You can't tell me you don't want it," he whispered in my ear.

I did kind of want it. Actually, there was no kind of about it. I wanted his cock right now.

"I'm wearing a romper," I hissed.

"It's thin fabric," he murmured in my ear. He reached down and tore the crotch, his fingers pushing inside to stroke my pussy. I bit down on a whimper. Owen unzipped his pants. I felt his thick cock tease my pussy through the ripped slit in my clothes.

"I love how wet you are," he whispered, that deep voice sending shock waves straight to my pussy as he teased me with his cock. He ripped open a condom packet, rolled it on, then thrust into me. I moaned.

The sound system blared "All I Want for Christmas."

All I wanted was Owen's cock, and he was giving it to me. I bit down another moan as he thrust into me. My tits tingled as his cock filled me. I whimpered again, and he ripped the romper a little more so he could rub my clit.

I gripped the edge of the bench, hoping I didn't get chocolate on anything as Owen fucked me from behind. I spread my legs as much as I could, needing him to go deeper. I let out a cry. Owen clamped his hand over my mouth again, the other digging into my hip as he fucked me.

Just the fact that we were in a semipublic place and could get caught any minute heightened the pleasure for me. I bucked against him. I felt myself tighten, and then I came, Owen finishing quickly after.

"See," he breathed. "Quick and dirty."

I adjusted my coatdress. My face was flushed. "I think I'm the only dirty one."

Owen still looked cool and collected as he readjusted his suit.

"That was good," he growled in my ear. "But I think I'm going to need more."

CHAPTER 50

Owen

"I'm sort of impressed that you didn't get chocolate all over your suit," Holly said as we walked back into the thick of the party. "Though I'm also kind of sad. I wanted to lick it off of you." She giggled.

I got her another drink. She fielded questions from my employees, and I went to schmooze. I did actually need to have some face time. I spent the next few hours avoiding Sloane and trying to find an excuse to get close to Holly.

Around nine, Dana motioned to me. "We're making the announcement," she said.

I went back to the judges' table with Anu and Nick.

Anastasia tapped on the microphone. "Thank you to the contestants and to everyone who voted. We have a clear winner: Holly with her Christmas cookie shots!"

All my employees cheered.

"Thanks, everyone, for an awesome holiday party!"

Most of my employees left, but a few stuck around. By the time I'd finished talking to the last one, Holly was gone. I seriously hoped she was upstairs waiting for me. Our quick and dirty sex had only dumped gasoline on the fire of my lust for her.

I waved to the cleaning crew then went to collect Rudolph and take him out for a walk. He was a little more coordinated now. It was insane how fast puppies grew, and I jogged beside him, hoping to expend more of his energy.

"Especially after you ate enough food for an adult man," I told the puppy. "You need to work all of that off."

"What in the world!"

Crap.

My parents came out of a restaurant.

"You see?" my mom said to my father. "She's corrupted him. It's just like Sloane said."

"I have other things to do tonight," I snapped at them.

"It's that baker. She's degraded you," my mother said, shaking her head.

"You can't trust women like Holly," my father added. "Sloane is perfect. She loves you. Holly is just using you. Haven't you seen the pictures she posted on social media? You'd never see Sloane pulling a stunt like that."

"Holly is a grown woman," I said, trying to stay cold and calm. "What she does is her business."

"But you know you can't trust her to be a good mother."

I thought about her with the Svensson brothers, how patient and loving she had been.

"Actually, I think she would be a great mother. As to whether you two would be good grandparents, well, that's up in the air."

"Honestly, Owen!"

"It's all that sugar," my father said. turning up his nose. I turned on my heel and left, not even saying goodbye.

Jack had been right. I needed to take a break from them. They were liars. They lied about the fact that Belle had been the one who paid for my college education, not them. They had been lying about Sloane, and now they were trying to act as if Holly was a terrible person, even though she was the best thing that had ever happened to me.

My phone buzzed with a message from her.

Holly: *Ready to come lick the chocolate off of my cookies?*

There was a very erotic picture of her with her face cropped off. I would have known her body anywhere, even with her full tits covered in chocolate. She wasn't wearing anything else.

Holly: *Better come hurry before this gets all over your bedspread.*

I went up to the condo. I was half undressed by the time I got upstairs to the bedroom.

"You sure came in a hurry," Holly said, swiping a finger down the chocolate sauce on her tits and popping the finger into her mouth. She was still wearing the Santa hat, and she rose seductively up on the bed.

"I want to ride your sleigh," she said as I undid my pants and dropped them to the floor.

CHAPTER 51

Holly

I could never get enough of Owen's big cock and washboard abs. Seriously, I was obsessed. It was too bad I wasn't an artist, or I would have drawn pictures of them.

"But maybe I'll make a cock-and-ball cookie, full sized," I said, thinking out loud.

"A cock-and-ball cookie?" Owen said, burying his face in my tits, licking the chocolate sauce off.

"Why not?" I gasped as his fingers pushed between my legs, stroking my aching pussy. "Sometimes I just want a frosting-covered cock in my mouth."

Owen growled and pushed me back on the bed. "You keep talking dirty like that, naughty girl, and you're not getting anything nice for Christmas."

"I already have it," I said, moaning as he stroked me, his large hand rubbing the wetness around, teasing my clit. I spread my legs wider for him and whimpered as he kissed

286 · ALINA JACOBS

me, his tongue tangling in my mouth while his fingers made little rolling motions in my pussy.

It was enough to put me teetering on the edge. Owen's hand moved to rub my clit, sending me free-falling over.

"Oh my god," I whimpered as I sprawled on the bed.

Owen licked the last of the icing off me. Then he kissed his way down, down to press his mouth against my pussy. I moaned, needing to feel him inside me. He grabbed my hips, taking his time as he brought me close to the edge again.

"I want your cock this time," I whispered, pushing him off before he could make me come again.

I shoved him back onto the bed, and he went willingly. My pussy was aching for him. I straddled him.

"I told you I want to ride your sleigh."

He wrapped one hand around my waist, the other caressing my tit and rolling the nipple between his fingers. I took his cock in my hand, sliding my palm along it greedily, needing his length in my pussy. I rubbed his cock in the silky wetness, moaning as the length slid along the hot, tight flesh.

Owen grabbed a condom, rolling it on with one hand as he swiped three fingers in my pussy.

"Better hold on, Santa, because you're in for a wild ride."

I pushed him back down on the bed. "We're going to the North Pole and back," I said, angling myself then sliding down on his length. His cock was huge inside me.

"Oh my god, Owen, this feels so good. You feel so good in my pussy," I moaned. I rose on trembling thighs then slid back down, his entire length filling me.

Owen grabbed my hips, fingers digging into my ass. He held me up then rose slightly to meet me as I came down.

I tipped forward to press my mouth to his, my tits rubbing against the ridges of his muscular chest. Owen pushed me up then slid me down on his cock again, making sure to angle me so that the length slid against my clit. I moaned, needing it harder and faster.

He flipped us over, and I wrapped my hand around his neck and my legs around his waist as he jackhammered into me, his cock robbing against my clit with every thrust. As he fucked me, Owen tipped his head down to nip and roll a nipple in his mouth.

He licked his way back up to kiss me, taking my mouth as he filled me with his cock. I whimpered and strained against him as wave after wave of pleasure cascaded over me. My body was still trembling as Owned finished soon after.

"If I could bottle that up and sell it," I said against his neck, "I'd be richer than you!"

All I wanted to do was lie in Owen's bed and have him do that thing with his tongue again and again. But the bake-off called. Literally.

"Heller?" I mumbled into the phone when it rang early the next morning.

"Where are you?" Morticia said.

"Uh, half on Owen's cock," I said, shifting my legs. "Why do you ask?"

"You can't see me, but I'm crossing myself right now," she said. "We have to go shopping."

"I'm going to be perfectly honest with you: I drank a lot of alcohol last night," I said.

Owen sat up and ran a hand through his hair. Even after sleeping and copious amounts of sex, he still looked like the god of winter. I, however, had a Santa hat literally glued to my hair with a combination of hair spray, chocolate, and lord knew what else.

Owen pressed a kiss to my neck.

"I need to wash my hair," I complained.

"I know," Morticia said smugly. "That's why I woke you up an hour and a half early."

After spending the next forty-five minutes using a variety of cleansers to get the chocolate out of my hair, I made it down to the lobby just in time. There were only four of us left: me, Fiona, Amber, and Jamila. Rita had been sent home the night before. She hadn't been able to make enough of her coconut cream pie snowmen.

"You think I didn't see you," Amber hissed in my ear when we assembled. "I see everything. I'm always watching him."

"Okay, Ms. Creepy," I said, slurping my peppermint mocha latte and wishing I were back in bed with Owen. It was Saturday. Why did I have to be out on a Saturday? And so early too.

"I'm going to make you an herb compress for your face," Morticia said. "You look puffy."

"Thanks, dear friend, for that confidence boost."

"Also, I'm going to make an herb bath for your hoo-ha. It's seen a workout. And if you're putting cupcakes, cookies, and God knows what else down there, you need to clean it out."

"It's self-cleaning."

"Not that self-cleaning," she said. "I have a good recipe I got from the old Korean lady down the street from me."

I needed a showstopping dessert to win. On the walk to the store, I deleted several nasty email and text messages from the credit card companies about all the debt I had accrued.

Millions of people were watching *The Great Christmas Bake-Off*, and I had new people signing up for my subscription baking box every day. Even though I had more customers, I was nowhere near breaking even, let alone turning a profit.

"Ugh, it was such a stupid idea," I said, loading up on apples in the grocery store.

"Maybe you can start a new business," Morticia suggested.

"I did have this idea for candy-cane dildos."

"Or Penny might give you a job. Your videos drive a lot of traffic to the *Vanity Rag* website. You could do a little baking channel."

"I should probably try and get a real job," I said dejectedly. "And start chipping away at my debt." I took a breath. "Or maybe I'll win the bake-off. I made it this far, right?"

"You're spending a lot of time with Owen. Don't let him distract you," Morticia warned.

"I'm not! Besides, he's not a distraction, he's inspiration! Really, though, I want to dress him up as Mr. Darcy."

The next *Bake-Off* episode was Regency themed. That meant Jane Austin and Mr. Darcy and ices and baked apples. Now all I wanted to do was curl up in front of a fire with a mug of rummy eggnog and a Jane Austen novel.

I sighed as I walked with Morticia, looking for nice fruits. In the Regency period, Great Britain had been flexing its world power. People were experimenting more with spices in baking, though not much. Cooking and baking were still done in the home, at least in upper-middle-class homes like Austen's. Desserts like apple dumplings and pudding were popular. Ices were a big thing, too, as were starchy desserts.

Planning my dessert gave me a boost. So did the caffeine hitting my system.

When we went back to the tower, I put away my ingredients. Then I changed into a sexy costume and went out to take pictures. I had plenty of baking leftovers, and I did a photo shoot in the park of me eating cookies in a dress too revealing for the cold. I uploaded the best of the pictures to Instagram and ate a piece of cake as I walked back to the building.

An elf grabbed me as I was turning onto Owen's street.

"Stay away from him," the elf warned.

Amber? Sloane? Nope. It was Owen's mom.

"As I've said multiple times," I said in exasperation, "Owen's an adult. He can make his own decisions."

The elf smiled cruelly. "Oh, I'm not telling you to stay away from him for his sake. I'm telling you for yours."

"Is that a threat?"

"Hardly. Owen's just using you. He's never going to marry you."

"I haven't really thought about marriage," I retorted. "I'm just here for a good time."

"Good, because so is he. He has every intention of marrying Sloane. He's just using you. Sloane is going to guarantee him a win in the *TechBiz* competition. They already have a deal. You don't stand a chance."

CHAPTER 52

Owen

Since Holly was out shopping, I went down to my office. There were a few people in there working as well. They waved happily when they saw me. That was new. Usually my employees were a little tense around me. Holly's ideas seemed to be working.

It was relaxing in my office. The minimalist Christmas decorations Holly had put up had a nice vibe. It was, dare I say, cozy. It would have been nicer if Holly were there, though. I managed to complete several hours of work before Walker popped his head in.

"I'm heading out to Harrogate. Several of my brothers are on winter break from college. Your brothers should be out too."

"They're doing a special engineering class, so they have to stay on campus for a bit longer. I expect I'll see them soon," I said.

It would be nice to see my two youngest brothers, I thought after Walker left. They were almost done with university. We did need to find them something to do. What was not going to happen was them running around partying and spending money.

My phone beeped. Holly had uploaded a new picture to her Instagram. She was wearing a poofy white skirt with a low-cut top. Perched on her head was a black top hat. She was blowing a kiss to the camera. In another picture, she was biting into a cookie.

My phone vibrated with a text from her.

Holly: *Don't get jealous of the picture! I saved the extra-special outfit just for you! When you're done working, come and get it.*

That was all I needed to be done.

One of my employees waved to me on the way out. "Hey, Mr. Frost."

"Owen is fine."

"You said yesterday at the holiday party to let you know if there was anything you could do to make it better to work here?"

I nodded, trying to keep the impatience off my face.

"Well, we were thinking that if we had a restaurant here, that would really help productivity."

"The hotel has a restaurant," I reminded him.

"It's fussy and slow," his coworker interjected. "Frost Tower has that awesome restaurant in it."

"I'll see what I can do," I stated. The engineers flashed me a thumbs-up, and I hightailed it upstairs.

Holly was waiting for me in the bedroom.

"I had the nice snowgirl costume and the naughty one," Holly said.

The lingerie she was wearing was one piece, but that was where the wholesomeness ended. The whole thing was made out of white fishnet. A black silk belt encircled her waist, emphasizing the hourglass shape of her curves. The outlines of her nipples were visible through the fine mesh. The piece ended in a high white lace collar. Framing her pussy was another panel of lace. She was wearing thigh-high white stockings held up with garters attached to the black silk belt. Three black buttons pointed a trail down to the curve of her tits. The top hat was perched jauntily on her head.

All I wanted to do was rip the outfit off her.

"I definitely don't want you posting this online," I said to her.

"This is all for you, Owen," she said, doing a sexy little dance that enticed me to the bed.

She didn't have to coax. My shirt was already on the floor, and my pants weren't far behind. I pushed her back on the bed, sending the hat rolling aside. I kissed her hard, pressing my aching cock against her. Holly moaned and strained against me. I nuzzled her neck then kissed down to suck her tits through the fabric.

"I might have to rip this off of you," I said hoarsely. "I hope you don't have any strong emotional attachment to it."

"It's Christmas themed!" she said as I caressed her thighs, nibbling and teasing her nipples through the white fabric. "I love all my Christmas outfits equally."

"I'll buy you a new one," I growled, needing her immediately.

"But this one has an extra-special surprise."

She gasped as I kissed my way down to the lace panel that framed the V where her legs met. I spread them, pushing my hand against her pussy as I kissed her. Holly moaned, fingers tangling in my hair. Then I noticed the surprise.

"Crotchless!" Holly said, winking up at me. "For your convenience."

"You're the one who's going to benefit," I told her as I stroked her, satisfied when she let out a loud moan. She whimpered and pressed herself against my hand. I ripped the thin white fishnet; her tits spilled out. I caressed one and kissed down the white lace to her pussy, pressing my mouth to the hot flesh. I held her hips down as she wiggled against me.

I hooked one stocking-clad leg over my shoulder then took my time as I explored every inch of her. I knew Holly was close when her breathing became more erratic and her legs trembled. I flicked my tongue against her clit then licked her hard, feeling smug when she cried out as she came.

"I'm going to be inside you the next time you do that," I told her as she lay on the bed, gasping from the aftereffect of the orgasm. I put on a condom, stroking her. I wanted her to be aching and pleading for me.

When I grabbed her hips and pushed inside her, she whimpered. She clung to my shoulders as I fucked her, making sure to hit her clit with every stroke. I thrust into her a few times more, then Holly came with a cry, her arms wrapped around my neck. She panted sloppy kisses along my jaw.

"Merry Christmas," she said. "I actually had another present for you."

"Oh yeah?" I kissed her neck. It was finally the weekend, and I wanted to stay in bed with her all day.

"We're doing a Regency theme for the next episode of the bake-off. I was going to buy you a Mr. Darcy outfit since Jane Austen's novels are mostly set during the Regency period."

I tried to keep the panic off my face.

"But I figured you'd like a tasty meat pie instead!" she said with a laugh at my horror.

"Good choice," I growled, pushing her back onto the bed.

After showering, I followed Holly downstairs. She petted Rudolph then opened the oven. The smell of something delicious wafted out.

"Ta-da! By the magic of TV, I bring you meat pies."

"I can't believe you had this cooking while we were upstairs. You could have made poor Rudolph homeless."

"Good thing you were on your A game then! But then I'm not the one that incinerated cookies," she retorted, sliding the small meat pies onto a cooling rack. Then she did some trickery with two plates and flipped the pies around, and suddenly they were all neatly out of the pans. "Good thing you worked up an appetite!"

CHAPTER 53

"I can't believe we're doing the bake-off on a Sunday," Owen complained early the next morning.

"I'm excited," I said. He pulled me back down on the bed. I kissed him then lightly batted his hands away. "I have to change."

"You look fine."

"I'm literally not wearing anything."

Owen chuckled. "Just how I like it!"

For the Regency Christmas bake-off episode, I was wearing an Elizabeth Bennet costume. With the empire waist and minimal petticoats, it was a lot roomier than my other outfits. I'd even begged Morticia to put my hair in an updo like the women in *Pride and Prejudice*.

"Welcome to another episode of *The Great Christmas Bake-Off*," Anastasia said. She, too, had dressed up in a long flowing gown. "It's a rite of passage for every girl to read and fall in love with Jane Austen novels, and Mr. Darcy is, of course, the dream man."

Fiona whistled.

"Too bad none of the guys dressed up!" Anu called out.

Nick shrank in his seat. The camera's panned to Owen. He shrugged.

"While Jane Austen was fairly sparse in her descriptions of food," Anastasia continued, "we do have historical records of what was served during the Regency period. We're all looking forward to some inspired Regency Christmas desserts. Let's start baking!"

In the Regency period, people tended to do a lot of boiling—boiling meats, boiling fruits, boiling puddings. It made sense, as they didn't have antibiotics or filtered water. But still. Boiled dough wrapped around apples was not the most enticing dessert.

I hadn't fully planned my dish because I had been busy with Owen, but I did know that in addition to the dumplings, I was going to make ices and ice creams. Though overdone, the Regency period was obsessed with flavored ices. Jane Austen even mentioned apricot ices in her novel *The Beautiful Cassandra*. The thing I loved most about Jane Austen's novels was how idyllic they were. A few well-to-do families in a cozy village—that was how I liked my romance novels, thank you very much.

I looked over at Amber. She was going very avant-garde. She had a distillery set up, and judging from the smell, she was charring fruit in the oven.

I was going to go in a less-crazy direction with my dessert. The plan was to make an apple dumpling with a honey pistachio ice cream, to capture the nuts that they ate a lot of back then. I was going to boil the apple dumpling first, weirdly enough, but then I was going to deep-fry it and crack it open like an egg, nestling the ice cream inside with gooseberries for tartness, like a cozy little winter nest. The presentation might not be the most extravagant, but I was going to make it look pleasing with how I arranged the little bites. To give it an extra flair, I had special china I'd found at a thrift store. It was old porcelain with hand-painted birds and flowers around the edges.

Since the dumpling was the start of the dish, I first made the dough. Instead of pastry dough, I was going authentic; in Jane Austen's time they'd used suet, which is animal fat and flour. I rolled out the dough as thin as I dared. Then I chopped up apples and put them on the stove to stew with cinnamon, nutmeg, brown sugar, and other spices. I also chopped up a pear and added that with a splash of lemon juice. The filling bubbled away. If it was too moist, the dumpling would be mushy, so I needed it to reduce. I added some cognac then stirred some more and lowered the heat.

I needed to start my ice cream. To make it super creamy, I was going to use liquid nitrogen, which was so cold that it didn't give water crystals a chance to form in the ice cream. I chopped up the pistachios and mixed in the local honey I'd bought.

Anastasia was going around to each station, Zane following her with the camera, filming her as she talked to each contestant.

"And what are you making?" Anastasia asked Amber.

My stepsister had been passing me dirty looks all morning. I knew she was going to try to sabotage me again. At least since she was talking to Anastasia, she couldn't do anything right now. She was saying something inane about the Regency period.

I tried to tune her out and concentrate on the ice cream. I needed everything to be perfect before I made it. The liquid nitrogen could freeze skin instantly. I'd used it in the restaurants where I'd worked and had had safety training. I knew Amber was going to try something while I used it. I was not going to have her freeze one of my fingers off.

"I'm using these oranges for the Smoking Bishop cocktail," Amber was saying. "See the oranges I charred? Oops! Ha ha! Dropped a couple. Good thing I made extra!"

A Smoking Bishop—now there was a Christmas drink. *Owen might actually like it*, I thought. It was similar to a mulled wine that used roasted oranges with cloves and had a smoky, masculine taste. Maybe for the Christmas party that I'd hinted about throwing? That reminded me, I needed to run through the checklist of the Quantum Cyber winter festival.

As I measured out the heavy cream, I smelled something acrid burning. Amber had sure screwed up those oranges.

"Oh my God!" Anastasia shouted.

Wildly, I looked around then down. "My dress!" I screamed. The hem of the long dress was in flames, a smoking orange scorching the floor next to it. "Help!" I panicked, searching for a fire extinguisher.

Suddenly, Owen was *there*. He picked up the pot of water and dumped it all over me.

"Are you all right?" he said, holding me, searching my eyes for pain.

"I'm fine," I said, refusing to act as shaken as I felt. "I'm a baker. I get burned, no big deal. Though I don't usually have people trying to kill me in the kitchen!" I said, raising my voice at Amber.

"No I didn't!" her eyes glittered with crocodile tears. "We're stepsisters! I would never hurt you."

CHAPTER 54

Owen

I felt sick looking down at Holly's dress. She was acting unconcerned, but I could tell she was freaked out. I was furious. But almost losing her to the bake-off, of all things, did cement that I definitely wasn't going to survive the rest of my life without her.

"That was close," Anastasia said.

"Thankfully Owen was here to save the day!" Holly hugged me. She was soaking wet and shivering. I wrapped her in my arms.

"Maybe you should just call it quits."

"The bake-off must go on. But hey, at least the food's not ruined!" she quipped, wringing out the dress.

I had been planning to go up to my office and work, but after Holly's narrow escape, I stayed in the studio, my eyes on her the entire time.

Morticia brought her a new dress, and Holly finished the rest of her dessert. I was a little concerned that the stress had

304 • ALINA JACOBS

affected her when I saw her boiling her apple dumplings. But when they had cooled, she dunked them in a tempura batter and deep-fried them.

"I'm interested to see the finished dessert," Anu said.

"She doesn't seem all that frazzled for almost burning alive," I remarked, still concerned that I'd almost lost her.

"Please," Nick snorted. "The amount of time's I've almost set myself and my kitchen on fire? It's insane."

"It's all part of being a chef," Anu told me.

Though she hadn't been part of the fire incident, Jamila seemed the most frazzled.

"She's trying to make an ice," Anu said. "She doesn't have enough time left for that. It's flavored water that you have to churn."

Her ice still wasn't quite frozen when it was set before us. Poor Jamila was in tears, and Anu sighed as she looked at the dish.

"It's beautiful," she said, "but you have to be conscious of the clock. Normally you all are given an entire day, but today I understand that it was only a couple of hours."

"Add a little alcohol to this and call it a cocktail," Nick said, slurping a spoonful.

"That is the other thing," Anu told her. "When things go awry, you have to accept it then readjust. Just be honest with yourself when you miscalculate."

Holly was next.

"This is exquisite," Anu said, admiring the dessert. The large deep-fried apple dumpling had been split open like a geode. Nestled inside was a greenish ice cream, cubes of gooseberry gelatin, and a little sphere of a milky custard. It was garnished with a drizzle of a tart red sauce.

"This is so refined yet composed, and the flavors are magnificent." Anu congratulated her.

"This is how you do ice cream," Nick said.

I took a bite; it was good, not too sweet. "Refined" was a good word for it.

Holly beamed.

"It does sort of feel like reading a Jane Austen novel, if that makes any sense," Anu added. "It's a dessert you can just enjoy exploring."

Amber was next. "I have a cocktail for you to enjoy with your fried pudding."

"This is a very strong cocktail," Nick said, taking a sip.

"Worth almost burning down the studio for?" I asked.

"I'm not sure about this pudding. It's a little bit dry," Anu said. "You should have seen what Holly did when she reimagined a boiled apple dumpling. This is just boiled fruit bread that you used to make French toast."

"It's a little off-putting," Nick said as I picked at it with my fork. "It's dense and dry and a little too eggy."

Fiona's dessert was nice. She'd made a sugar basket filled with chocolate truffles, candied fruit, and meringue cookies.

"This is whimsical and beautiful," Anu told her in admiration.

No surprise, but Holly was the winner; Jamila was sent home. I felt like Amber should have been the one to go, but I knew Dana and Gunnar wanted to keep her for the drama. I hung around and waited for Holly to finish with the post-bake-off interviews.

"You don't have any plans," I told her when she was done.

"Well, actually, I—"

"It's not a question," I said, taking her by the hand and leading her upstairs.

CHAPTER 55

Holly

Once we were back in Owen's condo, I took a shower. I still smelled like burnt fabric and smoky oranges. Though I wanted to spend a lazy, sexy afternoon with Owen, I really needed to do some planning for the Quantum Cyber winter festival; it was in a few days. I wanted to make sure we had all the finishing touches. Too bad Sloane would be there.

Owen had ordered food and had it waiting for me when I came downstairs.

"Wow! The star treatment! I was going to cook, but okay, I'll take it," I said as I opened the container of cheesy bacon-and-potato soup. There was also a grilled three-cheese sandwich and a creamy Caesar salad.

"It's like all my favorite food groups," I said, taking my plate to sit on Owen's couch. He followed me and sat down next to me. I rested my head on his shoulder for a second, and he kissed my hair.

"I do actually need to work on your winter festival," I said, turning on my tablet. "Especially since you are technically paying me. I feel like I haven't done anything yet except decorate your office with Christmas cheer."

"You had the Christmas Bake-Off holiday party."

"That was more Penny's idea."

"You decorated," he insisted. "Everyone liked it. My employees are much friendlier now."

"Copious amounts of free booze and their CEO not acting like a sociopath will do that!"

I hung out with Owen for the rest of the evening. I made him watch Christmas movies with me while I went through the catering menu and the day's programming. I was planning it like a mini conference, where there would be several sessions going on simultaneously. Owen's employees had been submitting topics for panels about various projects they were working on. We were planning to hold the talks in the company's lecture hall. We would also have people in the atrium of the Quantum Cyber office along with two sessions in the main lobby of the tower. Demonstrations of the more dangerous technology like the human-sized drones would take place out in the park. That was where I was also planning my extra-special surprise.

I also had a holiday feast planned with turkey, beef Wellington, and other traditional dishes. To celebrate the fact that Quantum Cyber was an inclusive company, we also had foods from other religions like potato latkes, challah, along with foods from around the world that people ate in December, such as *vitello tonato*, mince pie, and *Stollen*. There was a large catering kitchen in the tower. Fiona and Morticia were going to help me cook.

I sent out the last email then snuggled next to Owen, turning up the volume on the TV as *Holiday in Handcuffs* started.

"I love this movie," I said as he wrapped his arms around me. "I watch it several times a year."

"You watch Christmas movies all year round?" Owen said in confusion.

"Duh, yeah, of course. What else are you supposed to do in July?"

"I don't know. Go outside?"

"No way! Christmas movies all day every day."

"I think I might jump off the balcony. I can barely stand them in December, let alone all year round."

"I seriously doubt there's not one single Christmas movie you like," I said, shoving him playfully. He hauled me onto his lap, making me squeak. I kissed him and smiled. "We're going to watch one next that you'll love. It's called *Bad Santa*."

"If I'd known it was going to take you away from me, I'd have never asked you to help with the *TechBiz* competition," Owen said, pinning me to the front door and kissing me.

"I have to make cupcakes," I said against his mouth, "and a crap ton of food."

"No you don't. Just have it catered. The grocery store caters, and they have cupcakes."

"What kind of baker would I be if I *bought* cupcakes?" I demanded as Owen finally opened the door for me. "If you're good, maybe I'll bring you a cupcake," I called over my shoulder.

I pulled out my phone in the elevator.

Morticia: *These cupcakes are about to be not happening if you don't hurry up.*

Holly: *Once you land your own dream guy, you'll understand.*

Morticia: *Never.*

My friend was standing in the kitchen, arms crossed, when I walked into the penthouse.

"You need to do something with your stepsister. She's in there being weird," Morticia said.

"Hard pass," I said. "She's trying to ruin me in the bake-off."

Unfortunately, I had to go through the living room to go upstairs and change before I could start baking. Amber was sitting in the living room scrapbooking. She was cutting out pictures of Owen very carefully then pasting them onto a page. She already had several pictures of herself cut out and was doing some sort of demented scrapbooking Photoshop to make it look like the two of them were together.

"I'm going to pretend you aren't down there seeing him," she said, looking up at me. "You've been drugging him with all those sweets you give him."

"I'm not drugging him!" I shouted. "You're delusional. You were always like this when we were teenagers. You were obsessed with the high school quarterback. He kissed you once behind the bleachers, and you were convinced you two were going to get married. Then there was the foreign exchange student who you were convinced was going to take you back to France with him to his château, even though he lived in a cramped apartment with his mom in one of Paris's outer-ring suburbs. Now you think Owen is your soul mate. I don't even see how. He has never given you the time of day."

"He's the one keeping me in the bake-off," my stepsister said dramatically. "It's because he knows we're supposed to be together. He's looking out for me and making sure that I advance to the next round."

"Are you seriously feeding her delusions?" Morticia said, stomping into the room. "Spoiler, Amber, you're not making it past the next round."

"I will," she insisted. "Owen will protect me."

"I have to make two thousand cupcakes. I literally do not have time for this."

My stepsister started crying. "I don't understand why you can't just let me be happy."

When I came back down from changing, Amber was gone.

"She left," Morticia said when I asked.

"Did she say where? What if she goes after Owen?" I said with concern.

"Owen is a grown man and a large one at that. I'm sure he can handle himself."

I smiled a self-satisfied smile. "Yes, he *is* large."

"Ugh. I did not need to know that," Morticia said, adding the flour to the batter.

For the themed cupcakes, we were making chocolate cupcakes decorated like elves, white vanilla cupcakes with buttercream frosting like snowmen, and red velvet cupcakes decorated like reindeer. I'd even found muffin tins that looked like the bottoms of snowmen and reindeer and elves, so the cupcakes would be extra unique and festive.

"These are going to be super cute!" I gushed as I started spooning the batter into the muffin tins. Morticia dumped a bag of confectioners' sugar into a bowl of softened butter for the frosting.

"You know what," I said thoughtfully. "Maybe we should make some extra. I never did get to lick frosting off of Owen."

CHAPTER 56

Owen

I took Rudolph out for a walk after Holly left then went up to my office.

Workers were already setting up for the winter festival, as Holly called it, checking the sound systems and putting up lecterns. My employees were chattering about the event as well. Walker kept forwarding me emails of the speculation going around about what sort of crazy activity Holly had planned for me.

Christmas was a week away. I wondered what Holly was doing. I knew I wanted her to stay with me. I wondered if it was too early to propose marriage. I'd known her, what, a few weeks? But I figured she might like a Christmas proposal.

"Did you read through that report yet?" Walker asked.

"Uh—"

My COO peered at my screen before I could close it. "Dude, are you seriously looking up engagement rings? It's not for Sloane, is it?" he asked in horror.

"Of course it's not for Sloane!"

"Holly then?" Walker said, sitting across from me. "Dude, you literally just met her."

"I'm a hundred percent confident in my decision."

"Have you even talked to her about it?"

"I will."

"You can't just have the proposal be the first time you tell her you want to spend the rest of your life with her."

"I know that. I'm not an idiot."

"I mean sometimes I wonder."

I glared at him.

Walker sighed. "Beck wants to talk about the quarterly projections soon, don't forget."

I had settled into reading through the financial projections for the next quarter, which Beck had sent me, when I looked up to see my youngest brothers plastered against the glass.

I opened the door, and Matt and Oliver tumbled inside. My third-youngest brother, Jonathan, waited outside to finish his phone call.

"Owen!" they exclaimed as I hugged them.

"How was the drive?" I asked.

"Would have been nicer with one of your sports cars," Matt said.

"Don't touch my cars."

"Well, can you give me a job?" Matt asked. "I'm going to graduate in the summer. I can totally work for you."

"Why don't you go work for Jonathan's hedge fund?" I asked him.

"No more room at the inn," Jonathan said, sauntering in and tucking his phone away. "We came by to see Belle but thought we'd bother you first."

"I'm sure you could find something for Matt to do," I said to my brother while he rummaged in my desk. "What the hell are you doing?"

"Where are all the cookies?"

"What cookies?"

"Belle said you were dating one of the Great Christmas Bake-Off bakers, and I want cookies."

"Is she going to come cook?" Oliver asked as I herded them all out of my office to the elevator. "Jack said Chloe was too busy to party plan. She has that new franchise opening up. Jonathan said you and Holly were going to host."

"I'm not sure," I admitted as the elevator took us down to the bake-off studio.

Belle was in the studio, arguing with Gunnar about the editing of the latest episode. My sister had been more of a mother to Matt and Oliver than our own mother had been, and they ran to her when they saw her.

"How's the bake-off?" Matt asked.

"Two more episodes, then that's a wrap," Belle said, patting his hair.

Jonathan opened his mouth. "Are there—"

"Cookies?" Belle raised an eyebrow.

Jonathan nodded happily.

"No."

He looked deflated.

"If you want free cookies, you can be in it next year," Gunnar said.

"Or help Owen with the holiday party he's hosting," Belle added.

"I thought that was tentative," I complained.

"Jack did it last year. It's only fair to rotate," she said.

"Guess you've been voluntold!" Jonathan joked.

As I walked back to my office later, a woman in an elf costume jumped out from a doorway, snapping pictures.

"Owen, I love you!" she yelled before scampering away.

I seriously could not wait for Christmas to be over. The holidays made people crazy. Though if Holly wanted to wear a sexy elf costume, maybe I wouldn't mind celebrating all twelve days of Christmas.

My phone buzzed, and I looked at it. Holly had sent me a picture of herself holding up two cupcakes as if they were boobs.

Holly: *Want a sweet treat tonight?*

Of course that meant I had trouble concentrating for the rest of the day. Unfortunately, Holly was not waiting for me wearing nothing but frosting when I went back to my condo after my last meeting of the day.

Instead, I took Rudolph out for a walk. It was snowing, and he was happy to be out in the cold. He wanted to sit out on the balcony when we returned. I took off my jacket, loosened my tie, and checked my phone. Where was Holly? I'd already grown so used to having her around that the condo felt empty without her.

Holly: *How about a late-night sweet treat? It took a lot longer to finish cooking for the winter festival than I planned.*

Owen: *You don't even have to cover yourself in frosting.*

Holly: *I was planning on smothering you in frosting.*

Owen: *Can you come now?*

Ten minutes later, she showed up at my door with frosting on her cheek.

"No cute costume?" I asked, slipping two fingers down the front of the bodice. She had a streak of frosting across her chest.

"I have fun panties on."

"Are they crotchless?"

"I guess you better find out," she said.

I crushed my mouth to hers, tasting sweet frosting and nutmeg. She was warm and soft in my arms. I ran my hands along her body as she moaned against me. The thin fabric of the dress ripped easily under my hands when I tore the bodice.

"Look at you, Mr. Big Strong Handsome Man, giving me the true bodice-ripper romance," Holly purred. She unzipped my pants as I pulled the torn fabric back to expose her tits. Something plunked on the ground.

"Is that part of a Christmas cookie?"

"Oh!" Holly exclaimed. "I wondered where that went."

"Please don't eat it," I told her, kissing her tits so she wouldn't bend down and pick it up.

"I'm not," she said breathlessly. As I rolled her nipple around in my mouth, sucking her full, soft breast, my hand snuck under her skirt. I could confirm that the panties were indeed crotchless. Holly whimpered as I stroked her pussy, already wet and aching for my cock.

"You gonna fuck me?" she moaned as I knelt in front of her. "Or are you going to eat that cookie?"

"I'm going to eat a cookie, but not the one on the floor," I said, pushing up her skirt.

She moaned, her legs trembling, as I pressed my mouth to her pussy, lazily licking her. Her nails dug into my shoulders through my shirt as my tongue flicked her clit. Her breath came faster. She was close, but I wanted to draw it out.

"What the hell? Why'd you stop?"

"You said you wanted my cock," I reminded her. I rolled on a condom and hiked her up against the wall, thrusting into her.

She moaned, her hips wriggling against me as I fucked her, her legs wrapped around me to coax me deeper. She had been so close when I put my thick cock inside her that I knew she would come just from my entry. I made sure she was angled so that my cock stroked her clit with every thrust. I kissed her as I fucked her, her nipples hard as they brushed against my chest.

Holly bit my jaw as she came. I continued to fuck her, gritting my teeth as her body spasmed around me. She panted and cursed as I continued to fuck her. She bucked against me, and I could see that she needed to come again. I felt her body tighten as the second orgasm crashed around me, sending me over the edge as well.

She leaned against me, and I carried her to the couch. Rudolph padded in from the balcony, sniffed, then sprinted to the cookie on the floor.

"Boys!" Holly said with a laugh. "Always want to put their mouths on cookies!"

CHAPTER 57

Holly

The winter festival started bright and early the next morning. I'd been up for hours already. Morticia, Fiona, and I had cooked all of the previous day and into the night. Now we had a feast ready for Owen's company. I was downstairs doing last-minute checks and making sure everything was perfect.

Holly: *I wish Sloane wasn't going to be there.*

Morticia: *Show your dominance. Pee on Owen in front of her like a polar bear.*

Holly: *Uh, I don't think that's how anything works.*

Morticia: *So sue me. I went to a public school in a dying rust-belt town.*

Holly: *Harrogate isn't dying! The Svenssons are investing a lot of money. You could land a billionaire.*

Morticia: *Gag. No thanks. I'm allergic to douchebags with too much money and huge egos.*

The workers had been setting up the stages and chairs the night before. It all looked a little corporate, but this wasn't a boozy holiday party. Oh, we were going to have alcohol, but not garbage cans full of hard liquor. Just wine, punch, and beer, something to keep people talking and receptive but not falling-off-the-balcony drunk.

"Everything looks amazing," Owen said, wrapping his arms around me and kissing me.

"I feel like I didn't do much," I said with a laugh.

"You did a lot," he said, turning me around and looking at me seriously. "Thank you."

"Think it's enough to shoot you all to the top of the *TechBiz* list?"

"He's going to score high marks for sure," Sloane said, sauntering over to us. "Because that's what I promised, didn't I?" She pressed herself against Owen, reaching up to kiss his cheek. Someone might have been able to make the case that it was professional, but I knew it was anything but. Owen's face remained a cold, professional mask.

"Why don't you show me around?" Sloane said, taking Owen's arm.

I bit back a protest. It was business. The whole point of the winter festival was to schmooze overpaid magazine editors to land Owen's company at the top of a vanity list. I was a big girl. I could handle it.

"Don't forget to grab a snack! I have cupcakes I made myself!" I chirped. "They'll be out for lunch. For breakfast, we have cheesy breakfast burritos."

Sloane turned up her nose. "I don't eat breakfast."

Well then.

"It's the most important meal of the day!" I quipped.

"I do intermittent fasting," Sloane sneered. "You should try it."

"Willingly fasting is not my style," I replied.

"I can see that."

"Are you seriously going to let that hussy walk off with your man?" Morticia said in my ear. I shrieked. She'd just appeared like the Ghost of Christmas Past.

"It's fine."

"I don't trust either of them," Morticia said with a sniff. She was drinking some sort of bitter-smelling brew. "Cleansing tea?"

"Ugh, no thanks. Though I might need another of those Korean sitz baths later. Owen has been very impressed with the quality of things in the South Pole. I want to keep him happy and everything tight as a clam."

Morticia rolled her eyes.

"Thanks for your help, but I don't want to keep you from your actual job of working for the *Vanity Rag*."

"We're basically done," Morticia explained. "There are two more contests. One of them is with the Weddings in the City girls. Penny's out doing specials with each of them to put on the *Vanity Rag* website."

I took in a deep breath. "That means it's almost Christmas!" I made sparkly motions with my fingers.

"Spare me. I should go hibernate until it's over," Morticia said as we walked around.

I grabbed a breakfast burrito, and we watched the kickoff presentation in the atrium up in the Quantum Cyber offices.

Owen, Walker, and Beck were talking about the company. His employees hung off the balconies, watching.

We listened to Owen and his CFO and COO joke around. Then Morticia and I went to start setting up for lunch. To keep a clog from forming in the food lines, we had several tables set up around the office.

"We really went all out," Fiona said happily as we set out the trays of food for the feast. There were racks of beef Wellington, along with roast turkey and gravy. There was puffy Yorkshire pudding and creamy cheddar-and-chive mashed potatoes. Best of all was the lobster mac and cheese. There was also a roasted-pear-and-goat-cheese salad, because I had figured we needed something green that wasn't the green bean casserole.

"So good," I said, sneaking a plate of pasta. Morticia stole a bite.

Owen's employees seemed pleased with the food. In addition to Sloane, several other *TechBiz* magazine representatives were at the winter festival. Owen drifted through the groups of his employees, answering questions and being friendly and personable.

"I'm so proud!" I said dramatically, wiping a fake tear out of my eye when he passed me. "My baby's all grown up and being sociable!"

After the final sessions in the late afternoon, Morticia, Fiona, and I put out snacks and alcohol in the main lobby.

"Are we ready for the big surprise?" I asked Walker.

"It's all you," he said, handing me a microphone.

"Thank you all for participating in the Quantum Cyber Winter Festival," I said, stepping up onto the stage. "And thank you to the *TechBiz* committee for your time. I just came in to help decorate and bake and convince Owen to free-flow the booze!"

There were several cheers.

"I'll eat your cupcakes!" someone yelled.

I laughed. "In the restaurant business, we like to pride ourselves on having a close-knit culture, from the family meals before dinner service starts to helping out our fellow chefs in need. While working with you all at Quantum Cyber, I see the same type of relationships, the desire to innovate and be creative. And yes, you all do drink as much as any crazy restaurant workers!"

There was more cheering.

"Open a restaurant!" several guys in front of the stage chanted. I grinned at them.

"We have one more surprise. Since your CEO recently adopted a puppy, and I hear that dogs are very popular here, we have a little contest set up outside to raise money for the local animal shelter."

I turned to look at him.

"Owen, I hope you brought your swimsuit!"

CHAPTER 58

Owen

I followed Holly outside with the herd of employees. We went across the street to the park.

Near the fountain, a giant dunking tank had been set up with a chair affixed to a lever above the tank. A layer of ice coated the water.

"Are you okay with this?" Holly asked. "I guess we could always make Walker do it."

"Uh, no. No way. I'm a summer person," my COO said, backing away.

"Really? With all that blond hair?" Holly teased.

"I tan. I'm of Scandinavian descent!" Walker retorted.

"I'm good," I assured Holly, stepping behind a curtain to take off my suit and pull on the swim trunks Holly handed me. They were decorated with multiple Santas lying on lawn chairs, shirtless, with beers in their hands.

"Owen, if you could please take a seat," Holly said, her voice reverberating around the park through the sound system.

"Now, everyone, if I can direct your attention to the screen. As you can see, the counter is set at one million dollars. This is the amount the local animal shelter needs to expand its facility. The aim is to help keep more dogs off the cold streets. We have this event livestreaming, so all you viewers can donate as well. Once the counter hits the goal, Owen goes into the water."

"What if no one donates?" I asked Holly out of the side of my mouth.

"They will," she said confidently. "I've been pimping it out on social media. I told everyone it would involve you wet and shirtless. There are several mom groups that are very interested."

"Yeah, but that's a lot of money." I was about to offer to just give her the money, but when I looked at the screen, I noticed that the numbers were already creeping up.

"Besides," Holly added with a smirk, "Jack said he really wants to see you fall into the water."

I looked out into the crowd. All my brothers were pointing and laughing and taking pictures.

"So I'm not worried."

The counter climbed up and up. The crowd chanted. "Two hundred thousand! Three hundred thousand!"

Rudolph barked.

"I think a few of the Svenssons are also donating big amounts," Holly said innocently. I peered down.

Dana was standing near Holly and Walker.

"The Holbrooks are also donating," Dana said with a toothy smile. "My cousins are very excited."

"Of course they are." I sighed.

Walker snickered. "Greg said he normally hates the dog-pound people, but he's giving money just to watch Owen fall!"

I looked down at the ice. I guessed we were going to test just how much cold I could withstand.

The counter ticked up another big jump.

"Eight hundred!" The crowd cheered.

"Do you think we should break the ice?" Holly asked in concern.

Walker looked up at me. "Owen's a big guy. And he's high up. He'll just crash right through."

"Thanks, Walker," I said. It wasn't actually that bad outside. It was snowing, the flakes landing in my hair. There was another big jump, and the counter ticked to $930,000.

"Just a little more to go!" Holly said in excitement.

The counter crept up then made another big jump to $1.1 million.

The buzzer sounded, the chair collapsed, and I fell, cracking through the ice into the freezing water. It wasn't that cold. It was actually pretty refreshing. I did a lap in the tank and waved to the camera.

"Geez, you're freezing!" Holly exclaimed when I climbed out of the pool and flashed a thumbs-up. The crowd roared.

"We have bourbon-spiked hot chocolate, very boozy eggnog, and mulled apple cider inside in the lobby if you all want to warm up," Holly said into the microphone.

"Or you can take a refreshing swim," I added, gesturing to the tank. "It will really get the circulation going."

"Yeah, I don't think there are any takers," Holly said as my brothers and sister pushed up to the front.

"He's a frostscicle," Walker said. "Don't you want a blanket or a heater?"

"I feel fine," I said. "Actually, really good. See?" I held out my hands. "My fingers aren't even blue."

"Maybe Mom was experimenting on you when you were a baby," Jonathan joked.

I hugged Holly, and she shrieked when the droplets of freezing water landed on her neck.

"Your hair is coated in ice," she said with a laugh, raking her hand through it.

"You can help warm me up," I said, sticking my hands under her dress and making her scream.

CHAPTER 59

Holly

I t was the morning of the second-to-last episode of *The Great Christmas Bake-Off*.

Owen's money for the work on helping his company win the *TechBiz* contest had appeared in my bank account then immediately disappeared, filtering away into the ether of all my debt payments. I had been able to pay some of it to the storage facility, so they were going to hold my grandmother's items until the twenty-third of December. I hated to admit it, but I was starting to panic.

"I have to win," I chanted to myself, trying to stay in the zone. There were three of us left. I couldn't believe Amber was still in the competition.

"There's something about Christmas," Anastasia said when Dana gave her the signal, "that really sparks the romantic in me. And that's today's theme: romance—or rather the wedding that comes after. Today, each contestant is going to bake an elaborate winter wedding cake. To judge, we have two of the girls from the Weddings in the City collaborative, Zoey and Gracie. They plan, cater, and decorate the weddings of everyone who's anyone in New York City. Care to give our contestants some tips?"

"The trick to a wedding cake," Gracie said, "is that it needs to be visible from everywhere in the entire wedding venue, and that means lots and lots of tiers. The biggest cake I ever baked had twenty layers. You have giant ovens, which is good, because you'll need them."

"You have until midnight," Anastasia said.

"You'll need every minute of it," Gracie said with a laugh. "I'm typically working up to the eleventh hour decorating the cake, making sure it's perfect for the bride's big day."

I loved weddings. When I got married—if I got married—I wanted a Christmas wedding, with a huge white dress and a fur cape. I would take pictures in the snow. We'd have the whole venue decked out for Christmas. Hell, I might even have a live reindeer. But that was a big if. I couldn't even manage to keep my baking company afloat for three months. Did I really think I could handle a serious relationship?

What about Owen?

What about Owen?

I couldn't shake what his mother and Sloane had said, that he was only with me for fun. Maybe he didn't actually care about me. Maybe I was just the fun, sexy girl he brought to his bed, not the one he married.

But he was smiling softly at me before he left the studio for the day.

"Ready for your dream wedding cake?" he asked me.

"To be perfectly honest, it's probably going to be the nightmare wedding cake. The last time I made a wedding cake, it took me three days. Now I don't even have a full twenty-four hours."

Owen chuckled. "I have faith in you."

"I'm glad one of us does," I said.

He leaned over to kiss me. "I'll see you tonight."

After Owen left, I tried to focus. I desperately needed to win. I couldn't just show up with some three-tiered dumpy cake and call it a day. I needed height, drama, and a touch of something special.

I knew I was going to have every layer be a different flavor. On the bottom, it was going to be red velvet cake, because I wanted something red for a Christmas wedding. The red velvet layer would be the biggest. I was going to shape it like an abstracted snowflake. The next layer was going to be offset a few inches. It was going to be two layers of a citrusy cake with orange buttercream frosting. Layer three was going to be another round cake, and it was going to be chocolate with a fudgy frosting. The fourth layer would be tall, ten inches, and cut in a pentagon to add some visual interest so it wasn't just a stack of circles. For that tier, I was going to bake a seven-layer yellow cake with chocolate, raspberry, and butter crème between the layers. Layer five was going to be a smaller circular butterscotch-rum cake. For the final sixth layer: strawberry cake with layers of stewed fruit.

For the cake topper, I was going to blow sugar into a snowman groom and snowwoman bride. The decorations on the cake should evoke winter. I was going to have a few sugar-gum flowers but make them look frozen, as if they were covered in frost. I didn't want a lot of flowers. Sometimes wedding cakes with too many sugar flowers looked diseased. I just wanted a few tasteful bunches here and there. The rest of the cake would have intricate icing designs to evoke a frozen winterscape.

I had my sketch and my game plan. I checked the clock. "Let's do this."

I preheated the ovens then started several mixers going simultaneously. When I had worked in restaurant kitchens, I'd regularly cooked four of five dishes at once.

I made the bottom red velvet cake first, the cocoa powder frothing and turning red when I poured in the buttermilk and vinegar. I needed two mixers since the bottom tier of the cake was so big. The batter went into the largest pans, and I put them in the oven. Then I made the next three layers. The red velvet cake finished cooking while I was mixing up the final tiers. I took it out to cool then put the next pans of cake batter in to bake.

The actual making-of-the-cake part wasn't difficult; I could make cakes all day. It was the assembly and decoration that would be tricky. As the cakes came out of the oven, I carefully turned them over onto cooling racks. Once they were partially cool, I wrapped them in plastic wrap and put them in the fridge. While they chilled further, I started on the decorations.

The sugar snowman and -woman were going to take some time, so I heated up the sugar first. The cake toppers were going to be blown like glass. I couldn't just use the same sugar I would for candy; I had to add corn syrup and cream of tartar to make it thick enough to blow. I wanted the whole cake to feel minimalist and wintery. I kept the snow couple white and crystalline.

I was a little worried; the sugar was hot. I was wearing gloves, but still, last time, my dress had caught fire.

After the sugar had reached the correct temperature, I poured it out on a silicone sheet and rolled it into several balls. Then I stuck in a metal tube and started blowing. It was a delicate process. I shattered the first two before I got the hang of it. Using a blowtorch, I lightly melted the spheres and formed the snow couple. Then I colored the rest of the sugar, some orange for the noses, some black for the buttons, and some blue for a scarf. I was going to use blue and silver frosting as accents on the larger wedding cake. The accents weren't as difficult because I could just roll those out of fondant.

"Hard part is done," I said happily, running my hands under cold water. Amber passed by me, lugging a huge hand cart of ingredients. I watched her carefully to make sure she didn't throw anything into my icing.

"Please do not get too close to those," I warned Zane, who was shooting close-ups of the snow people. He flashed me a thumbs-up.

I made the frostings next, huge tubs of them. Once I had the cakes frosted, I was going to cover each in fondant as a protective coating and a clean, smooth base for the decorations. I rolled out the huge white sheets of fondant and set them aside. Then I took my cakes out of the fridge. They were nice and cold, and I easily trimmed them down to be flat and shaped like my templates.

Satisfied, I frosted and stacked the bottom red velvet layer, sticking in the dowels that provided the structural integrity, and then carefully laid the sheet of fondant over the top of the cake, smoothing it out so all the edges were crisp.

Then I assembled the next layer and the next. When I was done, I had a pristine white tower of cakes. I had to put on the final layer, then it would be ready to decorate. It was so tall that I needed a stepstool. I was carefully placing the final layer on when Amber rammed the hand cart into my table.

I shrieked as the cake tipped. I tried to catch it and stumbled off the stool, my hands raised. Somehow I didn't fall flat on my face. It truly was a Christmas miracle, especially since I felt something heavy and cake-like resting on my outstretched hands.

"I can't open my eyes," I said to Fiona. "How does it look?"

"Just hold on. We're going to right it," she said. She and I gingerly tipped the cake back upright. "Thank goodness you had the fondant on. It was like Spanx for your cake."

I was not in the mood for jokes.

"Seriously, Amber! You keep trying to ruin my desserts!" I turned and yelled at her.

"You're trying to ruin my life!" she yelled back. "You steal everything good in my life."

"*Girls*," Dana hissed, striding over, high heels clacking on the polished concrete. "I have two more days with you, then I am going to celebrate Christmas with all the alcohol. Stay away from each other."

"But she—" I protested.

"I don't care. Finish your cakes."

CHAPTER 60

Owen

The tension was high in the studio when I returned. During the day, I had caught up with work, taken Rudolph for several walks, met with my younger brothers about what in the world they planned on doing when they graduated, and now it was eleven p.m. and the contestants were still working on their cakes.

The Weddings in the City girls had already returned and were watching, enraptured.

"This is impressive," Zoey said.

"I need to hire Holly," her friend Gracie replied.

I didn't want Holly to have a job that would take her away from me for long stretches. She needed perhaps a café that closed in the early evening. But then, it was her life. I shouldn't try to dictate it.

Holly was carefully icing the wedding cake with intricate designs. On each tier was a different winter scene. The bottom was reindeer in a snowy pine forest. The next was a panorama of a countryside after a fresh snowfall. The next depicted little fairies riding snowflakes. Edged on the rims of each cake were icicles of icing.

It was exquisite workmanship. I respected technically perfect work. I demanded it of my programmers, and I appreciated that Holly also shared the same values. Though she acted fun, especially in bed, Holly was also very serious about the quality of the work she produced. I felt a renewed sense of conviction that she was exactly who I needed in my life, contrary to what my parents believed. Not that I cared. But it was nice to be right.

The buzzer sounded as Holly was inspecting the sugar flowers she had arranged sparingly on the cake. The production assistants very carefully wheeled each cake out to be photographed and videotaped, then they brought them to the judges' table.

Holly's cake was first.

"What amazing workmanship!" Zoey congratulated her.

"I appreciate it. It's all winter and no Christmas," I said with a slight smile.

"There's a bit of Christmas if you know where to look," Holly said.

"I'm just in awe that you managed to do all this in a day," Gracie said.

"I'm definitely ready for a drink," Holly replied with a laugh.

"You've earned it!"

"I don't even want to cut into it; it's too pretty to eat," Gracie said.

"I'm going for it," Zoey said, cutting a neat slice of the middle tier and taking a bit. "Good crumb, moist, great flavors, perfect wedding cake!"

Fiona had a great cake as well.

"I feel like I'm going to be up all night!" Zoey joked as she took a bite. That particular tier was espresso flavored. Fiona's cake wasn't as tall as Holly's, but she had done more with hers. It looked like a stack of presents in a leaning pile, but it wasn't hokey. The ribbons were made of pulled sugar. Fiona had lightly colored the cake presents and dusted the royal icing that she'd used to decorate them with patterns of fine silver and white gold dust.

Amber's cake was the worst. Also, the topper looked suspiciously like me.

"I had premonitions while making this cake," Amber said. "Premonitions of a wedding with a handsome ice prince."

"Okay," Zoey said after a moment. "First off, this cake is much plainer than the other two."

"It's simple and honest," Amber retorted.

"Naked cakes are in vogue," Gracie explained, "but they're more rustic, and honestly, a lot of people can make them. The theme of this episode is winter wedding. Usually weddings tend to be on the extravagant side. We don't want gaudy, but you did have a whole day to make a cake. I would expect something better, though this does taste pretty good."

Amber pouted as she left after hearing her criticism.

"So obviously we're sending Amber home," Gracie said. "But who should win?"

"What Fiona did was structurally more difficult," Zoey suggested.

"But Holly's cake was taller," I interjected.

"Ah, yes, rich men and their towers," Zoey said with an eye roll. "But Gracie is the wedding cake queen, so she should decide."

"I say we give it to Holly," Gracie said thoughtfully. "What she made is most like what a winter wedding cake should be."

Holly was as excited to win as Amber was devastated to lose.

"You can't do this to me! Please, Owen, you were supposed to save me!"

"What was that about?" Zoey asked as Anastasia led Amber away.

"It's the holidays," I replied as we listened to Amber shriek in front of the cameras. "People completely lose their minds around Christmas."

CHAPTER 61

Holly

breathed more easily after I won.

"You didn't honestly think Amber was going to make it to the finals," Morticia said after I'd given my interview. I was sure I looked a mess.

"Who knows." I yawned. "I'm exhausted. I'm going straight to sleep."

"You need to shower first," Morticia said with a sniff.

I showered and put on my favorite fuzzy pajamas with the cat wearing reindeer antlers, but I couldn't sleep. I missed Owen. Against my better judgment, I snuck downstairs.

When I was outside his door, I thought, *Holly, what are you doing? You're as crazy as Amber. Besides, Owen's probably asleep. You can't just knock on his door at three a.m. and wake him up; he has to work tomorrow. He has important things to do.*

As I stood there and debated with myself, the door opened. Owen was standing there shirtless, wearing grey sweatpants, the nice soft ones.

"I was hoping you'd come by," he said, deep voice sending shivers through me.

"Sorry I'm not wearing anything super exciting," I said. "But I did shower and wash my hair, so that's something."

Silently, Owen wrapped me in his arms, kissing me. Then he picked me up and carried me upstairs. He laid me back on the bed, kissing my neck. He unbuttoned my top as I ran my hands down the planes of his muscular chest, counting the washboard abs. I loved the feel of all that muscle and sinew against me.

Owen kissed my breasts then continued downward. He pulled the pajama bottoms off and slipped his hand under my panties while he kissed me. I moaned against his mouth, spreading my legs for him as he stroked me. He teased my clit, making me whimper. Then he tugged off my panties, planting kisses like snowflakes down to my pussy. I grabbed his hair as he licked me.

"I want you," I murmured. He ignored me, still licking my clit. I fumbled around in the nightstand and pulled out a condom.

"I want your cock," I said, ripping the packet.

He rolled the condom on then flipped me over so I was on all fours.

"Reindeer style!" I joked then moaned as he pressed his tongue against my aching pussy, holding my hips steady as he licked and teased me.

"Please," I whimpered.

Owen slid into me, caressing my tits, teasing my nipples. I ground back against him, needing the friction. He thrust into me again, and I whimpered.

"I need you to go faster."

"Why? You don't have to make it around the world to deliver presents," he said, slowly pulling out and thrusting into me again.

I reached down between my legs to stroke my clit. I needed more. Owen growled, thrusting into me harder then batting my hand away. He rubbed my clit while he fucked me, finally giving me all of his thick, hard cock.

I let out little cries every time he thrust into me. I was so close. I panted as he worked my clit, his cock filling me. His fingers rolled my clit, and I went crashing over the edge. Owen kept fucking me. His pace increased, and his cock hit me at just the right angle that suddenly I was seeing Christmas lights, and I came again. Owen followed shortly.

I started laughing as he lay down beside me.

"What?" he said, confused.

"Santa came down my chimney tonight!"

I woke up the next morning with a start. I'd had a horrible dream that I'd had to move back in with my mother and stepfather because my subscription baking box company failed and that Amber had won the bake-off. But she had been booted, and I was going to win the next round. So it was perfectly fine to ignore all the late notices and the nasty-grams about how my credit score was in the toilet.

"Too bad you have to work," I said, nuzzling Owen's bare chest.

"I did have a very important meeting scheduled for this morning," he said, smiling in a self-satisfied way.

"Don't let me keep you," I replied, sitting up. He pulled me down to him.

"It's with you," he said, kissing me.

"Just going to lie in bed all day and let me feed you Christmas cookies?" I teased.

"Hardly. I do have in itinerary. The *TechBiz* black-tie party is tonight. They're going to make the announcement about which tech company is best. I was hoping you would attend with me."

"Of course! How fun!"

"On one condition," he added. "Let me buy you a nice dress."

"You mean I can't show up dressed as a sexy Christmas tree?" I said in mock indignation.

He looked nervous for a second then saw I was kidding.

"I do have actual nice stuff, you know," I told him. "The costumes are part of my shtick."

"Come out anyway. I already had my secretary make an appointment at a boutique."

"You don't have to beg me to go shopping!"

"I think we're going to have a white Christmas," I said excitedly as I followed Owen down to the parking deck. "I've been checking the weather. It's supposed to dump a ton of snow a few days before Christmas Eve." I showed him the weather report.

"Glad I'm not traveling," he said with a grunt.

"Yeah, I hope I'm not too." If the spirits of Christmas were kind, I would win the bake-off and have enough money to pay off my debts and rent some cheap shared kitchen space. Then I'd have enough room to really take advantage of all the publicity with my bake-off win and the Taste My Muffins subscription service.

"Wow," I said as the elevator let us off in the parking garage. "Your employees sure have a lot of nice cars."

I wasn't really a car person, but I could recognize several of the brand decals. Plus the cars just looked expensive with their super-sleek, high-end designs. They were all black, though; none of them were in candy colors, which I thought was a missed opportunity.

"You need to have a Christmas-themed car," I told Owen. "We can put a ton of lights and Christmas decals all over it."

"Please don't put any stickers on my car," Owen said in alarm.

I laughed. "Which one is yours?"

He looked slightly guilty. "All of them."

"Geez," I said, turning around in a circle. There were a lot of cars. There were even a few that looked like antique racing cars.

"And I thought I had a problem with all my Christmas decor hoarding."

"I don't have a problem," Owen said. "I can quit anytime."

"Sure you can," I drawled.

He led me to a Bugatti Veyron. I ran my hands over the sleek sports car. Owen batted my hands away and polished away my fingerprints with a handkerchief.

"Can I drive it?"

"No."

"*Seriously?*"

"Can you even drive one of these?" he asked.

"I have a commercial trucking license," I bragged. "Needed it for a catering gig that went so, so badly. Until you've driven an eighteen-wheeler that was improperly loaded, *thanks Steve*, while it's pouring rain and your coworker's chinchilla is having an existential crisis in the seat next to you, then you don't know how to drive, my friend."

"I'm skeptical."

I made a "gimme" gesture with my hand. He sighed and held out the keys.

"Do not scratch it!" Owen warned.

I grabbed for the keys, but he jerked them away.

"If you scratch it, I'll—" he searched for an appropriate thing to say that didn't sound crazy.

"If I scratch it, I'll let you not only come down my chimney but all over my face any time you like!" I promised.

"Okay, maybe you can scratch the car a little bit, then," he said with a slight smile.

I laughed and took the keys then practically melted in the luxurious seat.

"Yum. I would ask if you ever had sex in this car, but it's actually not as roomy as you would think."

"I have not," Owen said tensely.

I started the car. It purred. "Better than a vibrator."

I pulled out of the parking space then slammed on the brake and made a car crunch noise with my mouth. Owen cursed and gripped the armrest. I laughed.

"Relax, I'm just messing with you," I said, pulling out of the garage.

CHAPTER 62

Owen

Holly wasn't a bad driver necessarily; she was aggressive, though. Whereas I like to keep several car lengths between me and the next car, Holly was right up on the bumper of the car in front of us.

"I can't believe how great these brakes are!" she remarked as she mashed the pedal for the umpteenth time, stopping about an inch before the car in front of us. The car moved, and in a flash, she pulled out in front of another car, zipping through traffic.

"I need a drink," I muttered.

"Don't these fancy cars come with special hidden alcohol compartments?" Holly asked, making a hard left turn at a yellow light then pulling up with a screech and zooming back to parallel park in front of the boutique.

I sat there for a moment in a daze.

"Ha!" Holly said, looking at her phone. "Google Maps said it would take us thirty minutes, but I got us here in ten."

"Good morning, Mr. Frost," the boutique manager said when we walked in. She took one look at my face and handed me a scotch.

"We're looking for a dress for a black-tie holiday party. And shoes," Holly said.

"She probably needs some sort of wrap and a purse," I added, the drink calming my nerves after that drive.

"You mean I can't take my bedazzled snowflake purse to the fancy black-tie holiday party?" Holly asked with a laugh.

The saleswoman walked Holly around the boutique while another associate brought out several dresses.

"These just came in," she said, hanging the dresses up.

"This is pretty," Holly said, inspecting a shimmery black, off-the-shoulder dress with layers of ruffles around the hem.

"This trumpet silhouette will look great on a curvy figure," the saleswoman said. "I know your boyfriend will be happy about that too."

I felt a rush of satisfaction at hearing them refer to me as Holly's boyfriend.

"I guess I'll try it on," Holly said.

"This fits pretty well," Holly said, coming out of the dressing room. I was a little surprised. As much as I loved Holly in the fun costumes, in this dress, she looked elegant and chic.

"Maybe wear your hair in a messy side bun?" the saleswoman suggested, holding up Holly's hair.

"You need shoes," another sales associate said, coming over with several choices.

"Black seems a little boring," Holly said, inspecting the shoes. Then she spied a pair of sparkly red, strappy stilettoes with huge bows to tie them around the ankles. Dangling diamond-and-ruby clasps sparkled. I saw Holly's eyes go wide.

"They have rubies on them," the salesclerk coaxed, holding them up.

"Seriously? Get out. I can't wear those."

She liked them, though.

"Buy them if you like them."

"It's not too gauche for your holiday party?" she asked me.

"You can't be too conservative," I told her. "It is Christmas after all."

"They look nice with the outfit," she said, slipping them on and tying the big red ribbons.

"Maybe some jewelry," I prompted the sales associate. Holly started to protest.

"You can't have a neckline like that without a nice choker at least," the associate said.

The store manager came back with an elaborate gold, ruby, diamond, emerald, and pearl necklace. "This would be perfect."

"It has some serious *Nutcracker* vibes," Holly said.

"Is that a good thing?" I asked.

"Of course! Nutcracker anything is a good thing."

"It does have a bit of a Russian-Austrian flavor," I said, studying it.

The store manager draped it around her throat then added the matching earrings.

"I don't know, it looks kind of pricy," Holly said nervously.

"It looks nice with the dress," I assured her. "Besides, you can't come to the holiday party wearing some sort of plastic snowman necklace. There will be a large number of billionaires there with their wives and girlfriends. We can't have them all looking down at you and at me for not providing you something nice to wear."

"If you put it that way." She chewed on her lip.

"It's your early Christmas present."

"I guess." She said, wrinkling her nose.

Another saleswoman came over with a white and silver fur wrap. "It's going to be cold, so you might want this as well."

"It's so soft!" Holly breathed.

"You look fantastic," I told her. I wanted nothing more than to take her out of that dress and show her how much she meant to me.

While Holly changed out of the clothes, the saleswoman gestured me into a side room.

"Why don't you see if there's anything in there that piques your interest?" It was a whole room full of lingerie.

"There are even some holiday-themed items," she said. The saleswoman showed me a piece that was mainly three little puffs of strategically placed white fur. The next option was several pieces of white lace with a subtle snowflake pattern. It came with a matching corset and garters. I wholeheartedly approved.

"Shall we wrap it?" the saleswoman asked.

"Sure."

"Also," she added in a conspiratorial whisper as she carefully took down the delicate lace, "we do have a nice selection of unique engagement rings. We partner with local jewelers who source ethical stones. Never too early to start thinking about it!"

Holly seemed happy when she bounced up to the desk while I was checking out.

"Thank you very much for your patronage, Mr. Frost," the manager said. She handed me the receipt, but not before Holly saw it.

She made a sound like a dying snowman. "I, um, you should probably put that back."

"They don't give refunds," I told her as I picked up the bags with her purchases.

"I really can't accept all of that. I didn't know it was going to be that much!" she said, horrified.

Taking her arm, I led her out to the car.

"It's way more than I spent on Christmas decorations for the whole lobby!" she said, looking up at me with wide eyes. "It's like an entire house."

I laughed. "Well, not in New York City, it's not." I peered at Holly. "You look like you're about to faint. So I guess I'm driving."

"I guess," Holly said.

I opened the trunk.

"Don't put that back there," she said. "Someone could steal it!"

"How—"

"I don't know, maybe there's a Christmas caper on the loose, or you could have people watching you…"

She trailed off, peering into the distance. Then she snatched the bag out of my hands and pushed me to the car.

"The party's starting in a few hours. I have to do my hair and shower."

CHAPTER 63

Holly

I couldn't believe Amber! She was there in the doorway of a nearby shop, dressed as an elf with a camera. She was totally stalking Owen or maybe me or maybe both of us.

I stewed as Owen drove us back to his tower in silence. This was my entire life—whenever anything good happened to me, Amber always found some way to ruin it. She was constantly in competition with me for every little thing. Now Owen was caught in her craziness.

"I'm sure they would take it back if you really don't want it," he said when he pulled into the garage.

"What? Oh, the clothes and jewelry and shoes. No, thank you." I leaned over and kissed him. "It was very generous of you."

He studied me carefully.

I grinned. "We just need to find you a red tux with a Christmas-themed bow tie so you can look half as awesome as me!"

When I dressed—after a few hours of answering fan messages on social media—I looked way better than I ever had before. I did a sexy, smoky eye, and my hair was even cooperating. Instead of frizz, I'd been able to tame it into loose ringlets and pin it into a messy bun with little tendrils framing my face.

The black dress looked amazing. It was mermaid shaped and accentuated my curves in a good way. My mother had always told me I needed to stick to A-lines and leave the more fitted dresses to girls with Amber's shape, but dammit if I didn't look good. The ruffles at the hem of the dress weren't too over the top, and they ended in an ever-so-slight train. The off-the-shoulder straps gave the dress a retro vibe. I slipped the red shoes on, fastening the ruby-and-diamond clasps, then I put on the necklace and the earrings. I glittered like a Christmas tree, but a nice, high-end tree.

Owen was waiting downstairs for me. His bespoke tux accented his broad shoulders and chest, which tapered to a narrow waist and very firm behind. He slipped the fur cape around my shoulders.

"Do I look good enough to rub elbows with billionaires?" I asked him.

"None of them better rub anything of yours," he snarled.

Waiting outside in front of the tower was an SUV limousine. Owen helped me inside then pressed a button. A hidden bar rose up, displaying chilled champagne and crystal flutes.

"Drink?"

"Yes, please!"

He popped the cork and poured us each a glass of bubbling golden champagne.

I took a long sip. "This is delicious. Probably shouldn't overdo it, though. I don't want to make any inappropriate comments in front of all your billionaire pals."

"I think a fair number of the Svenssons will be there," Owen said with a slight frown. "Archer will definitely be there, so inappropriate comments will be made."

"Better him than me!"

The black-tie party for the *TechBiz* announcement was being held in one of Archer Svensson's hotels. I gaped out the window as the limo pulled up in front of it. The historic limestone building had been decorated for Christmas in Victorian fashion, with candles in the windows.

"Do not trip over this dress," I ordered myself as Owen and I walked up a grand staircase to the ballroom. It was packed with well-dressed people; the women wore couture, and the men wore tuxes. The whole place was decorated like a Cinderella movie if it had been set during Christmas: a huge tree, chandeliers, miles of garland. A jazz band was playing retro Christmas songs on a low stage.

"You can tell who the tech billionaires are," Owen whispered in my ear, "because they look like they found their suits in a dumpster."

I giggled. "You're a tech billionaire! Did you ever dress like that?"

"Never."

I snorted.

"Okay, maybe when I first started out, but my sister, Belle, didn't let that go on for very long," he said. He snagged two red cocktails with green garnish from a tray and handed one to me.

"Belle and I should be best friends," I said. A passing server offered me a lobster croquette. "You definitely have a body worthy of a tailored tux."

I had just stuffed another of the croquettes into my mouth when Penny waved to me, her boyfriend, Garrett Svensson, on her arm.

"I love your shoes!" Penny gushed, hugging me. "Also, I don't know what you're doing after the bake-off, but you totally need to produce more pieces for the *Vanity Rag*. Everyone loves you!"

"You know what?" I said, snapping my fingers. "I was thinking of this sex-and-baking series, kind of like what *Cosmo* does but better."

Penny jumped up and down. "Maybe when celebrities come to be photographed for the cover, some of them could do drunk baking or something!"

"Sex baking?" Owen asked with a scowl.

"You should be a little more open-minded," Garrett replied. The two men stared mulishly at each other. Then they both looked out into the distance like two cats who refused to acknowledge the other's existence any longer.

Penny giggled. "Garrett didn't want to be here. He hates parties."

"I do not hate parties. I find them mildly intolerable."

"Owen likes parties." I squeezed his arm.

"I'm here because I want to find out the rankings," he said with a shrug.

"You better beat the Holbrooks," Garrett warned. "Greg and Hunter came here specifically to see them beaten. And both of my brothers are insufferable when they don't get what they want. And speaking of annoying people…"

"Hey, Archer," Owen said, shaking his hand.

Archer kissed my cheek then Penny's. "Ladies. Everyone's dressed to impress to watch Owen win. Especially me, because I'm tired of hearing about this stupid contest." He had a plate piled high with hors d'oeuvres.

"Where did you get one of those?" I said. "I want a huge plate of snacks!"

The woman next to him giggled.

"Hazel, this is Holly. Holly, this is Hazel, my fiancée and also a baker. Wait, isn't that a Christmas song? Garrett, help me out here. You're the freak show with the good memory."

"It's 'The Holly and the Ivy,'" I said, laughing. "Not the Holly and the Hazel."

"Well actually, maybe you two could call your new food sex line the Holly and the Hazel. Has a nice sort of innuendo to it, right?" Archer said, taking a huge bite of a duck slider.

"She's not making a sex food line," Owen stated.

"It's the twenty-first century, Owen," Archer said, stuffing a cracker piled high with caviar and sour cream into his mouth. "Sexy food is big business. Why, I've been trying to convince Hazel to bottle her edible body paint for months!"

"I'm not starting a sex food line," she said, shoving him.

"This is why I don't go to parties," Garrett complained. "Because there's no escape from my family!"

Speaking of no escape from family—across the room, I saw a woman who looked suspiciously like Amber. She half turned, and it was definitely her.

"Just give me a second, Owen," I said "Gotta use the little girls' room."

He nodded, and I scuttled off, grabbed Amber by the upper arm, and dragged her to an alcove.

"What are you doing here?" I hissed.

"I have every right to be here," she said, jerking her arm away.

"Do you even have a ticket?" I fumed.

"Do you?"

"I'm a plus one."

"You slept your way to a ticket and all those clothes and nice jewelry!" she argued. "Don't act like you're better than me."

"You need to leave," I said flatly. I refused to let her cause a scene. What would Owen think? He wouldn't want to be around me anymore once he realized Amber was a permanent fixture in my life, I was sure of that.

CHAPTER 64

Owen

I had a couple surprises planned for Holly for after the party. Since she was currently occupied, I went to a side hallway to make a call and make sure everything was on schedule. That was when Sloane pounced.

"Owen!" she exclaimed. Wrapping her arms around my neck, she pressed her mouth to mine, kissing me passionately. I tried to push her off, hoping no one saw. Sloane had her teeth sunk into my bottom lip and her hand shoved down my pants. It was a struggle trying to untangle her.

Tears pricked in her eyes as soon as I shoved her off me. "You don't understand. I love you. We're perfect together!"

"I'm with Holly," I asserted.

"You can't be serious," she spat. "Holly is nothing. She's homeless. She's failing as a baker. She has no career goals or aspirations. She's just using you for your money."

"She does have goals," I countered.

358 · ALINA JACOBS

"What, a sex food line?" Sloane sneered. "You and I belong together. I'm the type of woman a man like you should be with." She must have realized she was sounding unhinged, because she calmed her features. "Darling Owen," she said, sliding her hands back up my chest.

"I'm not doing this anymore. You can keep spiraling into delusions with my mother, but stay away from me," I warned.

Holly looked slightly flustered when I found her again.

"Everything all right?" I asked.

"Fine!" she said. She grabbed a glass of champagne from a server and all but chugged it. "I think they're going to announce the rankings."

The search committee assembled on the stage. Sloane sauntered to the front of the group and looked straight at me. Evan Harrington, whose hedge fund owned *TechBiz* and *Vanity Rag*, approached the lectern and leaned over to smile into the microphone. "Merry Christmas! Thanks for coming out."

Now there was a man I felt sorry for. He was engaged to a woman possibly even crazier and nastier than Sloane. Apparently she had even made him sell all of his cars. Evan's situation was dire, and he wasn't even married yet. No, I would much rather wake up to Holly every day. I leaned over and kissed her.

She squeezed my hand. "I'm so nervous!"

"It's just a petty pissing contest between CEOs," I whispered in her ear. "At the end of the day, it's not that important."

"You're talking to someone whose life goal is to win a Christmas bake-off. I live for petty contests."

Evan pulled a piece of paper out of a large envelope. "We have the rankings in. Please, before you all start calling your hitmen, remember I did not make any decisions," Evan said, earning a laugh from the crowd.

"Just to remind everyone, the rankings were determined by a combination of interviews with employees, surveys of existing employees, an inventory of the activities each firm has been engaged in over the year, and then our wonderful committee's work in visiting each company and getting a feel for the businesses' cultures and values. That being said, for the last couple of years, Holbrook Enterprises has dominated. However, now there's a new reindeer at the head of the pack!"

Everyone groaned.

"And that reindeer is Quantum Cyber. Some of the comments from employees were as follows: 'Coolest CEO, literally.' And yes, Owen, I did pay money to see you dunked in a tank of ice water. It's shocking that you're still alive and with us today. Now, we don't do trophies, because that's weird, but you get bragging rights and your picture on the cover of next month's issue. So don't eat too many sweets over the holidays, eh, Owen?"

"You did it!" Holly gushed, applauding. She rose onto her toes to kiss me.

"Thanks to you!"

"I wondered what your secret sauce was," Grant Holbrook said, swaggering over to me, hand outstretched. "Now I see it's her. Holly, you ever want to come work for me, just let me know. You already have a fan club in my house."

If Grant was implying it was because of all the sexy Instagram outfits, I was seriously going to punch him.

But Grant seemed to know what I was thinking. He smiled wryly. "Every woman in my family is now subscribed to the Taste My Muffin baking subscription box. When I tried to take a cookie, because I mean it was a whole box of baked goods, I was told that I should have bought my own."

"Of course you should buy your own," his wife Kate exclaimed. She patted me on the arm then clinked her glass to Holly's. "Maybe you can open up a café, Holly."

"I was hoping to convince Chloe to open a Grey Dove Bistro location in my tower," Grant continued, "but I hear she's not opening any more franchises at the moment."

"Yes," I confirmed, "she said she's tapped out and doesn't want to dilute the brand."

"Sounds like an opportunity for you then," Grant said to Holly. "You ever want to open a restaurant in my tower, let me know. You can have as much space as you want! Because I'm definitely taking the title back from you next year, Owen!"

We milled around and talked to people for the rest of the evening. Everyone seemed impressed with Holly. Apparently they were all watching *The Great Christmas Bake-Off*. Several people were even subscribed to her Taste My Muffin subscription box.

"Man, my feet hurt," Holly said after the crowd had thinned considerably. "And I was expecting more dancing for a holiday party."

"People just get together and schmooze," I said. "And talk about potential business deals."

"I barely got to eat any food."

"There's a lot left," one of the servers said, coming by with a tray. "Eat up!"

Holly took several of the mini crab cakes and two more drinks.

"You don't want one?" she said, holding up one of the cocktails.

"I need to be alert for the next surprise."

"Oooh! I thought this and the clothes were the surprise."

"This was work. I have something special planned for the two of us. You're going to love it. Are you ready?"

"Take us away!"

My silver Aston Martin One-77 was waiting in front of the hotel. I helped Holly into the passenger seat then pulled the car out onto the road. It was late and traffic was fairly light, mainly Ubers taking people to nightclubs.

"What is the surprise?" Holly asked. She'd taken a large plate of snacks to go and two cocktails that one of the servers had poured into a to-go cup.

"We get a lot of these requests," the server had said. "Guys don't want their tipsy girlfriends spilling their drinks in their expensive cars."

I had generously tipped the server because one, it was an ingenious idea, and two, I didn't want ants in my car.

"Are we going to a petting zoo?" Holly guessed. "Like a Christmas-themed one with penguins and reindeer and I don't know what other Christmas animals there are."

"No," I snorted, "we are not going to a petting zoo."

CHAPTER 65

Holly

We were leaving the city. The skyline glowed behind us as the car roared down the highway. Owen had one hand resting lightly on the steering wheel, the other on my leg, caressing it. He pulled off several exits from town. "Ignore the fact that I'm taking you to a suburb," he said. "But in my defense, it's a nice one." He slowed down as we drove into a more residential area. There were huge fancy houses and—

"Christmas lights," I breathed.

Owen slowed the car to a crawl and turned on the radio. "Silent Night" played softly from the sound system.

"It's so magical," I said, tearing up. "When I was a little girl, I always helped my grandmother put up Christmas lights. She never took them down; we would just add more and more every year. But I haven't put up Christmas lights since she died. My mom and stepfather were not big Christmas people."

"My mom would make us all put up lights," Owen said in the dark. "She wanted the house to look perfect. She would stand out there with a level and make sure the lights were exact. It was miserable. She was like that with everything; you had to be perfect to be worthy of her love. She's still like that, I suppose."

"I'm sorry," I said, holding his hand.

He squeezed my hand. "But these lights are pretty, especially since I didn't have to put them up!"

While my grandmother's lights had had wholesome charm, the lights in this neighborhood were otherworldly. Every house was framed in lights. Several even had whole Christmas scenes in their yards. The softly falling snow made it feel like I was in another world.

"That one's beautiful," I said, pointing to a house that had all blue and white lights. The homeowner had carefully outlined the tree branches in lights. The roofs were trimmed in icicle lights, with the windows outlined as well. "This is unreal. They must have spent forever."

"Yeah," Owen said, "and speaking of petty competitions, they all try to one-up each other for the holidays."

"Still," I said, "it's nice that people can enjoy it, you know. You just make something beautiful for everyone to enjoy."

We drove around for several songs more. Every house in the neighborhood was decorated in lights.

"This was lovely. Thank you," I said to Owen. "It's nice to be reminded of what Christmas is all about. That it's about reaching out to your family and your neighbors and doing something to make the world a more beautiful, happier place."

"Yeah, I guess you're right," Owen said quietly after a moment.

"I do have one, okay two more presents," Owen admitted as we headed back to Manhattan.

"You don't have to keep doing stuff for me," I protested.

"Really, part of this present is for me."

"Oh, it's that kind of present!" I teased.

The fast car made the trip in no time. It was also a short trip, I realized, because we didn't go all the way to Owen's tower.

"Why are we stopping here?" I asked as we pulled up in front of a fancy historic building.

"We're staying a night in a hotel. I need some time with you just to myself, No Rudolph, no bake-off."

"You just left your puppy at home by himself!"

"Walker went to go stay with him. I'm sure they're passed out on the couch. Apparently there was a lot of wedding cake left. Walker's probably eaten a whole tier all by himself," Owen said as he handed the keys to one of the valets. The valets seemed impressed with the car, and I heard them arguing over who was going to drive it.

"This is one of the Greyson Hotel Group boutique hotels," Owen explained as we walked into the grand building. "It was built in the twenties, right before the real estate crash."

The hotel manager greeted us and led us through the beautiful art deco building to the elevators. The Christmas decorations were, fittingly, in the opulent art deco style: swoopy lines of garland, dramatic lighting, and excessive amounts of glitter, gold, and feathers. The decor continued up the grand staircase and into the elevator, which had an actual elevator operator.

"I booked us the whole suite," Owen said as the manager opened the door.

"Please let us know if there's anything we can do for you, Mr. Frost, ma'am," the hotel manager said.

"Am I that old?" I whispered to Owen after the hotel manager left.

He nuzzled my neck. "You're sexy as hell, and he was a little intimidated."

I laughed, and Owen picked me up, swinging me around the room and kissing me.

"But what does the bedroom look like, I wonder," I said, slowly undoing my dress.

Owen picked me back up and carried me to the bedroom. On the bed was a large box wrapped in gold paper and tied with a big red bow.

"Is that for me?" I clapped my hands.

Owen watched in amusement as I carefully removed the wrapping paper. "Are you planning on saving that?"

"I might use it in a scrapbook." He raised an eyebrow. "Fine," I said. "I may or may not have a whole plastic container full of carefully folded wrapping paper that I am absolutely going to use. One day. In the very near future."

Inside the box was the most delicate and softest piece of lingerie I'd ever seen.

"Did you have little elves make it?" I marveled. "It's so soft!" Normally all the lacy costumes I bought online in drunken shopping binges tended to not be made with the best-quality materials, featuring instead itchy lace and stiff polyester.

I went into the bathroom to change.

"Thoughts and prayers that this actually fits!" I muttered. The lingerie fit like a glove. The delicate snowflake-patterned lace started high on my neck then curved around my tits, framing them. In between and down my torso was a delicate mesh. The larger snowflake mesh reappeared around my hips.

"I look like a sexy snowflake!" I undid my hair to let it bounce around my shoulders and walked out into the bedroom. Owen was standing there in only his boxer briefs.

"We have to stop meeting like this," I purred. "Though I bet I look a lot sexier now than I did in wet hair and a bathrobe."

Owen approached me and pressed the softest kisses up my neck and along my jaw as his fingers skimmed the lace.

"You still looked very sexy then," he whispered, kissing my mouth as his hands tightened around my waist. The kiss deepened, and he pushed one hand between my legs. I moaned, bucking against him.

"Your tits are amazing in that," he said, moving from my mouth down to the swell of my breasts, sucking my tits through the delicate fabric, his hand still stroking me between my legs. "I should have bought several of these," he murmured.

"Why?"

"Because I'm about to rip this off of you," he said, grabbing the fabric then ripping it right down the middle. My tits exposed, he returned to lavishing attention on them.

"You didn't rip the most important part," I whispered as my hips ground against his hand.

Owen kissed his way back up to my mouth then grabbed my hips and pushed me over the bed. Positioning himself behind me, he knelt, pressing his face between my legs and licking my aching pussy through the thin lace, his breath hot against me. He leaned back. His hand rubbed me through the lace. Then his fingers crooked, pulling at the delicate fabric. There was a tear, and then his tongue was back, licking me through the slit he'd just torn in the lace. I moaned, rolling my hips back against him. He held me steady, licking my pussy and teasing my clit.

"I want you," I begged.

Owen continued to stroke my pussy as he rolled on a condom. Then he grabbed my hips and thrust into me. I cried out; I was wet and aching for him. His huge cock filled me, giving me the friction I needed.

One large hand left my hip to rub my clit. I leaned on the bed, legs trembling, as Owen fucked me, letting out little whimpering pants every time he thrust his huge cock into me.

He leaned over me, his hand covering my tit, teasing and pinching the nipple as he fucked me. I moaned loud in my throat. I spread my legs wider, needing him to give me every inch of his thick cock. His hand moved back to my clit, rubbing furiously. My whole body tightened. I was so close! He jackhammered into me, my tits rubbing against the bedspread, two of his fingers on my clit.

I came with a loud cry and felt Owen come in me a second later. He pulled me up onto the bed with him, wrapping his muscular arms around me. I rubbed my nose in the valley between his pecs.

"That was a very nice surprise!"

CHAPTER 66

Owen

Holly was still asleep when I woke up the next morning. I eased out of bed to take a shower. I had one final surprise for her, and I wanted to look presentable for it. Once in the shower, I let the freezing water run down my back. Contrary to popular belief, cold showers are very good for one's circulation.

The door to the bathroom opened.

"Want some company?"

"If you are naked, you can come literally anywhere I am," I told her over the sound of the spray.

"I know you can make me come anywhere!" Holly teased, sliding open the glass door to the huge shower.

She waved a condom at me as she stepped in. Then she screamed and immediately almost slipped. I braced her and set her on the bench.

"Why is it so cold?" she chattered. The water temperature had made her nipples tight and erect. "Turn the hot water on!"

I leaned over her. "Let me warm you up another way. Sex is better in cold water. If it's too hot, you'll faint."

She clung to me as I kissed her. She made a needy sound when I leaned back.

"Warmer?"

"Much," she said and licked her lips. Then she stared not up at me but directly ahead. "I guess the cold water hasn't done you any disservice."

"The cold gets the blood flowing," I said.

Then she did look up at me. Holly was the picture of desire—her wet hair in her face, the fullness of her tits, her perky nipples. She leaned forward, her legs spreading slightly and giving me a flash of dark pink.

She put her lips around my cock. I hissed as she slowly took me into her mouth inch by inch then moved her head back, sliding my cock out of her mouth. I bit down a curse as she licked the slit on the tip then took me into her mouth again, her head bobbing as she hummed. It was all I could do not to combust. I gently massaged her scalp, loving the way her hair tangled around my fingers.

I blinked, the cold water running down my back. The humming echoed around the marble shower.

"Are you singing 'Jingle Bell Rock'?"

She looked up at me craftily and winked. That was it. I needed her now.

I pulled her off my cock. She squeaked as I pulled her forward on the bench, spreading her legs then stroking her pussy, the heat a sharp contrast from the cold of the shower.

She was wet, and she moaned when I rubbed her clit as I put on the condom. I grabbed her hips, angling her toward me as I thrust my hard cock into her tight, hot pussy. Holly wrapped her arms around me, kissing me.

"Your thick cock feels so good in my pussy *and* my mouth," she whispered, planting sloppy kisses along my jaw. "I want every thick, hard inch of you."

I kissed her hungrily as I fucked her.

"You like it when I talk dirty, don't you?" she panted in my ear.

I couldn't fuck her as fast as I wanted to, since I didn't need to slip and fall. I pulled out of her, and she moaned as I turned her around to get better leverage. I bent her over, and she spread her legs. I pressed my mouth to her hot pussy, licking her, teasing her clit with my tongue.

"Fuck me," she demanded, her hips making needy little circles.

I stood back up, grabbing her hips, then I jackhammered into her. Holly leaned over the bench, moaning loudly as I filled her with my cock. She begged for every inch, and I gave it to her.

I tangled my fingers in her hair as I fucked her. Another hand reached around, teasing her clit, making her whimper. I knew she was close from the way her pussy tightened around my cock. I hissed as I felt her come around me, then I came too.

"You're right," Holly said, panting as the cold water washed away the signs of our lovemaking. "Cold showers are very invigorating."

I wrapped Holly in a huge, fluffy bathrobe and carried her into the living room. There was a full spread of brunch set out along with pitchers of mimosas.

"I figured you might want a brunch that you didn't have to prepare."

"Hell yeah! Plus," she said, "all this sex makes me really hungry."

"So," I said carefully as we sat down to eat. "Any plans for after the bake-off?"

"I'm not sure," she said, taking a bite of her eggs Benedict. "It sort of depends on if I win."

"Several people seem like they have jobs for you."

"Yeah…"

"Thinking about opening a restaurant?" I asked, hoping she would declare that she wanted to stay in Manhattan with me.

"I don't know. Maybe I should travel. If I lose, I'm not sure I want to stay in Manhattan," she said nonchalantly. "Maybe I've flamed out. I was thinking I should take a sabbatical and try to land a job in fine dining in Paris or Milan."

I tried to keep my face neutral. *After everything we shared, she just wants to pack up and move to Paris? What the fuck.*

"Interesting."

She glared at me and said sharply, "What am I supposed to do? I can't just stay here and mooch off of my friends."

"I don't consider what you're doing mooching."

"I'm also not going to be my mother and just bounce from guy to guy, draining them dry."

"You can hardly suck me dry," I said, trying and failing to land a joke.

"Let's just have a nice brunch," she said, smiling at me.

I tried to remain relaxed and pleasant, but inside, I was a wreck. Was that the deal? Here I was thinking we were going to spend the rest of our lives together, and this was what, an experiment to her? A bucket list item for Holly?

You're acting paranoid and crazy. You just randomly put her on the spot, I told myself. *She's stressed about the bake-off. Just drop it.*

Walker was still asleep on the couch when Holly and I arrived back at my condo. Rudolph jumped up, tail wagging, and ran to me when he saw us.

"I took him out like three times last night," Walker said, yawning. There was an entire half of a cake beside him.

"Did you eat all of that?"

"Hell no! Little elves came in and ate all of that! It was a full cake an hour ago."

"Uh-huh."

"Let's not point fingers about who ate what cake. Instead, we should be thanking Holly for all her help," Walker said. "It definitely paid off. Greg has all the kids making Christmas ornaments showing the exact moment when Owen crashed into the water."

CHAPTER 67

Holly

I was sick with nervous energy the next morning. It was the final day of the bake-off. I needed to win—like *really* needed to win. Owen wasn't going to want to be with someone who couldn't manage a piddly little subscription baking business.

Worse, what if he thought I was only with him for the payday? I definitely had the means and motive. Shoot, if I was looking at the situation objectively, I clearly looked like a gold digger.

I paced around in front of the tower in the late-afternoon sun, hoping the cold would clear my head. But I couldn't stop thinking about Owen. I hadn't even decided what I was going to even bake.

"Ready to lose?" Amber said, jerking me out of my thoughts. She was dressed in a huge trench coat complete with sunglasses and a fedora.

"Ready to finally admit that you're a creepy stalker and Owen is never going to be interested in you?" I retorted.

"He's never going to be interested in you either," she said slyly. I narrowed my eyes. Amber pulled her tablet out of her bag, swiping the screen on.

"Take a look at that!"

There on the screen was Sloane and Owen kissing at the *TechBiz* holiday party.

"I've seen her do that before," I said, though it did sting a little. "She's after him. Just like you. I don't hold him accountable for your actions."

Amber pouted. "But he won the contest. The only reason he won was because Sloane pulled strings for him. And the only reason she would do that is because he's sleeping with her!"

"That's very convoluted," I said, rolling my eyes. Inside I was thinking, *Could it be true?*

No.

"I helped him win."

"Did you though?" Amber said. "You what, organized a half-cracked winter festival, and you think that was enough to win him the contest? Honestly, Holly, you are so naïve. You always were. Living in your Christmas fantasyland, watching your Hallmark movies, reading your holiday romance novels in the middle of August. Men like him don't want girls like you."

"They don't want girls like you either!" I shot back, hurt.

"I know," Amber said nastily. "And if I can't have him, I'm going to make sure no one can."

"Welcome to the final episode of *The Great Christmas Bake-Off*!" Anastasia announced. "For those of you watching on Christmas Eve when this airs, Merry Christmas from everyone here at the Great Christmas Bake-Off. We hope you're inspired by these amazing Christmas desserts."

Owen sat, back straight, at the judges' table. I still felt bad for getting snippy over brunch yesterday. But seeing Owen had given me the flash of inspiration I needed. I was going to make a dessert inspired by the Christmas lights Owen had taken me to see after the gala.

I didn't want to do something hokey like make cupcakes festooned with icing lights, though I was definitely going to do that whenever I got a chance to host another holiday party—which, since I was going to have to move out of the penthouse today, might be Nevuary.

No, I was going to bake something very delicate and light, with little bits of spun sugar. It was going to float in a sugar crystal lattice. The lattice was going to be a three-dimensional snowflake, and when someone looked at it from a certain angle, it would look like a house. Otherwise it was a beautiful form to hold morsels of little tarts and custards and tastes of sauces or a chocolate truffle. Inside, I was going to put tasty bites.

I made the lattices first, since I knew they needed time, and I didn't want to rush and break anything. Because the sugar needed to be clear and icy, I didn't heat it up too much. It took some time to carefully cut out all the little pieces and glue them together with melted sugar. The pieces of sugar were faceted like a diamond so that they caught the light. The dish should sparkle like fresh snow.

When I was done, I had four perfect snowflakes. I carefully cemented them to the plate with bits of white chocolate to hold them down. Then I made the decorations. There would be a mix of flavors and textures along with bright pops of color for visual interest. I made a bright-red hibiscus reduction, a glossy caramel, and a rich chocolate sauce and set them in the fridge. I could not have anything hot on the snowflakes.

Next I made several chocolate truffles and rolled some in purple lavender sugar and others in cinnamon and vanilla sugar. They glittered like gemstones. Next were salted caramels, the French sea salt providing the sparkle.

I also baked miniature chocolate, pear, and custard pastries. They were small, with thin, flaky crusts, and could be eaten in one bite. Finally, I candied flower petals and little pieces of fruit to provide even more sparkle and interest.

As I took my sauces out of the fridge, I looked at the clock. I had just enough time left to plate. I carefully composed each dish, sinking into the zone, making sure each snowflake was unique but still had a balance of flavors. I wanted them each to be different but not too different.

But not too different. Was that what was wrong with Owen and me? We were too different? He had the fancy cars and a huge company and lots of money. Maybe Amber and Sloane were right: maybe a man like Owen would never see a future with someone like me.

CHAPTER 68

Owen

A fter the camera guys took the footage they needed of the judges watching the opening of the contest, I took one last look at Holly then stood up from the judges' table.

Anu and Nick remained to watch, but I felt compelled to leave. Holly had seemed angry and annoyed that morning. Was it something I did? I'd thought I had a nice evening planned the night before, but maybe she would have rather gone to a play or a nice restaurant. Had I come across as cheap?

Maybe she was just nervous.

I went up to my office. The Christmas decorations Holly had hung up greeted me. I wished Holly was there too. That morning, she had said she wanted to go to Paris. Surely she didn't mean it. But what if she did?

"Someone's mopey," Walker said, strolling in. He had a huge piece of cake in his hand.

"I'm surprised you can even fit through the door."

"I went for a six-mile run today with a weight vest."

"Right."

"So I hear you're hosting a holiday party."

"Lies and rumors."

"That's not what my brother Liam says. Jack told everyone to be at your condo on the twenty-fourth. And let me just say that I am expecting a cookie with my face on it."

Holly had seemed nervous before the contest, which she normally never was. But when I returned to the studio later in the day, she seemed to be in her element. She was carefully plating her dish, balancing each element.

"I see you brought the Christmas bling!" Anu said when the plates with the snowflakes were set in front of us.

"Did you 3-D print this?" I asked.

"Nope. Handmade it. Took forever!"

"It looks so good," Nick said, turning the plate this way and that to catch the light.

"I was inspired by the Christmas lights," Holly explained. My heart melted a little bit as she smiled softly at me.

Fiona was next. "Since it's Christmas, I made a dessert inspired by *The Nutcracker*," she explained.

I inspected the dish.

"Astonishing," Anu said.

Fiona had made a white chocolate egg and decorated it like a *Fabergé* egg. She had carefully removed a piece of the shell. Inside was a scene made out of formed sugar, cakes, little mousses, and chocolate that was very reminiscent of a scene from *The Nutcracker* ballet. It had the Eastern European elements.

"The Sugar Plum Fairy scene, if I'm not mistaken," Anu said. She took a dainty bite. "And you can taste the plum."

"This chocolate pot de crème is just so smooth and perfect," Nick gushed. "This is a Michelin-star-level dessert!"

"Thank you so much for this!" Anu said, giving a little bow to Fiona.

"Wow, what a way to end the season, huh," Nick said. He and Anu looked at each other.

"What?" I snapped. "Both of them had great desserts."

Anu took a deep breath. "Fiona's was probably better."

Dana came over, making a cutting motion to Zane.

"Look," she said to me, "Fiona needs to win."

"Why?"

"Everyone knows you're sleeping with Holly."

"I'm in a relationship with her," I insisted.

"Whatever. We can't have bad press about this. People really dug the romance, but there will be a Christmas bloodbath if they think the contest was rigged because Holly slept with a judge. She can have the fan-favorite award, and Fiona wins. Everyone is happy. No one is lambasted on social media."

I glowered.

"You and Jack," Dana said, shaking her head. "If you all weren't so handsome, I'd never have another Frost brother on this show."

I dreaded having to tell Holly the news. She handled it very professionally when Anu told Fiona that she'd won. Somehow that made me feel even more like a piece of shit.

Holly hugged Fiona, clearly struggling to hold back tears and smile for her friend.

"You deserved it," she whispered.

"Thank you, everyone, for another Great Christmas Bake-Off," Anastasia said, "and everyone have a Merry Christmas!"

I was not having a merry anything if Holly was mad at me. I turned in the microphone then hung around for the postcontest interviews, hoping I didn't miss Holly. I saw her hurrying away after filming was over.

"Wait!" I called out to her.

"I have some stuff to do. I'll talk to you later," she said, trying to move around me.

I felt like shit. I should have insisted she win. That was what a good boyfriend would have done.

"Stop looking so guilty," she snapped. "I don't need you to just hand me stuff because you feel sorry for me. I'm a big girl. I can handle some disappointment. Fiona's dessert was better than mine. I'm a chef. I know what quality is. Hers was better. Someone wins, someone loses. I would have made the same choice. That's the way the cookie crumbles."

CHAPTER 69

Holly

I couldn't freaking believe it. I'd lost. Not just the contest but everything. When the judges announced that Fiona was the winner, I realized the weight of my loss would ripple into an implosion of epic proportions. I tried to keep it together in front of the cameras as my world crumbled around me.

What was I going to do? I had no money. I hadn't paid off my debt. My grandmother's decorations were going to be auctioned off in the next few days because I couldn't make the payment. I was a cold, hard failure. Again. I should really take down the webpage that had the sign-up for the sub-scription baking box, since I had nowhere to bake it. I didn't even have anywhere to live. I needed to find a job though, like right now. But all I wanted to do was curl up in bed and drink a gallon of hot chocolate and watch Christmas movies.

"Oh my God, I'm so sorry you lost," Fiona said, running to hop into the elevator with me after I blew off Owen.

I didn't want his pity. He'd just spent all that money on me. Any sob story I gave him would just make it seem like I was begging for more handouts.

"It's fine. Your dessert was awesome; you deserved the win," I assured her. We rode upstairs in silence. I felt bad that Fiona felt bad for winning.

"Are you going home for Christmas?" she asked.

"With Amber? No way. I don't know where I'm going," I admitted.

"Come stay in my apartment! You can use the obnox-iously tiny kitchen to bake the rest of your subscription boxes," Fiona said, grabbing my hand.

"I don't know…"

"Come on! It's Christmas. It's the season of giving," she said as we stepped off the elevator. "I would love to have you."

Owen called me. I sent it to voicemail.

"Or you could just move in with your boyfriend," she said slyly.

"I don't know, I'm not really the moocher type," I replied as Fiona unlocked the door.

It opened before she could pull the handle. Morticia stood there.

"Dana said we have to be out in one hour. Apparently Owen wants his penthouse back."

I looked around at all the Christmas decor. "We have to take all this down?" I asked, starting to panic.

Morticia snorted. "You can if you want to."

I didn't.

I ignored the text messages and other calls from Owen while I hastily packed.

"You can come back to Harrogate with me," Morticia offered.

"You're going back now?"

"In a few days." Her face softened, and she hugged me, the buckles on her jacket poking me. "You'll be fine. It's like *American Idol*. Everyone likes the runners-up better."

I groaned and lay down on the bed. Morticia pushed me aside and stripped off the sheets.

"Come on," she said. "I had to order an extra-large Uber to fit all your stuff. They're going to be here soon."

A half hour later, Fiona, Morticia, and I had hauled out all my possessions, which mostly consisted of my costumes, baking supplies, and the Christmas decorations from my grandmother I had managed to keep out of the soon-to-be auctioned storage unit, outside to the Uber.

I looked back up at the tower to where Owen's office was. His light was still on. I could tell it was his because of all the garland I'd hung on his balcony. I should go up and talk to him. That would have been the adult, mature thing to do. Instead, my friends and I rode across town to Fiona's tiny but very cute apartment.

"Wine," Fiona ordered, setting a box on the coffee table after we set all my stuff by the door. "You need wine and sugar."

"I think I'm all sugared out."

"Nope," Fiona said and stuffed a mini chocolate cupcake into my mouth.

"That so good," I said through the mouthful of icing.

We drank boxed wine and sat on the couch, watching *The Muppet Christmas Carol*. That segued into *Elf*, another box of wine, Christmas-cookie-flavored Lay's potato chips (which were a terrible idea), and then we rounded off the evening with *The Polar Express*. I fell asleep with the nightmarish, animated, uncanny-valley face of Tom Hanks as the conductor.

CHAPTER 70

Owen

I didn't know what to do about Holly. She wasn't answering my calls or returning any of my messages. In a fit of desperation, I dressed up Rudolph in a doggie snowman costume and sent her a picture, but not even that earned a reaction. She must be furious at me.

I was playing fetch with Rudolph when my sister, Belle, let herself into my condo.

"Your penthouse upstairs is cleared out," she said. "They left the decorations up, since apparently you're volunteering to host a large Christmas party."

"I was voluntold to do it," I grumbled. "I thought Holly was going to help."

"Ah, I see. You're dating her so she'll throw parties and cook for you." Belle gave me that look that older sisters give their younger brothers when they feel they've been complete idiots and they're stunned their brother can even function.

388 · ALINA JACOBS

"You make it sound bad," I complained. "I appreciate her for other stuff too."

"So she cooks, throws parties, and sucks your dick wearing those ridiculous outfits. Does she clean as well?" Belle asked, raising an eyebrow and crossing her arms.

"It's not like that!" I protested. "I bought her a very nice dress."

"And yet she's not here. I'm shocked."

"She's busy."

"The bake-off is over," Belle reminded me.

I was deflated. "So I fucked up."

"Who knows, but probably," Belle told me. "You're kind of an asshole sometimes, Owen."

I knew Belle was referencing when my parents had refused to pay her university tuition. She had gone to community college and worked nights. Then she had paid my Harvard tuition because our parents refused. She'd also paid for my younger brothers' schooling by day trading and working contract coding jobs. She had lived at home until Oliver, my youngest brother, was out of the house.

I didn't realize that was what had happened until later. I should have done more to get Belle out of our parents' house. She was my sister after all. But she was my big sister, and she always seemed to have her shit together. I'd assumed if she wanted to leave, she would have. But she had stayed to help take care of my younger brothers and be a buffer between them and our parents. As soon as Oliver was in college, she'd split.

I was definitely an asshole, and an oblivious one at that.

"I'm going to fix it," I said firmly.

"You better," Belle said, "because I'm not eating anything you cook."

After she left, I went through my condo, collecting all my belongings to take upstairs. I found the dress and cape I had bought for Holly. They still smelled like her, all sugar and spice. I half didn't want to leave this condo. Holly had been here with me. But I hauled all my stuff upstairs.

My penthouse had been freshly cleaned. The cleaner had even left all the windows open, just the way I liked it. It was freezing inside. I opened the fridge, hoping to find some of Holly's cookies. But the cleaner had removed any food.

I went upstairs to the master suite, where Holly had lived for a month, and lay down on the mattress.

The next morning, Holly still hadn't responded to any of my attempts to contact her. I dressed and went down to my office. I needed the distraction of work.

I was reading through some of the employee comments that *TechBiz* magazine had picked out to provide to each company. Several asked for a café in the tower. There was a fine-dining restaurant attached to the hotel, but the employees didn't like it, and they weren't shy about complaining.

I took a deep breath and called Svensson Investment. They managed the ground-floor retail space in the tower.

"You want a what?" Greg said in a clipped tone. "A restaurant? There's no street-frontage retail spots left."

"It doesn't need it. Word of mouth will generate traffic to the establishment, and my employees will use it. They've been begging for a fast casual restaurant in the tower. I think we might be able to carve part of the lobby space out for a café."

"Is this for Holly?" he asked.

"She helped win us the contest," I countered.

"I highly doubt that." I could hear the annoyance in Greg's voice.

In the background, Hunter said, "You can't just put a permanent restaurant in the middle of a lobby. Would the city building department even allow it?"

"They do it in France," I said into the phone.

"No."

Time to use my trump card. "If it's not built in the Quantum Cyber tower, the Holbrooks are going to build her a restaurant in their tower."

There was a sharp intake of breath from the other end of the line, followed by frantic whispering.

"We will invest one million dollars to build her a café," Greg said. "But you need to put up the other half."

"I don't need the money, I just need you to do the legal work to carve up the space, but sure, deal."

I looked up architects after the call. I wanted Holly to have the perfect restaurant. Surely this was what she wanted, right? She had that subscription baking company. She was entrepreneurial.

"Owen."

Crap. Sloane. I had left my secretary strict instructions not to allow Sloane into my office. Unfortunately, my secretary was already out for Christmas break.

"Can I help you?" I asked firmly.

"Of course," she said, sauntering over to me. Her blouse was unbuttoned several buttons too many, her cleavage pushed up.

"We had a deal, Owen."

"We didn't have a deal."

"Yes, we did!" She pouted. "I gave you the contest, and you give me everything I want!"

I threw my head back and laughed at the ridiculousness of the situation. "I'm not marrying you," I retorted.

"I don't need marriage," Sloane said, unbuttoning another button. "Maybe just a little early Christmas present." She pulled my face down into her cleavage. "I just want my reward for helping you."

I tried to scramble up, but she kissed me.

There was an explosion of glitter. As it cleared, it revealed Holly's angry face.

CHAPTER 71

Holly

I woke up the next morning half on the floor, chocolate frosting in my hair. The TV was still blaring holiday movies. Several elves were running around on the screen in a panic. The counter in the corner said two more days until Christmas. I started as a key turned in the door.

"I ordered us croissan'wiches," Morticia said as she set the borrowed keys in the little dish on the bookcase. "Though, mainly I bought them for you. You have a gallon of wine in your stomach."

I checked my phone as I ate the croissant. There were several texts from Owen. One was Rudolph dressed up as a snowman. Another asked if I was going to come to the holiday party he was apparently hosting on Christmas Eve.

Owen: *Please don't move to Paris. I'll miss your cookies.*

There was another text from Amber with the pictures of Owen kissing Sloane.

Morticia peered over my shoulder. "Is that—"

"I think she ambushed him."

"She seems to be doing that a lot," Morticia said, her eyes narrowing dangerously.

"It's not his fault!" I protested. "Sloane is crazy."

"He's a billionaire," Morticia said flatly. "He could have nipped that in the bud a while ago."

"I can't believe you're agreeing with Amber," I said.

Standing up and balling the empty wrapper, Morticia sighed. "You're my friend, and I don't want to see you get hurt. Also, I have a baseball bat in case he screws up."

"I appreciate that," I said, rolling my eyes, "but I'm not taking a baseball bat to Owen."

"Missed opportunity."

"I'm going to see him," I insisted, throwing away my trash. "We'll have an adult conversation. I still have his credit card anyway; I should give that back."

"You're going like that? You have frosting in your hair, and you smell like a bar."

I hopped out of the Uber in front of Owen's tower. I felt much better after a shower and some coffee. It was almost Christmas! I was wearing a sweater with holiday corgis on it. Owen had wanted me to help him with a holiday party, and there was nothing better than throwing a party!

Owen's office was mostly empty. A temp worker filling in for the receptionist was sitting at the front desk, sipping tea out of a giant mug shaped like a penguin and watching holiday movies.

"Just go on up," she said when I asked about Owen. "His secretary isn't there. She went back to Texas."

When I arrived on Owen's floor, I snuck up to his door. I wanted to surprise him, but I was the one who got the nasty surprise.

Owen was in his office, alone, with *Sloane*. She smiled and said something, then Owen tipped his head back and laughed.

I held my breath, not daring to believe what I was seeing. Surely there was a logical explanation for all of this, right? Then she leaned forward, grabbed him, and pulled him into a passionate kiss. I wanted to turn tail and run. But I would regret it forever if I didn't make some kind of scene.

I picked up one of the decorative pine cones I'd put on the secretary's desk. It was practically shellacked in glitter. And it was flaking. I flung the door to Owen's office open and chucked the giant pine cone at the two of them. It hit Sloane square in the shoulder. Sloane shrieked as she and Owen were covered in a puff of glitter.

"You lunatic!" she spat, trying to dust herself off. "This was a very expensive blouse!"

I was pretty proud of myself for the shot. All that whipping cream by hand had given me some muscle under the liquefied sugar.

"Holly," Owen said, "this isn't what it looks like."

"Really?" I said "What is it then?"

Sloane smirked. "He's giving me the payment for winning the *TechBiz* competition."

I tried to keep the despair off my face.

Sloane was triumphant. "You honestly didn't think your stupid little parties were what won him the contest, did you?"

"That's all I need to hear then," I said, fumbling in my purse to throw the credit card at him. "I hope your Christmas sucks, Owen Frost."

CHAPTER 72

Owen

"**G**et out of my office," I ordered Sloane.

"But we're made for each other, Owen," she said, flinging herself at me.

I tried to pull her off; it was difficult, as she had her nails sunk into my suit jacket.

"It's better this way," Sloane insisted. "You had your fun with the baker, but now it's time to settle down."

I finally disentangled myself from her. I was furious. "When I come back, you better be gone," I warned. Then I ran after Holly. She was walking quickly through the lobby to the front door when I caught up with her.

"Holly, stop!"

She whirled around. "I don't get you," she said. "Like what the hell?"

"Sloane just surprised me," I insisted.

"Yeah, she seems to be doing a lot of that," Holly said, eyes narrowing.

"Why can't you just accept that I'm telling the truth?" I snarled at her. "I did all those nice things for you."

"You mean like buying me expensive jewelry and outfits and paying me to throw parties that apparently you didn't need. Oh, wait, I forgot, there's totally nothing going on between you and the person who is handing out the prizes."

We glared at each other.

"See, this is why I hate Christmas," I declared. "People get overly emotional."

"I'm not emotional!" Holly screeched.

"I didn't say you were," I yelled. Then I clenched my jaw shut. I sounded like my father. I did not want to be anything like my father.

"I need to go," I said. *Before I say something I really regret.*

I left Holly standing there hurt, surrounded by the Christmas decorations. It felt cruel. I knew it was.

Cold, dispassionate.

I needed to calm down. Then I would figure things out with Holly.

"Did Sloane leave?" I asked the temp receptionist when I went back up to my office.

"Stormed out of here," she replied.

"Please don't let her back in."

Rudolph had found my credit card and was chewing it when I went back into my office.

"I need this," I told him, tugging the drooly card out of his mouth. "Apparently I need to plan a holiday party."

Belle had been right. I shouldn't have just expected Holly to do it, just like I shouldn't have assumed that she would want to stay here and open a restaurant in the lobby of my tower. There wouldn't even be a window. Paris would be nicer, of course. Maybe I could go visit her if I hadn't screwed up too badly.

Rudolph pawed at my legs, and I scratched his head and took out my phone.

Owen: *How many people are coming for the Christmas party tomorrow?*
Jack: *You're just now trying to figure this out?*
Jack: *Also doesn't Holly know what's going on?*
Owen: *I think she's done with me.*
Jack: *… Dude*

I searched the internet. If my secretary has been here, I would have asked her to help me find a place to cater at the last minute. Surely that wouldn't be impossible? I called a place that said they did high-end parties.

"You need what?" the owner asked incredulously when I called. "We've been booked for the twenty-fourth for months."

It was the same at the other places. I was screwed in more ways than one. I'd fucked up with Holly, and now I had screwed up the Christmas party I didn't even want.

Owen: *None of these places cater. I think I need to cook a turkey. Could your brother Remy give me a crash course on how to use a smoker?*
Walker: *Lol you're going to cook? I can't believe Holly didn't give you an easier dish to make.*

Owen: *Why does everyone assume she's doing all the cooking?*

Walker: *Please don't tell me you screwed up. I was going to put in a special request for that wedding cake she made.*

Owen: *You already ate the whole thing?*

Walker: *You know the holidays stress me out.*

Walker: *Hey you know what I'll bring a shit ton of beer and potato chips. Everyone will be so drunk it will kill the food poisoning you give them when you fuck up that turkey.*

I went back to praying I could find a place to cater the party but was interrupted by my phone ringing. It was Greg Svensson.

"I was just informed that you screwed up the restaurant," Greg said.

"I didn't screw anything up," I said icily.

"That's not what Walker said," Greg retorted. "I can't believe you. I already rubbed it in Grant Holbrook's face. I saw him at Cameli's. I can't have this coming back to me."

"You know I can't stand the Holbrooks after what they did to us," his brother Hunter said into the speaker. "I better not see Holly opening up shop in the Holbrook Enterprises tower. Has she confirmed with you on running the restaurant in the Quantum Cyber tower?"

"I don't know," I said brusquely.

"You don't know? Owen. This has to happen. I can't look bad," Greg insisted.

"Why does everyone get so petty and emotional around Christmas?" I complained.

"Because it's a terrible holiday."

I hung up. I had several problems to solve. The main one was Holly. I tried calling her again. No answer. I looked around my office; I needed a grand gesture. But I didn't even know where she lived. I bet I knew who would, though.

I scrolled through my phone until I found the number. I hated to do this—it felt like making a deal with the devil.

Owen: *I need to ask you for a favor.*
Garrett: *No.*
Owen: *It's not a big favor. I need to know where Holly is.*

My phone rang.

Garrett's voice was annoyed. "You lost Holly?"

"I didn't lose her."

"You better not have!" Penny yelled at the phone. "I have months' worth of *Vanity Rag* content for the New Year planned around her!"

"Just tell me where she is, and I'll fix it," I insisted.

"I don't know," Penny said. "I have to ask her first."

After ending the call, I paced around the office. I felt crazed and angry.

I was even sympathizing with Hunter Svensson, who always seemed to be some flavor of miserable and angry. Walker had filled me in on what had happened between him and Meghan. Now that I was in the throes of losing the love of my life, I realized how agonizing it was.

But unlike Hunter, I wasn't giving up without a fight— or, more accurately, a groveling apology. Christmas was going to be miserable enough, but Christmas without Holly? Intolerable.

I couldn't stand being cooped up anymore. I grabbed my keys and went down to the garage, Rudolph in tow. Driving would help clear my mind while I waited for Penny's response.

When I pushed through the door into the garage where all my cars were parked, something whizzed past my head and splatted on the floor. Rudolph pounced. I looked down to see him take a big bite of something red, green, and white.

"Is that a cupcake?"

CHAPTER 73

Holly

"**S**crew Owen!" I shouted when I flung open the door to Fiona's apartment. She and Morticia stopped their heated argument about whether *The Nightmare Before Christmas* was a Christmas movie or a Halloween movie.

"Owen is a Christmas-hating, cold-hearted bastard. I can't believe I wasted my whole December with him!" I sank down onto the couch. Fiona poured me a shot. I downed the whole thing.

"Was it Sloane?" Morticia asked.

"It was everything—the lying, the manipulation, the fact that he's so closed off. Most of all is the fact that he hates Christmas! I thought I could make him love it, but I think he was just tolerating it because, I don't know, he wanted to sleep with me, I guess. I was used. I mean, it felt really good," I said, remembering being with him, "but still. I have to have standards. He literally ruined Christmas for me!"

"Then we need to ruin it for him," Fiona insisted.

"How? He doesn't like Christmas."

"Everyone has something they love," Morticia said, face a little scary in her dark makeup.

"I'm not going after his family or his dog," I added.

"Billionaires are like Ebenezer Scrooge. They have weird emotional attachments to money and nice things. Does he have golf clubs you could throw in the Hudson River? Tacky bronze replicas of himself?"

"No," I said, "but he does have all his cars."

"Perfect," Morticia said, handing me a baseball bat.

"I'm not going to smash his cars!" I said, horrified, shoving it back at her. "They're expensive, and the only thing worse than spending Christmas in the company of all my debt collectors would be spending it in jail."

"You can't just let him off scot-free. At least make your exit a memorable one," Fiona said, pouring all of us another round of shots.

While it was fun to think about getting revenge, I would never actually go through with it, I promised myself as I downed another shot.

"God, this vodka is disgusting."

"I won it in a raffle last year," Fiona said. "It's eggnog flavored."

"It's nasty," I said as she poured me another.

"How about we do a little cake decorating," Fiona said. "Now?"

"Yes. We'll throw frosting and smear cake, chocolate sauce, marshmallows, and sprinkles all over his cars. Nothing a little carwash can't fix. Harmless fun and petty revenge!" she said.

"You know what?" I said, standing up and pouring myself another shot. "Turn on the oven. Let's bake!"

"You don't have to make it perfect," Morticia complained as Fiona carefully measured out flour. "No one's eating it."

"But I'll know if it's not good!" she wailed.

The mixer whirred as I made royal icing. Fiona carefully spooned the batter into cupcake tins.

"Can you make me some green and red frosting? I want to make swirled tops," she said.

"I want marshmallows," I slurred, pouring us all another round of shots. It was definitely getting a little blurry in here. I was really starting to think smearing cake and candy all over Owen's cars was a totally fantastic idea. Hey, he was a lying, cheating, Christmas-hating bastard, right? Really, if I thought about it, I was showing considerable restraint.

By the time the cupcakes had been baked, cooled, and decorated, the eggnog vodka was gone and we had started on the Yule log vodka, which was supposed to taste like chocolate mousse but tasted like reindeer roadkill.

"The frosting is done," Morticia said, scraping a bowl into an overflowing five-gallon bucket.

"We need disguises," Fiona suggested.

"I have the perfect thing," I said, snapping my fingers, or trying to. That vodka was messing with my hand-eye coordination.

From one of my boxes of costumes, I pulled out three elf outfits.

"Why do you have three?" Fiona asked.

"They were on sale." I shrugged, pulling on the red tights and little shorts. I put on the jacket and tightened the belt. Then I helped Fiona lace up the bodice on her elf costume and adjusted Morticia's collar. With our elf hats and sunglasses, my friends and I could be any mall Santa's little helpers.

"We can't just walk in with this stuff," Fiona said, gesturing to the boxes of sprinkles and the bags and buckets of icing.

"We'll wrap it," Fiona decided. "I bought all this Christmas paper from the dollar store and never used it."

"We should use it. I have bows too!" I said as we sat on the floor, wrapping the boxes of sprinkles, icing, sauces, and cupcakes.

"Now who's taking too much time?" I said as Morticia carefully wrapped the boxes of cupcakes.

"It has to look legit," she said as she carefully lined up the patterns on the silvery wrapping paper.

When everything was wrapped, Fiona took the boxes of cupcakes. I had the bags of royal icing and boxes of sprinkles, marshmallows, and other small, sugary objects. Morticia had the bucket of buttercream frosting and bags of chocolate sauce and red syrup. As we were about to leave, she picked up the bat and added it to her load. She had wrapped it neatly in green-and-red paper and tied a large bow on it.

"Just in case you want to really let loose."

We hauled the baked goods across town to Owen's tower. After all the physical exertion, I was a lot more sober when we arrived there and snuck into the garage.

"Maybe we shouldn't do this," I said apprehensively as I surveyed the rows of expensive cars. Morticia and Fiona were unwrapping the bags of frosting. "We could just eat the cupcakes instead."

"You shouldn't eat so many carbs," Owen's mom said, appearing out of the shadows, the bells on her elf costume jingling softly. "Carbs make you fat and break out your skin. I should know. I have two PhDs."

"Well, good for you," Fiona shot back, hefting a container of icing.

Was Owen's mom going to call the cops? *Holly, this was such a dumb idea.*

Diane frowned as she surveyed the boxes of cupcakes and frosting. "Are you here to do some sort of crazy sex activity with my son?"

"Of course not!" I said just as Morticia said, "Yeah, we totally are."

"*Morticia,*" I hissed.

"What?" she whispered back. "We can't admit we're here to cake-smash his cars."

Diane Frost smirked. "Oh, you poor, stupid, heartbroken girl. Did you actually think my son was in love with you?"

I bit my lip. Yeah, actually, a part of me kind of had.

"He was just using you," Diane continued. "He's been with Sloane the whole time. You know, as a scientist you have to remain dispassionate in order to see the truth. That's how I operate. Don't let your emotions cloud your judgment. I'm right. Look at the facts."

I did. I had. And the conclusion was that Owen had definitely been using me. I looked around in anger. Was I just another thing that Owen had acquired because he could? Did he collect women like cars?

"This is your big moment, Holly," Morticia said. She pressed a button on her phone, and the Russian dance from

The Nutcracker broke out, echoing around the parking deck. I pulled out a bag of royal icing and dumped it over the nearest car. Fiona handed me two cupcakes, and I hurled them at two more pristine black cars.

"More icing!" Fiona cheered.

I dragged the bucket of buttercream frosting and dumped it all over a silver Porsche, covering it with red. For good measure, I lobbed handfuls of red and green sprinkles onto the frosting. They stuck, speckling the car.

"Have fun licking that off, dick!"

I smashed several cupcakes on a Lamborghini, smearing the red and green frosting all over the windshield, cake crumbling on the sleek hood of the car. White chocolate went all over the Bugatti that he'd driven me around in, then came fistfuls of red sugar, the crystals raining over the car like angry snow.

"Stop it!" another woman shrieked. Amber raced toward me in an elf costume that was a lot sexier than mine. She had on mile-high stilettos and was hobbling along as she approached. "That's my boyfriend's car." She ran to Fiona and tried to wrestle the cupcakes out of her arms.

"I made these! Get your own cupcakes!" she hollered.

Morticia picked up the bat, comically wrapped in Christmas paper and a bow, and swung it around.

"Keep going, Holly! Finish the job. I'll hold her off!"

Amber managed to snag a cupcake. She hauled back and threw it at me. I ducked, squirting a nice stream of frosting along the length of a white McLaren Lotus. The cupcake barely missed me and instead hit Sloane in the face.

"Where did you come from?" She, too, was wearing a sexy elf costume.

"My future daughter-in-law!" Diane Frost said, pleased to see her.

"I was coming out here to give Owen a little surprise," Sloane said, "but clearly you animals ruin everything for people who are just trying to make their men happy."

"Because nothing says 'I love you more' like pimping yourself out to win a magazine award," Morticia shot out.

Sloane plunged at me, wrestling me for the icing. "Give it to me! I'm going to kill her!"

"All of you need to make your own baked goods!" Fiona shouted. "We spent hours on these! *Hours!*" She smashed a cupcake in Amber's face. Amber lunged at her.

I hoped Morticia had it under control. I was too busy avoiding Sloane. She had several inches on me, and unlike me, she did real workouts, not the "How fast can I shovel these chips and dip into my mouth?" kind.

Sloane finally wrestled the frosting from me, squirted it in my face, then ran to Morticia. I lunged at Sloane's ankles, and we both went down in the icing and destroyed cupcakes.

Morticia was still swinging the bat around. Dr. Frost did some sort of jujitsu move and took the bat, throwing it away. She tried to punch Morticia, but my friend ducked. Fiona was trying to throw a cupcake at Amber, but her aim was off, and Owen's mom scored a cupcake to the face.

Slone kicked at me then ran to the group. I raced after her, slipping and sliding in the icing. I grabbed a cupcake. I was furious at Sloane and the whole situation. Raising my arm, I hurled it at her. She ducked, and I watched as the cupcake flew through the air right at a very confused-looking Owen.

CHAPTER 74

Owen

looked up to see what looked like Santa's toy shop dumped out in my garage. Elves were everywhere.

"Owen!" my mom called.

"Baby!" Sloane cried.

They raced toward me, covered in frosting. In fact the garage looked as if an industrial baking accident had occurred. Icing, cake, chocolate sauce, and sprinkles were all over the floors, walls, and ceiling.

"My cars!" I said in shock. They were covered in desserts.

"It was Holly!" another elf exclaimed running towards me in mincing little steps.

"Shit," several men chorused behind me.

"Mom?" Jack said as he, Jonathan, Matt, and Oliver peered around me at the dessert carnage.

"My darling sons!" my mother said, trying to hug my brothers. The youngest two shrank away from her.

"This is private property," I said tersely. "I'm calling the police."

"Holly's the one who needs to go to jail!" Sloane howled.

I pushed through them.

Holly looked at me defiantly, picked up a cupcake, and threw it at the nearest car.

"You don't get to just use me like I'm some sort of funny little holiday experiment that you can brag about to your friends," she said hotly.

"I would never! I love you," I insisted.

"No you don't."

Holly looked as if she was about to cry.

"Of course I do," I said, reaching out and swiping at some of the frosting on her face.

"He's in love with me!" Sloane yelled.

"No he isn't," Belle said, shoving our brothers out of the way. "Honestly, Sloane, don't send incriminating emails from your work account. I had Garrett Svensson call up Evan Harrington and make him hand over your emails." My sister handed Holly a stack of papers.

"That just proves that Owen and I had a deal," Sloane countered.

"No, it explicitly shows you were talking to Diane about it." Belle pointed to the email.

"Belle is lying!" Sloane shrieked. "I didn't do any of that."

"Are you kidding me?" Belle said. "I literally have proof." She turned to Holly, who was leafing through the papers. "I'm sorry you got sucked into the middle of our family drama."

"And I'm sorry you got sucked into the middle of mine," Holly replied, jerking her head to indicate Amber. She smiled at me sheepishly. "So fair's fair? Sorry I ruined your cars. I'll buy you a drink to make it up to you?"

"You can make it up to me right now," I said, leaning over her, tasting the sugar, vanilla, and cake as I kissed her.

"Yeah, I think that might work," Holly breathed against my mouth.

I pulled her into a kiss, not caring that all the cake and frosting were going to ruin my suit. I kissed her long and hard.

"I think I love you too," she said when I released her—well, tried to release her.

"I think we're glued together," she said, peeling herself off me.

"Does this mean you accept him back?" Jonathan shouted. "Because supposedly we're eating raw turkey and beer for Christmas."

Holly wrinkled her nose.

"I'm cooking," I explained.

"You?" she said in shock.

"I couldn't book a caterer."

"Of course not! For Christmas Eve? You'd have had to book way in advance."

"Well," I said, "I didn't." I looked at Holly. "But maybe you want to have beer? Christmas is about spending time with people you love."

"Yes, but call me old-fashioned, I like food on Christmas." She looked at me then looked around. "The least I could do after destroying your cars is host your Christmas party."

Belle threw our mom, Sloane, and Amber out of the tower. She tried to eject Morticia and Fiona too.

"No, they're with me," Holly said.

Belle peered at them. "I didn't recognize you two under all that cake."

"We probably shouldn't track all that into the building," Holly said, stopping in the doorway.

"I'm going back home to shower," Fiona announced. She took a bite of the last remaining cupcake.

"Same," Morticia said from behind a cake-covered car, where she was recovering her baseball bat.

Holly waved to them then followed me to the elevator.

My brothers and Belle exited the elevator two floors below to adjourn to Belle's condo.

"I am sorry about everything," I apologized once we were in my penthouse. I pulled Holly to me, kissing her, little flakes of dried icing raining on the freshly swept floor.

"I think I might have *slightly* overreacted," she said against my mouth. "The holidays, right? Makes people crazy."

"You aren't crazy," I said seriously. "I love you."

"I love you, too, Owen."

I wrapped her in my arms again. She was exactly where she belonged. "I have a favor to ask," I said after a moment.

"Of course I'll help you with your holiday party," she told me. "And I'll even wash your cars off. I have a Christmas-themed bikini!"

"Not that I wanted—" I ran a hand through my hair, streaking the platinum silver with red frosting. Holly tried not to giggle. I looked down at my hand wryly.

"I know you said you wanted to go to Paris if you didn't win," I said. "And if you still want to move, I'll help you as much or as little as you want."

She opened her mouth, but I held up a hand to stop her.

"But I was thinking maybe you'd like to open a restaurant here in the lobby? I have money allocated for it. My employees want it. So do the Svenssons."

"What do they have to do with it?" she asked, confused.

"They have these weird feuds... Never mind them. You don't have to give me an answer now," I assured her.

"Yes."

"You can take time to think about it—"

"Yes!" she practically shouted.

"It doesn't have a window, because all the retail space is used up," I said.

Holly shrugged. "It will be a secret. Internet influencers love that stuff. We're building a building within a building! It will be totally cool!"

"I'm glad you're staying!" I said in relief. I grinned broadly then kissed Holly.

"Yum," she said. "I love the way you taste covered in frosting."

CHAPTER 75

Holly

undid his tie, the frosting smearing on my hands.

"I think this suit is ruined," I said as Owen took off his jacket and dropped it to the floor. I threw his tie next to it and unbuttoned the top button on his shirt then pulled. The buttons all popped off, springing around the room.

"I thought that shirt was better made than that."

"I beat a lot of meringue," I said. "All of me is soft with the exception of my chef's arms. They're disproportionately strong and good at fine motor control."

He threw off his undershirt, and I licked the frosting off his chest while I undid his belt.

"I need my Frost and frosting fix," I joked.

He hissed as I took his cock out of his pants. It was thick and big, and my pussy ached with need for him. He undid my elf costume as I stroked his cock, getting frosting on it.

"Nuh-uh," I said as Owen bent down to press his face to my now-exposed tits. "From the moment I first saw you, I wanted to lick frosting off your cock. Now is my chance. Don't ruin this for me."

He bit down a curse as I bent down and licked my tongue along the length of his cock, anticipating how it would feel to have his huge dick inside me. I slid the whole length into my mouth, tasting the frosting. His hand rested on my head, gently rubbing my scalp. Then his fingers tangled in my hair and pulled me up to kiss my tits.

"I want to fuck you in that ridiculous elf costume," he said, hand pressing between my legs.

"Feeling the Christmas spirit! Also, I come covered in frosting, so you get a two-for-one kink deal!"

"If you're going to continue to dress in those outfits, I think Christmas might be my new turn-on," he mumbled as he licked and kissed my nipples. He pushed me back onto the large couch, pulling down the little shorts I was wearing under the elf jacket, then tore off the tights.

I moaned as he spread my thighs and pressed his mouth against me, licking me, teasing my clit, stroking along my pussy. He rolled on a condom. His chest had a streak of red frosting on it.

Sticking out my tongue, I licked him, making him growl. Owen crushed our mouths together then slid into me. He fucked me slowly, purposefully, making me feel every inch of his hard length. I tipped my head back and moaned as Owen trailed his tongue over my skin to the mounds of my breasts as he slowly fucked me.

One hand snuck between my legs to stroke my clit. I whimpered, my tits brushing against his chest as he thrust into me. I panted, and he moved up to kiss me, taking my mouth as he filled me with his huge cock. I moaned, my hands in his hair. I knew I was getting icing in it, but I didn't care. I spread my legs wider, needing to feel him, needing his cock.

He increased the rhythm, and I whimpered and panted against his mouth, kissing his strong jaw. One hand braced on the couch, the other went to my hip, fingers digging into my ass as he went faster. My tits bounced as he fucked me, his thick cock rubbing against my clit with every thrust. My breath came out in pleading little pants until finally I crashed over the edge, Owen coming quickly after.

"Yum," I said, licking a stripe of green frosting off his cheek. "Sex is definitely sweeter with a little baking!"

After showering, I had dragged Owen out to grocery shop. The store was crowded with last-minute shoppers.

"You should have really planned ahead," I told Owen as he loaded several hams into one of the three carts we had commandeered.

"Why are we buying so much food?"

"I told you, I am not having a repeat of the chicken tenders incident. There will be leftovers."

"Did you have to invite all the Svenssons?"

"Yes," I said in disbelief. "They're our friends. That's what Christmas is about—spending time with family and friends."

"There's an awful lot of them."

"And that's why you have the big penthouse. Fortunately, it is already decorated." I added various cold cuts to the cart.

"You could have ordered this online," Owen said.

"No way. Who knows what they'll try and sneak past you? No, I have to inspect my food. I have standards," I said as I attempted to pick up a frozen turkey as big as Owen's dog and put it in the cart. He took it from me then grabbed another one.

"Are you sure you want two?"

"You ate my Thanksgiving leftovers. Besides, in England, they eat turkey during Christmas, so it seems like it should be considered a Christmas food for our purposes," Owen said. He pushed his two carts behind me as I guided mine to the dairy section.

"Look at you being a Christmas expert!" I exclaimed, squeezing his arm. "I need to buy you your own collection of sexy holiday outfits."

"Uh… Change of topic," Owen said. "How's the restaurant?"

"Speaking of, I should ask Fiona if she wants to go in on it with me," I said happily as I loaded armfuls of European butter into the cart. "It's going to be too much for one person. I have big ambitions."

"Did you think of a name yet?" Owen asked.

"Names are so hard," I complained as we headed to fruits and vegetables. "I'm not even sure what kind of food I want to serve," I said as I placed several squashes into the shopping cart.

"I know I want to serve happy-hour cocktails, especially if there's a hotel in the building. Oh, you know what? I totally want to do bento boxes. Just something portable and yummy people can quickly pick up and take away. I guess I'll also need to find a closer apartment. Fiona's been letting me stay in her apartment, but it's super tiny."

"I was thinking," Owen said then trailed off. I looked up at him. "I mean if you want, you're free to live with me. I have a lot of room," he offered.

"I don't want to impose."

He took me in his arms. "There's nothing I want more than to have you in my life, in my home, in my bed every day," Owen whispered.

I melted against him as he kissed me. "I don't know if you want to live with me and all my Christmas stuff," I said with a laugh after he released me.

"How much can it be?" he teased. "I have a three-story penthouse. I can spare a closet for you."

"I might need a whole suite," I admitted.

"I thought you said you had all your stuff with you in a tiny apartment."

"Eh, yeah?" I looked up at the ceiling. "I have all the Christmas stuff from my grandmother in storage. Like her entire house's worth of Christmas stuff. It was all my good childhood memories. She made Christmas fun and warm and lovely," I said, remembering the happy Christmases spent in her home. "She would invite all her friends over who would otherwise be alone for Christmas, and we'd have a big party on Christmas Eve. Then on Christmas Day, we'd visit people in nursing homes or pay house visits to people who were sick."

Owen was quiet a minute.

"Or I can throw most of it out. I just have to sort through it."

"It's fine; bring it here."

"Really?" I said, delighted. "There's so much cool stuff! She used to collect antique Christmas paraphernalia. She even had a piece of cake from a Christmas party Queen Victoria hosted."

Owen tried not to make a face. "That sounds—"

"Excessive? Yes, I know, but it's a piece of history, and you can't throw it away."

"You keep it in storage?"

"It's a special storage unit. Very pricy unfortunately." I tried not to feel sad. Would I even be able to retrieve all the decorations before the storage facility auctioned everything off?

Owen looked at me in concern. I wasn't going to burden him with my issues. I hadn't paid the bill. It was my own fault. I refused to have Owen think I was solely after him for his money.

"I don't think I brought enough reusable shopping bags for all of this," I said as the cashier rang up all the food.

❆ ❊ ❆

Owen's siblings were waiting in the garage with a luggage cart when we returned.

"Wow, Owen took you in the only practical car he owns," Jack remarked.

"This also happens to be the only car I own that is not covered in sugar or one of its derivatives," he said dryly.

"Again, I am sorry about that. Though the bikini car wash offer still stands!" I elbowed Owen. "That perked you up, didn't it?"

Owen's brothers snickered and finished loading up the cart.

The penthouse was just as large and airy as I remembered it. We lugged all the food in. The Christmas decorations were up, and the tree sparkled. It felt homey and festive.

Jack's dog, Milo, was playing tug-of-war with Rudolph. They growled playfully around a squeaky snowman toy.

Owen's younger brothers went back to watching the soccer game on TV while Jonathan poured drinks.

"I was told that there was a Christmas party tomorrow and that you make amazing cookies. I humbly offer myself in service," Jonathan told me seriously.

"Ignore him," Jack said. "He can't even cook an egg."

"Chloe sent you over here by yourself?" Owen asked Jack.

"She's coming later. I told her about your restaurant," Jack said to me. "She said she'll be happy to help you in any way possible."

Owen's phone rang, and he went to take the call.

His sister, Belle, smiled at me. "I'm glad you're here. You make Owen really happy."

"He makes me happy too!"

"The last episode of *The Great Christmas Bake-Off* is airing later," she reminded me. "If you're not all baked out!"

"I will never have too much baking. We are so having a viewing party!"

CHAPTER 76

Owen

L istening to Holly talk so warmly about her grandmother had given me an idea for a good Christmas present. This was the call I needed to make it happen. I drank a sip of whiskey then answered the phone.

"Thanks for calling me, Morticia."

She didn't say a word. Her disapproval wafted through the phone.

"I called you because I need a favor," I continued.

"I did you a solid by not taking a baseball bat to your fancy-pants cars," she retorted. "I think I showed considerable restraint."

"Look, we both care about Holly, correct?"

She sighed. "Correct."

After I did some more begging and promising to never hurt Holly and to treat her like a princess, Morticia finally gave me the information I needed. As I obviously couldn't summon Holly's grandmother here for Christmas, I was going to do the next best thing.

After calling the storage company where Holly's grandmother's things were being held, I was especially glad I'd had the stroke of inspiration. The storage facility said they were owed thousands of dollars on the unit and they were going to auction the unit off in the next few days. I paid the balance due then found a moving company that could have everything at my penthouse by Christmas Eve—tomorrow.

Holly was mixing up a big batch of cookies when I was done with my phone calls.

"Are those the famous sugar cookies?" Oliver asked, padding over to the kitchen island. He reached for my drink. I slapped his hand away.

"You're too young."

"I'm an adult!" he said, puffing his chest out. Jack and I doubled over laughing.

"Why don't you drink and stir this batter," Holly said, handing me another bowl. It smelled like gingerbread.

"I'm going to serve some of these as is," Holly said. "The others I'm using to make gingerbread rum balls. So if you have any rum on hand, give it up!"

I found several bottles and put them on the counter, shoving Oliver out of the way.

"He doesn't even have a palate refined enough for this rum," Jack scoffed.

Holly took a batch of sugar cookie dough out of the fridge and started rolling it out.

"You can help decorate in a little bit, Oliver," she said. "I'm making a ton of cookies. We have over a hundred people coming over for the Christmas party."

"Half of them are the Svenssons, I'm sure," I said.

"I invited the Holbrooks too!" Holly said with a grin.

"You didn't!" Jack said, horrified. "There is going to be a real fight, not a cute icing fight."

She laughed. "Kidding! I don't know the whole story, but I know enough that they probably shouldn't be in the same room for long periods of time."

When the first batch of cookies came out of the oven, Jonathan snagged one.

"They aren't even frosted," Holly chastised.

"Still amazing."

After the cookies had been baked and stacked to cool, Holly made cheesy potato gratin for dinner along with herb-crusted beef tenderloin with horseradish cream sauce and green beans.

"Something smells amazing!" Chloe called out. "Hi!" She and Holly hugged.

"This is Jack's almost-fiancée," I said. In my mind, I was thinking, *I'm totally proposing to Holly before Jack does to Chloe.*

"I brought some Christmas cupcakes and mini pies I made," Chloe said, holding out a box. "I didn't bring any savory food, though, so hopefully the boys don't starve!"

Holly giggled. "Don't worry, I made dinner!"

"Did you decorate too?"

"These are left over from *The Great Christmas Bake-Off.*"

"I didn't know you were living with the contestants, Owen," Chloe said.

"I wasn't living here during filming, thankfully," I replied.

We ate while watching the final episode of *The Great Christmas Bake-Off.* My brothers laughed whenever I was on the screen.

"Believe it or not," Belle said, "these are actually his more intelligent comments."

"I hope you're all good and inspired," Holly said, "because we have towers of cookies that need to be frosted."

"Heh. Frost Tower," Jack said with a laugh.

"You're a Neanderthal," I told him.

"Chloe, you can drink wine and watch," Holly said. "I'm sure you're tired of dessert and decorating cookies."

"Honestly, not really. I've been doing administrative work lately," she said. "It's really relaxing to bake and decorate cookies. I even came prepared." She pulled out a monogramed canvas bag embroidered with cookies and holiday wreaths. She unpacked it, revealing several icing tips and a mini icing gun.

Belle handed Jack, Jonathan, and me aprons. "Don't want icing on those expensive suits! Owen's already ruined one today."

"That wasn't totally his fault!" Holly said, kissing me.

"I've definitely been practicing," Jack bragged as he started decorating cookies.

"Have you?" I asked. "Because that one looks wonky."

Jonathan slathered frosting on three cookies then mashed them all together and took a big bite.

"It's a Christmas sandwich," he said, crumbs flying everywhere.

"It's hilarious," Chloe said, making a neat little icicle pattern on a Christmas tree cookie. "We have several powerful men who run successful, valuable companies and they can't manage to decorate one little cookie."

"Jonathan's hedge fund is iffy," I said.

"Hey, I just bought all those distilleries. My hedge fund will have the last laugh. This time next year, Belle," he said confidently, "I'll be sponsoring *The Great Christmas Bake-Off*. Everyone's going to be talking about how my hedge fund is the biggest power player in the northern hemisphere. Let it be known there will be booze," Jonathan assured us as he slathered way too much icing on another cookie, globs of it dripping on the counter.

Matt scooped some up and was about to flick it at Oliver.

Belle raised her arm, and my brothers and I collectively flinched. She smirked and continued the motion to tuck a strand of her hair back into her braid.

"Now that's power!" Holly said.

"The power of the older sister!" Chloe added.

After Oliver, Matt, and Jonathan had gone off to play video games, Jack and Chloe went home, and Belle went back to her condo, Holly and I sat in the living room in front of the fireplace. I lit a fire and threw a few logs on to burn cheerfully.

"For some reason, I thought this was decorative!" Holly said, snuggling under a large furry blanket. "Who has a working wood-burning fireplace in New York City?"

"I bought this building for a steal a few years back. I went in on it with the Svenssons. The building was built while you were still allowed to have wood-burning fireplaces, and the architect kept the ones here when she designed the penthouse. This used to be a smoking club. High-level employees of the insurance company that previously had its office here used to wine and dine clients up here."

Christmas carols played softly. The light from the fire reflected off the Christmas-tree ornaments. Holly lay her head against my chest.

"I think this is going to be the best Christmas ever," she said happily.

"It already is."

CHAPTER 77

Holly

I woke up the next morning bright and early. It was Christmas Eve! Owen was still asleep, and he rolled over next to me. I snuck out of bed and threw open the curtains. It was snowing. I whistled the first bars of "White Christmas," put *A Christmas Story* on TV, then started cooking.

First, though, I needed coffee. I was going to make peppermint mochas and a big breakfast for Owen's brothers. Fiona, who had said she was happy to help with the restaurant, had already gone home. Morticia was in Harrogate but was going to be back for the Christmas Eve shindig. I needed all hands on deck.

"Want a peppermint mocha?" I asked Owen as I mixed the chocolate and peppermint into the coffee then topped it with a generous helping of whipped cream and more chocolate sauce.

"Um..."

"Don't make that face. You drink Bulletproof coffee. This is basically the same thing!"

"Is it?"

Owen took Rudolph out while the breakfast casserole baked. I went and changed. As I was putting on my apron and fixing my makeup, Owen appeared in the doorway. Rudolph was next to him wearing little reindeer antlers.

"Thought you might need some Christmas inspiration."

"Aww!" I said, touched. "You dressed up Rudolph all for me!"

"Enjoy it, because he's been itching to scratch them off and chew them up," he said as he pulled me in for a hug and a kiss.

The timer beeped before we could go too far. The breakfast casserole was done. As I took it out, Owen's younger brothers slumped out into the living room and went for the remote.

"Don't you dare turn that channel," I said. "The football game doesn't start for hours. Let the Christmas spirit move you!"

They sighed dramatically. I prepped the turkeys for roasting. Owen's kitchen was huge. It held several ovens, more than enough space to cook all the meat and the sides.

"Don't you need help?" Owen asked. He sucked in a breath as if he was about to bellow at his younger brothers to come cook. They were pretending to be playing games on their phones, but I could see they were enjoying the Christmas shows.

"Just leave them. It's just assembly," I said as I mixed up the filling for the stuffed mushrooms.

Owen's phone rang, and he stepped out of the kitchen for a moment. I heard him say, "Yes, please have them bring it up." He came back into the kitchen, grinning. A few minutes later, he said, "I have a surprise for you! Come on!"

I wiped my hands and followed him to the front door. Owen opened it, and several men carting boxes walked in.

"Oliver," Owen called. "Can you show them to the east rooms on the second floor?"

"What in the world?" I said, half in shock. "Those are—" I looked at the labels on the boxes; they were custom Christmas labels in my own handwriting. I opened one of the packages.

"These are my grandmother's decorations!" I started sobbing.

"Merry Christmas," Owen said softly, petting my hair. "Do you want to put anything up?"

"Just the ornaments," I said, sniffling and shaking through the sobs.

One of the movers found the box of carefully packed crystal ornaments and set it by the tree.

"These are really pretty," Owen said as I carefully unpacked them, hanging them on the tree, where they glittered. "Better keep them up high so Rudolph doesn't break them."

"Thank you," I said. "This is the nicest thing anyone has ever done for me." I blew my nose.

"You deserve someone who will do nice things for you," Owen replied.

I wrapped my arms around him, kissing him. "I love you so much."

"I love you too." He kissed me again. "Now let's throw a crazy holiday party!"

The holiday party truly was going to be crazy, I decided several hours later as the guests spilled in.

"How was the drive?" Owen asked Walker Svensson as he herded his younger brothers into the penthouse.

"Say hello to Ms. Holly and Mr. Owen," Walker ordered, "before you descend like locusts onto the food." The two dozen blond-haired boys were all dressed in slacks and shirts, hair freshly combed above festive little bow ties.

"They're so adorable!"

Davy waved to me. I bent down to his level.

"It's so nice to see you again!"

"Thank you for inviting me," Davy said and hugged me.

"Did you make chicken tenders?" Henry asked.

"Geez, no," Walker said, pushing him lightly. "I swear, I don't know what they're doing over there in Harrogate. It's so backcountry. We should move you all to Manhattan."

"Yes," Isaac said, pumping his fist.

"No," Greg retorted, shooing away his remaining younger brothers then abruptly ending a phone call.

"You're in an aggressive mood for Christmas," Owen remarked.

"That was my brother Crawford," he spat, "who is not invited to this party."

"Hi, Holly," Dana said, hugging me.

"I thought you said no Holbrooks at the party," Jack said, smiling. Dana kissed him on each cheek, and Gunnar shook Jack's hand.

"We missed you at the bake-off this year," Gunnar said to Jack.

"Did we though?" Owen asked wryly.

Jack elbowed him. "It's Christmas, Owen, be pleasant." He slapped a Santa hat on Owen's head.

"Very sexy!" I told him, giving him a thumbs-up.

"You didn't tell me there would be children," Morticia said with horror. She was in all black but had on a red scarf in a grudging recognition of the Christmas holiday. Her identical twin, Lilith, had come too. She hugged me.

"*The Great Christmas Bake-Off* was good to you!" Lilith said, jerking her head in Owen's direction.

"You're a lot more chipper than Morticia," I remarked, giving Lilith a hug.

"I've been around all this Christmas for the last month," Morticia complained as more Svenssons spilled in.

"Are these all of your brothers?" I asked Walker, trying and failing to count all of the blond men.

"Not even close," he replied.

Owen handed me a drink. I'd made cranberry old-fashioneds and white-chocolate peppermint martinis.

"Ready to party?"

The heavy-metal strains of Korn's rendition of "Kidnap the Sandy Claws" from *The Nightmare Before Christmas* blared over the sound system. I downed the rest of my drink and sprinted over to where Morticia and Lilith were rocking out.

"Oh my god," I said, switching the music back to Paul McCartney singing "Wonderful Christmas Time." "We're having a nice Christmas party."

"You mean you aren't going to set up your candy-cane stripping pole?" Morticia asked loudly.

"Shhh!"

"You have a candy-cane stripper pole?" a woman with crazy brown hair asked.

"This is Josie," Owen said, introducing us. "Mace's girlfriend."

"I love candy!" she said excitedly. "I didn't even know you could buy a candy-cane stripper pole!"

"We were all pregaming on the ride over," Hazel said, coming by with a drink in each hand. Archer, her fiancé, reached for one. She clutched them both to her chest. "These are mine."

"Seriously? I had to ride in a bus all the way over here," Archer complained.

"You rode in a school bus?"

"It is the Christmas bus because the whole thing was repainted for Christmas, because, Christmas," Penny said with a shrug.

Owen came by with a tray of drinks. The dogs and kids were chasing each other around the penthouse.

"Maybe we should not have brought them," Hunter said, narrowing his eyes.

"And instead have a civilized adult evening?" Garrett said, his voice dripping with sarcasm. "Impossible."

"Stop running," Hunter ordered. His low voice carried around the room. The kids stopped and stood at attention.

"You have them trained," Chloe said, hugging Hazel, Josie, and Penny.

"Need another drink?" Owen asked me, tugging me away.

Matt and Oliver were talking excitedly to the college-aged Svensson boys. I heard the words "billion-dollar company" and "make a shit ton of money."

"You two need to act better," Owen reprimanded them. "It's Christmas. No swearing."

We went out onto the large outdoor roof deck. Snow was falling. The strains of Bing Crosby singing "White

Christmas" filtered out of the speakers. Owen danced me slowly around the rooftop.

"I wish it was Christmas every day," I said with a sigh.

Owen leaned down. Before he kissed me, he said, "With me, it will be."

The End

TASTING HER

Chocolate Cake

A SHORT
ROMANTIC COMEDY

CHAPTER 1

Holly

There's a super-boring zone between Christmas and Valentine's Day during which January stretches on forever. Outside, it was grey, cold, and snowy. I was looking over the preliminary design for the restaurant, while Owen was sitting next to me, reviewing potential corporate acquisitions.

"This is the perfect time of year," Owen said happily.

We were sitting in front of the fireplace in his living room. Owen's husky puppy, Rudolph, now much bigger, was on the balcony to escape the heat. I was under a giant fluffy blanket because Owen had the windows wide open. It was a compromise: I got a roaring fire and he got an open window.

"Really? It's so long and boring and cold." I sighed.

"Yes. Perfect."

"I wish there was a big holiday in January," I said.

"Just invent a new holiday."

"That's dumb," I complained.

"There's probably a random holiday in January," Owen suggested. "Maybe you could elevate it."

I scrolled through a list I found on my phone. "There's a lot. We're definitely celebrating Something on a Stick Day in March."

Owen smirked. "Sounds like my kind of holiday."

I swatted him playfully. "I'm trying to make this a family-friendly holiday. Oooh, there's Chocolate Cake Day on January twenty-seventh. We're totally celebrating that!" I said, starting to make a list. "We can invite all the Svenssons."

"We just had them all over," Owen countered. "Surely once a year is enough."

"Yes, and now it's a new year, so we can invite all the Svenssons again. Cheer up, Owen! I'm going to bake more chocolate cake than you've ever seen in your life. All different kinds! We can have chocolate soufflés, chocolate lava cake, chocolate mousse cake, and chocolate cheesecake."

"Do you want anything not chocolate?" Owen asked. "That sounds like a lot. The Svenssons will be pretty put out if we load their younger brothers with chocolate and caffeine."

"Obviously I'm serving food too," I scoffed. "You can't come to one of my parties and just eat cake! I'm totally making a ton of dips, though. We're not having a sit-down meal. You should have seen me when I was working at this pub on 31st Street. I made amazing dips! I had pizza dip and white pizza dip, spinach and artichoke dip, jalapeño dip, and taco dip, and barbecue pork dip."

Owen leaned over and kissed me. "That sounds fantastic."

"Oh, and crab dip. Forgot about that!"

Fiona and Morticia were waiting for me in the lobby the next morning. I wanted their opinions on the design of the restaurant in the lobby.

"Did you settle on a name?" Morticia asked me.

"I was thinking the Sparrow and Thyme Bistro," I said, taking the plans out of my bag and spreading them out on a table. The Christmas decorations had been taken down, and the lobby felt empty without them. I resolved to add some Valentine's Day decorations.

"Not bad," Morticia said. "I like it. It's a little Victorian. I'll make you a chic logo."

"I'm a little worried about not having street frontage," Fiona said, inspecting the plans.

"I think it will be fine; it will be like a little surprise. We'll really hype it as a hidden gem on Instagram," I assured her.

"We need Instagram-worthy foods," Fiona said, pulling out her notebook. "I'm thinking a rotating list of signature drinks, along with some French bistro-inspired foods like omelets, savory tarts, and hot sandwiches."

"I'm trying out some Instagram-worthy chocolate cake if you want to come by for a party. It's Chocolate Cake Day in a few days! Owen has done a lot for me, and he works hard. I want to host a nice party for him where he can see his friends. Also, you know me. Any excuse for desserts!"

CHAPTER 2

Owen

"Are you paying attention?" Walker Svensson, my friend and COO, asked me, snapping his fingers in front of my face.

"Marginally," I said.

"Repeat back to me what I just said," he ordered.

I tried to concentrate on what he and Beck had just been talking about.

"You want more money for... something?" I said.

"Wrong. We're asking you your opinion about moving to purchase that company that's doing AI pattern recognition."

"Oh, right, yeah. That's fine."

"What is going on with you? You need to get your head in the game," said Beck, my CFO and Walker's brother.

"He still has a Christmas hangover." Walker snickered.

"I don't have a Christmas hangover." I was glad Christmas was over. Now we had reached the long stretch of winter. It was much colder, and I approved. Who knew? I might even need to start wearing a coat. All Holly's talk of the party had given me the perfect idea. I started plotting in my head but then forced myself to concentrate on what Beck and Walker were discussing.

Walker turned to me. "What do you think, Owen?"

"I think I'm going to ask Holly to marry me."

"Uh, okay, one, that was not the question. Two, What the hell? You've known her for two months."

"That does seem early," Beck said slowly.

"We'll have a long engagement," I said with a shrug. "Besides, it takes years to plan a wedding, or so I've heard. Additionally, I don't want my little brother engaged before me. Jack would never let me live it down."

"And I thought our brothers were competitive," Walker said under his breath.

"What if she says no, it's too early?" Beck asked. "She could see it as a big red flag."

"I am confident in my decision," I said. "It's like Bitcoin. You all thought I was crazy. Now my net worth is ten figures."

But what if they were right? I thought later that evening as I took Rudolph out for a walk. He had grown much bigger, but he still acted like a puppy.

Maybe Holly would feel we were moving too fast, that it would be strange for me to propose to her so quickly. We'd barely been living together for three weeks. But when I walked back through the front door, there she was, and I fell in love with her all over again.

"Drink?" she asked, placing a pitcher of warm cocktails on a tray with glasses and garnishes. I picked up the tray and followed her to the French doors that led out to the roof deck.

"You actually want to sit outside?" I asked as I placed the tray on the low teak table.

"I like the firepit outside," she said, waving her hands over the flame. "I can't wait for summer! I'm going to have a ton of plants growing out here. It's going to look like a jungle!"

"So you're planning on staying until the summer?" I asked, pouring the drinks.

Holly toasted me then took a sip. "Of course I am!" she said in shock. "Also, brace yourself, because we're renovating this penthouse."

"It's not going to look weird, is it?"

"What's wrong with making it look like the inside of Santa's workshop?" she asked, eyes wide. "Morticia has several animatronic puppets that she has generously offered to gift us. One is a monkey that has tambourines. I can modify his costume to make it look like an elf."

She must have seen the shock on my face, because she burst out laughing then started coughing.

"Some of that went down the wrong way," she said, taking another sip of her cocktail. "I'm not seriously going to do the whole penthouse in a Christmas theme, just a few rooms."

"A few rooms how?" I replied cautiously, trying not to scowl at my drink. I'd thought Christmas was over.

"I totally want it to look like a little winter wonderland," Holly said, gesturing wildly to describe her vision. "There's going to be a Christmas tree in every room. The bathroom is going to be like the inside of a Nordic sauna. My grandmother even had an antique rocking-horse reindeer, which is going front and center. It will be super cute when we have kids. I can take totally adorable pictures of them on it."

I felt a rush of warmth and love for her. She was thinking about children. Our children. The children she and I would have together! I tried to stay composed and not propose to her with the curl of citrus peel.

"I'm sure they would be very nice pictures," I said formally.

CHAPTER 3

Holly

I wasn't sure about Owen's comments. What did he mean, was I planning on staying until the summer? Where else would I be? Was he tired of me? Tired of the baking? Tired of my stuff in his space? And then the comment about kids. He seemed very noncommittal.

"I'm not sure this is going to work," I confessed to Morticia. She was in a rented studio space painting a sample logo for my new restaurant.

"You said I could make it a little Gothic," she complained. "It's not like the sparrow is in death throes or anything."

"It's not that," I assured her. "It's Owen. I think he's tired of me."

"Tired of you? That man barely has a personality. You greatly increase the quality of his life," she retorted.

"Owen is great; he has his company, loves his family, he's dedicated to his business, participates in charity functions, and has close friends. What's not to love?"

Even as I said it, I wondered if maybe that was enough for him. Maybe he was worried that he would be distracted if he and I became more serious.

"Am I a distraction?"

Morticia's hand jerked. She peered at the canvas and sighed dramatically.

"Yes. Yes, you are. Now let me finish this logo. You need to have something for branding. You're meeting with the interior designer soon. Plus you need to start hyping the restaurant on social media, and you have to have a kick-ass logo that will make people think this is the coolest restaurant ever. Besides, you said you were planning a party."

"That's right, I am."

"So go do that and leave me to my creative genius."

I went back to the Quantum Cyber tower and borrowed one of Owen's cars. They had all been thoroughly detailed after the Christmas cake-fight incident. I took the SUV and drove to the grocery store.

I had some serious shopping to do. I needed a gazillion pounds of chocolate, for one thing. I added heavy cream, my weight in butter, more flour, cocoa powder—the good kind imported from the Netherlands.

I also bought what I needed for all the dips and snacks I was going to have to cut all the chocolaty sweetness. I stopped by the fish counter for smoked salmon—I made a mean salmon cream cheese dip. Next I perused the produce. The store had a variety of nice citrus fruits, along with tart fruits like berries. I also selected crisp vegetables to serve as the token healthy item. But of course I would make a tangy Greek yogurt dip to go with them.

After checking out, I loaded everything into the car. I couldn't wait until I had my industrial ovens in my new restaurant. But until then, I would have to bake bread in Owen's kitchen.

While driving back to the tower, I passed by the little boutique where Owen had taken me shopping for the gown. Though the party would be fun, I wanted to give Owen an extra-special present to show him that I cared about him and appreciated him.

I bit my lip, worrying about the food. It was cold, and I would be quick. I let the windows down on the SUV and climbed out, jogging inside the boutique. The salespeople greeted me.

I waved then said in a rush, "I need something super sexy!"

"Do you want to see what we have?"

"Just surprise me! I have food in the car."

A woman pulled out an outfit and stuck it in my face. I barely looked at it and said, "Perfect."

After paying, I grabbed the bag and ran back to the car. I didn't want the fish to go bad.

After putting away the groceries, I collected Rudolph from the doggie daycare. I liked having the not-so-little husky around.

"We have a lot to do for the party," I said to Rudolph when we were back in the penthouse kitchen. He wagged his tail at me and sniffed the refrigerator. "We are going to cook something amazing!"

CHAPTER 4

Owen

My mode of operation was to make a decision and then pursue it. I was going to marry Holly, and we were going to have several children—not as many as the Svensson brothers, but at least two, maybe three. But first I needed an engagement ring.

Holly: *I took Rudolph FYI. He's helping me bake.*

Owen: *Is he adding that extra flavor of dog hair?*

Holly: *Ha! No, I brushed him good beforehand.*

Owen: *Ginny's still mad at him. I think otherwise I'd take him to her. She has the magic touch on removing loose hair off of huskies according to Jack.*

Holly: *Maybe I can bribe her with dessert!*

It seemed Holly was occupied. Perfect. I was going ring shopping. I went to the garage to grab one of my cars. They'd been detailed, and they gleamed under the lights. Choosing a Porsche, I opened the door and noticed something glittered—a grain of sugar. Maybe I needed to have the cars detailed again. The interior still smelled faintly of icing.

There wasn't anyone in the boutique when I arrived. Of course, it was the middle of the afternoon, and the weather forecast included sleet.

"So glad to see you again, Mr. Frost," the saleswoman said. She and her associate giggled.

"I need a ring," I said determinedly. "Last time I was here, you mentioned you carried several options."

"What kind of ring?" she asked. "I assume it's for a special occasion?"

"Yes," I said. "It's for an engagement."

"Congratulations!"

"It's for Holly, the woman who was in here the last time with me," I clarified so they could find something that she would love.

"I hoped so, but you never know!" the associate said as she unlocked a glass cabinet. "Yesterday there was an older man in here buying an engagement present for a woman he met on one of those online dating sites. Hadn't even known her a few weeks."

"Er—" I decided to let them think Holly and I had been together longer than that. Was this a crazy stupid idea? It was a risk. But I was used to taking calculated risks and winning the big payout.

"We just had a ring come in that I think she would love," she said, taking out a ruby-and-diamond ring. It glittered under the lights. The huge oval ruby was a deep red, flanked by two large diamonds. The three stones were outlined in smaller diamonds that continued to wrap around the band.

"I think she'd like this," I said, inspecting the piece of jewelry. It felt like Christmas without me going out and buying a ring with a snowman or other kitschy character on it.

"We also have a wedding ring that goes with it," the saleswoman added. "They were designed together."

"I'll take it."

"Both?" she asked.

"Sure, why not." If Holly didn't want it as the wedding band, she could just wear the ring on another finger.

As I paid for the jewelry, I thought about how I was going to present the ring to her. Obviously I needed to make a big production of it. The Chocolate Cake Day celebration tomorrow was perfect. However, I couldn't just get down on one knee and give it to her. I had to plan something that demonstrated that I knew her intimately and respected her as a unique individual.

What did Holly love? Cake. It would be perfect.

My phone beeped as I started the car.

Holly: *Gone to meet with Morticia.*
Holly: *Have to make sure she doesn't turn the restaurant theme into the house of horrors.*
Owen: *I'll see you when I get back.*
Holly: *Dinner is in the fridge.*
Holly: *I would say don't wait up, but I have a little tiny surprise for you *wink**

Perfect. She would be out, and I would bake a cake.

456 · ALINA JACOBS

I stopped at the store on my way back. Obviously it would be chocolate. Could you bake a ring into cake? I looked up information on my phone while I wandered the aisles. It said to wrap the ring tightly in aluminum then put it in the cake batter. Easy enough.

We had tons of flour at home. But did we have chocolate? I wracked my brain, trying to remember what Holly used as I surveyed the aisle of a thousand different kinds of chocolate. Then I texted my younger brother.

Owen: *I need to bake a cake.*
Jack: *Que?*
Owen: *It's for Holly.*
Jack: *I don't think she wants to eat anything you can cook.*
Owen: *I'm proposing.*
Jack: *Kind of soon???*
Owen: *This is going to be the best decision I've ever made. But I need to make a cake.*
Jack: *I can ask Chloe to do it. She loves a sappy romantic gesture.*
Owen: *I have to do it. Otherwise it's not special.*
Jack: *Then I humbly offer my services. I live with a world-renowned baker. I've picked up a little something.*

❋ ❋ ❋

"You severely oversold your skills," I growled at Jack as I looked up at the batter all over the ceiling.

"My company made this mixer," he complained. "It is definitely not supposed to do that."

"Sounds like operator error," I replied as some of the batter dripped down, narrowly missing my shoulder.

I made Jack clean the ceiling while I made another batch of chocolate cake batter. For the proposal cake, I was taking the easy route—just a small, plain chocolate cupcake with chocolate frosting. I put one of the little silver liners in the muffin pan and scooped the cupcake batter into it. Then I gently poked the foil-wrapped ring into the batter and put the muffin tin in the oven.

"Now to make the frosting," I said, pulling out the egg-beaters. The fire alarm blared.

"Dude, what the hell!" Jack yelled as we raced to the oven. The cupcake looked half raw, but the empty muffin tins were smoking.

"Shit!" I cursed, pulling the pan out of the oven and setting it on the stove.

"Fail!" Jack said.

"Shut up," I retorted, fishing the ring out of the batter. It was unharmed by the ordeal.

"What are you doing?" I asked as he texted on his phone.

"Asking Chloe what happened." His phone rang.

"What are you two up to?" Chloe asked, voice suspicious through the phone speaker.

"Just testing out some stuff," I said.

"Stuff?"

"Yeah," I said, "stuff."

"Well, for the 'stuff' you're doing, don't just put an empty muffin tin in the oven. You need to fill the empty cups with water."

"You're the smartest person I know, Chloe," Jack said. "Love you."

"Love you!"

"Okay, water," I said, moving to fill the empty tins.

"You should start over," Jack suggested. "That one might taste smoky."

After dumping the smoky cupcake, I popped in a new liner, added batter, hid the ring, filled the cups with water, and slid the pan into the oven.

I was making the chocolate buttercream frosting when the fire alarm went off again.

"Shit!" There was a fire in the oven.

"You need to go buy a cupcake!" Jack yelled at me as I took the whole pan out and dumped it in the sink. Some of the batter had overflowed.

"You're an idiot! You put too much in," Jack complained as I used a metal spatula to scrape the blackened chocolate batter out of the oven.

"Attempt three," I said, armed with a new muffin tin. Put in the paper, fill with batter, but not too much! Add the ring, water in the empty tins. I stood in front of the oven.

"It can't go wrong if I watch it," I said.

The cupcake rose beautifully. I carefully removed it from the oven and let it cool then frosted it.

"Not going to be winning any contests," Jack said as we looked at the cupcake. "But it will do for a proposal."

"Should I add sprinkles?"

"Nah," Jack said. "Leave it *au naturel*."

I hid the iced cupcake in a Tupperware container and tucked it into a cabinet that was out of the way in the large kitchen. I'd never seen Holly go into it. She shouldn't find the surprise.

Jack poured us each a generous glass of whisky.

"To my soon-to-be-married big brother," he said, clinking our glasses together. "Also, that was incredibly stressful."

"I'll say."

I drank another glass after he left, hoping that my plan didn't spectacularly fail.

CHAPTER 5

Holly

The penthouse was dark when I came in. All the windows were open, and a freezing breeze flowed through the open kitchen and living area.

I wondered where Owen was; I still had my surprise for him. He wasn't in the bedroom, so I quickly pulled out the bag I had gotten from the boutique and took it with me into the large master bath.

I laughed when I pulled the skimpy lingerie out of the bag. It was a sexy winter dominatrix outfit, I assumed, based on the snowflake-studded collar and the riding crop the outfit came with.

"This is so extra!" I giggled, studying the lingerie. "Guess I should have actually looked at it carefully before buying it."

There were little sheer panties that had a lace-up opening at the crotch, and the outfit also included a white corset with a bra that was really just a series of white leather straps.

I was really proud of myself for being able to put it on; all the straps were a little complicated. But I did look hot, I decided when I looked in the mirror. To complete the look, I dug a pair of silver platform heels out of the closet and added some shimmery silver eyeliner. Go big or go home! And there was something big I definitely wanted.

I strutted around the penthouse looking for Owen. He wasn't in his office. He wasn't in the library. Yes, his condo had a library. Nuts, right? I finally found him in the den.

"Want a drink, Holly?" he asked, putting down the newspaper he was reading and turning toward me. His tie and jacket were off. He was barefoot, and his shirt was unbuttoned. His eyes practically bugged out of his head when he saw me.

"Surprise!" I said, striking a sexy pose.

He looked me up and down. I shivered. Owen looked as if he could eat me up right about now.

"I can't even tell what you're wearing, just that I really like it," he said. He stalked over to me, tipped my head back, and kissed me. I moaned as he caressed my body through the thin, soft lace. He took off his shirt, and I greedily ran my hands over the ripples of muscles on his chest.

"Honestly, I think I could just stand here and stare at you all night."

I smacked him lightly on the chest with the riding crop. "Don't you dare. You better fuck me with that big huge cock," I said, unzipping his pants and palming the hard bulge in his boxer briefs.

He grabbed the leather strap that crisscrossed my boobs and dragged me to him, crushing his mouth to mine.

I moaned as Owen nuzzled me, his breath a hot trail to the mounds of my breasts, which were pushed high in the corset. He carefully undid it, letting the fabric fall to the ground, then he kissed my tits. My nipples were hard, and the sensation of his mouth was making me wet. I whimpered as his hand moved between my legs. I spread them for him, and I felt him smile against me when he realized the ribbon was the only thing between him and my pussy. Owen pulled at the thin ribbon at the crotch, letting it fall to the floor.

"Very convenient," he said in the deep voice that always made me want to do naughty things.

Owen knelt in front of me, tongue darting out to lightly flick my clit. I whimpered, needing more. I grabbed the back of his head, and he chuckled, grabbing my thighs. Spreading my legs, he licked my pussy lightly again.

I smacked him on the back with the riding crop.

He cursed. "That's dangerous to do when I'm down here," he said, his voice slightly muffled.

"I didn't mean to hit that hard," I said then shrieked as he stood up, turned me around, and pushed me over the side of the couch. My ass was in the air, and my back was arched because of the high heels.

"You gonna punish me?" I purred, feeling weirdly aroused from the whole thing.

"Absolutely," he said. He pulled my panties down, threw them to the floor, and then stroked my aching pussy.

"I want you to punish me," I moaned.

Owen grabbed the riding crop, trailing it down my back then teasing my pussy with it. I whimpered, needing him.

"Hit me," I pleaded.

"Are you sure?"

"Yeah," I breathed. Owen hit me lightly with the riding crop across my bare ass. I whimpered.

"Again."

He hit me again, slightly harder.

"I want your cock," I moaned, tossing my head back.

"I'm still punishing you first," he said, tossing the riding crop in front of me. "Better hold on."

My fingers grasped at the couch as Owen pressed his face into my pussy, licking me, his tongue stroking expertly across the swollen, hot flesh.

"I need you," I whimpered as he flicked my clit with his tongue. I ground back against him. He growled and held my hips steady. I moaned helplessly as he licked, me bringing me almost to the edge. Then he stopped.

I swore.

Owen bent over me, grabbing my tits, pinching and teasing a nipple as he rolled on a condom. Then he grabbed my hips and thrust into me, his huge cock filling me, giving me everything I was craving.

I cried out as he slid that huge cock out of me then thrust back in, my tits bouncing with the force. He didn't touch my clit, which was probably a good thing, because I was about to snow globe all over his cock. I moaned loudly as he fucked me, keeping me right on the edge, teasing me, driving me crazy.

"I need you to fuck me harder," I pleaded as he thrust into me again with his hard cock. I welcomed every inch of him, whimpering as he buried himself me.

He tangled a large hand in my hair, tipping my head back. I arched into him as he fucked me hard, jackhammering into me, turning me into a pleading, moaning mess.

I felt my body tighten, and I panted as he kept me right on the edge. Again and again, Owen drove his thick cock into my aching pussy as I pleaded for him to make me come.

His hand moved from my hip to my clit, stroking me hard, then I was gone. I came in a screaming jumble of ohmygods and cursing. Owen kissed my neck as he thrust into me a few more times, drawing out my orgasm then finishing in me.

"I love you, Holly," he whispered in my ear.

"I love you, too, Owen."

Owen left for work early the next morning. After kissing him goodbye, I finished cooking. I had to make all the dips and finish baking the bread. I had made the various chocolate cakes the night before. Because they needed to be served hot, I would make the lava cakes at the last minute. Though the fridge was packed, I was still worried that there wasn't going to be enough food—particularly enough cake.

"We need cupcakes," I said aloud, face-palming. "That's what I didn't make. You can't have Chocolate Cake Day without cupcakes."

The bread was in the oven. We still had a few more hours until the party. I had enough time to quickly whip up a batch of chocolate cupcakes with chocolate buttercream frosting. There's nothing sexier than a huge tower of cupcakes.

Morticia called me as I lined the muffin tins and spooned in the batter.

"I have Fiona on the line," she said. "We need to talk about the bistro's menu. She wants me to do a sample."

We discussed the menu while the cupcakes baked. Fiona was giving me a rundown of what she thought the boxed lunch menu should be.

"It needs to be Instagram-worthy," I said, "like those Japanese bento boxes but with more food, because this is America and we eat too much."

The timer dinged and I pulled out the cupcakes and laid them out to cool.

"Are you baking while we're trying to have a business meeting?" Fiona said.

"I have the Chocolate Cake Day party. I'm making cupcakes," I replied, checking the cupcakes to see if they were cool enough to frost "We should serve flourless chocolate cake at the bistro. I made some for the party," I said as I started smearing icing on the dark chocolate cupcakes. The looked pretty, though a little rustic.

"We also need to serve quiche," Fiona said. "I think Owen's workers would like that."

"They need to be huge pieces—like, you should get a quarter of a quiche. I hate it when restaurants don't give you enough food."

Speaking of eating too much, somehow I had already moved way too much baking gear into Owen's kitchen. I couldn't find my fancy tiered cupcake stand. As I chatted with Fiona and Morticia, I opened cupboard after cupboard, looking for it.

"I want to do paninis too," I said as I reached the last row of cabinets. "Really big ones. Owen said that a lot of his employees complained about the fact that all the nearby lunch places skimped on food."

Rudolph padded into the kitchen and rose on his hind legs to sniff the cupcakes. I ran back to shoo him away then returned to my hunt in the cupboards.

"Ah, found it!" I said. I took out two of the pieces of the multitiered glass platter and set them on the counter. I took out the next batch of cupcakes from the oven then went to retrieve the rest of the platter pieces.

"Geez, I'm losing my mind," I told my friends. "Can you believe I put a cupcake in here for some reason? I definitely need to stop multitasking." I had even put it in its own special Tupperware container. Clearly I needed to pay more attention. I shook my head then placed the lost cupcake on the platter with its siblings.

CHAPTER 6

Owen

The cupcake was missing.

"What the fuck!" I muttered. I was back from work. The guests were coming in an hour. I had a big proposal planned. This was supposed to be one of the most important days of my life, and it was already in the toilet.

Somehow the cupcake with the very pricy engagement ring was gone. I had hidden it in the cupboard yesterday, and now it was not there.

I texted my brother.

Owen: *Emergency. Lost the cupcake.*
Jack: *Maybe Rudolph ate it.*

I looked down at the dog. Holly had had him groomed, and he was sporting a big bow around his neck.

"You and I will no longer be friends if you ate that ring," I warned the dog.

"I have a lot of the desserts in the other room," Holly said, scurrying into the kitchen to take a large platter of crab dip out of the oven. "Can you take them out and arrange them on the dining room table please?"

I went into the other room and found an abundant display of chocolate desserts of various types. Front and center? A huge tiered platter of chocolate cupcakes with chocolate buttercream frosting.

Shit.

"It's fine," I pep-talked myself. "There's only a handful of them." Then I looked to an adjacent side table and saw another hundred identical chocolate cupcakes.

Fuck. How was I going to search all of them?

Holly was preoccupied, so I snuck a toothpick from the kitchen and started gently poking it into each cupcake.

"Owen!" she called.

Shit. Shit. Shit.

I carried the tiered glass platter and another tray of cupcakes into the main entertaining space.

"Can you go take the spinach-and-artichoke dip out of the oven, please? Also put out the ice for drinks," she asked, gesturing to the kitchen.

"Sure."

This wasn't good. I needed to search the rest of the cupcakes. This proposal was not going according to plan.

The doorbell buzzed.

"Come on in!" Holly yelled.

"It's just us," Jack called out as Milo ran inside.

"Hi!" Chloe greeted us. She hugged Holly and looked over her shoulder at me with a questioning look. I subtly shook my head and drew a finger over my throat.

"Are you sure Rudolph didn't eat it?" Jack said under his breath as Chloe helped Holly arrange the rest of the food.

"I don't know. He doesn't seem sick or ninety thousand dollars more expensive." We looked at the dog.

"He looks a little pukey," Jack said.

"Holly made other cupcakes," I whispered to my brother. "I think it's in there."

The doorbell rang again. My younger brother Jonathan sauntered in with several of the Svenssons who were partners in his hedge fund.

"Hey, bro!" he said. "Big day, huh!" The Svenssons snickered.

So everyone knew, and they were all going to witness my failure.

"Thanks for coming and celebrating this auspicious holiday with us!" Holly said, hugging them.

"I'm not going to miss Chocolate Cake Day," Jonathan declared. "Can I start, please?"

"Wait for everyone else," Belle yelled at him, pushing her way through the growing crowd.

"Don't eat the cupcake," I hissed out of the corner of my mouth to my brother.

"How about some of this delicious dip?" he said loudly. I gave him a thumbs-up.

"Belle," I whispered to my sister, "can you distract Holly? I need to test the cupcakes."

"For poison?"

"He lost the ring," Jack hissed. "It's in one of those." He gestured to the sea of chocolate cupcakes.

"Whoo, boy," Belle said, squaring her shoulders. "Holly, I never did see what you did with all your Christmas stuff!"

"Oh my goodness! Let me show you!"

My big sister had come to my rescue again! I grabbed another toothpick, but before Holly and Belle could leave the room, the doorbell rang furiously. Someone on the other side yelled, "Stop it!"

"The kids are here!" Holly said as she ran to the door. "They're going to love this!"

I hastily poked three more cupcakes. Nothing.

The Svensson brothers tumbled in. "Cake! Cake!" the little kids chanted.

"I have real food too," Holly assured Hunter and Greg. "We even have veggie platters!"

"Did you hear that?" Mace Svensson said to his younger brothers. "You need to eat some healthy food, not just cake."

His girlfriend, Josie, took pictures of the table. "This is so pretty!"

"This is my new favorite holiday!" Archer, Mace's twin said, grabbing a cupcake.

"Don't eat that!" I said, snatching the cupcake out of Archer's hand.

"He can have it if he wants to," Holly said reproachfully, taking the cupcake back from me.

I watched Archer unwrap it and take a huge bite. I winced, expecting to hear a *clink*.

CHAPTER 7

Holly

"Owen's being really weird," I said to Morticia. The party was in full swing. The dips were a hit; I had made quadruple amounts of the recipies. The cakes were flying off the table. Morticia was helping me prep the lava cakes for the big finale.

"I thought being weird was part of his charm," she said.

"No, he's being cagey. Do you think he's going to break up with me?"

"I still have the baseball bat if he does," she promised.

"I don't think I can take it if he breaks up with me," I said, wringing my hands.

"Stop it," she said, slapping my hands. She stuffed a spoonful of chocolate lava cake batter into my mouth. "Eat that. Feel better?"

I nodded. "Probably going to contract salmonella, but life's too short not to eat raw batter."

I surveyed the spread of food. Most of the cupcakes were gone. I was doubly glad I had made them.

"Still want more chocolate?" I called out. "I'm getting ready to start the lava cake."

Owen was prowling around the room, watching everyone carefully.

"What is his problem? Is he policing the food?" I wondered aloud.

"You can't have kids if he's going to be territorial about food. You can't have a food-aggressive man in the house," Morticia said sagely as she slid the lava cakes into the oven.

I went to clear a space on the table for lava cake. I scooped up a chip full of some of the spinach-and-artichoke dip as well. I was jittery from too much sugar and caffeine.

Davy, the youngest Svensson brother, waved to me when he saw me. He was solemnly eating a cupcake, one hand glued to his older brother Garrett's leg. Garrett looked down.

"Davy, you have frosting everywhere. That better not be on my pants."

"Here," I said, handing him the wet rag I was carrying around.

"He's probably had enough cupcakes," Penny, Garrett's girlfriend said, trying to grab the cupcake from Davy.

"No!" he shrieked.

I was regretting the sheer amount of sugar I'd given all the kids. They were running around the penthouse like wild monkeys, playing tag with the dogs.

Garrett tried the snatch the cupcake, but Davy stuffed the whole thing into his mouth, chewing defiantly, cheeks puffed out like a chipmunk's.

"Well, that's the last of the cupcakes anyway," I said as Garrett looked down with disgust and Penny tried not to laugh.

Owen looked sick.

"You can't be the type of dad who doesn't let their kids have any sugar!" I said to Owen, exasperated. "That's no way to live. Also, if you keep them from sugar, it just makes them go crazy when they actually do have it. Honestly, I don't know what's gotten into you. You've been tense all evening."

Morticia came over to stand behind me for moral support. Too bad she didn't have the bat.

"It's not that," Owen said, looking slightly pale. "Holly, I have a confession to make. I really screwed up."

The music stopped comically.

"Sorry!" one of the younger Svensson brothers said, holding up a broken cable. "I didn't mean to do that! I'll fix it just a sec."

"What did you do?" I asked Owen. Had he cheated on me? Was he breaking up with me? My stomach churned. I regretted everything I'd eaten that evening.

"Ouch!" Davy cried, goopy half-chewed cupcake oozing out of his mouth.

"Davy, stop it," Garrett reprimanded, wiping his brother's face with the rag. Davy used that moment to spit all the contents of his mouth into Garrett's hand.

"Apologies," Garrett said. "He was raised in a polygamist cult in the middle of the desert. He's basically an animal."

"Still better than Archer," Hunter remarked.

"Hey!" Archer protested around a mouthful of flourless chocolate cake.

"That is true." Garrett peered at the mess in the rag.

"I think you forgot a frosting bag tip," he said. We peered at the metal thing in his hand.

Owen fist-pumped the air, and Jack, Jonathan, and Chloe cheered. Jack slapped Owen on the back.

"I'm confused," I said.

"And I'm relieved," he said, taking the metal thing out of the chewed-up cupcake.

Morticia looked horrified. I was a little grossed out.

"We can just toss it," I said. "It's not important."

"But it is," Owen said.

Penny pulled a handkerchief out of Garrett's suit pocket and handed it to Owen. He cleaned off the metal thing and unwrapped it.

"Oh my gosh!" I exclaimed, staring at the ring. It glittered in the firelight.

"Holly," Owen said, sinking to one knee, "I swear I had this planned better, but at least no one ate it. Now, before I tempt fate anymore, will you please marry me?"

"Yes!" I shrieked, jumping up and down.

Owen slid the ring onto my finger. It was a huge ruby surrounded by sparkling diamonds. I teared up.

"It's like Christmas! You *are* the perfect man for me!"

He stood and hoisted me up, swinging me around and kissing me while everyone cheered.

"I even baked it in a chocolate cupcake," he explained, setting me down, "but Davy got to it first."

"You were lucky," Garrett said. "If Archer had taken it, he eats so fast he wouldn't have even noticed the ring."

"I helped!" Davy said proudly. Owen patted him on the head.

"I love you so much, Owen! I can't wait to spend the rest of my life with you," I gushed.

"I love you, Holly, and I want to spend every day with you. Especially and including Christmas," Owen said, smiling happily at me.

"Celebration time!" I called out.

Jack started handing out champagne.

"Lava cake should be done," Morticia said. "Anybody up for more chocolate?"

We all looked around. No one was all that enthusiastic.

"Are you a little chocolated out?" Owen asked with a smile and leaned down and kissed me. "Say it isn't so!"

"I mean sort of, but I never say no to chocolate cake!"

The End

Sugar Cookies

Everyone who eats these cookies says they are absolutely amazing, even people who don't normally like sweets. Enjoy!

For the cookies
Makes 3-4 dozen

Ingredients:
- 1 3/4 cup flour
- 3/4 tsp baking powder
- 1/4 tsp salt
- 2/3 cup butter
- 1 cup sugar
- 1 egg
- 1/2 tsp vanilla
- 2 Tbl milk

Directions:
1. Preheat oven to 400°
2. In a food processor, cream the sugar and butter.
3. Add eggs and vanilla. Mix.

4. Sift flour, baking powder and salt.
5. Add dry ingredients to food processor, alternating with milk in two or three portions.
6. Put in a bowl and chill 1 hour.
7. Put parchments paper down on an air-insulated cookie sheet.
8. Roll 1/8 inch thick on lightly floured board or pastry cloth.
9. Cut out with a cookie cutter and place on parchment paper.
10. Bake 8 minutes. Should be barely golden.
11. Let cool completely before frosting with fluffy icing and sprinkling with large colored sugar.

For the fluffy icing
Makes 7 cups. Can be stored up to 8 weeks in fridge.

Ingredients:
   2/3 cup water
   4 Tbl Wilton Meringue powder
   12 cups (about 3 lbs) powdered sugar
   1 1/4 cups Crisco (solid, not flavored)
   3/4 tsp salt
   1/2 tsp clear vanilla extract
   1/4 tsp butter extract

Directions:
   Beat at high speed water and meringue power. Add four cups sugar, one cup at a time, beating at low speed after each addition. Add salt and flavorings. Alternately, add shortening and remaining 8 cups sugar. Beat at low speed until smooth.

Acknowledgements

✳ ✳ ✳

A big thank you to Red Adept Editing for editing and proofreading.

And finally a big thank you to all the readers! I had a great time writing this book, and I hope it put you in the Christmas spirit!

About the Author

If you like steamy romantic comedy novels with a creative streak, then I'm your girl!

Architect by day, writer by night, I love matcha green tea, chocolate, and books! So many books...

Sign up for my mailing list to get special bonus content, free books, giveaways, and more!

http://alinajacobs.com/mailinglist.html